'My favourite author used to be Catherine Cookson . . . but without a doubt you are n

'I have just finished *Tomorrow's Promises* and thoroughly enjoyed it. That now makes twenty-one I have read in the last two/three months' A reader

'I love your books' A reader, New South Wales

'I could not put them down and was sorry to see them come to an end.' A reader, Canada, on *A Pennyworth of Sunshine*, *Twopenny Rainbows* and *Threepenny Dreams*

'Thanks again for your lovely storytelling . . . I raced through the books SO quickly – I couldn't put them down!' A reader, South Africa

'Compulsive reading' A reader, South Wales, on *Tomorrow's Promises*

ANNA JACOBS

Freedom's Land

HODDER

First published in Great Britain in 2008 by Hodder & Stoughton
An Hachette Livre UK company

First published in paperback in 2009

1

A CIP catalogue record for this title is available from
the British Library

ISBN 978 0 340 95404 1

Typeset in Plantin Light by Palimpsest Book Production Ltd,
Grangemouth, Stirlingshire

Printed and bound by
CPI Mackays, Chatham

Hodder & Stoughton policy is to use papers that are natural, renewable
and recyclable products and made from wood grown in sustainable
forests. The logging and manufacturing processes are expected to
conform to the environmental regulations of the country of origin.

Hodder & Stoughton Ltd
338 Euston Road
London NW1 3BH

www.hodder.co.uk

This book is dedicated to all the brave, hard-working group settlers who helped build the town of Northcliffe in Western Australia – and also to the people of today's Northcliffe, who made me welcome, generously sharing information so that I could create this story.

ENGLAND, LATE 1923

Norah

I

Norah Webster looked up from her machining as the charge hand stopped next to her.

'You're wanted at home, lass. Urgent.'

She shoved her chair back and stood up. 'Do you know why?'

'The lad didn't say. I'll have to dock your pay for the time you're away from your machine, mind.'

But she wasn't listening. She grabbed her coat and ran all the way home with it flapping open.

She'd moved back in with her parents after the war when she lost her job as a porter at the railway station to a returned soldier. She was ashamed at having to seek their help, but as a widow, she found it impossible to earn enough to run a house of her own on women's peacetime wages, let alone provide properly for her eight-year-old daughter Janie. But she consoled herself with the thought that her money helped her parents out, too, so she was still paying her way.

When she got there, Norah saw a group of solemn-faced neighbours gathered near their house. They greeted her in subdued voices but avoided her eyes. Pushing open the front door, she heard her mother's anguished weeping coming from upstairs and her steps faltered.

She climbed the stairs slowly, stopping in the doorway of the front bedroom, still panting from running home. Her mother was kneeling on the floor by the bed, weeping loudly and unrestrainedly, holding the hand of the still figure lying there. She didn't even notice her daughter.

Norah went forward and knelt to put an arm round her. No need for anyone to say her father was dead. You couldn't mistake that look. 'What happened, Mum?'

Annie clung to her. 'He dropped dead at work, just keeled over and died, they said. They fetched the doctor straight off, but it was too late, so they brought him home. The first thing I knew was when they knocked on the door. Oh, Norah, he's gone, left me! How can I bear it?'

More sobs erupted from her and all Norah could do was hold her and let her weep for a while. She looked over the top of her mother's head at the calm face of her dad. Such a lovely man. So hard to believe he was dead. Tears welled in her eyes, but she didn't give in to the desire to weep. Someone had to stay strong, do what was necessary and organise the funeral. Her mother was a weak woman, who'd depended on her husband. What would become of her now? What would become of them all?

After a few minutes Norah decided this couldn't go on and said gently, 'You have to stop crying now, Mum. We've things to do.'

But Annie went into hysterics and couldn't be calmed. In the end they had to send for the doctor, who gave her something to make her sleep.

Norah sent a neighbour's lad round to tell her sisters what had happened, and almost as an afterthought, told him to go to the slipper factory afterwards to tell them she'd be taking the rest of the week off to bury her father.

Her sisters arrived and they went to see their father, then wept together. But neither of them was prepared to lay him out, so Norah did it.

By the time her daughter came home from school, she'd done that and made arrangements for the funeral, too. Well, that was easy enough to do, wasn't it? Her parents had taken out burial insurance a long time ago, paying threepence a week to ensure they had a decent send-off, not a pauper's funeral. The insurance company only dealt with one funeral firm, who offered a standard service to those insured, so you didn't get any choice about the details unless you could pay extra.

And they couldn't. Neither she nor her sisters had any money to spare because times were hard.

Janie fell silent when she heard what had happened and whispered, 'Like Daddy.' She cried softly and sadly. She'd been her granddad's favourite and maybe he'd spoiled her, but they both had so much fun together that Norah hadn't tried to stop him indulging the fatherless child. She tried to comfort her daughter, but what could you say, really? Death was so final.

After her daughter had sobbed herself to sleep, Norah lay awake for a long time in the back bedroom, lying very still in the double bed they shared, staring bleakly into the darkness. Was it possible to provide for herself, her mother and Janie without her father's wages?

However carefully she did the sums, it wasn't. The pennies didn't stretch that far, with her wages little more than half a man's. That meant they couldn't keep this house, or any other.

On the Saturday afternoon of that same week, Andrew Boyd knocked on the door of his fiancée's house and waited for Betty to answer it. For once, she wasn't smiling, didn't invite him in.

For a few moments they stared at one another then he asked the question whose answer he'd already guessed from her expression. 'Did you read the pamphlet I gave you?'

'No. I threw it in the fire.'

He was shocked by that. 'You didn't think I might want it back?'

'It was all lies. I don't know why you believe them.'

Her voice was shriller than usual and he wished she'd chosen somewhere more private for this confrontation, but that was Betty all over. She never thought before she acted.

He repeated what he'd been telling her for a while now, only he said it more strongly. 'It wasn't lies. It was a chance for us, and a good one, too. You know how I hate my job, hate this town as well. I feel stifled here after going overseas during the war. Other countries are warmer, brighter, more cheerful.'

For a moment he turned his head to scowl at the long row of shabby little houses built up the hill in steps, each dwelling exactly fourteen foot wide. Folk here lived on top of one another. Soldiers had lived together even more closely in the barracks. He longed for space and air and bright sunshine, and the freedom to do as he wanted with his life, to be on his own if he wanted. 'I've tried, Betty. God knows I've tried. But I *can't* settle down here. And why should I when there's a better alternative?'

She took a step backwards, the tears she seemed able to produce at will running down her face, and said in a voice throbbing with emotion, 'Not even for me? You said you loved me, Andrew, but you can't have meant it.' Pulling out a lace-edged handkerchief, she dabbed delicately at her eyes.

'I did mean it. You know that. And even if I stayed here, jobs aren't safe these days.'

'You're the charge hand at the foundry. You'll always have a job. They don't lay off charge hands.'

'Don't be so sure about that. They had to put people on short time at the spinning mill this week and they cancelled a big order at our works. So now *we* have to put our men on short time, too.'

She waved one hand impatiently. 'It's always been like that. Full on with work, then short time, and later things start picking up again.' She pressed one hand to her breast in a theatrical gesture. 'If you love me, you'll—'

'Love won't make jobs for people. You should read your father's newspapers instead of wasting your money on that stupid *Picture Show* magazine.'

She abandoned the pose to glare at him. 'It's only

twopence a week and if you men can go and waste your money watching football matches, I don't see why I can't take an interest in the cinema.'

It was an old argument and he shouldn't have raised it again, but when she started posing and acting like those silly film stars she adored, it really got to him. Especially now. 'No one will be able to afford to go to football or the cinema if things go on like this. Business is bad all across the north and getting worse. You'd think we'd lost the war, not won it. And anyway, that doesn't change the fact that I can't *stand* being shut up inside that damned noisy workshop all day.'

She gave him one of her soulful looks. He'd thought them beautiful when he first met her, but knew now she was play-acting half the time, modelling herself on her favourite film stars. It was starting to irritate him, but still he wanted her, couldn't help himself, she was so soft and pretty.

'If you insist on going to Australia, I can't marry you, Andrew.' She pressed one hand against her breast and bowed her head.

The silence was broken only by the striking of the town hall clock in the distance and a dog responding with a couple of half-hearted barks.

Get it over with, he told himself. *You know she'll never change her mind about this.*

He could see her watching him out of the corner of her eye, knew she was hoping her dramatic ultimatum would force him to stay. Only he'd told her the simple truth: he couldn't face staying. Still, it was hard to say the words.

When he'd met her, six months after his wife died, he'd fallen madly in love. Betty was not only pretty, but cheerful and lively. She made him laugh and feel whole again. What man who'd been through the war wouldn't enjoy the prospect of a rosy, smiling woman like her to brighten his days? It had seemed like a miracle that the prettiest girl in town loved him in return.

But love wasn't enough, not for him, and he steeled himself to look away from those big blue eyes. 'So you never even read the pamphlet or tried to find out about what it's like in Australia. It's a wonderful country, Betty. A man can make a good life for himself and his family out there. Just think, we'll own our own land.'

'What use is that to people like us? It's farmers they need to work the land. You're not one – you know nowt about farming, *nowt*! And I'm not going to be a farmer's wife. Let alone I like living in town, it's back-breaking work, farming is. Besides, I've told you before and I meant it: I'm *not* moving away from my family, not for anything. I've brothers and sisters here, Andrew, and my father's a widower.'

She spoke in broken tones but he could see no tears and there was a watchful look in her eyes. It was as if she'd turned suddenly into a stranger, someone he didn't know, someone very different from the woman whose kisses drove him mad with longing, the one who snuggled against him in the cinema, warm and soft.

He pushed those memories away. He'd made his decision. It was the only one possible because there were his sons to think of as well as himself. Taking a deep, shuddering breath, he took a step backwards.

Her mouth fell open in shock and she stretched one hand out towards him. 'Andrew, love, don't do this. You'll feel better about everything once we're married, I know you will.'

'I won't change my mind, Betty. They're *giving* land to ex-servicemen out there in Western Australia, just giving it away for the asking. And I'm going to ask for some.'

He watched as she fumbled for her ring finger and took off the engagement ring he'd given her, an extravagance she'd coaxed out of him. She held it out, mute now, her lips a tight thin line, anger rather than sorrow in her face.

When he took hold of it, she didn't let go for a minute and he realised in shock that she expected him to let her keep it. Well, he wasn't going to do that. He'd spent far too much money on her over the past few months already. He jerked it away from her and put it in his pocket.

She stepped back, scowling blackly, no longer pretending to weep.

'I wish you well, Betty.' He turned away and strode off down the street, not looking back. It was over, his brief dream of a happy married life, a life more satisfying and exciting than his placid first marriage had brought.

The only dream he had left now was to move to Australia, make a better life for himself and his sons, and by hell, he was going to make it come true, whatever he had to do.

And surely a government wouldn't lie about something as important as giving land to ex-servicemen?

After the funeral, Norah's family gathered at the house for a conference. They put all the children in the back room and forbade them to go outside and play on such a solemn day. It had poured down during the funeral and although it had stopped now, the skies were heavy with more rain.

Norah kept her head bowed as her eldest sister's husband stood up. She didn't want them to see how bitter she felt about the blows fate kept dealing her, losing her husband, losing her war job, now losing even her home.

'No need to tell you all why we're here. We have to decide what to do for Mum and Norah.' He paused, cleared his throat, then said it. 'Me and Emily can take Mum in, give her our front room, but we can't take you and Janie as well, Norah love, well, not for more than a few days, any road. I only wish we could. And we can't help you with the rent, either, because I'll be on short time from next week.' He paused as there was a murmur of sympathy. 'So, unless you've got any ideas, keeping Dad's house is out of the question.'

She shook her head, her throat aching from holding back tears.

Her youngest sister gave her an apologetic look. 'We've got Phil's father living with us already, so we've not an inch of room left at our place, either. You can always come to us in an emergency, but not permanently. Sorry, love.'

Norah could only manage a quick nod. She knew they'd help her if they could.

'You an' Janie will have to find lodgings,' her sister Emily said. 'I'll ask around.'

'Thanks.' She listened as they went on to discuss how to sell the furniture, how to get every extra penny for it they could, so that Mum would have a little something behind her.

Only once did Norah interrupt. 'Some of the furniture is mine. I'm sorry, but I can't let you have that. I may need it, or if I have to sell it, I'll need the money it brings for me and Janie.'

There was silence, then her brother-in-law said, 'Sorry, love. We weren't thinking.'

'Me and Mum will start sorting through our things tomorrow, separating hers out,' Norah said. 'If we're out by next Friday, it'll save paying another week's rent. I'll ask at work if I can store my stuff in the old shed for a few weeks, just till I see how I'm placed. I'm sure they'll let me. They're not using it just now.'

After that she let them talk, didn't dare open her mouth in case the sobs burst out, as pieces of her mother's furniture that she'd polished and cared for nearly all her life were shared out or priced.

She hadn't many pieces of her own left. Her life didn't seem to add up to much, even though she'd always worked hard.

She felt quite desperate inside, but tried not to let it show.

★   ★   ★

Andrew walked his sons to Sunday school, usually one of his favourite activities, because it gave them time to chat about their week without the rest of the family listening in. Today, however, he answered the lads mechanically, still feeling upset.

He'd told his family yesterday that he wasn't going to marry Betty after all and they'd been shocked. His sons were more worried that this might prevent them going to Australia, which they both regarded as a wonderful adventure, than about losing Betty, whom they'd merely tolerated.

His biggest worry was how he was to get accepted for the West Australian government's Group Settlement Scheme if he didn't have a wife. The information he'd been sent made it very plain that a man who had children needed a woman to work alongside him and care for them. There were schemes for single men, but not, it seemed, for widowers like him. He'd sent for another pamphlet to replace the one Betty had burned, just to be sure of the details. But he knew most of them by heart, really.

A little lass pushed past them and ran helter-skelter down a steep part of the path. She let out a shriek as she slipped on a damp patch and fell heavily against a low granite wall that guarded the grave of one of the richer families. Immediately she began to wail, clutching her knee and he could see the blood trickling from a bad graze, even from where he stood.

He moved to help her but a woman got there first, so he held back. Within seconds she had the child sitting on a nearby gravestone and had taken a clean handkerchief out of her pocket, passing it to her own lass, who ran off to dampen it.

Andrew turned to his sons. 'Off you go to Sunday school, lads.' He watched in pride as Jack and Ned ran down the hill, then slowed to walk sedately through the side entrance of the church hall. At ten and seven years old, they were a fine, sturdy pair. All three of them were living with his cousin Lyddie at the moment, had been since his wife died. But Lyddie was expecting her first baby, a miracle after years of trying, and she wasn't well. She was finding it hard going, caring for them all, so whatever happened, he had to make some changes and find a permanent home elsewhere. He'd been holding off doing anything because of going to Australia.

The lass came running back with the handkerchief, dampened now, and stood to one side watching while her mother cleaned the gravel from the child's knee. The woman waved her daughter off towards the church hall, then attended to the wound. She talked cheerfully the whole time to distract the injured child, asking her name and where she lived. Such a capable woman, bonny too in a wholesome way, her brown hair cut short and curling in the nape of her neck underneath the brim of her hat. He couldn't imagine Betty doing this sort of thing for a stranger. But he couldn't imagine this woman stirring a man's senses as Betty did, either – or even trying to.

He sucked in his breath on this thought and turned away, striding along the narrow streets to his cousin's house. When he got there, however, he found that her parents-in-law had arrived earlier than usual for Sunday tea. Somehow, today, he couldn't face sitting with them in the front room that Lyddie kept so neat, a room where you hardly dared move in case you knocked over an ornament. He didn't want to make laborious conversation or hear the old couple saying the same things they said every week.

He felt he needed to be free of such restrictions today, free to have a think about his future, so called out, 'I'm going for a walk till it's time to meet the lads, Lyddie love. I only came back for my coat because it's a bit parky outside.' Winter was coming on quickly. He was dreading it. He grabbed his overcoat from the hall-stand and was out again before anyone could protest.

In spite of the intermittent showers, he pulled his collar up and went for a brisk walk, heading up to the moors' edge. No time to go further or he'd have enjoyed a real tramp across the tops. He had a lot to consider and always thought better in the open air.

He wasn't giving up. He was going to Australia and getting his own land, whatever it took. He'd never wanted anything as much in his whole life.

After she'd helped the little girl who'd fallen, Norah decided to go for a walk. She'd spent the last four days shut up in the house, sorting through their possessions. Her mother had alternately wept and snapped at her; she'd tried to be patient because it was hard to lose your home and become dependent on your own children, she understood that.

But today Norah reckoned she'd earned a quiet

hour to herself, so went to walk briskly round the new park. Only that was too tame, too full of people, so she made her way up the hill to where the wind blew freely across the moors and she didn't have to pretend about anything.

Stopping where the streets ended, she stared wistfully up the narrow track that wound between two farms. Beyond them the moors rolled away into the distance, empty, bare, beautiful. She loved to tramp across the tops, wished she had time to go further now. *Ah, why torment yourself?* she thought. *You can't get away, so you must just paste on a smile and get on with it.*

She turned abruptly, bumping into someone so hard he had to grab her to steady them both.

'Sorry. I wasn't looking where I was going.' As he let go, she looked up at the man, who was righting his cap now. She'd seen him outside the church hall earlier with two lads. It was rare for her to look up at a fellow, because she was tall for a woman. Her husband had been shorter than her.

'That's all right. No harm done.'

He smiled, but the smile was forced and she could see that like her, he was upset about something. The town hall clock struck the hour just then and they both stopped to look down at it over the sloping rows of rooftops.

'Sunday school won't be out for another half-hour,' she said, thinking aloud.

'I saw you taking your daughter there,' he said. 'She looks like you.'

Norah smiled. 'Yes. I hope she doesn't grow as tall

as me, though. It's a disadvantage for a woman. I've seen you outside the church a few times with some lads. Your sons?'

'Yes.'

'They look a fine, healthy pair.'

He smiled, his eyes shining with love. 'They are.' As the wind whistled round them, he shivered and rubbed his gloved hands together briskly. 'Best to keep moving in weather like this.'

'Yes.'

'I'll walk back into town with you, if you'd like a bit of company.'

She nodded and he fell into place beside her.

'I don't really need to meet my lads,' he said after a while. 'They're old enough to come home on their own. But we're living with my cousin for the time being and I like to get out of the house as much as possible, to give her a bit of time with her own family. My wife died last year, you see.'

It seemed easy to confide in him in return. 'My husband died early in the war, so I've been on my own for a while. I live in Varley Street at the moment.' She sighed. 'It'll be a wrench to leave it.'

'You're moving?'

'I was living with my parents, but my father's just died. Mum and I can't manage the house on my wages so she's going to live with my sister and I'll have to find lodgings for me and Janie.' She saw him glance at the black armband, which was all the mourning she could afford.

'I'm sorry.'

She shrugged. 'I'll manage. You have to, don't you?'

'You've no other relatives who can take you in?' It was the usual solution.

'No. One sister's taking Mum and the other already has her husband's father living with them.'

There was still ten minutes to go when they arrived back at the chapel, so they walked past it by unspoken consent.

'Shall you look for a house of your own now?' she asked to make conversation.

'I've not decided what to do, yet.'

She shivered and dug her hands into her coat pockets. 'Winter's coming on fast this year.'

'Aye. I'm not fond of the cold weather, not in a town anyway.'

By the time they got back, the scholars were coming out of Sunday school. He waved his sons over, said goodbye and left her.

Nice man, she thought, then forgot him as Janie came out, talking earnestly to another little girl. Janie always had a best friend to cling to, didn't like to do anything on her own. She was a pretty child, and healthy looking, which always pleased Norah.

This was what mattered. Her daughter. Somehow, she'd find a way to make a decent life for the child. Maybe she could take in sewing and work on it in the evenings to earn a bit extra – if they found lodgings with enough room for her sewing machine, that was. The places she'd looked at so far offered only a tiny bedroom and limited access to cooking facilities. She'd have to sell everything to live in such a small place, which upset her. And she hated the thought of living in another woman's house, having to ask to do anything! Absolutely hated it.

What can't be cured must be endured, she reminded herself for the umpteenth time, and took Janie's hand, forcing back the unhappy thoughts and talking as cheerfully as she could manage. Janie had been very close to her granddad and was taking his death and the coming move very badly, clinging to her mother and crying for the slightest thing.

Norah was trying to be patient, but it was hard when she was grieving and upset herself.

2

When he got home from work on the Tuesday afternoon, Andrew was pleased to see that the new pamphlet about group settlement in Australia had arrived by the second post. It looked even more smudged than the previous one. They must have made a lot of copies. Perhaps all the places offered by the scheme were full up, all the land taken.

He greeted his cousin Lyddie, then took the pamphlet into the unheated front room, reading every word of it again.

But he'd remembered it accurately. With a groan, he buried his head in his hands.

Lyddie came into the room. 'Are you all right, love? You've been looking down in the dumps lately. Is it because you've finished with Betty?'

'No. Well, not exactly. It's mainly because I need a wife to get a place in Australia. I'd set my heart on going. Stupid, I know, when I haven't even applied to the scheme yet to see if I'm suitable.'

She frowned, opened her mouth as if to speak then shut it again.

'Say it! Tell me I'm a fool to dream like this.'

She sighed. 'All right. You're a fool, Andrew Boyd.

But not for dreaming of a better life for yourself and the lads – for dreaming of going to Australia with that Betty. I never believed *she* was the right woman for you, never. She only wanted you because you're tall and good-looking.'

He could feel himself flushing at this compliment. They weren't given to tossing praise at people in his family.

'And can you really imagine her on a farm? I can't. She's such a frivolous piece, I'd feel sorry for any man she married and when it was you, well, I was that upset. She won't stay faithful, you know. That sort never do.'

He stared at her in shock. 'You never said anything.'

'When you got engaged, I bit my tongue many a time, because you seemed happy.' Another hesitation, then she laid one hand on his arm, looking up at him earnestly. 'Are you sure it's over with Betty?'

'Quite sure.'

'Then why don't you marry someone else? There are other women who'd jump at the chance of wedding a decent fellow like you, yes, and they'd go to Australia with you in a blink.'

'Now you're talking nonsense. Let alone I can't just walk out on to the street and ask a stranger to marry me, there's not many who'd want to leave their families and go to live on the other side of the world.'

'There might be.'

'You know of someone?'

'No. But I could ask the curate's wife for you. She knows everyone in this part of town, Mrs Reddish does. I could go and see her about it.'

'Don't be daft!'

'What's daft about it? You've got problems and getting wed would solve them.'

He couldn't think straight, he was so surprised by this suggestion. Maybe that's why he agreed that Lyddie should speak to the curate's wife.

But after she'd gone out, he wished he hadn't. He couldn't do it, he just couldn't attempt anything as intimate as marriage with a complete stranger. Still, he consoled himself with the thought that no decent woman would be that desperate and he wasn't interested in women who weren't decent.

He was horrified when his sister came back looking smug. 'Never say you've found someone!'

'Of course I haven't, you fool. But Mrs Reddish thinks she might know someone. The woman's a widow and a hard worker. It seems life's dealt her a few blows lately. She's got a daughter, though, so I'm to let the curate's wife know if that puts you off. But if you *are* interested, you could meet the woman and see if you'd suit.'

'I'm not interested. I don't know what got into me earlier even to consider it. It'd never work.'

'Mrs Reddish thinks it's the perfect solution for both of you. She says if she was twenty years younger, she'd go out to Australia like a shot.'

'The only sort of woman who'd accept an offer of marriage from a complete stranger is a lunatic.'

'Or one who's desperate to give her child a better chance in life,' Lyddie said quietly. 'You're not the only one to want that, you know, Andrew. Meet this woman, at least, before you say no.'

'Don't push me, our Lyddie.'

'Someone has to. You've been restless ever since the war, but your wife was dying and you stayed in your old job for her sake. I respected you for that.' She linked her arm in his. 'It'd cost nowt to meet this woman and see if you take to one another. Go on, give it a try, love. To please me.'

And some madness made him agree.

She stood on tiptoe to kiss his cheek. 'I'll go back and tell Mrs Reddish straight away.'

When the door knocker sounded that evening, Norah was in the kitchen, sitting with a cup of tea she'd just made, toasting herself by the fire. Her mother had moved out this afternoon and most of the furniture had gone with her, so the house no longer felt like home. And now that Janie was in bed, the place was quiet – far too quiet.

She was surprised to find the curate's wife at the door.

'Can I have a word, Norah?'

She realised she'd been staring rudely. 'Sorry. I'm a bit – preoccupied at the moment.'

'No wonder.'

When they were sitting in the kitchen, she poured Mrs Reddish a cup of tea and waited to find out what she wanted.

'I know you've got to break up your home and find lodgings, dear.'

'Yes.'

'I may have a better answer to your problems.'

And hens might bark, Norah thought, but tried not to show how much she doubted this because Mrs Reddish was a kind woman, a sincere Christian who'd helped a lot of people, unlike the vicar's wife, who was a stuck-up snob.

The other hesitated. 'It's – a bit of a drastic solution I'm offering, Norah, so I'll just come straight out with it. I know a man who wants to go and live in Australia. They're giving away land to ex-servicemen out there, you see. He's a widower with two lads. He's just broken up with a young woman he was engaged to, and a good thing too, because she's a flighty piece. But he can't go to Australia unless he has a wife to work alongside him and – and well, I thought of you.'

If a flaming devil had jumped out of the fire and started dancing on the table, Norah would have been no more surprised than she was by this suggestion. Struck dumb, she could only gape at her visitor.

'I know it's a bolt from the blue, but it'd solve both your problems.'

'Are you – serious about this?'

'Yes, of course I am. You don't think I'd come here if I wasn't.' Mrs Reddish waited and nudged gently, 'Well? Are you willing to consider it?'

Norah should have said no straight off because it was a ridiculous idea. But she'd felt so low tonight at the thought of going into lodgings that heaven help her, she couldn't dismiss it out of hand. 'I don't know. I can't seem to take it in.'

Mrs Reddish clasped her hand and looked earnestly into her eyes. 'Let's concentrate on the facts. That's always a good way to start. The man is a widower with two sons. He was engaged to that Betty Simpson, who works in the draper's shop, but she wouldn't go to Australia with him so they broke up.'

Norah glanced across at the mirror and let out a snort of derision. 'Well, he wouldn't even look at a plain maypole like me after her. I know her by sight. She's the prettiest lass in town.'

'And one of the silliest, too. It'd have been a disastrous match. He's not only got a good brain, but he's a sensible, caring sort of man who wants to give his sons a better life than they could have here. If you married him, you could do the same for your daughter.'

'I can't—'

'Shh! Don't say no. Think about it overnight.'

'But I—'

Mrs Reddish stood up. 'I'm not listening to anything you say now. Consider your future carefully, then come and see me first thing tomorrow morning if you're interested in pursuing matters, in which case, don't bother going to work. We'd need to act quickly, before you lose your home and he loses his chance of a place on this scheme. Just remember: he needs you as much as you need him, so it'd be an equal bargain.'

And she was gone, leaving Norah so astounded she stood there in the hall for ages before the cold draught from underneath the front door made her shiver and she went back to her place in front of the kitchen fire.

It *was* a ridiculous idea.

Wasn't it?

★   ★   ★

Andrew slept badly. Why was he letting his cousin push him into this? And why was he getting so het up? He was probably worrying for nothing because what sensible woman would agree to go out to Australia with someone she hardly knew?

Only – what if this one did say yes? Where would that leave him?

He was being stupid.

No decent woman would possibly agree to it.

And anyway, they had to meet first and they might not like one another, probably wouldn't.

No, it was the daftest idea he'd ever heard of.

When he went downstairs, the boys were eating their breakfast. Lyddie beckoned to him and said in a low voice, 'Mrs Reddish sent a message round. You're to stay home from work this morning. If you don't hear anything by midday, it means the woman isn't interested. If she is, Mrs Reddish will send for you to meet her.'

All the air seemed suddenly to vanish from the room.

'Did you hear what I said, Andrew?'

'Yes.'

'Will you do it?'

He shrugged, couldn't frame a single word, it all felt so unreal.

Lyddie gave him a strange look, but didn't say anything else. Luckily it was a fine day, so after the lads had gone to school, he got out his tools and went into the back yard to repair a chair he'd bought for pennies, a fancy rocking chair that had been damaged.

It always soothed him, working with wood did. He should have gone into carpentry, not metal working.

By morning Norah had decided to tell Mrs Reddish she couldn't possibly consider her offer. But then the woman from across the road came over to look at the furniture that was left. She lingered to study Norah's sofa. 'I think I'll take this off your hands as well, but I'm not giving you more than three shillings for it.'

Three shillings for a sofa like this! And the pitiful offer came from a woman who was comfortably off, with a husband and three grown children in full-time work. Norah's gorge rose and she couldn't, *she just could not*, give her sofa away so cheaply. She'd set fire to it, rather. 'I've another offer to consider, so I'll let you know.'

'Take it or leave it now.'

'Then I'll have to leave it.'

The woman sniffed. 'Some people don't know how to accept help.'

'And some people don't know how to offer it generously.' There was a moment's silence, the visitor glaring at her, and Norah was sorry she'd lost her temper. 'I've got to go out now, I'm afraid. I have to see someone.'

'I wondered why you weren't at work. I hope nothing else is wrong?'

'No.' Norah held the door open. She couldn't dredge up a smile, however hard she tried. When she'd closed the door, she let out a little growl of anger and stared blindly at the wall for a few moments, then straightened her shoulders and muttered, 'Why not?'

To be offered so little for the sofa was the final straw. What had she to lose by going round to see Mrs Reddish? She could always say no to the man, if she didn't like the look of him.

And if she did like him, did want to go further with this . . . ?

She blushed, then clicked her tongue in exasperation. She'd think about that if it happened. Her dad had always said, 'Never meet trouble till it knocks on your door.' Eh, she missed his kindly wisdom, she did that. What would he have said now? The answer popped straight into her mind: *Find out more, Norah love. Don't do owt till you know what's involved.* So she would do just that.

She changed into her Sunday clothes and put on her best hat. After checking her appearance in the mirror she set off.

Halfway there she stopped, suddenly afraid. Was she making a fool of herself? Then she started walking again. She was just going to find out a few more details today, that's all. No need to get her knickers in a twist.

And anyway, no one would know about this except the curate's wife, who knew how to keep things to herself.

Mrs Reddish took her into the little sitting room at the back of the shabby curate's house behind the church. Norah sat nervously on the edge of the chair, wishing she hadn't come.

Mrs Reddish looked at her, eyes narrowed. 'You still haven't made your mind up, have you?'

'No. I don't even know why I'm here today. Begging your pardon, but it's a daft idea. This man might be anything, a wife beater, a drunkard, a—'

'I know his family because his cousin is a regular attender at our church and his sons come to Sunday school. They look happy when they're with him and his love for them shines out. He's well thought of by his employer, too. I knew his first wife because I used to visit her when she was dying and she could say nothing but good about him and the way he was looking after her.'

'Oh.'

Mrs Reddish passed across a crumpled piece of paper. 'Early this morning he brought this round for you to look at. It's information about the scheme he wants to join in Australia. I'll leave you to read it while I make us a cup of tea.'

Norah read the pamphlet carefully, then read it again. It did sound a good opportunity for an energetic man. But it'd be hard work for everyone concerned. Well, she wasn't afraid of hard work.

But she was afraid of saying yes out of desperation and then regretting it bitterly for the rest of her life.

She looked up as the door opened again.

Mrs Reddish was carrying a tray. She set it down and smiled at Norah. 'A cup of tea?'

'That'd be lovely.'

Not until she'd eaten a small currant bun and accepted a refill of her cup did Norah speak. 'I – don't know what to say. I came here thinking I'd probably refuse the offer, but I've looked at the pamphlet and – you're quite sure about his character?'

'Yes.'

And suddenly a wild longing to escape from a bleak future swept through Norah and she spoke recklessly, before she could change her mind. 'All right. I'll do it!'

After that things moved so quickly she could only sit in cold terror as Mrs Reddish took over.

Someone knocked on the front door and Andrew, who'd been lost in thought, jumped in shock at the sharp sound. He heard his cousin answer it, then the door closed and she came into the front room.

'Mrs Reddish has sent word for you to go round to her house. The woman is waiting for you there, wants to meet you.'

It was the last thing he'd expected. He didn't know whether he was happy about this or not, but he was definitely nervous.

'Oh, Andrew, I'm so glad for you.' Lyddie came and gave him an awkward hug, her belly coming between them, reminding him that he had to find a new home quickly before the child was born, as well as everything else.

'I must be mad,' he muttered.

'What does that mean?'

'It means I'll go and meet this woman. More than that I can't promise till I see what she's like.'

'That's all I ask, love.' She put up one hand to pat his cheek. 'I think this is going to work out well.'

He didn't. He couldn't imagine why he was even

doing this. How could he possibly marry another woman so soon after Betty?

'Tell me more about him, Mrs Reddish,' Norah pleaded.

'He's called Andrew Boyd. His older son Jack is ten and Ned's seven. He's a widower. It's better if he tells you the rest himself.' She reached across to grasp the younger woman's hand. 'Don't screw up that pamphlet. He'll want it back.'

Norah looked down in surprise at her clenched fist, then smoothed the paper out slowly and carefully. 'I shan't know what to say to him.'

'He'll be feeling the same, I dare say. Just tell him what's in your heart. It won't be easy, but if you're brave, I'm sure you'll manage.'

The door knocker sounded and before Norah could tell her kind hostess she wasn't feeling brave and had definitely changed her mind, Mrs Reddish had whisked out of the room.

There was no escaping now.

It seemed a long time before the door opened again and Mrs Reddish brought a man in. 'This is Andrew Boyd. Andrew, this is Norah Webster.' She left without another word.

To Norah's surprise it was the man she'd met the previous Sunday. From the look in his eyes, he recognised her too.

'Won't you sit down?' But her voice betrayed her, wobbling.

'Thank you.'

She studied him carefully. She remembered him

clearly from their walk but now she studied him more carefully. He was a fine figure of a man, tall and moved as if he was strong. His hair was a very dark brown and his eyes were a deep blue, fringed in long, dark lashes any woman would have killed for. And he had a gentle smile. It was the smile more than his good looks which attracted and comforted her. 'Please tell me about yourself, Mr Boyd, and – and about your plans for Australia.'

Andrew had been studying her just as carefully, liking her neat appearance and the light brown hair, with wisps softening her high forehead and curls nestling into the nape of her neck. She wasn't pretty, but pleasant enough looking, bonny, folk would call her. She looked healthy, with rosy cheeks and clear blue eyes. He remembered the kind way she'd helped the little lass the previous Sunday. He wanted someone who'd be kind to his lads. 'I didn't realise it was you Mrs Reddish was talking about.'

'No. We didn't exchange names.'

He was shocked to realise that for the first time, he was taking his cousin's suggestion seriously.

'I've read the pamphlet,' Norah prompted.

So he told her everything he knew about the scheme and about Western Australia, which was further away from Sydney, it seemed, than Rome was from London, a very isolated place where they wanted more settlers to create dairy farms.

When he ran out of facts, he took a deep breath and looked at her, waiting for a response.

'It sounds – interesting.'

'Mmm. Would you tell me something about yourself now, please?'

He listened as she spoke about her daughter, family and job. He smiled to think of her working as a porter during the war and a little voice inside his head said it'd be good to have a strong woman working beside him on a farm. Now he came to think of it, he must have seen her at the station when he came home on leave. But he'd never noticed her, had always been too eager to see his wife and boys, because it was his family he'd fought for, the only sane reason he could find for that vile war.

When Norah stopped speaking, he abandoned caution, because now that he'd met her, this felt possible. 'I think we both need to make changes in our lives. And I reckon we could get on all right together.'

'How can anyone tell that?'

He shrugged. 'You can't, not for sure, even if you're madly in love. But I feel comfortable with you and Mrs Reddish speaks well of you, so . . . I'm willing to get married if you are. If you're happy to come out to Australia, that is.'

Norah looked at him, thinking over what he'd said. Strange that he'd chosen that word. *Comfortable*. Yes, she'd felt comfortable with him on Sunday and even now, she wasn't uncomfortable with him.

'And I promise you, I'd try to be a good father to your Janie, and – well, I'd ask you to look after my boys, be a good mother to them. I think a lot of them.'

She studied his face again, saw only sincerity there, and yet it was such a big step to take that it was a few moments before she took a deep breath and said, 'All right, then. I'll do it.'

Not the most romantic of proposals, she thought afterwards, more like a business arrangement.

And what was wrong with that?

Only she'd married for love the first time and been happy, too. She wasn't sure whether an agreement like this would be enough for a lifetime.

Well, too late now. It'd been too late for anything but drastic measures when her father died.

And there was Janie's future to think about, as well as hers. She could put up with anything for her daughter's sake.

She'd miss her family, though she'd not miss living in a town. Her spirits lifted just a little at that thought.

It was one thing to tell Andrew she'd marry him, another to tell her family. Norah waited till her daughter got home from school and told her first.

Janie stared at her in shock. 'I don't want you to marry anyone, Mum! I like it with just you and me.' She burst into tears.

Norah cuddled her but when the tears stopped, she said firmly, 'If I don't marry him, our life won't be very nice. We'll only have a small room to share, no kitchen, no yard to play out in, nothing.'

Janie started crying again, clinging to her mother. She'd been crying on and off ever since her granddad died.

Norah sat the child up straight and said sharply, 'Be quiet now! It's not for you to decide something like this. I'm marrying Mr Boyd and that's it.' She watched Janie mop her eyes and look at her pleadingly and repeated, 'I'm your mother and I'm doing this for you. And you *know* you didn't want to live in Mrs Carson's house. You didn't like her at all when we went to see the room.'

Janie gulped. 'Is he a nice man? Will I like him?'

'I think he's very nice and I like him. Do you know two boys at Sunday school called Jack and Ned Boyd?'

'Ned's in my class, but the boys sit at one side and the girls at the other. I don't play with them or anything. And big boys are rough.'

'It's their father I'm marrying, so that'd make them your stepbrothers. Wouldn't it be nice to have brothers?'

Janie's bottom lip was sticking out and she was scowling. 'No. I don't want to share you with anyone.' She burst out crying again. 'We'll not be sleeping together if you get married. You'll be sleeping with *him*!'

'I used to sleep with your father and it made no difference to you.'

'I was only little then. Now I'm bigger I've slept with you for ages and ages. I don't *want* to sleep on my own.'

'Well, you'll soon get used to it. And think how exciting it'll be to go on a big ship.'

'Will my aunties be coming too, and grandma?'

'No. They'll be staying here.'

More tears trickled down Janie's face, but she caught

her mother's eye and didn't start sobbing. 'Will we have our own home again in Australia?'

'Yes.' Norah hugged her. 'It'll be all right, love. You'll see. Now, put your coat on. We have to go and tell your aunties and grandma, then tomorrow Mr Boyd is coming round after tea to meet you.'

'I don't want to meet him.'

'Don't start that again!'

At her older sister's house there was an uproar when Norah explained what she was going to do. Emily sent for their other sister and her husband, then all of them tried to persuade Norah to change her mind.

'You don't even know the man!' her mother wailed.

'Mrs Reddish does. She speaks well of him.'

Janie began sobbing again and crawled into her grandmother's lap, looking accusingly at her mother.

'How can you think of leaving us and going so far away?' Emily wept. 'We'd never see you again.'

In the end Norah took Janie home and left her family to talk things over, as she was sure they were dying to do. They'd already upset the child, made her sob and protest again.

'They don't want you to marry him, Mum,' Janie said as they walked along the street. 'Please don't do it.'

'I've agreed already. I don't break my promises. And as I keep telling you, we'll have a better life with Mr Boyd, much better than living in lodgings and scraping for every farthing. And you'll like him when you get to know him, I'm sure you will.'

'I won't! I hate him.'

'If you ever speak like that again, I'll turn you over

my knee and give you a good spanking, young woman!'

Janie stopped walking to stare at her in shock.

Norah stared right back. 'I mean it.'

She felt dreadful, but what did an eight-year-old child know about the harsh facts of life? Especially one who'd been spoiled as Janie had. This was the only chance she had to make a better life for herself and her child. And Janie would have to learn that the world didn't revolve around her.

Norah looked round at the smoky little town and then imagined a neat little farm with green fields and trees. They'd have cows and chickens, lots of fresh air and sunshine. Everyone said Australia was a sunny country. That would be so good for the children.

She had to hold on to that thought and not let her own fears, or those of an eight-year-old child, over-whelm the good sense of it all.

Both Norah's brothers-in-law went round to Andrew's house that very evening, without telling her, to size him up and question him about the Australian scheme. That embarrassed her when she found out from her sister Emily the next day.

Andrew came round to meet Janie in the evening after work, as agreed. When Norah tried to apologise for her brothers, he smiled. 'I'm not upset by their visit. I'd feel the same if it was my sister. I hope I was able to set their minds at rest.'

He turned to Janie and solemnly held out his right hand. 'I'm pleased to meet you, lass.'

Janie shoved her hands behind her back and scowled at him so darkly, Norah cleared her throat and gave her daughter a look. But Janie didn't take his hand, just said in a toneless voice, 'Pleased to meet you, Mr Boyd.' Which made it perfectly clear that she was anything but pleased.

After that, Janie said nothing. But she watched him. She always did watch people, that child did. And she was always nervous with strangers.

Norah was relieved that he didn't try to push Janie into talking to him but turned back to tell her about his hopes and plans for this venture to Australia.

When he'd gone, she realised in mild surprise that she'd enjoyed his company and found what he had to say interesting – more than that, it had roused excitement in her.

She turned to Janie. 'There. That wasn't so bad, was it?'

But Janie ran out of the room and could be heard sobbing in the bedroom.

Norah sighed, but didn't go after her.

This move was her decision, not that of an eight-year-old child, and the more she saw Andrew Boyd, the more she liked him. Moreover he talked like a sensible man who'd thought things out, not a fool rushing blindly into something. He'd even suggested they go out to a dairy farm whose owner he knew slightly the following weekend and try to learn something about milking and feeding cows.

It made sense to find out about the creatures who would be the basis of their livelihood.

And it would give her a chance to get to know him better, because they weren't taking the children with them this time. They were going to learn.

When she refused to change her mind about marrying Andrew Boyd, her family grudgingly admitted that he seemed all right, but they still thought going to Australia was a stupid, risky thing and begged her not to do it. They didn't want to lose her.

She didn't want to lose them, either, but they couldn't help her out of her predicament and Andrew could. And somehow, her family's opposition, not to mention Janie's continuing sulks, made her more determined to go through with it, though she woke a few times in the night in a cold sweat at the enormity of the step she was taking.

There was one thing that still worried her: going to bed with Andrew. He'd expect it, any man would. And she was prepared to do it because she'd quite enjoyed bed play – but she didn't want to do it yet, not till she knew him properly.

Strangely, it was he who raised the matter. He'd acted quickly to carry on renting her mother's house until they left for Australia and as they were checking through what was left by way of furniture, both his and hers, he said gruffly, 'After me and the lads move in, I think you should continue to sleep with your daughter and I'll sleep in the other room with my sons. I've got bedroom furniture for the three of us. Even on the ship – well, we'll see how we go. After all, we don't want to start our life in Australia with a baby on our hands. And by that time Janie will know me better and not resent me so much.'

Norah murmured agreement, but felt a bit disappointed. It seemed a cold way to approach a marriage. Maybe you could do that when you didn't love your spouse, be driven by your brain not your feelings.

She wished it was different, though, wished he was in love with her, wished he'd kiss her passionately and . . . Oh, she was stupid! She'd be wishing for the moon next.

The marriage took place on the following Friday afternoon, by special licence, with just her mother and sisters in attendance, together with the three children, kept home from school for such a special occasion. His cousin Lyddie had intended to come too but she'd started the baby early.

The ceremony seemed unreal to Norah. She repeated the familiar words dutifully, heard Andrew's deep voice making his responses, and when the curate pronounced them man and wife, she stood frozen in shock as her new husband kissed her cheek.

What had she done?

After it was all over, the two of them took their children back to the house. There was a cake to eat, a fancy one Norah had made herself, and she was glad to see the boys tuck in and accept her offer of a second piece.

'You're a good cook,' Andrew said, also taking a second piece.

'I like cooking.'

'Good thing, because Jack here likes eating.' He ruffled his older son's hair and smiled down at him.

She wished Andrew would smile at her like that. He was even more good-looking when he smiled.

As the days passed and they settled down together, each acted politely, as to a stranger. The three children were equally wary with one another, and Janie made no attempt to get to know her new stepbrothers, avoiding them as much as possible. And she continued to be sulky with Andrew, not always answering his questions and kindly remarks, which resulted in her being sent to bed early two or three times, and once, when she was downright rude to him, Norah smacked her on the bottom.

One day Norah met Betty Simpson in the street, and the other woman barred her path, looking her up and down with a scornful expression on her face.

'I can't think what he sees in *you*!' she said by way of a greeting.

'He sees his wife,' Norah snapped.

'You may be his wife, but Andrew will never forget *me*.' Betty tossed her head. 'But I've done better than him already. I'm marrying the owner of the cinema next month and I'll never have to work again. Tell Andrew that from me. And remember it when you're old and ugly from working your fingers to the bone on a farm.' With a laugh, she walked off.

Norah watched her go, saw men's eyes follow her and sighed. She wished men looked at her like that, or at least, that Andrew did, but he showed no signs of being attracted to her and that hurt. She went on with her shopping, enjoying the fact that she was only working part-time now.

She didn't say a word to her husband about her encounter.

And although the whole town was soon talking about the coming marriage between the balding, middle-aged widower of fifty who owned the cinema and the prettiest girl in town, Andrew said not a word about it to her.

He grew noticeably more distant, though, and frowned a lot.

She was glad of the distraction of more visits to a farm, this time taking the children. She hadn't had much to do with animals, but the cows seemed docile enough and had beautiful eyes. The farmer's wife was clearly fond of them and showed Norah how to milk, laughing gently at her ineptitude and standing by her until the milk started flowing.

The dairy was immaculately clean with stone shelves and big bowls for the cream. Norah could imagine herself managing a place like this.

Janie was very quiet during the visit and refused point-blank to go near the cows. The boys were just the opposite, wanting to touch the animals and have a go at milking. Jack didn't make a bad fist of it, either.

Three weeks later a letter arrived from Australia House by the morning post. Norah wasn't working at the slipper factory that day, so it lay there on the table until teatime and she was itching to see what it said. But it was addressed to him, so of course she couldn't open it as she'd have done with her first husband.

'There's a letter,' she said as soon as Andrew came back from work.

He stared at it for a few seconds then tore it open. She noticed the paper shaking as he read it. He didn't say anything, just covered his face with one hand. Her heart sank. It must be a refusal. What would they do now? He'd regret marrying her, that's for sure.

But when he raised his head, he was smiling, even if it was a tremulous sort of smile. 'I'm sorry. I was just – so relieved I couldn't think straight. I've been worrying myself sick about it, but it's all right. We've been accepted for the group settlement scheme.'

She smiled at him. 'I'm glad.'

'And because another family had just changed their minds about going, we can leave in early January if we can be ready in time. Here. Read it yourself, then tell me what you think.'

She read it carefully and as she passed it back to Andrew, he grabbed her and danced her round the kitchen, crying, 'We're going. We're really really going!'

She couldn't help laughing as they circled the kitchen again. 'You daft ha'porth! Let me go.'

But he didn't. When he stopped moving, he stared at her. They were pressed so closely together she could hardly breathe. And all the air seemed to leave her lungs as he bent his head and kissed her. Not a gentle kiss, this one, but the kiss of a triumphant male.

As he moved away, he stared at her so strangely she

guessed he hadn't intended that. Was he glad or sorry? She couldn't tell.

But *she* was glad. It gave her a small gleam of hope for them as a couple. She didn't want to hurry things, though. Not yet. But she did want that bit of hope, especially after Betty's sneers.

Irene and Freddie

3

Irene Dawson finished wiping the dishes after the Sunday family gathering, and dried her hands slowly, gathering her courage together to face what she was sure would be an unpleasant scene. She'd not said anything before, had waited till she got her mother on her own before speaking. But it was even harder to begin than she'd expected.

'I've, um, got something to tell you, Mam.'

'Oh?' Her mother swung round, expression suddenly eager. 'You're not expecting again?'

Sorrow stabbed through Irene, as it always did when she thought of the baby she'd lost. They'd not even let her see it and the doctor had warned her not to have any more babies for a year or two.

'No. I told you the doctor said we should wait a bit.'

'It's not natural, what you're doing. If Father Benson knew you were preventing babies, he'd be round here like a shot. I knew nothing good would come of you marrying a heathen. But you wouldn't be told. No, you had to marry him. You always go your own sweet way, you do.'

Irene bit back her usual argument that Freddie not

being a Catholic didn't make him a heathen. 'You agreed not to tell the priest.'

'Only because your da was so worried about you, he made a fuss.'

Irene swallowed a lump that suddenly seemed to be blocking her throat. If it was hard to tell her mam, it was going to be even harder to tell her beloved da.

'I'm still hoping you'll come to your senses and let nature take her course, my girl. And I won't lie to the priest, if he asks, which he will soon. It's been six months now since you lost the other baby, and he notices these things. I lost two, you know, but I got on with it and had more, which is a wife's duty, and that's what you should do.'

Yes, thought Irene. Twelve times you did it and just look at you now. Fat, with bad legs and still with a six-year-old to look after when our Bridget's nearly thirty.

'What would doctors be knowing about women anyway?' her mother said with a toss of her head. Her Irish accent was stronger, as always when something upset her. 'They're all men, so they are. You've been brooding ever since you lost the baby. You *need* something to take your mind off it, and what better than a new baby at your breast?'

'Mam! I'm trying to talk to you about something else.'

'Well, get on with it, then.'

'It's this scheme my Freddie's seen in the papers. It's for ex-soldiers, a really good chance it is for them to get their own farms.'

'You're never moving away?'

Trust her mother to leap straight to the main point of how it would affect the family.

'Yes, we are. I'm sorry.'

Silence, then. 'Where are you going?'

'Australia. It's—' But she didn't get chance to finish. Her mother let out a great long wail of anguish, and collapsed on the nearest chair. Her cries were so piercing they brought the rest of the family running till the kitchen was crammed with Irene's sisters and brothers and cousins, not to mention the children crowding the hallway and trying to peer in.

Irene saw her husband stop in the doorway and shoot her a questioning look. She edged round to join him while her eldest sister calmed their mother down a bit. 'I'd only just got started,' she whispered, 'but as soon as I said the word "Australia", she had hysterics, so I couldn't go on.'

Freddie put an arm round her shoulders and watched as his father-in-law abandoned soft words and gave his wife a shake.

'Calm down, woman, and tell us what's wrong. Where does it hurt? Shall I be fetching the doctor?'

'Ask her what's wrong!' Mam pointed one shaking hand at Irene. 'Ask her what she's doing. She's going away, leaving us.' Again she began to wail and sob, refusing to be comforted.

It was half an hour before they got Mam calmed down, after which Da took up his favourite position in front of the fire. 'Well, Irene. Is it true you're going to Australia?'

Irene reached for her husband's hand and Freddie gave hers a quick squeeze as he took over.

'I'll tell you about it, Mr Doyle. There's a scheme been set up for ex-soldiers by the government. If you go out to Australia, they'll give you a piece of land there and help you set up as a farmer. They'll lend you money for your fares, the farm machinery, the house, everything, and you can pay it back gradually. So I've applied. It's the best chance I'm ever likely to get.'

There was dead silence in the room, then Da bowed his head. When he raised it, he looked sorrowfully at Irene, who was his favourite, but his words surprised them all, no recriminations, just, 'Tell us about this scheme, then.'

They listened quietly.

'Each family is given a block of land, just *given* it,' Freddie said.

'No one gives away land,' one of Irene's brothers protested, 'not unless it's useless land, anyway.'

'It's written in black and white on a government pamphlet, so it must be true. The farm will have a windmill to bring up water and the boundaries will be fenced. Part of the land will be cleared and put down to grass, but we'll have to clear the rest. There'd be a house and we'd be given six milking cows, a horse and cart, to be paid for gradually.'

Da looked across at Irene, not Freddie. 'Is it what you really want?'

'Yes, Da.'

'But you know nothing about farming, let alone how they do it in Australia.'

'There's going to be a foreman for each group who'll

help you get used to how they do things there,' Freddie said. 'And I'm a quick learner.'

'Hmm.' Da didn't look convinced.

The younger man put one arm round his wife. 'There's something else, Mr Doyle, the main reason for going as far as I'm concerned. We went to see the doctor before we applied. You know what a weak chest Irene has, how ill she gets every winter. He said a warmer climate would be just the thing for her. She nearly died last winter. I don't want to lose her.'

There was complete silence in the room as everyone waited for Da to pronounce judgement and shrivel Freddie with harsh words, as he could when he was angry.

But he didn't. Instead, he nodded slowly, his eyes filling with tears. 'I don't want to lose her, either. But if I have to, I'd rather it was to Australia than to the pneumonia.' He held out one hand to Freddie. 'You'll look after her?'

'I will. You know I will.' The two men shook hands.

'Aye, no one would deny that you love her,' Da said in a quiet voice, then slapped one hand down on the table, making them all jump. 'And if I were younger, I'd be going out there myself, I would so.'

Mam looked at him, her mouth trembling.

'We have to think of what's best for them, not us, darlin',' he said gently, pulling her close.

She leaned her head against him, her eyes still leaking tears, but made no further protest. In all the major decisions of family life, Da's word was law.

Irene was warmed as always by the love between

her parents. She felt just the same about Freddie, though sometimes she didn't understand him, because he could be dreadfully moody, for no reason she could tell.

Pushing her way across the room she linked her father's other arm. 'Thanks, Da.'

'We heard this week that we've been accepted on the scheme,' Freddie said. 'We have to leave in early January.'

'That letter you got last week,' Ma said bitterly. 'I'd have burned it, I would, if I'd known what it contained.'

'Now, me lass,' Da said. 'None of that.'

She closed her mouth, but it trembled still and tears kept escaping and running down her cheeks. And his.

There were a few people crying that night. They were a close family.

But when they got to bed in the front room, Freddie was exultant. 'It went well, don't you think?'

'I suppose so.'

'I can't wait to leave.'

She was dreading it. Only now was it sinking in that she'd not be with her family, perhaps never see them again.

After that, it seemed the days flew by, there was so much to do. Freddie and Irene both continued to work as long as they could, because every penny counted. And even though it was winter, she stayed well, thank goodness.

In the evenings, Freddie spent a lot of time talking to Da about farming. Da was always happy to talk about the farm he'd grown up on in Ireland, which he still missed, even after twenty-five years in England. And he took Freddie to the pub to talk to a mate of his, who'd grown up on a dairy farm. It made sense to learn as much as you could, did it not?

Freddie was in a good mood all the time. Irene had never seen him so happy. That made life a lot easier.

Her sisters and mother did a great deal of sewing for her, not only clothes, but household linen, because as her mother said, 'If you're going off to some god-forsaken country at the other side of the world, you're going decent.'

Somehow the money was found for these items and no one would say how. Pieces of material would simply appear and be cut up into pillowcases or sheets or underwear. And there were blouses to be embroidered on the long voyage to Australia. Never mind that Irene wasn't a good needlewoman. She could learn, couldn't she?

It seemed that there wasn't a minute to spare and the day of departure came racing towards them.

That day, Mam wept solidly from the time everyone got up and Da's eyes were bright as he said his final farewell before he left for work.

It was a relief to Irene when she and Freddie got on the train and waved goodbye. She felt torn apart. Half of her wanted to jump out of the train and stay with her family, the other half was excited about this adventure.

As they pulled away from the station, she sat there numbly for a minute or two, feeling exhausted. Then she looked at Freddie and burst into tears, sobbing against his chest, not caring what the other passengers thought, until she'd wept herself dry.

After which, she blew her nose and dredged up a smile for him because he was looking so anxious. 'We'll make a fine new life for ourselves in Australia, won't we, Freddie?'

'Yes, love, we will. And one day there'll be enough money for you to come back and visit your family, I promise you.'

She nodded, though she didn't believe him. People like them didn't make enough money to travel round the world. People like them struggled to make ends meet. He was always too optimistic about his various schemes. She'd seen it time and time again. But this one was run by the government, so surely you could trust in them not to cheat you.

And not only were she and Freddie going to the ends of the earth, but they were getting themselves into debt to do it, because you had to pay back the price of the farm equipment and animals. They had precious little saved if things went wrong.

Still, Freddie was young and strong, and she was going to be better in a warm country, she just knew she was. It was a leap into the dark, exciting and terrifying at the same time. But they'd make it work.

AUSTRALIA, 1923

Gil Matthews

4

Life was never the same without Mabel. Gil still missed his wife, even five years after her death. She'd only been twenty-eight at the time, the same age as him. Not a long life, that. So unfair for her to die. If she'd lived in the city, she might still be alive, but they were too far away from help on the farm and she died of a ruptured appendix before they could get her to hospital.

He wasn't even there to say goodbye to her. He'd been away fighting in Europe, had heard about her death from his brother weeks after she'd died – *in a damned letter, two scribbled paragraphs!*

The war had ended soon afterwards. If only it'd ended a bit sooner, he'd have been home and maybe he could have done something to help her. He'd learned a lot about first aid in the Army, been on a training course and all. He preferred tending the wounded to killing any day.

They'd told him he was fighting for his country, but he was never quite sure what his country was fighting for. None of it made any sense to him.

He'd turned into a loner since he got demobbed, not wanting any close friends, not going back to the farm, just working here and there, finding ways to fill the time, wondering if it was worth even bothering.

He still had Mabel's letters, and every now and then he'd feel a desperate need to read them and hear her voice in his head again. Lovely letters they were, written just as she spoke. She'd had a real gift for words and in spite of her anger at him for enlisting, she'd written to him every week while he was overseas, telling him little stories about the farm and the other people in the town.

After he'd read as many of her letters as he could bear, he'd get drunk, not roaring drunk, he didn't want to be a trouble to anyone or to shame himself publicly. He just drank quietly on his own till he passed out and the pain went away for a while.

He'd expected Mabel to be waiting for him to come home, dammit, had needed her desperately after what he'd gone through.

He shouldn't have enlisted, really, still felt guilty about that. But after she'd lost the fifth baby, something had snapped inside him and when two of his friends enlisted, he did too in a fit of black misery.

He and Mabel had had such hopes this time that the baby would live. She'd reached six months, longer than ever before, and the baby had quickened, not vigorous like some but giving gentle little kicks and twitches. They'd joked that it must be a girl. Then it'd stopped moving and they'd begun to worry.

One day his brother had come running out to the paddock to fetch him and he'd stood helplessly outside the bedroom as Mabel lost the baby, screaming and sobbing and begging God to save it.

Gil hadn't believed in God since then.

A boy, it'd been, not a girl. Perfectly formed. But white and still in the bloodied sheet they'd wrapped it in. It had never breathed, had died inside her, they said.

The doctor had tried to stop him looking at it, saying it wasn't really a child yet. But it was. And it was the only son he was ever likely to have, so he'd looked his fill and named his son John, holding him close until they forced him to let go. It took three of them to do that.

Afterwards, while his cheeks were still wet from weeping, the doctor had told him there was no chance of Mabel ever giving him a child, and if he valued her life, they shouldn't even try to have another.

They took away the poor limp body, but he'd found where it was and retrieved it from the rubbish tip – that was the best way to think about it, *retrieved,* not dug up. He'd buried John surreptitiously in the family plot in the church yard, wrapping the poor little body in his mother's silk shawl and saying prayers over it before covering it up, not really believing them but it seemed wrong not to say the words. Babies that hadn't gone to full term didn't count, didn't get a proper burial, but his son had.

And at least if Gil enlisted, he'd not be able to get her pregnant again.

He'd soon wished he hadn't, because he hated Army life and missed her horribly. But to his surprise, he'd survived everything the Army threw him into, starting with Gallipoli in April 1915.

He'd never forgotten his first battle or how cold they'd been. He'd wake up shivering sometimes in the night, as he'd shivered during the hours before the landing. And all because some stupid bloody officer, all fancy braid and brass, had given orders to keep greatcoats rolled in packs and roll tunic sleeves up to the elbows so that flashes of white skin would identify their lads.

He still had nightmares about that battle and the good mates he'd lost there.

He had a lot of nightmares after the war. You saw things that you never spoke of to civilians. But you could never forget them. They were etched into your brain with acid.

One day in 1923 an advertisement in the newspaper caught Gil's eye and he decided to apply for a foreman's job on this new Group Settlement Scheme the government was setting up. It sounded like a worthwhile project, and he'd be doing something useful for lads who'd fought in the war. The idea of that gave him more hope than anything had for a long time.

Maybe he'd be so busy he'd not slip into his drinking bouts.

Maybe.

They accepted him for the position, but they weren't starting work yet, so he had to fill in a month or two before he was needed. They offered him temporary work but he decided to spend the time going down south to see the country that was to be settled, working his way by doing odd jobs. He was a handy fellow, if he said so himself, and could always find a way to earn a meal or a night's shelter.

He was appalled to find how little had been done to prepare for the settlers, raw lads from Britain most of them, by the sounds of it. It wasn't farming land they were being offered, either; it was forest mostly. Big trees, magnificent some of them, like gods of nature.

Why the hell did the authorities want dairy farming set up there?

He nearly quit the job in sheer disgust, because he didn't want to be part of something so badly organised that it would be bound to hurt the lads involved.

But something drew him back to Perth on the appointed date. After all, if the scheme was a muddle, they'd need practical fellows like him even more, to help sort it out. He didn't waste his time complaining, either. When had the authorities ever listened to anything they didn't want to hear?

A few days before he was due to go south, he shut out the world, opened a bottle of rotgut and pulled out Mabel's letters.

It was the last time he'd do this, he told himself, definitely the last.

It was two days before he could see or think clearly again.

This time, however, the drinking didn't bring the oblivion he sought. However much he poured down, he seemed to keep hearing Mabel's voice. She was angry with him, telling him to shape up, telling him to make something of his life not throw it away.

She'd have gone for him with the poker if she'd

found him drunk during their life together. She didn't believe in boozing, Mabel didn't.

Well, she might be safely at rest, but he wasn't. So if he wanted to booze, he damned well would.

5

The Boyds set off for Australia early one morning, well before it was light. The children had been excited the night before, even Janie, getting in the way of the final packing, unable to settle to sleep. Now they were subdued and yawning, which was probably a good thing.

They all walked through the dark frosty streets with their remaining worldly possessions piled on a handcart, pushed by her brother-in-law. Andrew was mono-syllabic, the boys were equally silent, but kept very close to him, Norah was fighting a desire to weep and Janie was clinging to her hand.

The journey south seemed interminable. On the train the boys grew restive and Janie wouldn't leave her mother's side. She'd stopped sobbing now but her face was white and anxious. She turned away from the boys when they tried to talk to her and she ignored Andrew's questions.

Jack was used to bossing his younger brother around and had expected to do the same with Janie, but she'd was adroit at avoiding or ignoring him. That baffled and irritated him. Ned ignored her back. He had a happy nature, was still a little boy unlike Jack who was growing up fast and tried always to emulate his father.

Andrew looked exhausted, which was no wonder, because he'd worked well into the night for the past few days, packing and repacking, finding ways to fit as many of their possessions as possible into the wooden crates which he was paying extra to ship out with them. They'd been deposited at the railway station the night before, ready to be loaded on to the train.

When her husband and the children fell asleep, Norah was glad of some time to herself. She stared across at his face. No need to study his features, she knew them by heart now, but she sometimes wondered what was behind the attractive mask. She didn't feel she knew him much better now than she had when she'd agreed to marry him. Oh, she knew what he liked to eat, that he kept himself very clean, was an extremely hard worker. But what was he *thinking?* How did he *feel* about being married to her?

She presumed they'd be sharing a cabin on the ship and she wasn't sure she was ready for that yet. But he hadn't said anything about it, so she hadn't either. That was one area of their lives that neither of them had talked about since he'd suggested they wait to consummate the marriage. But she still remembered that kiss.

After a long, weary day's travel they arrived at Tilbury and saw the ship they would travel on anchored midstream. They had to go on board by barge, together with a couple of other families. The novelty of this revived the lads considerably, but Janie didn't like heights and was white-faced and shivering as she clambered on to the ship.

Once on board, they were asked to stand in family groups on deck while their cabin luggage was carried on board, though the wind was cold and it was threatening to rain. An officer called for silence and introduced the two people beside him as the matron, in charge of women and girls, and the steward in charge of the men and boys.

'Will the women and girls move to this side of the deck, please,' Matron said.

Norah exchanged puzzled glances with Andrew, wondering what this was about. One of the younger women clung obstinately to her husband's hand, insisting she wasn't leaving his side.

Matron looked at the group and sighed. 'They didn't tell you that the women and girls would be sleeping separately from the men and boys, did they?'

There was a burst of indignant protest and when it didn't stop, the officer roared, 'Quiet!'

'Will you be all right?' Andrew asked in a low voice.

'Yes, of course.' Norah moved across the deck with her daughter. Janie had perked up considerably at the news she'd have her mother to herself. Norah was rather sorry about that.

After Matron had ticked off their names on a list and given them cabin numbers, she led the way down to the passenger cabins, where the women were to sleep in fours. The men and boys were to sleep in the hold, it seemed, which had been fitted up with bunks for the trip.

Norah and Janie were the first into their cabin.

'Can I sleep on the top bunk, Mummy?'

'Why not?' She lifted Janie up to try it.

'I'm glad we're not with *them*, aren't you?'

'No, I'm not. Families should stay together.'

'They don't feel like family to me.'

'Janie, you have to stop this—'

Just then a young woman came into the cabin and smiled at them shyly, so Norah stopped scolding her daughter, not wanting to air their private business.

'I'm Irene Dawson.'

'Norah Web— I mean, Boyd. And this is my daughter, Janie.'

'Are the other bunks free?'

'Yes.'

'I'll sleep on this top one, then.' She set down her suitcase and climbed up, smiling across at Janie.

Another young woman arrived and stared round as if suspicious of what she might find.

'That bottom bunk is the only one free now.' Norah pointed to it.

'Who told the child to take the top one?' the newcomer asked in a shrill voice.

'I did.' Norah replied.

Matron stopped in the doorway just then. 'Everything all right here?'

'No, it isn't!' the angry young woman snapped. 'They've given the top bunk to a child, and that's not fair. I'm not sleeping at the bottom.'

'I'll take the bottom one, if you like,' Irene said. 'I don't mind.'

Matron looked from one to the other, her expression grimly assessing. 'Very kind of you to offer, Mrs Dawson, but there's no need. Mrs Grenville can perfectly well sleep in the bottom bunk.'

'But I don't m—'

Matron held up one hand to stop Irene continuing and looked at the complainer. 'If you want to change to a cabin lower down the ship, without a porthole, Mrs Grenville, you can have your choice of bunks. We work on the principle of first come, first served and we've not started assigning those cabins because there are more people yet to arrive. Otherwise, you can stay here and take that last bunk. Decide quickly and be done with this fussing. I've got some real problems to sort out.'

The angry woman hesitated then said in an aggrieved voice, 'I'm not going into a cabin without a porthole. I'd suffocate in one of those.'

'No one has done so yet. But please yourself.' Matron hurried away.

Norah introduced herself and the newcomer said grudgingly, 'I'm Susan Grenville.'

Irene sighed. 'I didn't think we'd be separated from our husbands.'

'It's a cheat, that's what it is,' Susan grumbled. 'I didn't want to come anyway, but Bert insisted, and now look where it's got us. Separated. It's a bad sign, that is.'

Norah could see that the woman was a grumbler. It was going to be a long journey.

She found it wearing in many ways, the main one

being the way Janie still clung to her like a leech. And since she was used to working and keeping herself busy, Norah found the hours of idleness hard to cope with, in spite of the concerts and clubs and organised activities.

The sight of Irene, struggling to embroider a blouse, led her to start teaching her cabin mate sewing, and other women asked for her help, which led to a sewing group forming. The purser proved to have some material, thread and buttons for sale, and the women set about making garments by hand for themselves or their children.

'Thanks for doing that, Mrs Boyd,' Matron said.

'I couldn't have done it if there weren't sewing materials for sale.'

The other woman laughed. 'There's usually a sewing group starts up. And our Purser makes good money from his sales, one of the perks of the job. He has a fair idea of what's needed.'

Andrew grew friendly with a group of older men, some of whom had farming experience. He spent a lot of time talking to them.

Norah would watch him wistfully, wishing he spent half as much time talking to her, really talking, not making polite chitchat. Then she chided herself for being unrealistic. How could they have serious conversations when they were never alone, always surrounded by people?

And when Janie refused to leave her side.

Irene also complained of having little time in private with her husband. 'There's always someone nearby so you can't really have a conversation, let alone a bit of a cuddle.'

Norah would have settled for a private conversation. But when she one day insisted Janie stay with the other children and began to walk round the deck with Andrew, it wasn't long before another woman came to find her.

'Your Janie's upset. She's crying for you.'

You couldn't refuse to attend to your child when she was upsetting other people.

Andrew held her hand for a moment before she left him. 'We'll have time to talk in Australia, Norah.'

But she wanted to talk now, wanted to spend the lovely balmy nights chatting to him without Janie's scowls and sighs interrupting them.

The ship docked in Fremantle in early February. It was a searing hot day, because the seasons were the opposite to England here in Australia. The children complained about having to wear their coats, but it was the easiest way to carry them, since each had a bag to carry as well.

Norah saw Andrew's arms go round his boys' shoulders and wished he would hold and touch her as easily as he did them. As they stood waiting, she lost herself in her own thoughts. The main one was how glad she was that the voyage was over and she wouldn't be shut up in a stuffy cabin any longer. And she'd be relieved to see the back of Susan. Irene was a delightful young woman, but Susan had a very sour nature and nothing ever seemed to make her happy.

Norah knew she'd been sharp with her a few times, but give the devil his due, Susan never seemed to hold a grudge about that.

At last they were let off the ship, shuffling down on to dry land, where they were directed towards a huge metal shed. There was laughter as they found it hard to walk properly after so long at sea, then grumbling as they had to stand in queues again, waiting for medical and customs checks.

These didn't take very long, thank goodness.

After that, the group settlers were gathered together in one corner. A rather podgy young man, who introduced himself as a representative of the Group Settlement Board, began to call out their names in alphabetical order, ticking them off on a list.

'This seems to be taking a long time,' Norah said to Andrew with a sigh. 'I want to see something more of Australia than a big tin shed.'

'Tired?'

'Only of having nothing to do. I prefer to keep busy.'

'Me, too. Ned, come here and stand still!'

She was glad Andrew kept a firm hand on his sons. She didn't approve of children being allowed to run wild. No need to tell Janie to stay next to her. She was never more than a few inches away.

The young man and a clerk then gave them back their landing money. Andrew had had to deposit twenty pounds before leaving England, so that they wouldn't be destitute on arrival. She wasn't sure how much he had left after that. Money was another thing they hadn't really had an opportunity to discuss. She'd got some of her own and hadn't offered it to him, because it made her feel more secure to have something behind her.

And then, at long last, they were escorted outside 'into Australia' as Janie called it, and directed to a charabanc, which would take them to the old Immigrants' Home, where they were to stay until they could go down to their farms. Its top was open to the evening sunshine and she wished the drive had taken longer, because she was fascinated by everything, the little wooden houses with verandas, the strange trees and once, what she thought were parrots flying freely over the house tops, only the driver said they were white-tailed black cockatoos. But that was a sort of parrot, wasn't it?

So much to learn.

At the Immigrants' Home men and women were once again separated, which caused much grumbling. Females were to sleep in long dormitories and males outside on the wide verandas, which would be no hardship in such warm weather.

Norah was relieved when Susan was assigned to another dormitory and quickly found herself and Janie beds. Irene, looking a lot rosier than she had at the start of the journey, came to take the next one.

'Do you mind if I stay near you?' she asked. 'I don't know anyone else here.'

'Not at all.' The narrow camp stretchers they were sleeping on were set about four feet apart. Janie sat on the edge of hers with a tired sigh, suddenly losing her energy. 'Can I go to bed now, Mum?'

'Not till you've eaten, love,' Norah said.

'I'm not hungry.'

'Well, I am. And you must try to eat something or you'll be hungry in the middle of the night.'

'I thought I'd be with my Freddie tonight!' Irene said as she took her nightclothes out of the suitcase and then pushed it under the stretcher bed. 'I do miss him.'

'You'll be with your husband when you get to your farm.' So would she, Norah thought. And how would that go? After the one kiss, Andrew had made no attempt to touch her. Was he perhaps not a very passionate man? If so, that would be a big disappointment.

And what was she doing brooding, when she had a child to feed and was ravenous herself? 'Let's go down to the dining room.'

They rejoined their men folk and found a hearty lamb stew and fresh crusty bread waiting for them, followed by fruit – melons, which many of them hadn't tried before, and grapes, a luxury item in England. Here, it seemed, they were very cheap at this time of year and many people grew their own.

Before they went to bed, a roster was read out because the women had to take a share of the cooking and cleaning. Norah found she'd be on early duty, getting breakfast ready, which she didn't mind.

As soon as the meal ended, she turned to Andrew. 'It's been a long day and Janie's exhausted. I think we'll go to bed now.'

He looked out to where some of the bigger lads were

playing catchers. 'Those rascals of mine seem to have got a new lease of life, but I'm tired too.'

When would they be sent to their new homes? she wondered as she lay in bed. She was fed up with being ordered around like a schoolgirl, wanted to start her new life and try to pull the family together. They still felt like two separate families and that was no way to go on.

And Andrew never seemed to want to spend time with her. If he'd suggested putting the children to bed and going for a walk round the grounds, she'd have done it, been glad to talk. But he hadn't.

And she'd been hesitant to suggest it to him, fearing a rebuff.

What sort of life would they have together if they didn't talk? How would she go on a farm? There were all sorts of questions bubbling up in her brain, but very few answers.

Well, she'd made her choice now and there was no use grumbling. She just had to get on with it.

Gil and another man were sent down to Northcliffe to help set up a new group. Pete was Australian, another ex-serviceman. He was to take up one of the blocks and act as a sort of deputy foreman to a new group.

So many settlers had been sent out from England that the authorities had decided to release more land. Gil was assigned to be foreman of Special Group 1, which was a farce, really. He'd seen the general area, but didn't know where the land they were to be allotted was, or the exact facilities that were waiting there for the settlers. He too would be allotted a piece of land. He'd almost told them not to bother, then had decided to accept it. If he didn't want to stay, he could maybe sell it.

He met Pete at the railway station and since his head was thumping with a hangover, sat quietly in a corner of the compartment, making no attempt to start a conversation.

'Easy job this,' Pete said as the train set off, 'telling others what to do.'

Gil stared at him in surprise. '*Easy!* Teaching ignorant Poms everything about dairy farming here in Western Australia. You can't mean that.'

'Well, I read in that pamphlet that the farms are already laid out, so it won't be too difficult, surely?'

'I think you'll find yourself with more to do than you expect. I went down to have a look round a few weeks ago and they've hardly got anything set up down there, let alone cleared and laid out the farms. The town has a store and a couple of huts, and that's all. *They* can call it a town. I wouldn't. So unless they've had an army of workers down there in the past few weeks, I can't see much being ready.'

'But it said they'd surveyed the town site, marked out thirty-two quarter-acre blocks. There must be some people and amenities there,' Pete protested.

'There aren't, you know. They've only recently done the town site survey. They've not got any houses built or any businesses going apart from the one store.'

He'd brought some gear of his own with him, including a tent, to make sure he had somewhere under cover to sleep. He didn't even trust the Board to provide a roof. It was getting towards the end of summer now, and he'd been told it rained more in Northcliffe than in Perth, and was cooler, too, so he thought it best to be prepared. He wanted to buy a horse and cart too, if he could find them at a reasonable price, but would buy those locally.

Pete scowled at him. 'If the authorities haven't got things set up, why are they rushing this new group through and sending us down?'

'Beats me.' Gil thrust his hands into his pockets and stretched his legs out. He often found it hard to understand what those in charge were thinking of, they did such damned stupid things. Someone made a decision without thinking if it was possible, then left the poor underlings to try to carry it out.

He'd learned in the Army to keep his mouth shut and make the best of things in your own way. No use complaining, just get on with it.

Three days after their arrival at Fremantle, the settlers were notified that they'd be leaving the following morning. Their group was to travel by train to a town called Pemberton. A map was displayed and throughout the day there seemed always to be people near it, pointing, discussing, speculating as to what they would find down south.

Norah was glad that Irene and Freddie were in their group, but to her dismay, the Grenvilles were in it as well. She tried not to let her feelings show, but Bert was as sour-tempered as his wife and she didn't trust him, though he'd given her no reason for this.

They set off early in the morning, snatching a quick breakfast of bread and jam, and taking with them a package of sandwiches and metal bottles of water.

The journey seemed very long indeed and even with the windows open, the railway carriage soon grew unbearably hot. They'd got used to hot weather on board the ship, but there had usually been a sea breeze. Today the air was still and heat seemed to press down on you like a heavy weight. The children drank their water then complained about being thirsty.

'Keep hold of those bottles and we'll fill them every time we stop,' Andrew said. 'I've been in hot countries before and you need to drink a lot more water.'

Luckily the train stopped several times and at each stop they were able to buy something to eat and drink, pies, sandwiches or cakes, and cups of dark, stewed tea, which normally she'd have turned her nose up at. They were also able to refill their water bottles. Indeed, the station staff seemed to expect that.

Norah had never in her whole life felt as thirsty as this. But then, she'd never experienced such heat in England. Her face was glowing and her hair felt damp with sweat.

Some people grumbled, but one or two seemed to love the heat, and to Norah's surprise, Irene was one of those. Freddie, however, looked desperately uncomfortable and complained several times.

As if that would make any difference! It wasn't setting

a good example to the children to see a grown man grumbling like that.

The scenery between stops seemed to consist mainly of 'bush' as everyone called the countryside that hadn't been settled. There were trees with dull green leaves, some very tall, and sparse undergrowth, very unlike that in England.

The first time the children saw a kangaroo hopping across a piece of open ground as the train passed by, they got very excited, but after they'd seen a lot of them, they lost interest. It was a relief when they fell asleep one by one.

Andrew gave her a weary smile and said in a low voice, 'Bit of an endurance feat, isn't it?'

'It is rather.' She fanned herself with a newspaper they'd bought at the station, knowing her cheeks were still flushed.

'It only gets this hot in the summer, thank goodness. Eh, I'll be glad to get there.' He leaned his head back and soon he too was asleep.

Norah wished she could drop off so easily, but she'd never found it easy to take naps in the daytime so she stared out of the window and day-dreamed of having her own kitchen, of looking after her family, cooking, washing, doing all the familiar chores which added up to *making a home*.

And then there were the unfamiliar things ahead of her, not just milking cows and living on a farm, but sleeping with her new husband.

No wonder she couldn't sleep.

★   ★   ★

It was late at night and had long been dark when they arrived in Pemberton, because you didn't get long summer evenings nearer the equator, Andrew Boyd had said. They'd been expecting a town, but this place didn't seem more than a village to Irene.

She shook Freddie awake and they got ready to leave the train, but before they did, a man walked up and down shouting, 'Leave your luggage on the train. Leave your bags on the train. They'll be quite safe and you'll need both hands to eat and drink.'

They found some people from the towns waiting on the platform with corned beef sandwiches and cups of tea. The tea had been brewed in a big square tin labelled Laurel Kerosene. Irene hoped it had been thoroughly washed out. She accepted a cup from a smiling woman, who'd scooped it out with a jug.

'Where do we sleep?' Freddie asked a man who seemed to be in charge.

'On the train. There isn't anywhere else.'

A few feet away Bert Grenville exploded into anger at this news. '*What?* We've been travelling all day and we're tired. Surely you can do better than that for us?'

The man's expression tightened. 'The government didn't think it out properly. There *is* nowhere round here to put so many people up. And you'll be comfier on the train than on a hard wooden floor somewhere.'

Bert cursed.

'Mind your language. There are ladies present. We're volunteers, doing this as a favour to you. We've stayed up late to feed you and you might show a little gratitude.'

Susan tugged at her husband's arm and he stepped back, still scowling and with no word of apology.

Irene sipped her tea, welcoming its warmth because the night was quite cool, especially after such a hot day.

Standing next to them were the Boyds. Little Janie was so tired she had to be persuaded to eat and drink, and Irene watched wistfully. Surely one day she'd be able to have a child? She didn't want to produce as many as her mother had, but three or four children would be wonderful. It wouldn't be a proper family without children.

Freddie didn't seem to care about children half as much as she did, but he would once they arrived, she was sure he would.

And then, after they'd queued to use the lavatories, it was back to the train to sleep. She snuggled down with her head on Freddie's shoulder, thinking what a strange few days these had been. And would get even stranger, she was sure. But she didn't mind. They were here at last. Well, almost.

6

As soon as he had collected the things he needed, Gil set off for Northcliffe. He left early, once there was enough light to see the way, before the sun had risen, driving there in the horse and cart he'd bought for himself during the few days he'd spent in the south-west. He reckoned that form of transport would be easier to maintain than a car. He wasn't much of a mechanic, but he did know about horses.

Pete was glad of a lift out to the new town, but both of them were horrified by how rough the track was. Gil let Daisy move along it at her own pace. Like him, she was no longer young, but not old yet, a sensible mare, to whom he'd taken a liking at first sight.

In Northcliffe they found a clerk from the Group Settlement Board, who had arrived in a delivery truck. He'd been waiting there for their group, stuck for a way to get out to their blocks. Good organisation, that, but you couldn't blame a clerk like this one for what the higher-ups did. Gil offered the man a ride out and back again.

'Thank you. I appreciate that.'

'We try to help one another in the country,' Gil said

mildly. It was obvious this fellow was a townie. What would he know about settling the land?

They jogged along mostly in silence, but at a particularly bad patch, where they had to detour round a fallen tree trunk, Gil couldn't keep quiet any longer. 'Crikey! Couldn't they have done better than this? You can't call it a road, not by any stretch of the imagination, and what it'll be like in winter, I dread to think.'

The clerk, who'd got off and helped them at least, rather than expecting them to do all the work, shrugged. 'I just do as I'm told. But I will report this road as needing urgent attention.'

It wasn't hard to find their land, because they just followed the track and turned off where they'd been told. It was easy to see which block was meant to be the starting camp for the whole group, because there were piles of tents and equipment lying around, looking as if they'd been dumped there haphazardly.

Gil reined in his horse, cursing under his breath. The materials were there, wood and corrugated iron, but not a single temporary shack had been erected. And the first half of the group was due here later today. Where were the poor sods expected to sleep? A quick glance sideways showed him that the other two were lost for words. 'This can't be the right place, surely?' he said to the clerk. 'There's nowhere for them to live.'

'There've been so many settlers we're a bit behind on the building.'

'A *bit* behind!' Gil bit back angry words. It wasn't this man's fault. And shouting at him wouldn't do any good.

He and Pete fed and watered the horse while the clerk went round the piles of equipment, searching for something. Luckily there was a small creek to one side, easily identified by the greenery round it, so none of them would go thirsty. When Daisy was happily munching from her nose bag, with a bucket of water beside her, Gil went back to see what was to happen next.

'They did send some tents,' the clerk said, as if that was something to be pleased about. 'They're good tents, too. Ex-Army.'

'They didn't erect them, though, did they? And by the time the people get here, it'll be late afternoon – if we're lucky it'll still be light, but who knows?' Gil prayed for patience. 'Do you at least have a list of what equipment there should be?'

'The list is supposed to be here waiting for us, because they weren't sure what they could bring out this time round.' The man looked around as if expecting a list to waft into his hands.

So they walked round the piles again, lifting things and poking around, but there was no sign of any paper-work, let alone a detailed list, just crates and piles of heavier equipment, corrugated iron and wood for the shacks, all sorts of bits and pieces.

'I'll, um, have to go back to Pemberton and find out what's gone wrong,' the official said. 'Unfortunately, a foreman can't take responsibility for things without a list, so you can't use these yet.'

Townies! Gil thought in disgust. *Couldn't organise a washday at a laundry, that lot couldn't.* And he'd bet the people in Pemberton would send up to Perth for instructions. 'List or not, we need to get these tents up so that the settlers have somewhere to sleep tonight.'

He waited, but the fellow didn't make any suggestions about what to do next, so Gil had a quick think about the best way to sort things out since the settlers were already on their way here. 'You drive him back to Northcliffe, Pete, and while you're there you can see if anyone knows about this list. I'll stay here and make a start on finding out exactly what they've given us.' He smiled at the official. 'I can make my own list. Will that satisfy you?'

'But who's to check it?'

'I was a corporal in the Army and I've never been accused of dishonesty before,' Gil said through gritted teeth. 'Are you going to be the first to do it?'

The man looked at him nervously, opened his mouth, then shut it again.

'And bring some food back with you, Pete. I can't find any here. We'll have to feed them when they arrive.'

'I'm not sure there's authorisation for more food,' the official said. 'There was to be some left here. I'm sure if you look more carefully—' He let out a squeak as Gil moved to stand nose to nose with him.

'We've already checked that. There's *no – food – here*, except for those loaves we brought with us from Pemberton. Good thing we had a bit of gumption, isn't it? And the sense to put them in one of the big tin boxes we unpacked even without a list, or they'd be eaten by ants while we're waiting for the settlers to arrive. You'd better find a way of authorising some more tinned food and potatoes, because I'm not staying if you don't do that. Which will leave you to manage the settlers.'

'And if he doesn't stay, I won't, either,' Pete said at once, winking at Gil.

'No, no! Don't do that. I'll authorise it myself. I'm sure if I write and explain why to my superiors, they'll understand.'

'Good. You do that. Write them a nice long letter. They'll be able to file it carefully with all the other letters. My deputy can bring the food back in the cart this afternoon after he's dropped you.'

Pete had turned slightly sideways to hide another grin, which was nearly Gil's undoing.

When the others had gone, Gil closed his eyes and spent a minute or two listening to the birds and humming insects, letting the warmth of the sun soak into him. That cheerful chorus calmed something inside him.

It'd not be peaceful here for long, though, not when the settlers arrived and found nothing ready for them. They'd be angry – and they'd have a right to be.

Opening his eyes, feeling refreshed by those few peaceful moments, he decided to reconnoitre the whole area and see if there was anywhere better to set up camp. They'd passed a few of the blocks as they drove in, and he'd been glad to see that someone had cleared the first twenty yards or so next to the track. They must have planted it with grass, too, because you didn't get stretches of grass like that occurring naturally.

The track continued past the camp. He strode along it as it wound its way through more of this group's twenty farms.

Farms! There was a long way to go before you could call them *farms,* these pieces of mainly forest. The only good thing about how the blocks were arranged was that they were in a fan shape, and most of them seemed to have fairly short frontages, then to broaden out at the rear, so that people wouldn't have too far to go to see one another. Well, it'd seem a long way if you'd grown up in towns, but for those raised in the country, it was close, walking distance instead of driving distance.

The main camp ground was fairly central, which was another good thing. This land, the clerk had said, was to house a school one day. Gil would make a start there and then think about whether to build their temporary humpies or shacks all together or out on the blocks.

Hang what regulations said. He'd do what was best for his group.

As he walked, he checked the map he'd brought with him, muttering the numbers of the blocks to fix them in his mind and scribbling notes about the characteristics of each on a piece of paper with a stub of pencil. There were rough markers for each farm, wooden posts with numbers painted on. He reckoned the surveyors would have marked all four corners – they usually did, but he'd check that another time.

He'd expected fences and temporary shacks, at least. And though land had been cleared at the road edge of each block, there were some damned big trees further in on some of the blocks, trees that would take two men's arms outstretched to span the lower trunk. And there were a hell of a lot of smaller trees too. No wonder the Board paid settlers three pounds a week to clear their own land and do work for the group. They'd have to go on paying out for a while here, so much needed doing.

As he was allowed, he chose the block he'd take for himself. It had some higher ground and a little creek running through it, even now after a long spell of hot dry weather. Not all creeks ran in the summer, when there was very little rainfall, so that would be a big advantage.

After that, he stood for a moment looking at his land, feeling surprised at how good that made him feel. He hadn't been sure he even wanted to stay until now. But something about the huge trees, dappled light and birdsong was getting to him. This would be a good place to live one day, with hard work. And he'd never been afraid of hard work. Mabel would have really loved it here— He cut off that thought firmly. He'd spent enough time reconnoitring, time to get back to the camp ground.

First thing he did when he got back was set a couple of traps for possums, which weren't the best eating, but were all right. He'd be able to shoot kangaroos too. They were better eating, but you needed a gun to get them. The settlers probably wouldn't have guns, but he did.

He gobbled down the food he'd had the foresight

to bring with him, because he'd worked up a good appetite now, then set to work on the tents.

By the time Pete drove back with some provisions, it was half-past two and Gil had two tents laid out ready to erect, a job more easily done by two men on these bigger tents.

The two of them managed that without much difficulty, but then, they'd both been in the Army and Gil at least had erected more tents than he cared to remember, starting at his training camp. How long ago that seemed now!

'Still think it's going to be an easy job?' he asked as they sat by the camp fire for a smoko, even though Pete was the only one who needed a smoking break, because Gil had never liked the taste of cigarettes or the smoke that always seemed to blow in your eyes.

Pete carefully put out his cigarette butt, because they didn't want to risk forest fires, making a few unflattering comments about the intelligence of those who'd set this new scheme in motion too soon. 'You were right,' he told Gil. 'It won't be easy, anything but.'

Gil would have raised a glass to that if there'd been any beer available, but the authorities had banned the sale of liquor in the new town. He grinned. Finding something to drink wouldn't be easy but if there was one thing he was sure of, it was that some men would always find a way to get hold of booze and other men would make money selling it to them.

But he'd vowed not to let himself go on any more binges, not while he was working here. He wasn't going to make a fool of himself in front of other people. Surely this time he'd not fall into the pit of gloom?

He'd be too busy.

Irene was woken at dawn by someone banging on the train doors with a stick and shouting at them to wake up and hand in the blankets they'd been lent. She yawned and stretched as well as she could in the confines of the railway carriage.

'Breakfast will be served in ten minutes,' the same loud voice cried from the platform.

'I didn't expect to bring you to such hardship,' Freddie whispered as they walked across to get some food, after queuing to relieve themselves.

'Tea and bacon sandwiches. No hardship, that.' Irene smiled at the woman serving her. 'Thank you so much for feeding us. We really appreciate your help.'

The woman smiled back. 'It's a pleasure to help those who're grateful.' She threw a meaningful look at Susan Grenville, who was standing at one side, ostentatiously rubbing the side of her cup with a handkerchief as if it had been too dirty to use.

As she ate, Irene could feel Freddie watching her, almost urging every mouthful down. She knew how anxious he always was about her health and sometimes wished he wouldn't fuss over her. Actually, she hadn't felt so well for a long time. Warmer weather definitely agreed with her. The doctor had been right about that.

It was Freddie who suffered from the heat, poor thing, getting rashes in tender parts of his anatomy from sweating.

She tried to turn his mind to something more cheerful. 'I'm looking forward to seeing our farm, aren't you?'

His face brightened at once. 'Shouldn't be long now. And it'll be our very own home, this time.' He turned to the man who kept shouting instructions. 'Do we go on by train?'

'No, by truck.' He pulled a battered pocket watch out and studied it, then raised his voice, 'Better get your luggage out of the train now, folks. The trucks will be along soon to take you to Northcliffe.'

Everyone dispersed and began lifting cases and bags out of the carriages and then helping one another unload the trunks from the luggage wagon.

After that they stood around in family groups, some sitting on their luggage, and waited.

The man who seemed to be in charge kept looking at his watch and frowning. The air grew warmer as the sun rose and it seemed a long time till they heard the sound of motor engines and three trucks came into view, Red Reos. They were so battered and dusty everyone gaped.

When they drew up, one of the drivers called, 'Sorry we're late, folks! We had to move a couple of fallen trees from the track.' He stared round, as if assessing what to do with them. 'Need to get you into three groups, about even numbers. Pregnant women or those with babies can ride in the front of the trucks, everyone else rides in the back with some of the luggage.' He looked round, but no one was pregnant and only one had a baby. Then he turned his attention to their luggage.

'There's too much luggage for this trip, so we'll bring the rest on later. You'd better choose what you'll take with you. About half of what you've got, I reckon.'

'What about our crates from the ship?' someone called.

'Not arrived yet. We'll send them on when they do.'

Andrew saw Bert open his mouth to complain and dug him hard in the ribs. 'Shut up! They're doing their best.'

Bert scowled at him but kept silent.

The eight families milled round, getting in each other's way, and tempers grew shorter. One or two kept insisting that *their* luggage all had to go with them. When he could bear it no longer Andrew took over, roaring in his best sergeant's manner, 'Stay where you are, everyone!' He did a quick head count and then told them who would ride together to give the trucks roughly even numbers of people, and who would sit in the front.

'Who do you think you are to take over?' Bert snapped, the only one to argue with this.

'He's a man with a bit of sense,' the driver of the first truck said. 'And if you don't stop arguing and get on board, we'll have to leave you here.'

Andrew helped load the luggage, insisting on only one item per family till they saw how it went. He made sure Norah's trunk was loaded and later, when they could add a few more things, the boys' trunk. Then, by dint of careful arranging, he got all the people seated in the backs of the trucks. To his relief, the Grenvilles were in the second truck, not with him in the first, because he felt if Bert made one more complaint, he'd punch him.

That was the other thing about hot weather, he remembered, it made for shorter tempers in those who didn't like it.

There was a pile of trunks and boxes left at the station.

'Two of us will come back for them tomorrow,' the leading driver said.

'Who's going to keep an eye on them till then?' Bert demanded at once.

The man shot him a disgusted look. 'They'll be perfectly safe here. What do you think the people in this town are? Thieves?'

Bert muttered something, but the driver turned back to Andrew.

'Thanks for sorting it out, mate. What rank were you?'

'Sergeant.'

'Thought so. You've got that tone of voice. I never let them promote me, just did what they told me and prayed not to be killed. Now, let's get going. I have to deliver you to your foreman before nightfall – if I can.'

'*If* you can?'

The man shrugged. 'Punctures, break-downs, trees down across the road. It isn't much of a road at the best of times, but it's all we've got. There's always something going wrong. At least it isn't winter. We get bogged down regularly in winter round here, then it's all out to dig the trucks out. Sometimes you have to unload them completely to get them out of the bad patches.'

He paused for breath then continued, 'They've only cleared a rough track to your blocks, so even in dry weather, it'll not be a fast trip, especially loaded up like we are. I reckon the government's mad opening up such a lot of land for new groups all at once. We've got that many settlers coming in, there's no keeping up with them.'

On this cheerful note, he climbed into the driver's seat, yelled, 'Hold tight back there!' and set off.

It took them three hours to get to Northcliffe, and by that time, everyone was hungry, thirsty and tired of being shaken about, not to mention covered with the dust and fine grit thrown up by the truck. One child had been sick, and another had cried fretfully for most of the journey. The adults had endured the jolting and bumping in grim resignation and even the older children had lost their usual liveliness.

'This is the town,' called the leading driver. 'And that's the store.'

Norah looked round in shock as they stopped. It didn't look like a town to her, or even a village. The land might have been cleared but there was virtually nothing built on it, no rows of houses or shops, just a couple of what she'd call huts, and the store, which was little more than a tin shed with a tent next to it. This was fronted by an expanse of bare earth, with deep ruts criss-crossing it. What it'd be like here when it rained, she dreaded to think.

A horse and cart was standing outside the store but there was no sign of people till a man came to the doorway and yelled to their drivers, 'Water's heating. Tea will be served in ten minutes.'

'What's that building over there?' Andrew asked, pointing to one further away.

'A small timber mill. It's easier to produce the planks on the spot with all these trees around. Good timber country, this.'

'But the wood will be green, unseasoned!'

'It'll still keep the rain off come winter, so you won't be complaining that they didn't season it.'

A woman went up to the driver, holding a little girl by the hand, and whispered to him.

'Sorry. Shoulda told you.' He raised his voice. 'The lavatories are over there, women to that side, men to the other.'

They straggled across, and Norah walked behind a temporary fence of canvas, tacked to poles. Behind it was a pit with a pole over it for them to sit on and do their business, and that was it. Flies were buzzing round and there was no privacy whatsoever.

'I can't do it here, Mummy!' Janie burst into tears.

Norah summoned up her courage. 'You've no choice, love. Do it here or wet your knickers. See, I'll go first and then I'll help you.'

Janie wasn't the only one to protest, and even grown women were weeping in embarrassment, but when it came down to it, you could only wait so long. Carefully avoiding looking at one another, they did what they had to and encouraged their daughters to do the same.

When they went outside again, they found that the man from the store had provided two enamel buckets of hot, black tea and some thick chunks of bread spread with jam but no butter.

'Eat up quickly!' the driver called. 'We need to get on if we're to get you to your blocks before nightfall.'

People cheered up a little at that prospect.

Andrew, who'd been talking to one of the other drivers, came up to Norah. 'They're providing basic food for the next few days, but I think we should buy some stuff of our own as well, a few tins maybe, just in case. You'll know what to get better than me. We'll be a few miles from the shops, apparently.'

'How on earth will we do the shopping, then?'

He spread his hands. 'Who knows? Presumably they've thought it all out. The foreman is out at Special Group One already, apparently, waiting for us. And the brochure said that later on they'd provide us with a horse and cart as part of the deal. Maybe our group will need those earlier if we're a long way out of town.'

'Can you drive a horse and cart?'

'Not really. I drove cars and motorbikes in the Army. But I can learn, can't I?'

'Yes. And so can I.'

'Good lass. Come on now. Let's go and buy some supplies.'

A few people were buying food, but there were others in their group who bought nothing, people who clearly didn't have any money to spare. Maybe their landing money was all they'd got. She was glad she had some money of her own tucked away. That made her feel more secure.

She bought a huge tin of jam and some flour. A

26-pound bag was the smallest weight of flour they sold, and they didn't have any bread for sale because you had to order that and it came in from Pemberton. She and Irene agreed to share a bag and make soda bread. It grew stale quickly but hungry children wouldn't complain. She also got some tea, sugar and Oxo cubes. She hoped there would be some way of getting milk for the children. She hoped the farm would be pretty and the house well designed.

Happiness surged through her as she went out into the sunlight again. It cheered you up, sunshine did. And she was so glad they'd arrived, more than ready to start work now.

When they drove off again, the trucks were even more heavily laden with all the purchases, but the drivers said nothing. As before, they were strung out at about a hundred yards from one another to try to minimise the debris thrown up by the one in front. But the passengers still copped a lot of dust.

Irene sat holding on to Freddie, who was clutching the side of the truck. She'd been shocked by the sight of Northcliffe but had tried to keep cheerful because he was so angry. She wished he wouldn't fire up so easily.

'They told us a bunch of lies about this place,' he muttered as they bumped in and out of shadow and sunlight. 'That wasn't a town, not even a village.'

'You can say that again!' the man next to him said.

Freddie sighed. 'I was a fool to believe what that pamphlet said.'

'Oh, look at that pretty blue flower!' Irene nudged him, trying to distract him.

'What?'

But by the time he looked they'd driven past the flowers and anyway, Freddie was so lost in anger and his own thoughts, he hardly seemed aware of the scenery near their new home. A few of the others seemed to be in a similar sort of mood. Irene turned her attention to the scenery, which was pretty once they got out of the bare-earthed town.

They were all tired of travelling, so very tired, after over six weeks of it. It felt much longer than that to Irene. But she wasn't as exhausted as she'd have expected by the last two days and was looking forward to their new life.

Surely, there would be opportunities for themselves and the children here? It might not be quite as the pamphlet had said, but the land was there, land just for the taking. You could see that as you drove along. So much land and so few people.

She wasn't going to let things get her down. She was going to make a success of their new life, whatever it took. But she was glad she'd made friends with Norah. They'd be able to help one another.

7

It was late afternoon by the time the overloaded trucks chugged slowly up a slight incline where the land was cleared at each side of the track. The driver of the first one called, 'Here it is, folks, your new home!' A bit further on, he yelled, 'This is the main camp!' and everyone craned their necks to look at the place they'd come so far to live in.

The car breasted the top of the slope and turned off the track on to some cleared land, following faint wheel marks across ground still littered with small branches, twigs and dead leaves.

Two men were working there, erecting tents. They had two up and were fitting poles together for a third one.

The first truck rolled to a halt nearby, then the second and third pulled up behind them. The drivers stayed where they were, stretching and easing their shoulders.

Without the noise of the motors, the silence was broken only by distant birdsong and the buzzing of insects. People stayed where they were, not moving, staring, twisting their heads from side to side, unable to believe this was it. The cleared space was surrounded by forest. There were no chequered fields or hedges, no cattle grazing, no green grass even, only trees that made them feel tiny and a sky whose huge blue arch was unbroken by clouds.

The burning sun was moving inexorably down towards the horizon, yet even now, in the late afternoon, it was hot and the faces of the people in the trucks were reddened by the sun, their shoulders drooping like flowers in the heat.

Then the men erecting the tents broke the silence by shouting a greeting and striding across to the trucks.

'Welcome to Special Group One! I'm Gil Matthews, your foreman, and this is Pete Hessel, my deputy.'

'This can't be our land!' Bert exclaimed. 'It *can't*!'

Gil looked at him sympathetically, remembering from his war service how neat and tidy England and Europe had been, how firmly under man's control nature was there. Here men were tiny and nature was dominant.

Suddenly there was a mad scramble to get off the trucks, with parents shouting instructions to children to stay close by, husbands and wives moving to stand together until all the adults were gathered round the lean, foreman with his tanned face and sun-bleached light brown hair. He looked as if he was used to hard physical work.

He was of middle height, shorter than some of the other men, but he had a presence that made them pay attention to him as he pushed up the sweat-dampened bandana round his forehead. 'Welcome to Special Group One, though it isn't the welcome you or I expected, I'm afraid.'

'Where are the farms?' someone shouted.

Gil waved one hand to encompass the surroundings. 'The blocks of land are spread along the track, marked out with boundary pegs. They'll need more land clearing before you can farm them properly. The Board has sent some tents and equipment to start you off, and the material for temporary shacks will be coming soon, though we'll have to erect them ourselves. The proper houses will be built later.'

'But they said there'd be a farmhouse, pastures, outbuildings!' an older man protested, his voice breaking with the depth of his disappointment.

'There will. But this group has been put together in a hurry, and there's no denying that those doing the organising have let us down. Governments promise a lot of things, but it's people who have to carry them through. Everyone's been working flat out round here, because there are other groups besides yours. We've not got your houses up yet and we won't for a while but the shacks will at least give you shelter. And the Board will pay you to clear the blocks, so you won't be without a means of earning a living in the meantime.'

This was greeted with another silence. Men's fists were clenched, knuckles white, one woman put a hand across her mouth, a tear ran down another woman's face and the children stood looking from one grownup to another, knowing something was badly wrong, but not sure what.

Gil let the information sink in for another moment or two, then turned and gestured to the piles of boxes and equipment spread out across the dry ground. 'We need to finish setting up the tents, so that you've somewhere to sleep tonight. We'll have to dig latrines too. Ladies, there's bread and tinned meat and potatoes, and cooking pots. Can you prepare us some sort of meal?' He squinted up through the trees at the long slanting shadows of early evening. 'If we work hard, we men can get enough tents up to give us all shelter, though some of you will have to share tonight. Fortunately, it doesn't look like rain.'

There was another hubbub as people spoke to one another, shouted questions at him and at least two of the eight women started crying in earnest, which set off some of the children too.

Norah waited a moment to see if anyone else volunteered, but as they didn't she moved forward. 'They reckon I'm a fair cook, so if you'll show me the food and light me a fire, Mr Matthews, I'll see what I can organise.'

'Gil. We use first names in Australia.'

'Gil,' she repeated obediently. 'And I'm Norah.'

'Norah.' He smiled at her approvingly. 'We've got some loaves, at least. If you're careful, there should be enough for tonight's meal and breakfast, but we'll need to bake some more tomorrow. I can show you how to make damper bread, which doesn't need yeast, but there are only three camp ovens to bake it in, so it'll be an ongoing job till we get better organised.'

He looked round as two lads started yelling at one another and raised his voice again. 'Someone needs to keep an eye on the kids. Until me and Pete can teach them what's dangerous and what isn't, they're best staying close to camp. They can gather twigs and branches for the fire, but they'll need to watch out for spiders and scorpions, so kick the branches before you pick them up, kids.'

Gil watched as his words sank in. It all hung in the balance, with some people still looking absolutely furious, two or three complaining to one another and the sun sinking inexorably. Which reminded him. He needed to find the hurricane lamps.

Then an older woman stepped forward. 'I'll help you with the cooking, Norah. Come on, you lot. We've families to feed.'

She's another good 'un, Gil thought. 'Get the lamps out, Pete.' He didn't waste time seeing that done, but turned back to the group. 'Can anyone erect tents? Good. You're in charge of that one,' he gestured to a pile of equipment. 'What's your name? Andrew. Right. And we need someone to dig latrines, one for the ladies and one for the men.'

To his surprise, the man who had been complaining most stepped forward and said sulkily, 'I'll see to that, if someone will help me. Name's Bert Grenville.'

'Spades are over there. Someone help him.'

Gil hadn't the energy to jolly them along, so he lit another cooking fire for the capable looking woman who'd first volunteered, ignored the grumblers and concentrated on providing shelter, food and sanitation. Nights could be quite cool here, even in summer. He helped those dealing with the tents to pick out suitable level ground and left them to it. Pete had found some hurricane lanterns and oil, thank goodness, and one of the women was filling them and setting them out ready for lighting.

He nipped across to check the latrines.

'We didn't want to go too far away and we couldn't put the latrines too near the creek, so this is the best place,' Bert said even before Gil reached him, looking as if he expected an argument.

He was surprised by the competent job the sour-faced fellow was doing. 'You're right. It is the best place. I can see you've done this before.'

'Show me a soldier who hasn't! But how can we give people privacy? The ladies won't want to do it in public, you know.'

'We can't do anything about privacy tonight,' Gil said. 'Just dig the trenches and tell people who's to use which. No, it's no use arguing, that's how it is. There's too much to sort out before it gets dark.'

Gil walked off before the man could protest further. Already the weight of the responsibility was sitting heavily on his shoulders. What did the complainers think he was? A miracle worker?

He was relieved to see that the women had made a cup of tea for everyone in one of the big cooking pots and the older children were fetching in branches and twigs to feed the fires. A young woman with a pretty face held out a cup for him. It had no milk and tealeaves were floating in it, but they'd sweetened it and it went down easily, soothing his dry throat and putting warmth in his belly. He realised suddenly that it had been several hours since he'd eaten.

'Did you find something to cook for tea?'

She smiled at him. 'Oh, yes. Corned beef hash. Norah's overseeing that and I'm in charge of making cups of tea. There aren't enough cups but we're taking it in turns to drink. Is there some water I can use to wash them out and another bucket to fetch it in?'

He should have realised they'd need several buckets. He sorted those out and an enamel jug to use as a dipper for the tea, then led her to the side of the block where the creek trickled. Frogs were croaking already and cicadas creaking out their nightly choruses. 'Careful. It's marshy here. Come round this way.'

Without thinking he held out one hand to help her and as she set hers in it, he paused for a moment in shock, because for the first time since Mabel's death, the very first time, he was aware of a woman's attractiveness. He carried on speaking, hoping she hadn't noticed his reaction to her, but she had, he could see a hint of a smile in her eyes. Some women seemed to be born knowing the effect they had on men. Not that this one seemed a flirt, nothing like that. Just – a very attractive woman.

'Get your water there. You'd better dip it up with the jug. Don't disturb the bottom or the water will be cloudy. Tomorrow we'll dig a deeper hole in the creek so you can put your bucket in more easily. I'll put these branches as markers to show you the best path when you need more water.' As he picked up a dead branch, something scuttled off into the undergrowth and she squeaked. 'Nothing to harm you here, except snakes and they usually slither away unless you attack them.'

She shivered. 'I'll not do that.'

'Stamp your feet when you're walking in areas with debris and low plants where they might be hiding. They'll feel the vibrations and get out of the way.'

'I never thought of there being snakes,' she said wonderingly. 'We've a lot to learn about Australia, haven't we, Mr Matthews?'

'Gil.'

'And I'm Irene.'

A voice called his name sharply and he sighed. 'I'd better hurry. You hold the lamp and I'll help you get a bucket of clean water first.'

While she held the lamp up, he dipped the water up carefully then carried the bucket back for her. By that time the voice was calling out for him again, sounding extremely indignant. 'Got to go. Will you be all right now?'

'Yes, of course.'

There were six tents up by the time it grew dark. As the eight families gathered round the two camp fires, Gil noted who sat there waiting for someone to tell them what to do next and who got on with things of their own accord.

'We've got some bush rugs to keep you warm at night,' he said once they were settled down and eating their corned beef hash, drinking tea from any kind of receptacle they could find to make up for the shortage of cups. 'We've not unpacked all the boxes, but so far we've not found any groundsheets, so you'd be best sleeping in pairs with one bush rug under you and one over you. We call them blueys, by the way, for obvious reasons.'

Silence and a few nods greeted his words. The poor devils looked exhausted. Well, he was pretty tired himself.

'I shall complain about this to the authorities,' Bert said.

'You go ahead and complain, mate. If they take any notice, I'll get you to do my complaining too.' Gil didn't know what to make of that fellow. He'd worked hard and done a good job with the latrines, not the most pleasant of jobs – but had never stopped complaining. 'In the meantime, we have to do our best with what we've got. Now, if you've all finished eating, I reckon we'd better sort out who sleeps where. Some of you will have to share tents tonight, but at least you'll be out of the cold.'

He was going to sleep in the open near the fire. Not a hardship at this time of year and he'd had enough of being surrounded by people for one day. Pete could sleep where he wanted.

To his annoyance, Gil found himself watching Irene as she helped clear up then got ready for bed. That puzzled him. Why her? Why had being close to her roused his body after years of not desiring anyone or anything? She was happily married, from the way she looked at her husband, and at least ten years younger than Gil. Ah, he was a fool.

He fell asleep, still wondering about Irene, what had brought her here, how she'd get on as a settler.

Norah laid out the blankets in their half of the tent, arranged for Janie to sleep with a girl from the other family sharing with them, then went out for a stroll to let the other adults get ready for bed. Strange that the first time she'd be sharing a bed with her husband would be in such circumstances.

She felt shy as she went back to the tent and used the darkness to slip a nightdress on over her underwear. She'd stopped wearing corsets on board the ship and loved the freedom of not being constrained. It'd be foolish to sleep all night in her outer clothes, though, and make them even more crumpled. She didn't know how she was going to get washed in the morning, though.

As the foreman had said, it had grown rapidly cooler as it grew dark and she shivered as she lay down beside Andrew, closing her eyes with a tired sigh.

'You need to move closer,' he murmured near her ear, 'otherwise the blanket won't cover us both.'

'I'm sorry.'

'No, it's me who's sorry.'

'Whatever for?'

'Getting you into this mess.'

'It is a bit of a muddle, isn't it? We'll laugh about it one day, I suppose.' The warmth of his body was so tempting she moved closer.

His hand encountered hers and he wrapped his fingers round it. 'You feel chilled through. Come here, let me hold you properly. I rarely feel the cold.'

She moved gratefully into his arms, letting his warmth wrap around her, feeling his breath gently disturbing her hair.

There was silence, then he said suddenly, 'You're

taking all this without making a fuss or complaining. I really appreciate that.'

'Well, it's not *your* fault. And anyway, weeping and wailing wouldn't change a thing, would it?'

'It *is* my fault because I'm the one who got us into this. I'll do my best to sort things out quickly and get you a proper home.'

'*We* shall do our best.' She'd admired the way he'd got on with things tonight, instead of whining and complaining like that Bert Grenville. Her first impression of the man hadn't changed. She neither liked nor trusted him. She yawned and felt sleep creeping over her body, gave into it willingly.

The next thing she knew, grey light was filtering into the tent and she could hear the sound of someone hammering outside. But Andrew's arms were still round her, so she waited till he woke up to move. It'd been a long time since a man held her like this and she'd forgotten how good it felt.

Then a little ant ran across his cheek. He twitched and as it continued to run round his face, opened his eyes and shook his head to dislodge it, staring at her in surprise for a moment. He pulled away suddenly and she realised why with a blush.

She didn't comment on the change in his lower body but was glad for this proof that he did desire her. It had been worrying her more than a little that he'd showed no signs of wanting her except for that one kiss before they left England. Edging away, she reached for her clothes but quickly abandoned the attempt to dress under the blanket and after checking to make sure the others were asleep, got up to do the job properly, standing up.

The combinations she was wearing under her night-dress reached only to her knees and she saw Andrew's eyes linger on the swell of her full breasts, which she knew showed clearly under the fine cambric. She'd never be able to achieve the slender boyish look that was fashionable now, that was sure, not with her figure. Feeling warmth in her cheeks but not trying to hide herself from him, she slipped on her petticoat and a sensible, sleeveless cotton frock. It warmed up quickly here and even at this hour of the morning she didn't feel the need for a cardigan.

When she went outside, she saw to her immense relief that the women's latrine was shielded from view. The hammering she'd heard had been Gil. He'd stuck poles into the ground on three sides with a plank joining them, and was just finishing nailing leafy branches to this.

He took a step backwards to check his work, then turned and saw her watching. With a grin, he flour-ished an invitation to her to use the convenience before starting building the same sort of fence round the men's area.

When she'd finished her ablutions, she smiled up at the weak morning sunshine. Would she ever get enough of it after the grey, rainy weather she'd experienced so often in Lancashire? Then she thought of how much there was to do and went to wash her hands and face in the creek at a place their foreman had marked out, just below where they took their drinking water.

She flapped her hands to dry them as she walked back to the tent to rouse the children.

It was going to be a very busy day, she was sure. Well, she didn't mind that.

Bert woke early, or rather, he was woken by someone hammering away, on and on. No consideration, some folks hadn't. He'd slept badly, as usual, but at least he hadn't had one of the yelling, shouting nightmares that were his legacy from the war. He stared at Susan, still asleep next to him. Even now, she was frowning. She'd changed so much since their marriage.

Well, so had he. The war was to blame for a lot of unhappiness in the world. Now he'd survived it, he intended to get what he could for himself and his family, if they ever had any family, that was. Susan wasn't very fond of bed play, damn her.

She was still asleep, but he decided to get up and start work. No use lying here thinking. He hoped things would go better here today, but didn't feel optimistic. So far, this group settlement thing had been one big mess after another.

When he left the tent, he saw what had caused the banging. Gil was screening the latrines. Bert nodded approval and went to use the men's, then began to help him, picking up suitable branches and handing them to the foreman. 'What are we going to do today?'

'Start building the humpies.'

'Humpies?'

'The temporary shacks for you to live in. You need them as much to shield you from the sun at this time of year, because we won't get much rain till April. That's what that pile of corrugated iron is for, walls and roofs.'

'They cheated us.'

'So you said yesterday. How long are you going to harp on that? What's done is done and we have to make the best of it.'

Bert scowled at him but continued to hand him the leafy branches. 'What do we do when the leaves drop off these?'

'Pick more branches and thread them through. There's no shortage of branches round here, but our leaves are leathery, especially the gum leaves, so they'll last longer than the soft English leaves would.'

Bert took a leaf or two and tested that out by tearing them up, then continued helping.

Gil bit back a sharp comment.

They worked in silence for a few more minutes, then Gil stood back. 'That should do for now. Let's go and get a cup of tea. Thanks for your help.'

Bert nodded and followed him to the fire, where Norah Boyd was once again in charge. Capable woman that, but too tall for his taste, Bert decided. He could see no sign of his wife, so went across to the tent and found her still sleeping, the only one left in bed. He shook her hard and she jerked awake with a squeak of shock.

'Wake up, you lazy bitch! Everyone else is working.'

She looked at him dopily, then sat up and yawned. 'I'm no good in the mornings.'

'They get up at dawn here, so you'll have to change your ways. It looks bad, you lying in bed like this. Did no one try to wake you?'

She frowned, then nodded slowly. 'I told 'em to leave me alone.'

He could imagine it. She had the sharpest voice he'd ever heard when she was annoyed about something and she'd no doubt used language that had shocked the other women. He pulled the cover off her and she complained in that whiny voice he hated. 'Damned well get up or I'll tip a bucket of water over you.'

She called him things his mother wouldn't have known the meaning of and before he knew it, they were off again, quarrelling. Well, he wasn't going to let a woman talk to him like that, wife or no wife. In the end he pulled the other blanket from underneath her for good measure, tossing them out of the tent as she squealed in protest.

Still angry, he went across to join the rest of the group, who were standing around eating breakfast and pretending they weren't listening to the quarrel. As if anyone could miss it! He avoided their eyes. What did he care about them anyway? When Norah held out a steaming cup he took it from her gratefully. 'Thanks.'

He tipped some of the hot liquid down his throat and watched his wife stumble across to the latrines, looking like a sleepwalker.

'She's always dopey in the mornings,' he said to no one in particular. 'And bad tempered.'

Gil let out a huff of laughter. 'When you get your farm set up and the cows arrive, she'll have to get up at dawn every day. Cows need milking early and late.'

Bert nodded. Susan had been eager to come when he showed her the pamphlet, eager to get on his good side again, more like, because he'd threatened to throw her out when he found out what she'd been doing during the war. But he knew her eagerness was also because she was imagining herself like the farmers' wives in their town, comfortably circumstanced, with maids to help out.

He hadn't enlightened her. If they'd stayed in England, her family would have continued to interfere in their marriage. Those brothers of hers weren't afraid to use their fists if they thought anyone had hurt their little sister.

Ha! It was more likely that she was the one doing the hurting. She was cunning, Susan was, nothing like the sweet girl he'd thought he was marrying. She'd stopped hiding her true nature within days of the wedding, but he was stuck with her by then.

He sighed. He'd never had anyone to stand up for him – and neither would she have here. See how she liked that.

In the meantime he'd do the best he could for himself and sod everyone else.

While they were waiting for people to gather for breakfast, and two women were cutting up bread on the top of someone's tin trunk, Gil showed Norah how to mix and bake a batch of damper. He helped her embed one of the camp ovens in the hot embers at the edge of the fire.

'It's a good thing those pots are made of solid iron,' she said as he scattered more hot embers on its lid.

'Aye, they're tough all right. Think you can make some more batches now?'

'Yes. It's like soda bread. I just needed to know how to cook it, really.'

'You might keep an eye on the one that's started, and turn it round later, so the other side gets the heat.' He turned to assess the other settlers. In spite of a night's sleep, some of them looked bone weary. Not used to sleeping on the hard ground, he thought.

He let them finish eating breakfast then called them to order. 'Come and sit down. We need to plan how we're going to set up the camp and farms.'

He waited till they were settled, then explained. 'We're supposed to conduct a ballot for the blocks, with everyone present, only the rest of our group hasn't arrived yet. But as we don't know when they're coming, I suggest we do it anyway. We'll walk along to see the blocks, then we'll put all twenty pieces of land into the ballot and assign them by number. When the others arrive, they can draw for the numbers.'

'How do we run it fairly?' Bert asked at once.

He would ask that, Gil thought. Bert seemed to suspect everyone of trying to cheat him. 'The government has sent us forms to record the result of the ballot, and we have to do it properly, in public. There are numbers for each block on the map I've got, and we can put the same numbers on pieces of paper. *You* can do that, if you like, Bert.' He hid a grin at the man's solemn nod and saw others smiling as if they understood why he was singling out Bert.

'We'll put the pieces of paper into my hat and let

the youngest member of each family draw one and that's the block they get, no arguments. Afterwards, we'll keep the rest of the block numbers in a sealed envelope for when the other families arrive.'

A short time later Gil set off, walking them to see the nearest blocks, but not leaving the road. To his surprise, all of them came, carrying small children if they had to. He pointed out his own block and when they asked why his wasn't in the ballot, he said simply, 'Foreman's privilege.'

'I suppose you've taken the best block,' Susan Grenville sneered.

'I've taken the one that best suits my purpose, yes. And I'll earn the privilege, believe me.' His had a narrower road frontage but with quite a big stretch of the creek running through it. He preferred that one because it was a bit more secluded than most. He'd build his house further back, didn't want to live in his neighbours' pockets.

Within a couple of hours he had them back at the camp and insisted they eat dinner first, a scratch meal of bread and tinned meat from one of the big tins. He'd sent Pete into Northcliffe in the horse and cart to order regular bread to be sent in from Pemberton, and extra provisions for the time they'd have to spend living together as a group. Once they had their own humpies they could make what arrangements they wanted for feeding themselves and it'd be deducted from the money the men earned by clearing the land.

He'd claim they were working from today onwards – and who was to know when exactly they'd started now the clerk had gone back to report that the first half of this new group had arrived safely? Selecting their blocks counted as working for the scheme, in Gil's book anyway.

No one lingered over the meal and afterwards they gathered round him in a tense silence. He'd be tense too.

Bert solemnly wrote out the names, cut them up into bits of paper and screwed them up, with the other man Gil had chosen watching every move. Whether you got one of the better blocks or not would make a big difference to your chances of success, though some of this lot looked too soft to last it out to him. And the surveyors might claim they'd divided the blocks fairly, but you couldn't change the nature of the land. Some blocks were definitely more promising than others.

Gil carried out the ballot grimly, letting a three-year-old lass pull the first piece of paper out of the hat.

When the numbers were read out, Gil was disappointed, though he'd tried not to show it. He'd hoped Andrew Boyd would get a good block. The man was a hard worker if Gil had ever met one, and his wife was just as capable. But Boyd had got the worst block of all.

Irene and her husband had got the block next to it, which was only marginally better, while Bert had got the best block of all.

Life just wasn't fair sometimes.

8

After the draw, Andrew, Norah and the children walked up to their new block in silence. The children kept quiet as if they'd sensed the mood of their parents.

When they got to the block, Andrew said curtly, 'Don't go beyond the cleared part, children and don't go poking your fingers into anything. You heard what Mr Matthews said: there are poisonous spiders and scorpions. Your mother and I are going to have a look round.'

When they were out of the children's hearing, Andrew said bluntly, 'This is the worst of all the blocks. No creek to give water in summer and more big trees to fell than on other blocks.'

'We won't be short of firewood, then,' she said, trying to look on the bright side. 'And I like that group of huge trees. Can we build our house in their shade?'

He shook his head. 'Didn't you hear Gil yesterday evening talking about how that sort of tree drops branches and kills people. He called them "widow-makers".'

'No. I was clearing up after the meal. We'd better ask him where would be best, then.'

'I want to walk the boundaries today and I think you should too. After all, it's going to be your home as well as mine.'

'Is there time? I have to get back and help cook tea.'

Words exploded from him. 'To hell with cooking tea for everyone else!' He closed his eyes for a few seconds, then opened them and said in a calmer voice, 'We've come all this way and we both ought to know what our land is like.' Seizing her hand, he pulled her along. As they reached the edge of the cleared land he looked back to check on the children and called, 'Your mother and I are going to walk the boundaries. Jack, you're in charge. Don't let me down, now.'

The older boy nodded.

Janie looked at her mother, her mouth getting that square, I'm-going-to-cry look. Norah said sharply, 'Behave yourself, Janie, and do as Jack tells you, or I'll tan your backside.' It was a threat she rarely carried out, but Janie knew it meant she was very serious about the orders she was giving.

Relieved, Andrew went on, 'You three can make yourselves useful by collecting firewood and piling it over there. Look for dead, dry wood, not green branches. Put small pieces for kindling in one pile and bigger branches in another. And bash them with a big stick before you pick them up to make sure there are no spiders hiding in them. If you find any pieces that are fairly straight, like poles, set them on one side for fencing. Now jump to it!'

'Yes, Dad.'

From the way his sons nodded and set to work,

it was clear he was strict with them and even little Ned was used to working. Janie was still looking at her mother pleadingly, but Norah repeated, 'You heard your father, Janie. Do as he told you.'

A short distance beyond the cleared land Andrew stopped.

'How are we to be sure of finding our way back?' Norah asked. It was as if they'd stepped into another world. The bush seemed untouched only twenty yards from the cleared part and it had closed around them as if it never wanted to let them go. It made her feel nervous, but at the same time, she found it beautiful. She'd never been alone in the countryside before, she realised in surprise.

It even smelled different here, a faint tangy scent. She picked a gum leaf off a lower branch of a tree and crumpled it in her fingers, sniffing them. 'Eucalyptus oil.'

He looked at her.

'It smells of eucalyptus oil. My mother always keeps a bottle of it handy for when anyone has a cold. If you put some in hot-water and breathe in the steam, it clears your nose. Or you can gargle with it for a sore throat. Fancy me seeing the trees it comes from! Sorry, I'm going on and we have to hurry if we're to walk round the block.'

He smiled at her. 'That's all right. It's exciting to learn about our new country, don't you think?'

'Yes. And I like being out of doors, I always have. But I don't want to get lost.'

'We'll break off branches or pull down saplings to

leave a trail as we go. And I've got this as well.' He pulled a small compass out of his pocket.

It took them almost two hours to walk round the boundaries in this way and she'd have gone astray if it weren't for him and his compass, because try as they might, it just wasn't possible to walk in a straight line.

When they got back they found the children still in the cleared area, with several piles of branches and twigs collected. The boys were in the middle of a mock sword fight with two straight branches and Janie was sleeping on the ground in the shade of a tree.

'I'm hungry, Dad,' Ned complained, abandoning the sword fight to run over to them, 'and we're all thirsty.'

'We are too. We should have brought some water! We'd better remember that next time.' Andrew looked at the children apologetically. 'Sorry.'

Norah shook her daughter awake and studied the children's sunburnt faces. 'You three had better stay out of the sun as much as possible for the rest of the day, or you'll get badly burnt.'

The boys eyed her rebelliously and looked at their father.

'You heard your mother,' he said. 'Do as she tells you.'

But it was clear to her from the dirty looks they gave her that they resented this command. So far she'd not had much opportunity to deal with them, but she would have to from now on. She didn't need anyone to tell her that only by pulling together as a team would they make something of their new life. And if she expected Andrew to make Janie part of the family, she had to treat his boys like her own sons.

Only she still wasn't sure how they felt about their father's second marriage. Jack at least had looked at her resentfully a few times, and Janie was still not reconciled to her mother marrying Andrew, or sleeping with him.

Three blocks away, Bert and Susan were quarrelling again.

'You didn't tell me it'd be like this,' she raged. 'It's a proper swizzle, this scheme of yours is. These aren't proper farms and it's *jungle* out there. I want to go home. I'm not staying here.'

'Don't be stupid! How will you get back to England? We don't have enough money for the fares. Anyway, I don't want to go back. I've nothing to go back to. And we've been lucky, got one of the best blocks in this group. It'll be worth something, that will.' And he might be selling it sooner rather than later, though he wasn't telling anyone about that.

'Well, I won't—'

'Won't what? If you don't cook, you won't have anything to eat. And your mother isn't round the corner here to help you now.' His anger overflowed and he added, 'You're bone idle, you are.'

Her hand flew out to hit him, but he caught it and gave her a hard shake. 'Stop that! I'll not put up with it here – and you've no brothers to run to and whine.' Her brothers had beaten him up on more than one occasion for ill-treating their spoilt young sister, on her word, not because they'd seen anything.

Susan burst into loud, angry sobs, but when he walked away instead of comforting her, she soon stopped crying and trailed after him.

She hadn't gone far into the untouched bush before something slithered past her. For a moment she stood frozen in fear as she saw a long dark snake. It went on its way unheeding, as if she were just another tree, and not until it had vanished from sight could she move. Then she screamed at the top of her voice.

From a hundred yards away, Bert heard her clearly and something about the tone of her voice told him there was a real problem this time, not one of her fusses over nothing. He ran back to find her shaking and in hysterics, and it was a few minutes before he could calm her down and find out what had happened.

When she told him, he pulled her into his arms, soothing her. Then he put his arm round her shoulders, walking slowly back to the road.

They were the first to return to the camp and he went straight across to tell Gil what had happened.

The foreman asked Susan exactly what she'd seen, then pursed his lips. 'Sounds like a tiger snake to me. They can kill you if they bite you.' He looked down at her flimsy shoes. 'You need a good pair of boots, Susan. Those shoes are only good enough for walking round inside a house.'

'I haven't got a pair of boots!' she wailed.

'Then you'll have to get some. You can order a pair

from Perth through the shop.' He looked at Bert. 'Worth the money, for safety's sake.'

'I gave her the money to get some before we left, and I thought she had done.'

Susan scowled from one to the other. 'They're ugly, boots are. Only common women wear boots.'

Gil shrugged. 'Your choice. Wear them or risk getting bitten. And since you're back, you can make a start on cooking tea.'

'Me?'

'You expect to eat, don't you? So you'll need to share in the cooking. We all have to pull our weight here.'

Bert hid a smile as she stamped off and began opening one of the huge tins of corned beef. But he knew only too well how bad a cook she was, so he was relieved when Pam Beeston came back. She watched what his wife was doing for a minute or two then took over, relegating her to the role of helper.

He was even more relieved to see Susan obeying the older woman's orders, though she had a sulky look on her face.

He'd made a bad mistake when he married her, the worst of his whole life. Been bamboozled by a pretty face, and wasn't the first that had happened to. It made him feel angry all the time, being lumbered with her did. If she didn't start pulling her weight, he'd leave her and hang the vows he'd taken.

The rest of the day was spent in putting up the first humpy on the camp ground. The group would be formed of about twenty families, but the clerk had said the others weren't due yet. This humpy would be used for keeping the stores dry and safe.

It had been decided quite quickly to put one humpy on each block of land that had been allocated, rather than putting them up at the camp ground and then having to move them later. They all wanted to be on their own land, and Gil didn't blame them. He'd stay at the camp ground for the time being, so his humpy could go up later.

He warned people that they might have to share with the newcomers, if the others arrived before proper farmhouses were built. He was thankful for his horse and cart, but when Bert started treating it as a piece of group property, he quickly put a stop to that.

'They're mine, the horse and cart are. I'm supposed to be issued with a horse, but no one's got round to that yet. I'm letting the group use them to get things started quickly, but I'm not having poor Daisy over-worked. You need to look after a horse of her age properly if you want to get the best out of her.'

Bert stared at him. 'She's yours? I hope they're paying you to use her, then.'

Gil couldn't hold back a grin. 'When you're complaining to the authorities about the other stuff, you can tell them that. Maybe they'll send me some money for hiring her. I shan't rely on it, though.'

'You don't think much of how this has been organised, do you?'

'No. Do you?'

Bert shook his head and scowled mightily, then said, 'Thanks for the loan of the horse and cart, then.'

It had sounded very grudging, Gil thought, but the man had said the words at least. And he must have told the others, because one by one they thanked him. He didn't want their thanks, he just wanted to get things started here. It made him feel so much better, having something worthwhile to do with his life. Mabel would be pleased with what he was doing, he was sure.

That thought brought a lump into his throat. 'Eh, lass,' he muttered under his breath. 'Why were you taken from me?'

He went back to working on the first humpy. They'd erected the wooden frame by hammering the uprights straight into the ground. If they were building to last, they'd put the uprights on stumps, protected by over-hanging pieces of metal so that white ants couldn't get in, but these were temporary structures and wood was abundant and easily replaced. The roof timbers had arrived cut to size – well, more or less – so they'd gone on quite easily. Now, they needed to cover the whole frame with corrugated iron.

He looked up at the sky, blue and cloudless. They'd been lucky so far. It'd not rained on their precious food supplies. But he wasn't pushing his luck any further than he had to. If the settlers had to stay in the tents another day or two to make sure the stores were safe, then so be it. The store humpy would be built first.

He smiled on another thought. And if he had to put up with more grumbling from Bert about that, well, too bad.

★　　★　　★

The following day the men began to work the full nine hours required to earn their wages, starting at seven in the morning and finishing at five, with an hour's break for the midday meal.

Seven of the eight women voted to have a washday, because there were two boilers among the equipment sent out. Susan said nothing, just scowled at them all impartially.

The women persuaded Gil and Pete to set the boilers up over fires and tied ropes between the trees to hang the washing on, then set to work, fetching water, chatting about their families and hopes.

As usual, Susan soon started complaining, spoiling the pleasant mood, and when she could stand it no longer, Norah spoke to her very sharply.

'Who are you to boss me around?' Susan asked shrilly, stopping work and folding her arms.

'Someone who's doing her full share of the work, unlike you.'

'I'm not a great strong workhorse like you.'

'Then you'd better get stronger. Weaklings won't survive here,' Pam snapped.

But Susan continued to work slowly and grudgingly, and as the day passed, she found ways to do less than the others. They grew angrier and angrier. If sent to fill a bucket at the creek, she didn't fill it completely and dawdled back, her thoughts clearly on other things. She went to the latrines more often than anyone else and was found lying down in her tent after one trip there. When dragged outside, she claimed she was too exhausted to work non-stop.

'I know how we'd have treated her if she'd tried that on in the orphanage where I grew up,' Pam muttered as Susan vanished yet again.

'How?' another woman asked, not stopping rubbing her clothes on the washboard.

'We'd have tipped her clothes out on the ground and left her to do what she wanted.'

'Good idea,' another said. 'We're ready to start pegging out the first lot of whites. Come and get yours, everyone. The ones that are left will be hers and if she isn't back in time . . .' She grinned at them and pointed her index finger downwards.

When they'd all taken their dripping washing, they worked in pairs to wring it as best they could, since no clothes wringers had been thought necessary by the people equipping the camps. They were left with a small pile of clothes.

'She hasn't come back,' Pam said.

'No.'

For a moment all hung in the balance, but they looked round and saw the wall of the Grenvilles' tent move slightly.

'I'll do it.' Pam tipped the white underwear out on the ground and went to peg out her own family's clothes.

When Gil passed by, he saw the pile of wet clothes on the ground and looked at it in puzzlement. Just then Susan came sauntering out of her tent. He saw one of the group of women nudge another and they all paused to watch.

Susan stopped, stared down at the wet clothes, then let out a shriek. 'Who did this?'

'We all did,' Norah said quickly.

'You've dirtied my clothes again.'

Pam stepped forward. 'Oh, dear. Well, you weren't around – *again!* – and we needed to use the washing tub for something else.'

'We're fed up with you nipping off and avoiding the work,' another woman said.

The others nodded agreement.

Susan stared from one angry face to another, but saw no hint of softness in them. Sobbing loudly, she picked up the clothes and turned to look for a bucket.

Gil had seen this sort of rough justice before and didn't blame the women. In circumstances like these, everyone had to pull their weight. And even then, some hard-working people were beaten down by the random harshness of life. He saw Susan put the clothes in a bucket and start towards the creek, so called out, 'If you're intending to rinse them, make sure you do it downstream from where we get our drinking water. I'm sure you don't want muddy water to drink.'

She scowled in his direction, then glared at the women again. 'Think you're clever, don't you? Well, you're fools. You'll grow old before your time in this horrible place. I'll find a way out of it one day, see if I don't, and then I'll laugh whenever I think of you. Yes, I'll laugh at you for the rest of my life.'

She was not only lazy but a fool to antagonise them, Gil decided. No wonder her husband was so grumpy all the time. Anyone would be, married to her. He doubted that pair would ever fit in here.

When he turned, he saw Bert watching from the group of men, but he made no attempt to help his wife, only turned back to hammer the next lot of nails in with unnecessary force.

Gil had been keeping a closer eye on all the group members than they realised, not saying anything, trying to size them up. There was another fellow who wasn't strong. Poor sod did his best, you had to give him that, but he soon got out of breath. Gil doubted he'd make it here. He'd seen the same sort of thing among the farmers he'd grown up with. If you were physically weak, you just couldn't put in the hard work necessary to make a living.

By nightfall the stores humpy was finished. It was twenty feet by twelve, and had corrugated iron walls and roof, with the gables open to the elements for ventilation and light. There were no windows and the door consisted of a piece of corrugated iron hanging on loops of wire fixed to the doorposts. Inside there was a head height partition across the middle, also made of corrugated iron. Such huts could be erected quickly but weren't meant for permanent homes.

Everyone had come to inspect it, falling silent as they saw how small it was. Wives muttered to husbands, children hung around the edges of the group, feeling the unhappy currents.

'I know it's small,' Gil said, 'but it'll keep off the rain in the winter and shelter you at night. If all the other families were here, we'd have to put two families in each. As it is, you can have a full humpy each.'

'This isn't – the farmhouse they promised us, is it?' one man asked.

'No. Those are proper wooden houses with four rooms and a veranda front and back. But it'll take time to get them built and for the moment we can put these up quickly and at least give you better shelter than a tent. When it rains in winter it sometimes buckets down, and nearly all the rain falls during the winter months. It's different from where you come from.'

He saw Susan frown and open her mouth. Bert jabbed her in the ribs to stop her. Gil didn't give anyone else time to comment but turned to ask the men to carry the perishable stores inside. Once the food was under cover, he felt a lot happier.

Pete would be sleeping in a corner of the store room but Gil intended to keep one of the tents for himself to be going on with. He didn't want to sleep with others.

He was so disgusted by how this was being done by the Board, he'd seriously considered giving up the job – only these people truly needed him and his skills desperately.

That thought made something hard inside him soften a little, just a little.

Four days later, by working from dawn to dusk, they'd erected a humpy on each block, again drawing lots as the fairest method of deciding which would be built first. People moved into them one by one. The floors were bare earth, wind and insects moved in and out of the open gables easily, the makeshift doors rattled and had gaps around them – yet the humpies were a big improvement on the tents. He suggested they build lean-to kitchens, using green timber they cleared from their blocks and when they got wood-burning stoves, they put them into the humpies for heating.

There was as much timber as they could use. They'd have to saw it into planks and slabs themselves, but it came free at least. He'd get a saw pit dug on the camp ground for them all to use.

Norah and Andrew were the last family to move in, because once again, they'd not been lucky in the draw. She hoped this wasn't an omen.

They set to work to arrange their new home, unpacking anything useful and shutting the rest back in the trunks. They had stretcher beds now, to keep them off the ground and since there hadn't been time to put the dividing wall up and they'd wanted to move in, they used the trunks to separate two areas, making a smaller space where the children could sleep and a bigger one for the grown-ups, which was also the living area during the day, when they stood the stretcher beds upright against the walls.

'When our crates arrive, we'll be much better fixed,' Andrew said. 'I don't know what's holding them up. They came into Australia on the ship at the same time as us, didn't they?'

There were a lot of people saying the same thing. Why hadn't their possessions been delivered? No one except Susan Grenville blamed Gil for that, but then she blamed everything on others and seemed to target people quite impartially. You had to feel sorry for her, the poor woman was so desperately unhappy, so out of place here.

For all they had such primitive facilities, Norah was delighted to have moved into the humpy. She was not only able to undress behind a screen made of branches, but to have a proper wash all over, and made sure the children did the same before they went to bed. She shivered as she put on her nightie and got quickly into bed.

Andrew took her place behind the screen and she could hear the water they'd had to share splashing as he too washed himself thoroughly.

When he came out, dressed in his pyjamas, he smelled of soap. He looked ruefully at the two stretcher beds and bent to caress her hair with his hand. 'You've got beautiful hair.'

He trailed his finger down her cheek and her body responded. Hesitantly, she reached out to grasp his hand.

'Frustrating, isn't it?' he whispered.

'Yes, very.' It was more than time they became man and wife.

Janie suddenly began to cry and call, 'Mummy! Mummy!'

Norah and Andrew both froze, and he muttered a curse.

'What's the matter, darling?'

'I'm frightened. It's dark and I don't like this horrible place.' She began to sob.

Jack raised his head to shout, 'Shut up! You woke me up again, you stupid girl.'

That made Janie sob even more loudly.

'I'll have to settle her,' Norah said. 'If I don't, she'll make herself sick crying. She's always been frightened of the dark.'

Andrew sighed and got into his own stretcher bed.

It seemed a long time before Janie went to sleep and when Norah crept back to her own bed, Andrew too was asleep, his breathing deep and even, so they couldn't even continue their whispered conversation, which she'd been enjoying.

It was a long time before she could get to sleep. Her body felt unsatisfied, and her emotions did too. She'd enjoyed being held close, wanted to be a proper wife to him. She still didn't feel as if she knew Andrew as well as she'd like, because he kept his thoughts to himself, but what she knew, she liked.

She hoped he liked her too. Well, at least now she was more than certain he wanted her and that was one worry put to rest. You never really knew a man till you'd shared his bed.

When you married for convenience, it was even more difficult. Not only did they both have children, but Janie remained stubbornly hostile towards her step-father and new brothers. That had to stop. But how to stop it had Norah baffled. She didn't want to treat the child harshly. Janie'd had to face a lot of unhappiness in the past few years, losing her father then her beloved granddad.

But others had lost people they loved and they got on with things.

Norah was still agonising about whether she was

being too soft with her daughter when she fell asleep. She woke to find the next stretcher bed empty and sunlight pouring into the humpy through the open gable.

Work fell into a routine, with the men doing the various tasks needed to set things up, like improving the track, clearing more land and preparing for the cows which would soon be arriving. They had to build milking sheds on each block, but he said that could wait a bit, as only simple three-sided sheds were needed in a place with no snow or ice. The main thing was to clear the land for pastures.

Andrew started building a lean-to kitchen in his spare time, often working by lantern light. For this, he used rough planks and slabs that he and Freddie Dawson combined to saw themselves from trees felled on their blocks. They'd found some clay and Andrew used it like plaster to cover the timber walls near the cooking stove, which he'd bought at the store.

He made a rough bench for Norah to work on and two narrow shelves above it to store their supplies.

'Not the best of kitchens,' he said when he'd finished.

'I can work just fine in here.' She kept her voice cheerful, knowing he'd run himself ragged to provide this for her.

Gil was very insistent on them taking every precaution possible to prevent setting fire to all the wood that was around, not only the lean-tos, but the bush itself. He gave them a talk about how quickly fires could spread through the bush, how people stood no chance out in the open because they couldn't outrun a fire. A wooden house could be alight in a matter of minutes, burned to the ground in an hour.

They were to keep the land near their houses and sheds cleared of dry vegetation or fallen timber in the hopes that if a fire went through their block, they had some hope of saving their buildings – and possibly their lives.

They were all very solemn after his first talk, and no one complained when he repeated his warnings at regular intervals.

'He's a good fellow, Gil is,' Andrew said to Norah one day. 'If we didn't have him, we'd have been in a lot of trouble, because things are so different here. You'd think they'd put some Australian families in with the English ones, wouldn't you?'

'We'll just have to learn quickly, like we did about our shoes.' They were all used now to shaking their shoes in the morning before they put them on, to make sure no insects had crept inside, especially scorpions or poisonous spiders.

Gil would have echoed that sentiment. He was trying desperately to teach his group as much as he could in the shortest possible time. He'd never talked so much in his life and his idea of bliss at the moment was to sit silently in the late evening, staring into a fire and not saying a word.

Except for himself and Pete, all the families were from England and simply didn't understand some of the things that might be dangerous here. He was forever explaining this, that and the other, forever hearing the words, 'Gil, can you just—'

Since there were no schools and wouldn't be for a while, he'd roped in the older children and women to help whenever they were free, which wasn't often for the women, if they wanted to keep their families clean and well fed. It was hard work managing a household, washing or washing up outside in a tub set on rough planks nailed over upright pieces of log set in the ground.

They had to fetch water from the well or the creek if there was one on the block. No windmills had arrived yet to pump water up from wells. The Boyds had a dry block; the luckier ones had part of the creek running through. The duty of fetching water was assigned to older children, if there were any, and woe betide them if they stirred up the bottom of the creek and brought cloudy water back. People needed several buckets and had frugally made more from square kerosene cans or big jam cans. They used anything that would serve and didn't cost anything, hanging two cans at the ends of a sturdy pole so that two lads supporting the middle could carry them more easily.

Gil suggested they dig wells on dry blocks and showed them the best places. For the first time, Andrew found a job hard to face. He hated the penned in feeling of standing at the bottom of a hole shovelling muck into buckets that another man pulled up and emptied, praying the sides didn't fall in on him before they could wall them up with wood. But you couldn't ask another man to do that for you.

He hoped he'd hidden his fears, but Norah watched him sometimes, and he soon realised that she understood what it was like for him, would often touch his hand before he went down into the darkness of the hole or stand at the top when she was taking a break and chat to him.

He was greatly relieved when they found water without having to dig too deep. But even nineteen feet was too deep for him.

And every night their sleep was disturbed because Janie cried or had nightmares, becoming so distressed that in the end, Norah started sleeping next to her, putting her stretcher bed close enough to reach out and touch the child. The frustration of wanting his wife's body, of catching glimpses of her rosy flesh as she washed, was hard to bear and Andrew found his temper very short at times.

'When we get our farmhouse,' he told Janie abruptly one night, 'you'll be having your own room, young lady, and your mother won't be sleeping in it with you, however much you cry.'

The child stared at him mutinously, her bottom lip sticking out.

'I mean it.'

Norah came up to link her arm with his, in a gesture which was becoming familiar and which pleased him. 'He's right, Janie. Mothers sleep with fathers, not with the children.'

'He isn't my father.'

'He is now. And he's my husband. That won't change.'

Andrew put up his free hand to clasp Norah's for a moment and they exchanged wry smiles.

But she saw how her daughter scowled even more blackly at that and continued to worry. Janie could be a very stubborn young madam when she got some idea into her head and she seemed quite certain that Andrew and his sons hated her, would not be persuaded otherwise.

Norah also worried that Jack seemed somewhat resentful of his new stepmother, but his resentment took the form of avoiding Norah as much as he could, which was easier to deal with. She heard him taunting Janie a few times with being a mardy, a cry-baby and a softie but she didn't intervene, hardening her heart when Janie looked at her, mutely pleading for help. The children had to adjust to one another.

She might have taken steps about Janie more quickly, but most days she and Andrew were too tired to do anything but sleep at night. She'd never worked as hard physically in her whole life before, not even when she was a railway porter.

And had never enjoyed sunshine and bright, sparkling fresh air as much.

The other problems would work themselves out as they settled down together as a family and got used to their new home.

Surely they would?

9

One day a man turned up with a cow lowing dolefully in the back of a truck. The creature had been sent to provide milk for their group, especially the children. The driver had also brought some more boxes of basic food supplies for the settlers and a few bales of hay to supplement the cow's feed until the winter rains brought new grass.

Gil helped lead the animal off the truck, talking to it all the time in a gentle voice and seeming to know exactly what he was doing. When the cow was on firm ground, it pulled away, stared round for a minute then ambled over to a patch of nearby grass where it started grazing.

He beckoned some of the men over and as they unloaded the rest of the things from the truck, the driver handed him a letter from the authorities and accepted the offer of one of the enamel mugs of tea that contained a full pint and were very popular. In the warmer weather, people sweated more and even the children were getting used to drinking extra to make up for it.

As people drifted over to look at the animal, Gil opened his letter in case it needed a quick reply.

He nearly choked as he read it, but when he saw someone staring at him, he stuffed the letter into his pocket without saying anything about its contents. He'd attend to this later. No point in replying to the letter. In his experience you could never talk sense into people in authority once they'd made their minds up about some course of action.

As the truck pulled away, he went to slap the cow on the rump and looked at the bystanders. 'Anyone know anything about cows?'

Heads were shaken.

He bit back a sharp response. They'd come out here to be dairy farmers, hadn't they? Surely some of them had found out about their new trade?

'They said a foreman would be here to teach us,' one man volunteered.

'It can't be that hard,' another said. 'You feed the front end and the milk comes out from underneath.'

They all laughed. Gil wished he felt like laughing. The weight of responsibility for all these lives seemed to get heavier by the day. 'Well, we need someone to look after this lass and milk her. We'll share the milk out daily, but the person tending the cow gets an extra ration. I can show you what to do.'

'I don't mind having a try,' Norah offered. 'I had a couple of goes at milking a cow before we left England, but I don't really know a lot about them.'

'In that case, we'll take her over to your block and I'll help you get started.'

Pam stepped forward. 'If you're giving Norah lessons in milking, can I come and watch?'

'I'd like to watch, too.' Irene looked at the cow, her head on one side. 'What are we going to call her?'

'Blossom,' one of the little girls shouted.

'Good idea.' Gil smiled across at the child. 'Blossom it is.' The children always made him feel better and he loved the comical things they said and did. He thought of his son sometimes and wished desperately that the baby had lived. John would be nearly ten if he had.

All the women except for Susan said that they would like to come and watch the milking demonstration, which pleased Gil. He looked at her and raised one eyebrow but she shuddered, staring at the cow as if it was something to be afraid of. Shaking his head at how unsuitable such a woman was for this life, he turned back to study the animal's udder, which wasn't full yet. 'Blossom's not ready to milk yet. We'll do that before tea. I'll find you some buckets, Norah, one for the milk, one for water to wash her with, and one to hold drinking water till we can make her a proper drinking trough. We'll half bury the drinking bucket so she can't knock it over.

When he'd found the buckets, he walked her and Blossom to their new home. The sun shone down on them as they moved in and out of the long shadows cast by the afternoon sun. No hardship to take a stroll like this, Gil thought, especially with a woman who didn't try to fill every second with words. He seemed to have been working non-stop for days, rushing here, rushing there, always on call.

It didn't even matter that the cow was in a contrary mood and it took longer than he'd expected to walk along the track to the Boyds' block. He'd needed a bit of a rest.

'Cows are like that,' he told Norah. 'Pleasant enough usually, but when they get it into their heads that they want to stop for a feed, they do.' He slapped Blossom on the rump and gave her a shove. After flicking her tail at him, she condescended to amble forward again.

At the block, he looked round. 'Where shall we put her? Not too near the house and not too far from the well would be best.'

'How shall we manage without a fence?'

'Look! She's found some grass. If you put out some water nearby, she'll stay round here eating, I reckon, but we'll put her on a long rope attached to a stake to start off with. They're not roamers, cows aren't, and even if they do wander off, they don't move fast. She'll soon learn where her home is, especially when we build her a shelter for the cooler weather. And don't forget, you'll get the dung from her, as well as the milk. The land isn't highly fertile round here and you'll need as much manure as you can get for your vegetable garden. You should pile the dung somewhere and cover it with branches till you need it.'

Norah held back a smile at this, because he was so serious about it and she didn't want to upset him. Fancy being glad of cow pats! But then she'd seen men scraping up horse droppings in the street back home to put on their rhubarb, so she supposed it was the same sort of thing.

Strange new life, this, but it suited her. She looked at the cow who raised her head to stare steadily back.

Lovely eyes, Blossom had. Norah smiled, the cow swished her tail gently as if in response, and some of the nervousness about looking after a cow faded.

She turned slowly in a circle, studying their land. Theirs! Their very own land. That thought gave her such satisfaction.

If only Janie would settle down here, Norah felt sure she and Andrew could not only make a decent life for themselves but be happy together. And maybe have other children. She'd always wanted more than one.

The milking demonstration a little later attracted all the women except Susan. The other six left their children at the main camp under the eyes of the men and each brought a container for a share of the milk, as Gil had instructed. They stood round in a circle, watching and listening carefully as he told them exactly what to do and why. He washed the cow's udder first, explaining how vital it was to keep everything immaculately clean, then he rinsed out the bucket equally carefully before drawing down some milk. He borrowed a cup from Norah, dipping some up to give everyone a taste and smiling as they exclaimed at the creaminess of it.

'That's what we need, cream. It's the only thing the dairy company wants, to make butter with. You'll be left with the skim milk then, I'm afraid, gallons of it.'

They frowned at this.

'What do we do with so much?' one asked.

'Feed it to your families and get a couple of pigs to raise for bacon. They'll drink what's left of the milk

and grow well on it. Nothing need go to waste. Now . . .'
He gestured to Norah to try milking and watched her
critically, nodding approval as she gained confidence
and the milk began to spurt steadily. She had firm but
gentle hands. She'd do.

When the milking was done, they gave the cow some
hay to supplement the sparse grass on the block, leaving
it near the drinking bucket. Then Gil shared out the
milk as fairly as he could, giving the same amount to
each family and double to Norah.

'What about the Grenvilles?' Pam asked.

'Mrs Grenville didn't bother to attend the demonstration, so I reckon she's not earned a share this time.'

There was no sympathy only smiles and pleased
nods at that. Susan Grenville was a fool, Gil thought,
getting on the wrong side of everyone. He couldn't
abide lazy people. He hadn't thought much of her
husband at first, either, but Bert's hard work and
everyone's dawning understanding of what the poor
man had to put up with in his marriage had made
them a little more forgiving towards him.

No wonder he was sour about life. Anyone would
be bad-tempered, married to a lazy woman like that.

Only when he got the chance for a quiet word with
Pete, did Gil pull the letter out of his pocket. 'Look at
this.' He handed it to his deputy.

Pete cursed. 'They're stupid, them lot in Perth.
Haven't the sense they were born with.'

'Stupid or not, we'll have to cope. It's too late to
stop them doing this now.'

'When are you going to tell the group?'

'I'll let them have another night or two in peace, then we'll start making the necessary arrangements.'

But they weren't destined to have much peace. The man Gil had picked out as a weakling put his tools down at the end of the following morning, clapped one hand to his chest and keeled over without even a groan.

Pete ran across to him, kneeling beside him, then looked up with a shocked expression. 'He's dead.'

The men working nearby dropped their tools and hurried over.

'One of you fetch Gil. Quick! Don't say anything to the others yet.'

Pete closed the dead man's staring eyes and muttered a quick prayer, then stood and waited for the foreman.

Gil was too used to death not to recognise it when he saw it. 'I'd better go ahead and tell his wife. Two of you carry him back to their block.'

'Poor chap,' one man muttered. 'To come so far and then die like that.'

'What's his wife going to do now?' another asked.

No one answered.

Gil found Ernest's wife mending her son's breeches, which had got ripped in some rough play. He took off his hat and stood there, searching for words. But there was no easy way to say it except, 'I'm sorry, but your Ernest has just dropped dead.'

Flo sat like a frozen thing, then set her scissors down carefully and threaded her needle into the cloth to keep it safe.

Gil saw a tear roll down her face, then another, but after a minute or two she dashed them impatiently from her cheeks with the back of one hand.

'Why now?' she asked. 'He got here to Australia, came *all this way*. I thought he was getting better. He was certainly happier in the warmth.'

A lad of about twelve walked out of the nearby bush dragging a couple of fallen branches for firewood. 'What's wrong, Mam?'

'Your father's just up and died on us, that's what.'

Dropping the branches, the boy went across to his mother and stood beside her, not seeming to know what to do, at the age of thin bony limbs and clumsy, oversized feet.

Flo reached out to touch him, just once, then straightened her shoulders.

'We can lay him out in the store room, if you like,' Gil offered.

She shook her head. 'My Ernest's being laid out proper at home. He allus was a homebody and that's what he'd want.' She looked at Gil and added, 'After that, I'm leaving here. I never did want to come but he was set on it, and I thought—' She paused to take a deep breath. 'I reckoned it was his last chance, might do him good, because he wasn't a well man. Them trenches done for him. He got pneumonia twice. Coming here might not have helped him get better, but it made him happy and he enjoyed the time on the ship, so I'm glad of that now.'

'Where shall you go? Back to England?'

'No, up to Perth. There's only me and the lad now,

so I'll find a job and he can too. We've no one to go back to.'

The men arrived with the body.

Flo stood up and directed them where to lay it, then stood staring down at her husband. 'He looks peaceful. I don't think he suffered. I'm glad of that.'

'We'll have to take him to Pemberton tomorrow to bury him,' Gil said. 'There's not a cemetery in Northcliffe yet. I'll borrow a truck.'

She nodded, regal as any queen. 'Thanks. I'll go on from there after the funeral. I'll have to sell some of this stuff before I go.' She gestured round at their meagre possessions. 'Think anyone would want them?'

'I'll arrange a quick sale.'

As he walked away he marvelled at her. They said men were stronger, but he reckoned some women were just as strong in their own way.

The death cast a blight over the whole camp, with people talking in subdued voices. Andrew took up a collection for the widow. People who had almost nothing gave what they could, even if it was only a few pennies.

Later Gil conducted an auction of the larger possessions Flo couldn't carry up to Perth with her. There wasn't a lot to sell and she said there was no more stuff coming out. The sale made enough to pay her and her son's fares to Perth and her meagre savings would keep them till they found jobs, at least she hoped they would.

Gil gave her some advice and suggested she go to his cousin Nelly in Fremantle first, writing her a letter of introduction. Nelly often took in waifs and strays and if she had no room for them herself, she'd find someone who had.

He drove Flo and her son to Pemberton the next morning. The body was cursorily examined by the doctor, officially pronounced dead and a death certificate issued.

The widow looked down at the piece of paper, stony-faced. 'I don't need this to know he's gone.' Her voice wobbled on the last words, then she pressed her lips together and put it in her handbag.

Gil left her in the care of a woman he knew, a motherly soul who always had room for someone in trouble. While he was in town, he posted letters for members of the group, picked up some more letters for them, did some shopping and finally went to enquire at the station about their heavy boxes and crates, which should have been delivered by now. He found the boxes himself, clearly labelled, sitting in a big pile to one side of the station yard.

'No one's been authorised to take them into Northcliffe,' the stationmaster said in answer to his query.

'You must have realised we needed them.'

'They usually send word and then I organise it.'

'I'll find someone to do it.'

'Who's to pay? And anyway, I can't let you have them without authorisation.'

Gil leaned forward and said loudly and clearly, 'Are

you really going to try to stop me from taking them to their owners, folk who need them desperately?'

The man muttered something and turned away.

Gil found a couple of fellows to help him load as many of the boxes as possible on the truck, then slept beside it. He didn't think anyone would steal them, but he wasn't taking any chances. The weather was still warm enough that this was no hardship, but the nights would be cooling down soon. March was the first month of autumn, after all.

Ernest was buried first thing the next morning and Gil attended as a matter of courtesy, though he was itching to set off back.

The widow was dry-eyed and still had that grim, determined look to her.

She came and shook Gil's hand when it was over. 'Thank you for your help, Mr Matthews.'

'Will you be all right, Flo?'

'I shall have to be, shan't I? I've had to find jobs before when Ernest was ill, and I dare say it won't be very different here. I'm a good worker and I usually manage.'

Brave woman, he thought again as he drove the heavily laden truck home.

He couldn't forget her courage and it occurred to him very forcibly that he hadn't been as brave as her about losing his wife. He'd wallowed in his grief. For years. Maybe it was the aftermath of the war too. He'd hated all the killing. It'd left him with an ache inside him, somehow, stupid as that sounded.

It was a long drive back and all the time his thoughts

went round and round, but they always came back to the group settlement scheme. He hadn't expected to feel so much a part of it, so determined to make it succeed. Now, he realised in surprise, he was committed to staying in Northcliffe and making a new life for himself. But to do that properly, he needed a wife to help him run the farm he would create with the sweat of his own brow.

He pushed that thought hastily aside. It was the first time he'd seriously contemplated remarrying, though God knew there were enough spare women around after all the wartime losses, and more than one had shown him she wouldn't be averse to his attentions.

Thinking of marriage brought back painful memories of Mabel. It also made him smile. She'd have told him to find another wife, for heaven's sake and stop shilly-shallying about. Nothing if not practical, his Mabel.

And he hadn't had the urge to drink himself senseless since he'd come here, not the slightest flicker of it. That was good – wasn't it?

They'd have to get a cemetery authorised in Northcliffe and the sooner the better. Others would die and it was a long way to go to bury your dead. There wasn't much in the new town at the moment, though people were starting to come in. Some would fail and leave, but others would stay.

He drove through Northcliffe, idly noting the progress on one of the new buildings in the town centre.

When the rough camp came into view, it felt as if he was coming home. Some of the groupies still ate together there, others preferred to cook their own food and eat as a family.

He had to swallow hard because he got a lump in his throat at the mere sight of Irene laughing at something Norah said. Andrew went up to join them, and when Janie saw it she pushed between him and his wife. That lass did cling to her mother. She made her feelings about the marriage all too plain. You couldn't help noticing it.

His eyes lingered on Irene. The sunlight made her red hair gleam like fire. He wondered idly if it'd be warm to the touch. Her laughter pealed out suddenly as Norah said something else. He loved to hear that laugh.

Somehow he had to help make this place feel like home to all these Poms, as well. They hardly knew one end of a cow from the other, but had bravely travelled to the other side of the world to set up dairy farms.

And he was going to make it all work *in spite of* the bungling in Perth. He was thankful that someone up there knew his job every time a consignment of supplies came through safely, but he never relied on them, didn't dare.

After the meal was over, Gil gathered the adults together and told them the bad news that he'd been keeping to himself. 'They're sending the rest of the families in this group down here in two days' time. They've not sent any more humpies, though, so I'm afraid you're going to have to share your humpies.

There were murmurs of disappointment, groans,

even the odd curse, though the men didn't usually swear in front of the women.

'I can let you have the tents again if you want to put the children in those, or sleep in them yourselves, but there will be more than two families in each. We're in autumn now, so we'll have to have them all under cover. When it starts to rain, the tents won't be very pleasant to live in. We just have to hope they'll send us the materials for the rest of the humpies before then.'

He didn't dare hope that they'd send men to build the proper farmhouses yet. They weren't the only group starting up and they were the one some idiot in Perth had added as an afterthought, without making proper provision for them, so he'd guess they came last on every list.

He turned away, then swung back as something occurred to him. 'I need a volunteer either to drive my horse and cart into Northcliffe or the truck, which I have to return.'

Andrew raised one hand. 'I could drive the truck.'

'I'll come with you,' Susan said at once. 'There are things I need to buy.'

There were angry mutters at this.

'Any other women like to go into town?' Gil asked.

Every single one put up her hand.

'We'll draw lots, then. It's the only fair way.'

'But I spoke first!' Susan yelled, her voice even shriller than usual.

Gil glared at her. 'We do things in the fairest way we know in this group.'

But when they drew lots and he pulled out the

winning number, it was Susan's, to his annoyance. For a minute he debated pretending it was someone else's, but by then Pete had peered over his shoulder and called out the number.

Susan smirked at him, ignoring the way the other woman scowled at her.

'You'd better get a list of what other people want buying,' Gil said curtly. 'Anyone going into town will have to do the shopping for the rest.'

She shrugged. 'All right.'

The other women gave her their lists and money, some of it wrapped in bits of rag. Two women shook their heads when Gil asked them if they wanted anything buying.

'Can't afford it.'

'Got to watch the pennies.'

He nodded sympathetically. These families hadn't turned up their noses at his possum stew, as some had. They ate anything put before them and glad of it.

'We'll be leaving at eight o'clock in the morning,' he warned Susan. 'If you're not ready on time, I shall leave without you.'

'I'll be ready, don't worry.'

The following morning she was waiting next to the table they all sat round and on which the women prepared food. It was made from some of the smaller trees they'd felled, rough-hewn in two, and then fixed to pieces of trunk he and Pete had dug into the ground. They'd planed the cut sides as best they could, but it wasn't a smooth surface by any means.

He gestured to the truck. 'There you are, Andrew. I'll take old Daisy here and we'll come at her speed.'

'Can I go in the truck?' Susan asked at once. 'I've a lot of things to buy.'

Gil looked at Andrew, who shrugged. 'If you want. You'll be riding home in the back of the cart, though, so I don't know why you're dressed so fancily.'

'I like to look my best when I go out.'

She might think she looked good with her hair frizzed like that, but Gil thought she looked like one of those women who hung around in pubs looking for a fellow and possibly even charging money for her favours. And why was she wearing a coat when it was pleasantly warm today? It wasn't flattering, made her look fatter. And what did she have in that bag of hers? It didn't look empty to him.

Argh, what was he doing thinking about her? He had far better things to occupy his mind with.

He watched Andrew drive off, noting how capably he drove the truck.

When Daisy clopped into Northcliffe Gil shook his head. Call this a street! It would be a mud patch in winter unless they put in some better drainage. The horse came to a halt in front of the store without needing to be told. There was a motor car parked to one side and he wondered who was visiting.

Andrew came out to greet him. 'I've returned the truck to its owner and made my family's purchases. If you don't need any help, I'd just like to see how exactly they're building that house. I've no experience of weatherboard and if our houses are going to be built of it, I'd like to see how it's done. Give me a yell if you need me.'

Gil nodded and watched for a moment or two as Andrew started chatting to a man working on a new weatherboard house on one of the town blocks that had been sold recently. Someone had made a quick start on building. He admired the way Andrew always tried to learn new skills, wished all the groupies were like him.

Of Susan there was no sign.

Gil put a nosebag on his horse and went inside the store. As he started giving his order, he looked round again for Susan, because this was the only place she could be, surely? There was the sound of voices from the rear and he walked in that direction, stopping when he saw her standing outside chatting to a stranger, presumably the owner of the small motor car that was parked nearby.

Indignation rose hotly in him. She was flirting, had opened her coat and laid a hand on one hip, posing to show off her figure. The man was smiling down at her, openly eyeing the curve of her breasts.

'Can't abide married women who flirt,' Gil muttered.

'Did you say something?' the shopkeeper asked as he stood a 150-pound sack of flour next to the counter, and added a 72-pound bag of sugar, then a wooden packing case of the huge tins of jam and another of tins of corned beef, followed by a sack of onions.

'No. Just thinking aloud.' Gil turned back to finish his order. 'Did *she* put in her orders?' he asked, gesturing to the couple still talking outside.

'Yes. I've got everything ready over there. She hasn't paid me yet, too busy giving *him* the glad eye. He only came to see if there was any way to make money out of us, but when he saw that the town hadn't really got going yet, he said he'd changed his mind and would come back in a year or two. He'd be long gone if he hadn't met her. I doubt we'll ever see him again. He's a townie, that one, not the sort to settle in a place that needs work to make it worthwhile.'

'I can see that.'

'I'll give you a hand to load these on the cart.' The storekeeper laughed. 'I don't mind *you* not paying me till afterwards. You're hardly likely to run out on me, are you?'

'You think not?'

'Nah. I can tell the ones who're going to stay by now – well usually. There are one or two who surprise you, but mostly it's obvious.'

There were a lot of tins of food. Gil hadn't realised how much the women would be ordering and began to worry about the weight.

'That poor old horse of yours is going to be tired out by the time you get back.'

'We'll walk beside her going back.' Gil slapped Daisy's side affectionately then frowned as he remembered Susan's unsuitable shoes. He hoped she'd bought or ordered some more sensible ones. As he picked up the first crate of goods, he heard the stranger's car start up and drive off and thought good riddance to that sleazy fellow.

When they were loaded and ready to leave, he

signed for the group's official goods, paid for his personal purchases, then went to find Susan, annoyed that she was keeping them waiting. She should have been keeping a watch out for when he was ready to leave.

But she wasn't at the rear of the store and the stranger had driven off now.

'Has she paid you for the extra orders?' he asked as he walked towards the front of the store again.

'Not yet.'

Perhaps she'd gone to relieve herself. Gil waited. Five minutes passed. But there was still no sign of her. Angry now, he strode across to the women's latrines and called out, 'Are you all right, Susan?'

There was only silence.

'Is anyone in there?' No answer, so he peered round the canvas screen, ready to duck back. But no one was there.

He went back to the store where Andrew was waiting. 'Have you seen Susan?'

'No, she hasn't come this way. I thought she was inside the store.'

They hunted up and down the street and it was a man up on the roof frame who asked, 'You looking for a young woman with frizzy hair?'

'That's the one.'

'She drove off with the fellow in that car.'

'*She what?*'

'Saw them driving off about half an hour ago. She'll be well on her way to Pemberton by now.'

Gil stood stock still, gaping up at him, then pulled

himself together and thanked him before rejoining Andrew. 'She's legged it.'

'What?'

'That Susan. She's run off with the fellow driving that car. And unless I'm very much mistaken, she's taken the money the other women gave her.'

Andrew let out a low whistle. 'Hell!'

'I'd better go and pay for what they've bought.'

'Do you have enough money.'

'Yes. But some of them are going to be hurt by this when they have to pay twice.'

'I'm glad I didn't have to depend on a woman like her to buy our things.'

Gil nodded. It was the first bit of luck his companion had had. That was the only good thing about today. The Boyds were all right, at least.

They drove back mainly in silence, walking to ease the load on Daisy. Neither of them was looking forward to getting back.

When they arrived at the camp, they found four families gathered for their midday meal, the adults sitting on chunks of log round the big table, the children standing up to eat. They could have taken their food and cooked it individually, but these were the more sociable folk and the women had voted to share the cooking. They'd not have been able to do that if they weren't living on fairly close blocks and luckily, the main camp was in the centre of the group's blocks.

Gil looked at Andrew. 'I'll take Bert aside and tell

him about his wife. You get yourself something to eat. I'll tell the rest of them after dinner.'

Bert had been tucking into a plate of stew, but when he saw the two men and no sign of his wife, he got up and came across to them. 'Where's Susan?'

'Let's walk over to the creek to talk,' Gil said.

Something about his expression must have warned Bert that it wasn't good news. He turned pale, but said nothing, falling in beside the foreman and digging his hands into his pockets.

They walked in silence to the creek, then Gil said bluntly, 'She went off with a fellow in a car. He was going to Perth, we think.'

'Couldn't you have stopped her?'

'She'd been gone half an hour before we found out.'

Bert cursed and closed his eyes for a minute or two, then looked down at the water, rocking forward and backwards, changing his weight from heels to toes, not speaking.

'Are you going after her? I'll drive you into Pemberton tomorrow if you want.'

'No. She can go to hell as far as I'm concerned.'

Another silence then suddenly words poured out of Bert. 'She was unfaithful to me during the war, but her family persuaded me to give her another chance and she was all lovey-dovey, so I thought we could get over all that. But now it's happened again, only this time she's run off, and I won't even *try* to get over it.'

Gil hesitated, but knew he had to say it. 'There's something else.'

'What else could there be?'

'She's taken the money with her that people gave her for their orders. I had to dip into my own pocket to pay the man at the stores.'

Bert closed his eyes, saying in a low voice, 'I'll pay everyone back. I've got— Oh, no!' Suddenly he was off running along the track as if all the hounds of hell were after him.

Andrew came up to ask, 'What's he doing?'

Gil shrugged. 'I don't know. Will you go after him, make sure he's all right? I've got to tell the rest of them what's happened.'

There was dead silence when he explained what Susan had done. He couldn't think of anything else to say, so went to get the food that had been kept for him. But it tasted like sawdust. Afterwards he took his plate and scraped the leftovers into the big bowl for burying later, then went over to stand near the cooking fire, staring down at the flames, wondering what the hell was going to happen next.

Andrew hurried along the track after Bert, who had a nearby block, one of the best around. He found him inside the humpy, tossing things aside, not caring where they landed as he hunted through his trunk. Guessing what the other was looking for, Andrew stepped back and waited, still keeping an eye on him.

When he'd emptied the trunk, Bert continued to kneel there, staring down into it, hardly moving a muscle, then he groaned and buried his face in his hands.

Andrew cleared his throat and moved forward.

Bert looked up at him. 'She didn't leave me even a shilling. *Not even – a lousy – shilling.*'

'I'm sorry.'

'I rue the day I married her. I'm not going after her and I'm not taking her back this time.'

'What *are* you going to do?'

'Soldier on. See what I can make of life here.' He made a broad gesture with one hand.

'It'll be hard on your own.'

'I'm not staying on the land.' He began to put things back inside the trunk, but only his things. Anything feminine was tossed into a pile.

'Looks like we'll be having another sale,' he said when he'd finished, his voice harsh with anger. 'Maybe some of the others have enough money to buy these, or will take them in lieu of the money she stole. Some of these clothes are new, not even worn yet.'

'Won't she – want them back?'

'She might. She won't be getting them, though. I intend to pay back every single penny she stole.'

Andrew put one hand on the other man's shoulder and squeezed gently. There was nothing he could say. He helped carry the clothes down to the group then went across to Norah. 'Anything you fancy among that lot? She didn't leave him with a penny.'

'I'm bigger than her, so her clothes won't be any use to me. But I could unravel that cardigan and knit it up again as a sweater for one of the boys.'

Unfortunately, few of the others had any money to spare, so the sale went badly.

Bert gathered the remaining clothes together in

silence then turned to face them all, clutching the crumpled pile of clothes to his chest. His voice was choked,
his face white and set. 'I'll keep these till I can find a
way to sell them. I *will* pay back what she stole, every
single penny, however long it takes.'

Gil stepped forward. 'I've paid for the purchases,
so it's me you owe.'

There was a sigh of relief from some people.

Bert gestured to the small pile of coins on the table.
'There's the first payment, then. Let me know how
much I still owe you.'

'All right.'

The other stared at him for a moment. 'Do you
trust me? You're not afraid I'll run off like she did?'

Gil held one hand out. 'I trust you. We'll shake on it.'

As they did so, he could see how close Bert was to
breaking down.

The poor man didn't speak. Shoulders straight, head
held high, he walked away in the direction of his block
and wasn't seen again that day.

'I reckon he will pay you back,' Andrew said.

'I do too.' Gil raised his voice. 'Well, let's get some
work done here.'

Irene watched Freddie count their meagre store of
coins, then count them again. 'We'll manage.'

'We've no choice but to manage, have we? I'd never
have come if I'd known we'd be reduced to this.' He
gestured round with a look of distaste.

'I like it here.'

He stared at her as if he didn't believe her.

'I do.'

'But we're living like savages.'

She laughed. 'And I've not felt this well for years.'

His face cleared slightly. 'You're not – pretending?'

'No, Freddie. I'd never pretend with you. I do feel better. My cough's gone completely and I've far more energy these days, you know I have.'

With an inarticulate murmur, he pulled her into his arms and gave her a quick hug, heedless of what others might say. 'Then I've just got to hold on, however hard it is.'

She'd known it! He tried to hide it from her, but he hated it here, hated it with a passion, was desperately homesick as well.

And she could never think of going back to England. Would this destroy their love?

10

Bert got up before the sun had risen on the Sunday morning, the embers of his anger at his wife still glowing hotly within him. How could she have done this to him? He pushed that thought aside when he realised his anger was preventing him from thinking clearly. He shouldn't waste his time on thoughts of her – only how could you help it when someone had knocked the ground from under your feet, treated you so badly.

He'd spoken to one of the men building the new houses in Northcliffe and been told he could earn some money today if he could get into the town and labour for them. It was only a few miles, so he didn't need to ask a favour of anyone, but could simply walk there.

He set off, hunger growling in his belly, wondering what he was going to do about feeding himself. He didn't have time to bake loaves, even if he'd known how to do it. Maybe he could pay one of the women to do it for him? But he could only do that if he had some money and he hadn't, not a single coin. In the meantime, he ate at midday and the evening with the group and that had to do.

Gradually, as he walked, the sun rose and birds began to sing and flutter around the forest. It was pretty here when there were no people around to disturb things. He stopped once to stare at a particularly big tree. If you cut that down, six people could stand on the stump, he reckoned. He'd never seen anything like it. A small creature scuttled among the leaf litter on the ground. Good luck to it, he thought, and realised it'd brought a smile to his face.

In town, two men had already started work, needing to get the roof on before the rains came, even if it was the Sabbath. He went up to the fellow in charge and reminded him of his offer of work, was soon labouring alongside them.

In the middle of the morning they took a smoko, breaking for a cup of tea and a cigarette. One man had some bacon sandwiches and Bert couldn't stop his stomach rumbling. The man shot him a quick glance. 'Had anything to eat yet today, mate?'

'No.'

'Wife not treating you well?'

Usually Bert kept things to himself, but the sandwich smelled so good, words burst out of him. 'She ran off. Took all my money.'

'Oh. Heard about that. Didn't realise it was you. Sorry, mate. Here.' He thrust one of his sandwiches into Bert's hand.

That simple act of kindness brought tears to his eyes and he was too hungry to refuse. 'Thanks.' He bit into the sandwich, closing his eyes in pleasure at how good it was.

At midday they each gave him another sandwich, this time with cheese in them, and he had to thank them with a nod, because he didn't trust himself to speak without breaking down.

By the end of the day he was exhausted, but he'd earned five shillings and that was what counted.

'Come again next Sunday,' the one in charge said. 'They're not worrying about us observing the Sabbath – well, there's no one here *to* worry – and anyway, they need the houses built as quickly as they can.'

'Thanks. I will. What if it's raining? They tell me it's going to rain heavily soon.' It was certainly much cooler than it had been.

'We'll still be working inside the house.'

As he walked back, something hard inside Bert's chest softened just a little, and the coins clinked cheerfully in his pocket.

When he arrived at the main camp, he went over to Gil and handed him three shillings. 'I did some work in Northcliffe today.'

'Thanks. Look, me and Pete are just about to have our meal. Why don't you sit with us?'

Bert had never been at the receiving end of so many acts of kindness before in his whole life. Again, he could only nod as he sat down.

'How are you managing?'

'All right. I had a bit of a problem this morning as I had to set off before breakfast to walk into Northcliffe.

'You should have come and seen me about it. We'd

have found you some food to take with you. We'll have to work out something for your washing, too.'

'It's the money I'm most concerned about. I've never owed anyone before. Not even a halfpenny.'

'Well, you're paying it off, aren't you? That's what matters. I can wait, don't worry. I'm not short of a bob or two. Now, come and have a bowl of kangaroo stew while it's hot.'

As he walked home, Bert felt better than he had for a very long time. These people were so kind. He'd never met anyone like them. It made him doubly determined to pay back the money Susan had stolen – and to make good in Australia.

Three days later the other families assigned to their group arrived, bumping along in the same Red Reo trucks as the first eight families. It was an overcast day, which felt strange after so much sunshine, and clouds were racing across the sky, dimming the sun intermittently and threatening showers or worse.

Sound carried more easily in the damp air and they all heard the trucks coming well before they came into sight.

Gil wiped his sweaty forehead with the back of one arm and beckoned to the men, who had stopped work to listen. 'We might as well stop now. I need to go and meet these new folk. Someone tell the others we're stopping early for dinner.'

'Will there be enough food for everyone?' Bert asked.

'They'll have been given a piece of bread and jam, and a cup of tea at the store, so we don't have to feed them till teatime.' Gil looked up at the sky. 'We'd better unload their things as quickly as we can, though. It won't be long before it's raining.'

By the time the men reached the camp, the newcomers had got down from the trucks and were standing huddled together in groups. Most had a glazed look in their eyes, as if they couldn't believe what they were seeing.

'Did we look as shocked as that when we first arrived?' Andrew wondered aloud.

'Worse,' the foreman said. 'You'd nothing waiting for you, not even tents. This lot has it easy compared to you.'

Andrew watched as the women found cups of tea for the newcomers, then he went forward to join them. Janie was standing near her mother and gave him her customary resentful look as he approached. He ignored her, nodded to the family standing beside his own and offered his hand. 'Welcome to Special Group One. I'm Andrew Boyd.'

'Reggie Cheever.' The man shook hands, but his attention was still on his surroundings. 'I can't believe this is it! The government said they'd give us *farms*. Where are they?'

'Not made yet. We were surprised too. We've just had to make the best of things. At least they pay us so much per acre for clearing our blocks and that's enough to manage on till we get our cows and start producing the cream.'

The man turned with a sneering expression on his face. 'Oh, I'm sure you lot made the best of things.

You'll have taken all the good blocks of land just because you got here first. *You'll* be all right!'

Andrew felt anger rise in him at this undeserved accusation, especially as he had copped one of the worst blocks. 'Land was selected purely by drawing lots.'

The man made a scornful noise and dug his hands deep in his pockets, hunching his shoulders.

The woman standing beside him, who was heavily pregnant, scowled at everyone impartially and rubbed her back. She had a small child with a snotty nose whining and tugging at her skirts, and the whole family looked and smelled as if they and their clothes could do with a good wash.

'Why don't you sit down?' Norah said to her. 'You look tired. We use these logs as stools.'

Mrs Cheever greeted this with a curl of her lips. 'I'd rather be taken to our house, thank you. Have our boxes arrived yet? And they said we'd get stretcher beds to start us off. I need a lie-down. I have to have my lie-down in the afternoon, or I can't manage.'

'Er—' Norah was relieved when Gil shouted to gain their attention and she was spared being the one to give them the bad news.

When they'd all gathered round, Gil explained the situation and some of the newcomers exploded into angry protests, including Reggie. The foreman had to yell at them several times to quieten them.

Norah felt sorry for him. It wasn't his fault things had been so badly organised and he'd worked as hard as a man could to help them all, keeping going in circumstances where others would give up.

As the shouters calmed down, Gil spoke again. 'First we'll draw lots to give you a number each, then we'll go through the numbers from one onwards and draw lots again to give you each a block of land. After that we'll sort out who shares which humpy according to family size, because there aren't enough temporary shacks built to go round. I don't know how long you'll have to share for and we'll have to fit three families into some of the humpies until the materials arrive to build others – unless you'd rather sleep in tents. We've got several of those going spare.'

'We were promised *farmhouses*!' Reggie shouted.

'They haven't been built yet. The government has promised to send men and materials to erect the houses – and they will, eventually. Look at it this way: at least you'll be under cover.' He glanced at the sky, which was growing steadily darker. 'And since it looks like rain, let's get on with it.'

But Reggie and two other men started protesting again, and people had to shush them before Gil could conduct the draw.

Others waited more patiently and one newcomer on the other side of Andrew muttered apologetically, 'I'm sick of them lot complaining. Nothing's ever good enough for them. We aren't all like that and some of us can see that you folk are doing your best.'

When Gil got everyone's attention again, he took some paper and began to write numbers on it. Reggie instantly pushed through the crowd to stand where he could see what the foreman was doing.

By now Andrew was praying his family wouldn't

have to share with the Cheevers, and he probably wasn't the only one.

The block numbers meant nothing to the newcomers, but they clutched the bits of paper and took them across to Pete, who was writing them down on the official form.

Then Gil began to assign the families to share humpies.

Bert got the largest family in his, one with six children ranging from a strapping fourteen-year-old lad to a babe in arms. He said nothing, just nodded when introduced to them.

To Andrew's dismay, his family did get the Cheevers to share their humpy. His heart sank and he could see that Norah was also upset. It felt as if luck had been against them ever since their arrival here, and he didn't look forward to sharing such a small hut with mean-minded people. However, he put the best face on it he could and forced a smile when Gil pointed him out to them.

'Since the trucks had to leave, we'll have to use my horse and cart to take your things to the temporary homes,' Gil said. 'Is everything labelled? Good. You can walk there with the people you're sharing with and me and Pete will come round with your stuff as quickly as we can.'

'Norah and I will have to move our things to one half of the humpy,' Andrew said stiffly to Reggie. 'We didn't have time to do it before.'

It was a silent group who walked back to the block. When she saw the tin shed she'd be living in, Lil burst into tears and refused to be comforted. Reggie was no happier, stamping around and muttering remarks like, 'Worse than a cattle shed'. He saw Blossom and asked sharply, 'How did you get a cow so quickly?' He grunted at the explanation, scowling even more deeply, as if there was something wrong with them looking after the group's cow.

The Cheevers didn't offer to help move things, but went outside again to wait for the Boyds to clear their half of the humpy, predicting everything would be soaked if they didn't hurry up and wondering why they were always last to get anything.

'This isn't going to be easy,' Norah whispered.

'It's going to be terrible living in such close quarters with them.'

Reggie looked inside again to see how they were getting on, but still didn't offer to help them, just wandered back out, muttering to himself.

So be it, Andrew thought. He'd not offer to help them move in, either.

When the children saw how their sleeping arrangements had been changed, they became sulky, so that by the time Gil drove up with the Cheevers' trunk, some stretcher beds and blueys, Andrew had had to speak sharply to the boys and Norah had scolded Janie, for trying to move her bed right next to her mother's.

'Here you are,' Gil said cheerfully. 'Come and help me get your things down.' He looked across in puzzlement as Andrew made no effort to help the scowling, grumbling newcomer.

As Gil got back on the cart after unloading things,

Andrew moved over to speak to him privately. 'If there's any chance of changing our sleeping partners, I'd be grateful.'

'I'll bear it in mind. I can see you've got a problem there. Has he done anything but complain?'

'No.' Andrew went back inside, leaving the newcomers to arrange their sleeping accommodation as best they could. He could hear them grumbling, hear everything they said, because the central wall didn't reach to the ceiling.

He felt obliged to mention the time of the evening meal to them and as a result, the adults all walked down to the central camp together, the boys having run ahead, though Janie stayed beside her mother. He explained that some people were cooking for them-selves now, but the ones who lived closest were still sharing.

'After this, we'll cook our own, too,' Lil said. 'You don't know what other people put into it.'

Norah managed not to say something sharp, but only just. The women who were sharing were doing wonders with a very limited number of ingredients.

The meal wasn't ready yet and thunder was rumbling in the distance. People stood round the fires chatting as they waited. Some of the newcomers seemed already on good terms with the people they were sharing with. Others, like the Cheevers, stood apart and made no attempt to talk to anyone – nor did the Boyds stay near them.

It was dark by the time the food was ready and lightning was zipping across the sky. They ate quickly and set off back to their blocks. Those who had them used hurricane lanterns to guide their way. Even inside the humpy candles weren't much use in windy weather, because draughts abounded and they were always blowing out.

Before they got home, it started to spit with rain.

'Run for it!' Andrew yelled.

'Hoy! What about us?' Reggie called after him. 'My Lil can't run in her condition.'

Andrew slowed down. 'You go ahead with the children, Norah. I can't leave these people to stumble along a strange path.'

'We'll stay with you.'

'Why should we all get wet? You take the children back.'

When he eventually reached the hut, where a light was flickering in his own half, he was soaked through and Lil was sobbing loudly. He'd carried the little girl and left Reggie to look after his wife. The child smelled to Andrew as if she'd wet herself. Well, he'd not seen the mother make any attempt to take the poor little thing to the latrines, as other women did.

He felt duty bound to ask, 'Have you got matches and candles?'

'Yes, that foreman fellow gave us some.' Reggie led the way inside his half, striking a match and lighting a candle, then pushing the flimsy door shut without a word of farewell or thanks to the man who'd got soaked guiding them here.

Inside their half of the humpy, Andrew pulled the corrugated iron door across the hole, glad to shut the Cheevers out. It was rattling in the wind, so he pulled the trunk behind it to hold it in place.

When he turned, he found Norah smiling and holding out a towel. The three children were already in bed, their eyes gleaming in the candlelight as they watched him. 'I'll hold up a blanket and you can change out of those wet clothes behind it,' she said. 'Then perhaps you'd do the same for me?'

No complaints from this woman. Just practical help. He reached out to touch her cheek. 'Thank you.'

'What for?'

'Not complaining.'

'What good would it do? It's not your fault. You can't control the weather.'

'That doesn't stop some women.' He glanced at the dividing wall.

From the other side came sobs and bitter recriminations. It was half an hour before the Cheevers stopped quarrelling, by which time Andrew was in bed, wishing he could hold Norah in his arms, only they were each on a single stretcher bed.

She'd fallen asleep almost at once, but he couldn't seem to settle, not with their new neighbours still arguing and revealing all their secret grudges. It wasn't going to be very pleasant living in such close proximity to them.

In the morning there was no sound from the other half of the humpy. Andrew moved the trunk and opened the door, revealing another grey sky with wind thrashing the tree branches around. 'I think it's going to rain again. Let's make an early start.'

Norah got up quietly, dressed and went to milk the cow, who had indeed stayed close to the humpy, water bucket and her rough shelter, which was made of one piece of corrugated iron bent over a frame that curved over at the top. Other scraps of corrugated iron filled in two sides and left the other open. That would shelter Blossom from what Gil said were the prevailing winds.

By the time she'd finished the milking, Andrew and the children were ready to walk down to the camp with her. 'Shall we wake *them*?' she asked, looking back at the humpy.

He hesitated. 'I suppose so.' He went to bang on the door of the other half and called, 'Breakfast will be served soon, then the men have to start work.'

But there was no answer. With a shrug, he joined Norah, took the lidded bucket of milk out of her hands and they walked along the track together, avoiding last night's puddles.

Gil and two other men were already sitting at one end of the long communal table, cradling big enamel mugs of tea, and Pam was cutting up some bread. The camp ovens were standing in the embers, so she must have put some damper on to bake already.

Gil gestured to the huge teapot. 'Freshly made. You lot are up early.'

'Yes.'

'How's the milking coming?'

Norah smiled. 'I think I'm getting quicker. Blossom's

very friendly. She comes over sometimes to stand near the humpy. I think she'd come inside if I let her.'

'And how did your new neighbours settle in?'

'They shouted at one another.' Janie giggled. 'I didn't know what some of the words meant.'

She repeated a very rude word and the two boys tittered.

Andrew snapped, 'Don't you ever use that word again, young lady!'

There was a pregnant silence, with all the adults trying hard not to smile.

Janie scowled at her stepfather. 'I'm not doing what you say. You're not my real father.'

Norah dragged her to one side. 'If I ever hear you speak to your father like that, I'll spank you myself. The cheek of it, being rude to a grown-up! What would your granddad say to that?'

Tears came into Janie's eyes, but the mutinous look didn't leave her face. 'I don't care. *He* isn't my father.'

So Norah upended her daughter over her knee and gave her a few hard smacks. When she let Janie go, the child was crying and tried to run away, but Norah grabbed her arm. 'You'll stay here with your family, miss. Now, come and sit down with your brothers.'

If looks could have killed, Janie's would have dropped Norah where she stood. She was amazed and horrified. What had happened to her daughter? Janie had always been wilful, but never openly defiant and naughty like this.

She helped Pam make them some bread and jam,

their usual breakfast, making sure all the children got their share.

Andrew watched his wife, grateful that she'd made a quick, sharp point about Janie's misbehaviour. He'd have done the same to his sons if they'd been defiant or cheeky to Norah, whether in public or in private.

'How did you get on with the Cheevers?' Gil asked quietly.

Andrew turned, shrugging. 'As you'd expect. They didn't try to talk to us, too busy quarrelling with one another. I just hope they're going to have a washday soon.' The sour smell of unwashed bodies seemed to waft everywhere, even in the Boyds' side of the humpy.

'If they don't, I'll tell them to do it,' Gil said. 'But with so many in the group now, I think it's time we all did our own meals. I'll share out the flour and other stuff. I'll tell folk after breakfast. And if they don't bring your crates soon, I'll go to Pemberton and bring them myself.'

Norah joined them, sitting down with a smile as her husband poured her a cup of tea. 'It'll be good to have the rest of our possessions, but we've nowhere dry to store them now that we're sharing the humpy.'

'I'm sending off a letter to the Board this very morning,' Gil said. 'They have to do something about this group. Of all the stupid ideas, to add on an extra group!'

Irene woke with a start, feeling Freddie's hand reach for hers. Their beds were very close together, because their hut was housing three families now. She wished they hadn't chosen to do without a central partition when it was built, but it had seemed better then to have one big room. She smiled at her husband, then peered round in the grey light of pre-dawn to check whether anyone else was awake. She could hear that it wasn't raining now, at least. The noise of the rain beating down on the metal roof last night had kept her awake for ages.

She saw a man at the other end of the room stretch his arms and heard him yawn. As he got up, clad only in knee-length drawers and a short-sleeved vest, she averted her eyes quickly. He pulled on his trousers and walked outside. Reaching out, she pulled her clothes into bed with her. She wasn't getting dressed in front of strangers.

'I'll hold a blanket across this corner for you, love,' Freddie said. 'You'll tie yourself in knots or fall off that narrow bed trying to get into your things lying down.'

'All right.' She shivered in the cold air and scrambled into her clothes as quickly as she could, not bothering with her usual wash. She'd do that later in privacy.

By the time Irene had held the blanket for Freddie to dress behind, most of the others were stirring. A lad of about ten was still fast asleep and a little girl of four. The newcomers they were sharing with weren't too bad. She didn't envy poor Norah, who had to put up with that horrible complaining man and his slovenly wife.

It was so much cooler this morning, she shivered as she walked down to the camp area. Rain seemed so strange after all the warm, dry weather. But welcome.

She wouldn't have to water her vegetable garden as often now.

After breakfast, Gil set the men to work then gathered the women together and informed them that there were too many people to eat communally now. 'I'll share out this week's supplies and you can cook what you want at your own places. Since the bags of flour are heavy, I'll drive them out to you. But before we do that, we'll show all you newcomers how to make damper in a camp oven.' He held one of the heavy iron cooking pots up to show them what a camp oven was. 'We can't always get bread made for us, you see. No corner shops in the bush. Pam and Norah are dab hands at it now.'

'It's just soda bread,' Norah said. 'Not hard to make at all.'

They nodded, some looking happy enough, others frowning.

'Maybe those sharing humpies can share the cooking?' he suggested. 'Anyone who hasn't got a camp oven can get one from me, to be paid for from your earnings.'

Norah looked at Lil, whose nails were black with ingrained dirt and vowed that nothing that woman touched was going into her children's mouths.

That was easier said than done. As they walked back after a demonstration, Lil said, 'I'm not good at making bread. Maybe we can share the cooking?'

'I'd rather do my own cooking, but you can watch me if you're in any doubt, then do yours the same way on your own fire. If your husband wants to build you a lean-to kitchen, Andrew will show him how, but that kitchen is ours and so are the things in it.'

'You'd think a person would want to help newcomers.'

Norah didn't answer.

'You're walking too fast for me.'

'I always walk briskly. And you know the way home now.'

Lil began to cry.

Norah hardened her heart and pulled Janie along as fast as she could, holding the empty milk bucket in her other hand. It was a relief to have the well to get water from now. The Cheevers had even complained about that, but they hadn't had to dig it out as Andrew had.

Thinking of Andrew made her sigh and look down at Janie. When they got back, she spoke very sternly to her daughter. 'It upsets me when you're so badly behaved.'

Janie didn't say anything.

'I want your promise that you'll not shame us again.' She saw a tear roll down the girl's cheek, but wasn't going to soften, not this time. 'Promise me you'll behave in future.'

She thought for a moment or two that Janie was going to refuse, but in the end heard the promise made. 'Good. We'll say no more about it, then.' She set Janie to work collecting more firewood, put her buckets inside her half of the humpy, instead of leaving them outside. She just didn't trust the Cheevers.

She went to check on Blossom, who was standing out of the sun in her shelter, swishing her tail to and fro. Norah got the shovel and collected the manure, piling it up carefully and covering it.

'That's men's work,' a voice said behind her. 'They shouldn't ask a woman to do that sort of thing.'

She turned to see Lil. 'I'm the one looking after the cow, so it's my work.'

'Can you let me have some milk for my tea, and show me how to light a fire.'

'You got your milk this morning. I noticed you in the morning group.'

'I need more than that.'

'There isn't any more. When you get your own cows, you'll have all you need. Till then you'll have to manage without, like the rest of us.'

'*You* seem to have plenty of milk.'

'I get an extra ration because of looking after the cow.' She went to draw some water from the well and heat it up to wash a few pieces of clothing. They wouldn't be as well washed without a boiler and starch, but they'd be clean and if the rain held off, they'd dry quickly.

In the afternoon she walked across to Pam's block and when she got back, she found that her milk supply had gone down noticeably.

She went storming next door, to find Lil lying on a bed. 'Someone has stolen my milk.'

Lil shrugged. 'It wasn't me.'

'Who else could it be? There aren't any people walking past here.'

For a minute it seemed Lil would deny it, then she shrugged. 'I needed it. You'd think a person would take pity on a woman in my condition. The child was hungry.'

'If you steal any more, I'll tell Gil and make sure he doesn't give you a share the next day. And don't you dare set foot inside our half again.'

Lil burst into tears and covered her head with the sheet. The child was fast asleep on the floor, looking filthy and unloved.

Norah hardened her heart, but she ached to feed and clean the poor little thing. Only you couldn't help people like this, she knew from past experience with slovenly neighbours. They only expected more and more from you if you started and they rarely changed their ways, whatever you said or did.

By mid-afternoon all the humpies were partitioned into two halves and Gil had shown the newcomers how to clear the smaller growth ready for felling the bigger trees. It'd rained intermittently in the afternoon, but he'd kept the men at work because they might as well get used to it now winter was coming on. It'd not snow and there would be no heavy frosts, as he'd encountered overseas. He hoped he never saw snow again, had hated it.

During the day he'd kept his eyes on Bert, who seemed a bit less strained, and he managed not to tell Reggie what he thought of his carping and complaining, though he did speak sharply about the slowness of the man's work.

He was glad when everyone went off to bed. He always enjoyed the last half-hour of the day, sitting alone with the fire for company because Pete, who was extremely fond of his sleep, usually went to bed early.

Gil sat on a low stool made from an upended log, his back against a pile of crates on the sheltered side of the storage humpy, watching the dying embers and the patterns that formed and re-formed in them. He didn't bother to put more wood on the fire. He smiled as he heard the soft snoring and whiffling of Pete.

When he heard a noise he couldn't place, he listened intently, then got up, still hidden by the side wall. A shadowy figure was approaching the store entrance. The man clearly hadn't seen him. 'Who's there?' he called, thinking it was someone who'd got a family emergency.

The figure turned and ran off down the track, turning to the left, heading towards the town.

Gil was so surprised he didn't move for a minute, then decided it was too late to chase after the person. Why would someone run away when spoken to? Surely there wasn't a thief in the new group? He heard the sounds fade into the distance and sat wondering who it could have been.

Pete was such a heavy sleeper that if the thief came back, he'd probably not notice, so Gil went and shook his deputy awake. After telling him about the intruder, he suggested he put something across to bar the inside of the door.

After kicking out the fire, Gil made his way to his tent, which was up the slope from the camp. He'd not be moving to his own block till later, because he liked to be here to start the day. But he'd not let the new people use his humpy, because if he did, he'd have to stay there himself. He'd got some of his things stored there, but had others at his cousin's in Fremantle.

It was a while before he got to sleep, because his thoughts kept going back to the prowler. Damnation! He didn't need this as well as all the other problems.

He wondered which family the man had been from, counting off in his mind those whose blocks were to the left. But he couldn't pick on one who might be a thief. They'd all seemed decent enough folk. If the man had run to the right, he'd have suspected Cheever. He didn't know why, but he'd mistrusted the fellow on sight. Not because of his complaining, but because there was something shifty about him.

But the would-be thief had definitely run to the left, so that puzzled Gil. Could he have come from another group? What had he been after?

Gil decided to keep a careful watch on things from now on, though the group's tools should be safe enough. There was no one around to sell large items to, after all, and no way of getting them to the town without the others noticing.

He'd also put a lock on his own humpy.

How could anyone expect to get away with stealing in such a small group?

Norah waited until the children were asleep to tell her husband about Lil stealing some milk. He was angry, she could tell that, even though he kept his voice down.

'I was wondering – Andrew, do you think we could make some sort of lock for the door?'

'Yes. I've got the padlock from my trunk. That'd fit. And I've two keys for it, so we can have one each. You can lock it in the mornings before you take the milk down.'

So they did. But it felt strange after living so freely until now.

At the camp, Gil was waiting for the milk. 'We can't expect you to walk down with it twice a day,' he said. 'You have your own family to look after. I'm going to suggest a roster, with people coming to collect their own and their neighbours' milk in turns – or sending their children for it. How about that?'

'That'd be fine. There's a bit less today. I, um, spilt some.' She didn't tell him about Lil, but felt terrible lying to him. Still, things would be all right from now on. There'd be no chance for pilfering with the padlock in place.

But when Gil strolled up the track the next morning for his own and Pete's supply of milk, he saw the padlock on the door. 'Why've you put a lock on the door?'

She hesitated. 'I don't want to tell tales.'

'It need go no further than the two of us.'

She explained.

In return he told her about the person creeping round the central store humpy.

She shook her head sadly. 'I don't like to think of there being a thief among us. It's hard enough to manage without that.'

'Thieves,' he said, emphasising the final 's'. 'We have more than one. Lil stole your milk. The other was a man and he ran away when I called out to him, which brands him as guilty in my eyes. I should have kept quiet and nabbed him, but I thought he just needed something.'

Lil came sauntering across to join them, a patently false smile on her face. 'I'm so glad to see you, Gil.

I need extra milk and *she* won't give it to me, even though she gets a whole bucketful morning and evening. I have a small child to look after and in my condition, I need the extra nourishment.'

He didn't trouble to hide his scorn. 'Can't do it. We have barely enough to go round. But you can buy tins of food and evaporated milk at the store in Northcliffe, if you've not got enough in your rations.'

'How can I get into town in my condition? It's miles away.'

'Anyone who's going in collects the orders and fetches them back. People leave their orders with me or Pete at the camp ground.'

Lil abandoned her smile and glared at them both. 'You know very well we can't afford extras. I'll get my husband to complain to the Board. It's not right, the way you're treating us, *starving* us.'

Gil flourished one hand at her. 'Go ahead and complain. You'll find that the Board isn't very good about replying to complaints.' He was quite sure she'd not bother to do it. She was clearly bone idle. Look at the way she neglected that poor little child.

After a look that would have soured milk, Lil swung round and went back to the humpy, sluthering her feet along the ground as if she couldn't be bothered to pick them up.

Norah watched her go in silence.

'I'm sorry you've to share accommodation with them,' Gil said. 'If there was anywhere else to put them, I'd move them, but there isn't.'

'I know.' But Norah was worried. The padlock was

a flimsy thing and Andrew's money was in their trunk. If only there was a savings bank near here, she'd feel a lot safer about it. Maybe they should ask Gil to store it somewhere for them?

By the end of the week, most of the newcomers had been assimilated into the group and had got into a routine for managing their daily lives. Some women sharing humpies made friends and worked together, others preferred to manage alone. Norah sometimes visited Pam, but was tied to milking the cow. She didn't mind that, was learning a lot about caring for cows, would need that knowledge.

When someone suggested a sing-song on the following Saturday night, a get-together for the whole group, people agreed to it with pleasure. From then on, they kept eyeing the sky anxiously and asking Gil if he thought it'd stay fine.

The women decided to do a little cake baking, not easy in the camp ovens most were using. But one of the newcomers had proved more skilful than most and she took charge, pulling a face at the lack of eggs and sending her oldest son to the store in Northcliffe to see if they had any.

The lad didn't complain. The children were getting used to walking if they wanted to go anywhere and it made a change to go into the tiny town.

It felt good to be getting dressed up again, Norah thought on the Saturday as she put on a favourite dress she hadn't worn since they arrived here and made sure Janie and the boys were well turned out. She looked at them all when they were ready, and felt proud of her family. Her eyes lingered on her husband, who'd had a shave and looked positively handsome. He saw her looking and smiled back at her, a look that said he found her attractive too.

When they set off, he closed the door by hanging the new wire loop over the hook and fixing the padlock to it. Then he held his arm out to Norah.

She took it with a mock curtsey, but when they set off walking, Janie tried to cling to her other side. 'Walk with the boys, love.'

'Don't want to.'

Norah could feel Andrew's arm grow tense. But for once she wasn't going to pander to Janie's clinging ways. 'Do as you're told,' she snapped. She wanted to arrive at the gathering on her husband's arm, to look like a married couple, to sit next to him and sing. She'd already discovered that he had a nice baritone voice, and she knew she was a tuneful singer.

The Cheevers came out of the other half of the humpy just as they were leaving, but the child looked as neglected as ever, with a dirty face that wouldn't have taken a minute to wash. Lil began complaining after only a few minutes that the track was rough and hurt her feet but Reggie wouldn't let her go back.

'Let's speed up,' Andrew whispered in Norah's ear.

She smiled and did so, ignoring pointed comments from behind about unfriendly people.

Janie trailed behind and Norah decided to let her. It wasn't dark yet and there were no paths but this one to get lost on. When they turned a corner she smiled as she heard running footsteps behind them.

'I thought she'd not let us out of her sight,' Andrew murmured then began to talk about his favourite songs.

Once the Boyds were out of sight, Reggie took hold of Lil's arm and pulled her to a halt, saying quietly, 'You wait here. I'm just nipping back to have a quick look round.'

She stared at him in dismay. 'You said you'd left all that sort of thing behind.'

'How do you like it here?'

'I hate it.'

'Do you think you're going to change your mind about that?'

'No, I'm not. I never wanted to come in the first place. It was your stupid idea.'

'I needed to get away from England. I might have ended up in jail if I'd stayed there.' He looked round them in the moonlight. 'But I'm not staying in the middle of nowhere, working like a slave. They told us lies about giving us farms. You can sell a farm, but you can't sell a lump of uncleared land. But if we're to get back to Perth, we'll need some money. Now, you walk on very slowly. If anyone comes back say I was taken short. But I doubt they will.'

Before she could stop him, he set off back.

She couldn't hold back a whimper of fear. She hated all those trees, was terrified what might be hiding in the bush. She picked up her daughter, holding the child close and not moving anywhere.

It seemed a long time till he returned. 'Well?' she asked.

He grinned and tapped the side of his nose. 'Less you know, less you'll worry.'

'Reggie, what have you done?' She was terrified suddenly, because nothing he ever started seemed to turn out as he planned. And if he did something against the law here, if they put him in prison, what would she do then?

'What I've done is started collecting for the poor, which means us.' Whistling cheerfully, he took her arm and hurried her along, in spite of her protests that she couldn't walk fast and her repeated questions about what exactly he'd done.

When they got near the campsite, he stopped and shook her like a rat. 'Don't forget. Keep quiet about this. You couldn't walk fast, if anyone asks.'

To her relief, no one said anything and they found seats away from the Boyds, who didn't even give them a second glance, for all they were neighbours. Suddenly she was glad Reggie was stealing from them. She hated them, hated all these people who looked down their noses at her. But most of all she hated having babies. If it happened again, she was going to do something about it early on. This was the last one she intended to carry.

The child started crying and she slapped her. 'Shut up!'

One of the other women leaned forward. 'She wants to wee. I'll take her if you like.'

Lil smiled and nodded. 'Thanks. My back's hurting

after that long walk.' She watched the woman walk away with Dinny. When they came back Dinny was eating a jam butty. Lil wished she had one and wondered if she could pinch a bit of her daughter's, but the woman kept Dinny sitting by her till she'd finished eating.

None of the women made an effort to talk to her and after trying to start up conversations, Lil shut her mouth and listened to them. They all seemed good friends, even some of the newcomers.

Why did she have to be living next to the Boyds? They deserved all they got, stuck-up snobs like them.

The sing-song got under way, with Pam's husband Ted as master of ceremonies, Gil having declined the chance to run things. Norah laughed at Ted's introductory joke, leaned against Andrew who put his arm round her, then joined the singing.

They sang recent favourites like 'K-K-K-Katie' and 'Alice Blue Gown', then inevitably went on to songs the men had sung during the war, 'Long Way to Tipperary' and 'Keep the Home Fires Burning'.

She looked sideways at Andrew and saw that his eyes were bright with unshed tears, so took hold of his hand and squeezed it. She hated to think of what the men who'd fought for their country had gone through. There were nights when Andrew tossed and turned, muttering about 'snipers' and 'bombs'. Once he'd yelled, 'Look out!' and had curled up in bed, hands over his head.

Tonight he seemed carefree, for once. He squeezed

her hand in return and directed his singing to her and when she joined in, he harmonised effortlessly with her.

'Hallo there!' Ted called when there was a break in the singing. 'I think we've got a pair of star performers here.' He walked over to them and took Norah's hand, pulling her to her feet in spite of her laughing protests. 'How about you two giving us a couple of solos?'

Andrew looked at her questioningly and she nodded, used to leading the singing in her family. 'What do you want to sing?'

'Do you know "Roses of Picardy"?'

'Yes. It's one of my favourites.'

So they sang it, and it was as if they'd rehearsed, their voices fitted together so perfectly. Why hadn't they found this out before? She knew the answer. Because they'd hardly had a minute to spare from working.

When they'd finished, everyone applauded and asked for more, so they did 'Apple Blossom Time'.

Not to be outdone, Pete called, 'Here's one for Australia!' and started them off on 'Waltzing Matilda'. He had such a bad voice that there were calls of protest and Gil started singing loudly enough to drown Pete's tuneless drone.

Some songs were sung more than once, others brought tears to people's eyes and from time to time, someone would make an excuse of needing to use the latrine and leave the group to hide overflowing emotions.

When the singing died down, Norah still had

Andrew's arm round her. She looked down and saw her daughter scowling at her but ignored that.

As they walked home, they started singing again and the boys forgot their sleepiness and joined in.

Only Janie remained obstinately silent, which settled it for Norah. She'd made a start, but she wasn't going to let the matter drop. That child was going to be part of this family, whatever it took.

Irene and Freddie also walked home arm in arm.

'That was a lovely evening, wasn't it?' she said.

'Yes. But—' He broke off. He'd promised himself not to say anything.

'But what?' she pressed.

Suddenly it all came out. 'But I miss the pictures and chip shops and football matches on a Saturday. Don't you?'

'Not really. Oh, Freddie, love, I'm so sorry you're still so unhappy.'

'I didn't realise how homesick I'd be. It never even occurred to me.'

They walked in silence for a few minutes, then he saw the tears on her cheeks and stopped to kiss them away. 'It's not your fault, Irene love. It's your health that matters most to me. I'll get over the homesickness and we'll make a good life for ourselves here.'

'Yes. It's very boring work, isn't it, clearing the trees?'

'Tedious. It's not so bad when you're working with the group, but when you're on your own with nothing but those damned trees . . .' He broke off, shrugging. 'Has to be done.'

'When you've finished the group clearing, you'll be working on our own block and we'll be together more. Maybe you'll be happier then? I could help you sometimes with the clearing.'

'I wouldn't let you. It's back-breaking work. I can't believe they'll only be paying me four pounds ten shillings an acre for it.'

'But you don't have to fell the bigger trees and—'

'I have to fell every tree under eighteen inches in diameter *and* clear the roots so that the land is in a ploughable state before I get my money. You can't help with that! And I have to ringbark every tree over that size.'

She didn't say anything, just walked on beside him, head bent.

'Then I have to haul all the trees into piles for burning. And I *don't* have a horse and cart for that.'

'I thought the men were going to work together to do that. I heard Andrew saying he'd work with you.'

'I can't keep up with him! He's big and strong. I'm not.' He saw the distress on her face and closed his mouth tightly, holding in his anger. He'd said too much already. It wasn't her fault, she hadn't known what it'd be like here any more than he had.

At the door she raised one of his hands to her lips, kissing it gently. 'I feel guilty for spoiling your life.'

He pulled her close and sighed. 'I shouldn't have said anything.'

'Of course you should. We don't keep secrets from one another.'

But they did keep secrets, he thought as he continued

to hold her, rocking her slightly. At least, *he* had secrets. She might know he wasn't happy but she would never know how deep that unhappiness went. He was facing a lifetime of work that offered nothing to stimulate his mind.

He was already wondering if they could simply walk away and seek work in the capital. Surely in Perth life would be more interesting?

Only they had so little money. And the country air suited her. How could he even suggest that?

When the Boyds got home, they found the padlock on the door smashed by Andrew's own axe, which lay on the ground to one side. He stood in the doorway holding up the hurricane lantern and they saw their possessions scattered over the bare earth floor.

'Stay outside, kids.' He didn't wait to see if they obeyed, but went inside, going straight to their trunk, which had also been locked. This lock too was smashed and the trunk nearly empty because things had been flung out of it.

'Keep back.' He fumbled through the things still left in the bottom then hunted through the mess on the floor. When he looked up, his face was drawn. 'It's gone,' he said. 'Our money's been stolen. Every single penny.'

'Oh, Andrew love.' She ran to hold him for a moment, and he clung to her, then put her aside.

'I'm fetching Gil. Don't touch anything till we come back, leave it just as it is.'

Reggie and Lil had left early, but there was no sound from the other half of the humpy.

What sort of neighbour, he wondered, didn't come out to help in times of trouble?

He was quite sure in his own mind that Reggie had done this.

But how did you prove it?

Norah and the children stayed outside the humpy. She went in and pulled a blanket off the bed, then put the three of them to lie on the hay in the store shed. She stayed near the humpy door, the axe beside her for protection, though she was quite sure she wouldn't need it. Whoever had done this wouldn't be coming back because they'd already got what they wanted. Like her husband, she felt sure Reggie had done it, because no one else in the group seemed other than honest and friendly.

There were no noises from their neighbours while she waited for her husband to return. That in itself was unusual. There were usually arguments before the Cheevers got to sleep, and they didn't seem to care who heard them. Once they did get to sleep, Reggie snored. Lil would occasionally poke him awake and tell him to shut up, then they'd quarrel again. There was no snoring now.

Norah felt bitter acid roil in her stomach at the thought of those two lazy devils profiting from her and Andrew's hard work and frugality.

Gil came back with him, surveyed the mess and cursed under his breath. Then he looked at the partition and raised his voice. 'I'll find out who it was, Andrew lad. I won't give up till I get your money back.'

There was still no sound from the Cheevers.

Gil beckoned Norah and Andrew outside and moved away out of hearing. 'What do you reckon?'

They all looked at the Cheevers' half of the humpy.

'I reckon it was them,' Andrew said. 'Who else could it have been? And he's stupid enough to mess on his own doorstep. But how do we prove it?'

'You stay here and keep an eye on things. I'm going to fetch Pete and a couple of the other men. We'll search them and their half, and if we don't find the money, we'll search the whole bloody block if necessary. If they come out, stop them going anywhere.' He raised his voice. 'I'll be back as soon as it's daylight and we'll see if we can find any footprints. The ground's still soft. Don't walk about outside and mess it up.'

He moved away, walking more noisily than he usually did, calling out farewells.

An hour later Norah saw the light of two lanterns bobbing about in the distance, coming gradually closer, and nudged her husband.

Gil led the others to the doorway and gestured to the mess. 'That's what Andrew found.'

The three men standing behind him let out low rumbles of angry sound.

'Right. We'll do it now,' Gil said quietly.

'Do what?' Andrew asked.

'Search him and his humpy.'

'Isn't it against the law?' Andrew worried. 'We have no real grounds for our suspicions, after all.'

'It'd take too long to get the police here. We look after ourselves in the country, because you can't rely on the police getting to you in time when something goes wrong.' He moved to the next door and hammered on it so hard it rattled. Then he tried to open it. There was no lock on the door, but it didn't budge. 'They must have something jammed against it. Hoy! Open up, Cheever!'

There was the sound of someone moving around inside, then Reggie called out in a slurred voice, 'Who's that? What's the matter?'

Gil held up his lantern. 'You know damned well who I am.'

'Oh. It's you, Gil. What do you want? It's the middle of the night.'

'I want the money.'

Silence then, 'What money?'

'The money you stole from Andrew.'

'I never.'

'Prove it. Open that door and let us search your humpy.'

There was a mutter of voices, the words not clear but the tone argumentative, then Lil shouted, 'Why are you picking on us?'

'Because you're the only ones who could have stolen it.'

'We were at the sing-song with everyone else tonight.'

'How do you know it was stolen tonight?' Gil asked.

There was no answer to that.

Jack had left his temporary bed in the hay and spoke from behind his father. 'You might have set off at the same time, but you got there a long time after us. We'd had something to eat and started singing by the time you got there.'

'I can't walk quickly in my condition,' Lil said. 'We set off at the same time as the Boyds.'

Gil banged on the door with one clenched fist and kept on banging: thump, thump, thump. 'Open up.'

'All right, all right. But you won't find anything.'

As soon as the door opened, Gil dragged Reggie out by the front of his shirt and slammed him against the corrugated iron of the house, then searched him carefully. 'I'll go on looking till I do find it, believe me. Come outside, Lil, and bring the child with you.'

She came out with a blanket wrapped round her. 'I don't know why you're picking on my Reggie. He didn't do nothing.'

Gil looked at Norah. 'Keep your eye on her and the kid. Don't let her move away.'

She nodded.

The men went inside the humpy, hanging a hurricane lantern on a hook on one of the beams. They left one man outside to keep an eye on Reggie, who sat on a log and folded his arms, staring at them defiantly.

Lil smirked at Norah. 'They won't find anything.'

Norah didn't reply. She was waiting to see what the men discovered.

There wasn't much to search and it took them only a few minutes to check everything the Cheevers owned, throwing their possessions out of the door one by one.

Reggie jerked to his feet. 'Hey! You'll damage things.'

'And get them dirty,' Lil added shrilly.

'They're filthy already, like everything else you own,' Norah snapped. She turned to Janie and the boys, who had crept forward to watch. 'Stay back, you three.'

They nodded and took a couple of steps backwards. For once there was no trouble with Janie doing as she was told.

When the men had searched every inch of the bare earth floor to make sure nothing had been buried, they came outside again.

'He's hidden it somewhere else,' Gil said. 'So we'll wait until it's light and search everywhere nearby.'

Lil smirked and pulled her little daughter close, in an unusual show of affection.

Norah looked at her, surprised by this, because she'd never seen Lil cuddling the child, never seen her doing anything but complaining about the trouble children were. Suddenly she remembered how confidently Lil had said, 'They won't find anything.'

'I think I should search Lil,' she said suddenly, and caught a sudden look of fear on the other woman's face.

'Not on your own, you won't,' Gil said at once. 'We'll send for another woman to be a witness.' He turned to one of the men. 'Fetch the nearest woman.'

The man nodded. 'That'd be Irene Dawson.' He strode off into the darkness.

A few minutes later, Lil said suddenly, 'I have to go to the lav.'

Gil laughed in her face. 'Go here then, behind the hut. But Norah will be keeping an eye on you the whole time.'

Lil shot a pleading look at Reggie, who was sitting huddled up on a log. He didn't respond in any way. She stayed where she was.

It was starting to get light by the time Irene arrived and the chill greyness of pre-dawn made the whole scene look like a scene from a film, black and white and every shade of grey, no real colours around. Little Dinny was asleep now, wrapped in a dirty blanket Gil had found among the Cheevers' possessions. Gil had beckoned to Norah to search the child before he carried her across to the hay and told Janie to keep an eye on her.

Lil was sitting on a log now, her shoulders slumped dejectedly, all the defiance gone out of her.

Norah stood up and said to Irene, 'Let's get it over with. Come inside, Lil.'

'No. I'm not going anywhere with you. You're going to pretend you found the money on me.'

'Search her here, then,' Andrew said.

'Reggie, do something!' Lil yelled.

He stood up. 'I protest. I'm going to complain to the police about this.'

Gil repeated Andrew's words, 'Search her here, where there are enough witnesses.'

As soon as Norah touched her, Lil began fighting, clawing at the other woman's face and biting Irene's hand when she intervened.

Furious, Norah held the woman's hands and when Lil kicked out at her, Gil stepped forward and knocked Lil's feet from under her.

Norah knelt to hold Lil and Irene felt her body

through her layers of clothing, her nose wrinkled in disgust at the smell of the unwashed body. Her hands lingered at the waist. 'There's something here, I think.'

Lil screamed and redoubled her attempts to escape.

Reggie suddenly ran for it, but two men chased him and it didn't take long to catch him.

As they dragged him back, Irene hesitated, then lifted Lil's petticoats and there, fastened to her body by a strip of cloth, was a small bundle.

'Don't touch it, Norah,' Gil said. 'Let Irene un-wrap it.'

Inside was a pouch containing a roll of banknotes and some coins.

'That's mine,' Andrew said. 'You'll find my initials embossed in the leather of the pouch.'

Gil studied the pouch, keeping it in full view of the group. 'Yes. Here they are.' He showed it to the two men standing near him, and they both nodded. He passed it to Andrew. 'Is this yours?'

'Yes.'

Norah heard how husky Andrew's voice was as he said this and knew how relieved he was, how shaken he'd been to think of losing all his savings. She felt like weeping in relief herself. To face life without anything behind you was hard indeed, especially in a strange country.

'You rotten thief!' Reggie shouted at his wife. 'How could you shame me like that, Lil?'

She gaped at him. '*You* stole the money and gave it to me to hide.'

'Never.' He took a step away from her and folded his arms.

She jumped up so quickly the two women couldn't stop her and threw herself at her husband, pummelling and scratching him, weeping as she did so, cursing like a fishwife.

And though her husband was bigger than she was, he had trouble defending himself.

No one tried to intervene until Reggie punched her on the jaw and knocked her to the ground. As she lay there, he kicked her and drew back his foot to do it again. Gil dragged him off her then and she rolled away, groaning.

No one went to help her.

'You're the worst sort of scum,' the foreman told Reggie, his voice burred with loathing. 'The very worst. I'm taking you into Pemberton. The police can deal with you.' He looked down at the woman, moaning and weeping on the ground. 'Get up, you. You'll need to start packing.'

She fell silent and pushed herself slowly into a sitting position, wincing as she did so. 'What shall I do if he's locked away?'

'You should have thought of that when you started stealing from your neighbours.'

'I didn't even know he'd done it till he made me hide the purse. *I didn't!*'

'But you did hide the money for him.'

'He'd have thumped me if I'd refused.'

Norah stepped forward. 'Can't we leave her out of this? I believe her. I've seen and heard him thump her.'

Gil shrugged. 'We'll see what the police say.' By that time it was light, so he added, 'You lot can start work at midday today. I'll count your helping me catch this scum as part of your day's work. Take him into the camp and tie him up. I'll catch up with you in a minute or two. Keep an eye on Cheever. If he escapes I'll have your guts for garters.'

The men smiled at this phrase which everyone who'd served in the war had had thrown at them.

As the others walked off, Gil turned to Norah and Andrew. 'I'm sorry about this. They should have vetted applicants for the scheme more carefully.'

'Do you have the authority to chuck the Cheevers out of our group?' she asked.

He grinned. 'I don't know. But by the time anyone asks, I'll have done it and he'll be in jail.' He turned back to Lil. 'Get your things packed. I'll come back for you in an hour in the cart. Will you stay and keep an eye on her, Norah and Irene?'

'Yes.'

When Gil had taken both the Cheevers away, Andrew looked at the children. 'Go and get some sleep now, you lot.' When they'd gone into the humpy, he pulled Norah into his arms, holding her tightly against him, shuddering. 'I thought we'd lost everything.'

'Not quite everything. I've got some money and I keep it on my person. I hope you don't mind me keeping it back. It makes me feel – safer.'

He looked at her with a faint smile. 'I didn't marry you to take your money away from you, my lass.'

'It's only just over ten pounds that I've got, but it's there if you ever need it.'

'Thanks, love. And I'll make a better place to hide the family money than the trunk, buy a better padlock, too.'

'I doubt we'll need to do that now, or lock our door. Most of the groupies seem really decent sorts.'

'Yes, they do.' His voice came out muffled by her hair as he pulled her close again. 'Are you sorry you came?'

'No. I like it here.'

'You're a wonderful woman. I just wish—'

'What?'

'That we weren't living in such cramped conditions.'

No mistaking his meaning there. She smiled at him as warmly as he was smiling at her, then stood on tiptoe and kissed him, a gentle kiss, no more than a brief meeting of lips. But it seemed to link them more closely afterwards. She looked him directly in the eyes as she added, 'I wish so too.'

Janie appeared suddenly in the doorway. 'Mummy, Jack kicked me.'

A voice from inside the other room yelled, 'I didn't!'

'You did so.' She turned back to her mother. 'I don't want to sleep near him!'

Without turning, Norah said loudly, 'Get to bed this minute!'

'But Mummy, Jack—'

'Did you hear me?'

Janie began to cry loudly.

'That's enough.' Norah marched across, took her

daughter by the arm, and frog-marched her to bed. 'One more word from you, miss, and you'll feel my hand on your backside.' She didn't like hitting the child, but she was at her wits' end as to how to deal with her daughter, who seemed to get naughtier by the day. Janie hadn't shamed them in public again, but she was contrary and unco-operative in private.

Norah was fairly certain Jack hadn't laid a finger on Janie. It seemed as if that child sensed each time her mother and stepfather were getting close and did anything she could to stop it. She went back to stand next to Andrew in the doorway, but the spell was broken and after a minute or two, he yawned and said, 'We might as well get a bit of sleep.'

Norah looked up at the first sunbeams breaking through the nearby trees. 'I'd better go and see to the cow. People will be coming to collect their milk.'

He turned back as if to help her.

'You snatch some sleep. I can manage on my own. I'll have a nap this afternoon.'

'You're sure?'

She nodded.

He reached out to grasp her hand for a minute, then went inside.

She could feel the warmth of his touch for a long time afterwards, kept looking at her hand and smiling wryly.

It seemed as if fate was always stepping in to prevent them consummating their marriage.

Gil and Pete got ready to drive into Northcliffe with a sullen Reggie, who had his hands bound behind his back. A snivelling Lil had Dinny clinging to her skirts, but was ignoring her daughter.

Pam came across and looked at the child, then at Gil. 'Let me take her and feed her properly.'

'She's wet herself.' He could smell it from here.

'So would you if you were as scared as she is,' Pam said. She looked at Lil. 'Is it all right if I clean her up and give her some food?'

Lil shrugged.

Pam held out her hand to Dinny. 'Would you like a jam butty, dear?'

The child looked at her solemnly for a moment, then nodded.

Pam took her away, talking gently, and came back fifteen minutes later. 'Let me look after her till we know what's going to happen to those two.'

Gil frowned. 'They might not be coming back.'

Lil looked from one to the other, seemed to see something in Pam's face, and said suddenly, 'Take her.'

'You're sure?'

'I'm a lousy mother. Keep her.'

'I will, then.'

Gil took Pam aside. 'She means to leave the child with you permanently.'

'I know. And I think it'd be the best thing that could happen to the poor little thing. We've all seen how neglected Dinny is.'

'But – don't you mind taking on another? You've got four of your own already.'

Pam shook her head, smiling but with a deep sadness in her eyes. 'And didn't give birth to any of them.

I love children, Gil, but I can't seem to make any of my own, so I've gathered up the ones other people haven't wanted. No one's complained about it so far and I don't think the authorities will here – especially if we don't tell them.'

He turned to Lil. 'You're sure you want Pam to look after Dinny?'

She looked at him in irritation. 'I said so, didn't I?'

'What about you?' Gil asked Reggie.

'I don't care what happens to the damned brat. I'm not even sure if she's mine.'

Pam shook her head and walked back to take Dinny's hand.

Gil felt disgusted with the Cheevers and wondered what'd happen to the baby Lil was carrying. Well, that was none of his business.

When he got to Northcliffe, he had only to explain what had happened to be offered the loan of one of the builders' trucks to get him to and from Pemberton quickly.

Reggie said nothing as they drove along. Gil had tied him securely to the truck frame. Lil curled up on the floor in the back and went to sleep.

Gil felt bitterness etch his stomach with acid at the way they'd handed their child to Pam without a backward glance. He'd have given all he owned for a child of his own, or even an unwanted child to raise.

Perhaps later, he might find a young lad in an orphanage and take him in. Such places were always glad to get rid of their inmates.

He blinked in surprise at his own thoughts. Was he going mad? Or was he coming to his senses?

A few days later they heard that Reggie Cheever had escaped from custody on the way to Perth, jumping from the moving train while using the lavatories. He'd vanished, so he must have survived the jump.

Lil was now locked away, awaiting the birth of her child and her trial. It wasn't clear which would happen first.

No one came to make enquiries about little Dinny.

'That Cheever fellow probably got on a ship to the eastern states,' Gil said after the policeman had left. 'And good riddance to him.'

'What about poor Lil?' Irene asked. 'I never did believe she took the money.'

'She'll be taken care of by the authorities.' He grinned. 'They'll make her work for her keep, though.'

'I'm glad Dinny's stayed with Pam,' Irene said. 'Children should be loved.' She was hoping that she too was going to become a mother and unconsciously laid one hand on her own stomach. She caught Norah's eye and blushed but didn't say anything. She was waiting for the right time to tell Freddie and it was proving more difficult than she'd expected. He'd changed so much since coming here that she wasn't as sure of him as she had been. Not even sure that he still loved her in the same way.

Surely he'd gradually come to terms with their new life and she'd get the old Freddie back?

13

At the end of the week, during which it rained twice, two trucks arrived with a pile of corrugated iron and timber. They bumped slowly along the muddy track but luckily didn't get bogged down, which Gil said often happened in winter on such tracks.

Each vehicle carried two men, who consulted the foreman and then set to work to build humpies on every single block, helped by the groupies he sent with them.

Andrew was among the latter because he seemed to have a feel for working with wood. Structures he built, like his cowshed, were square and strong, while anything Freddie Dawson helped build seemed to sag and look weary even before it was finished. As did Freddie.

Andrew came home triumphantly when the first humpy was finished. This time they'd been more fortunate, or perhaps Gil had favoured them, because there hadn't been a draw. This new humpy had been built on the block owned by the young couple who'd moved in to share with the Boyds after the Cheevers left.

'We'll go tonight,' the young man said and his wife blushed. 'Can we borrow your cart to carry our stuff, Gil?'

'If you can get packed quickly. Daisy's wanting her food and a rest after a hard day's work.' Gil found he was talking to thin air as they'd both rushed into the humpy to pack, so he smiled and turned to Norah. 'Any chance of a cup of tea? It's thirsty work moving folk.'

'Of course.'

The young couple had their things packed and had left within the half-hour. They'd brought so little with them and were so cheerful about having no money that you could only marvel at their bravery and optimism.

'Thank goodness for that,' Norah said to Andrew as they stood waving goodbye. Although their new neighbours had been pleasant enough, she desperately wanted a house of their own again, even if it only had two rooms, a rough lean-to kitchen and a bare earth floor. Most of all, she wanted the privacy of her own bedroom, where she and Andrew could live as man and wife. She was surprised how much she wanted that, had never felt as strongly about sharing her first husband's bed.

'The children can sleep in the other half tonight.' Andrew lowered his voice. 'A married couple should have their own bedroom, don't you think?'

She looked at him and her breath caught in her throat because there was a message in his eyes, a very welcome message, and with it a question that needed answering. 'Yes, I agree.'

His smile was brilliant. She felt its warmth for a long time afterwards.

★　★　★

That night they sent the children to bed early, and as the boys were tired, there was very little grumbling from them.

Janie, however, was upset about the move and scowled at the bedroom she'd be sharing with the boys again. 'I don't like it here. I want to sleep near you, Mum.'

'Don't be such a baby,' Norah said crisply. 'Here, let me tuck you in.'

Andrew winked at her as they closed the door of their half of the humpy. He picked up a piece of canvas tarpaulin and gestured towards the floor, waiting for her nod of agreement before spreading it out carefully. A thrill ran through her as he picked up one bluey from his stretcher bed and spread that equally carefully on top of the canvas.

She took a bluey off her own narrow bed and laid it on top of his for a covering.

He stood up and smiled, then took a step backwards. 'I think I'll just get a breath of fresh air before I turn in.'

'Ten minutes?' she whispered.

He nodded and strolled outside. She caught a glimpse of the star-studded sky through the open door, then it closed. Normally she enjoyed watching the stars twinkle down on them. Tonight she cared only about loving Andrew.

She was grateful for his tact, because she'd never seen her first husband fully naked or he her. It was something decent women simply didn't do – in fact, her mother always said, 'I'd as soon walk around the house naked' when expressing the strongest possible disgust for the idea of doing something.

But tonight as she got undressed, Norah found herself wondering if the rest of Andrew's body was as firm and well-muscled as his chest, looking forward to feeling his hands on her skin. She sucked in a quick breath as this thought sent warmth running through her body, wondering if he'd find her body attractive? She hoped so, but she knew she was tall and more muscular than most women. Her waist wasn't tiny and her hips and breasts were full. Child-bearing hips, the midwife had said approvingly and she'd borne Janie easily enough. But did such hips appeal to a man?

After washing herself quickly all over, she put on a clean nightdress, her prettiest one, which she'd been saving for this moment. It had lace at neck and wrists, tucking down the front and rows of lace and more tucks round the hem. She'd made it herself for when Cyril came back from the war – only he hadn't, poor fellow, so it had never been used.

Andrew came back in and smiled at her by the light of the lamp. 'Pretty nightdress.' He touched the lace at her neck with one fingertip. The finger didn't even graze her skin, but still a thrill ran through her and she lifted her face for a kiss.

Janie chose that moment to start making a fuss, calling out that she was frightened of the dark, wanted her mother.

Andrew froze and muttered, 'Not again!' as the crying continued next door. He looked at Norah. 'Shall

I deal with her? It's about time I became a proper father, don't you think?'

'Yes, please.'

He went to the door of the other half of the humpy and she heard him speaking sternly in the same tone he used to chastise his sons. 'Settle down *this minute*, Janie!'

'Go 'way. I want my mummy.'

'Your mummy's in bed and she's tired. And look, you've woken Ned now. If you don't settle down, I shall be really angry with you. You're nearly nine years old, a big girl now.'

'Go to sleep, stupid!' Ned said in a thick, sleepy voice. 'Stop waking me up all the time.'

As Andrew shut the door and came back into their half of the humpy, Norah listened to her daughter's sobbing. It wasn't real weeping, she could tell that, but forced sobs, a way of trying to wear them down.

'Can you ignore her?' Andrew asked in a low voice, kneeling by the bed.

'Yes.' She raised her voice, knowing how clearly you could hear people in the other room. 'I've run out of patience with Janie. If she doesn't calm down soon, I'll go next door myself and give her a good smacking.'

It wasn't something she usually did. In fact, a couple of the other women had seen the trouble she was having with her daughter and had told Norah she was too lax. One had said she should get a strap and use it regularly. *Spare the rod and spoil the child.* But Norah didn't believe in straps or sticks, had only rarely needed to smack Janie until now. She hated it when people beat their children severely.

Andrew had the same attitude towards the boys, but they were far better behaved than their stepsister, so didn't usually need more than a quick word from their father to pull them back into line. And besides, like the other older lads, they enjoyed working with the men, doing real jobs, coming home dirty and tired, free from lessons and school. They had little energy left to be naughty after a day's work.

Norah realised that while she had been lost in thought, Andrew had started washing himself. Unlike her, he showed no signs of being bashful about his body. That probably came from being in the Army. The experience had changed a lot of attitudes and many women had said their men came home different and they had to get to know one another all over again. She stole a few glances when he wasn't looking at her and could feel her cheeks growing warmer as she saw the effect she'd had on him.

Janie's crying had gone quieter and then it ceased altogether, thank goodness.

When Andrew turned out the lamp and slid in beside her, he was still naked, which shocked her. Cyril would never have done such a thing. But then Cyril's body hadn't been as strong and manly as Andrew's.

'Do you really need that nightdress?' he whispered.

Her heart began to beat faster and she swallowed back a sudden surge of nervousness. 'No. No, I don't.'

'Let me help you out of it . . .'

He made it fun, undressing her, whispering, teasing

her into cuddles, which led to caresses until they were moving together in the ancient rhythms, moving on to an ecstasy she'd never achieved before.

She was shocked by her own responses, shocked and delighted at the same time.

'You're a grand lass,' he murmured in her ear and fell asleep between one breath and the next.

She smiled in the darkness and let herself sink into sleep too. The floor seemed comfortable enough tonight.

In the morning, Norah woke before her husband and lay studying his face, which looked younger when he was asleep. He was not only a strong man, but had proved to be a virile and considerate one, too. She had never experienced such a night, wondered where he had learned to pleasure a woman like that.

He stirred and woke up suddenly, staring round in a quick appraisal of where he was. Then his eyes returned to her face and he smiled. 'I feel we're well and truly married now. Don't you?'

She blushed. 'Yes.' Then she heard one of the children stirring. 'We'd better got the beds sorted out quickly before they come in here.'

He was up in a minute, holding out his hand to pull her to her feet and chuckling when she gave a squeak and tried to cover her naked body. 'Don't be ashamed,' he whispered. 'You've a lovely body.'

But she wasn't used to being undressed in anyone's company and slipped her dressing gown on till she could have a quick wash. They lifted the blankets back on to the stretcher beds and folded up the canvas groundsheet, then she washed quickly in cold water and while she was dressing, he followed her example.

After that there was no time to think, with a fire to light in the kitchen, breakfast to prepare and a cow to milk, not to mention the people who got milk in the mornings turning up to collect their supplies.

Janie was sulky but Norah ignored that and kept her daughter busy. Heaven knew, there were enough jobs, all done under difficult conditions. She missed the ease of cooking on gas and the convenience of a water tap over a sink. Fetching all the water from the well was hard. Andrew and the boys took their turns when they were home, but they were gone all day.

She managed to find time during the day to dig out more ground for a vegetable garden. Andrew was going to extend the fence for this, to keep the wild animals away. When that was done, she'd plant peas and cabbage and onions. She was so thankful she'd taken advice and brought packets of seeds with her.

That evening, when Andrew and the boys came home, the lads were their usual cheerful selves. She couldn't help noticing, however, that they didn't speak to Janie unless they had to, and when they did, it was scornfully. Her heart ached for her daughter, who was making such a mess of her new family life. She'd tried to have a little talk with the child today, but no matter what she said or how often she said it, Janie scowled and went her own stubborn way.

Well, there were no grandparents here to spoil her and jolly her along, so in time she'd surely learn to get on with others. She knew Janie was still grieving for her granddad and missing her grandma. So was Norah. Everyone lost people they loved, but nothing you said or did could change what had happened. Death was part of life, and so was getting on with people.

The next night, with another two humpies finished, Irene and Freddie were on their own again. They'd made love furtively on the ship too, crawling into a lifeboat together more than once. And they hadn't been the only ones to do that, either. The sailors had turned a blind eye to it as long as you kept quiet and left things tidy.

But they'd not even tried to escape into the bush once they were sharing the humpy. Indeed, Freddie hardly ever made love to her now. So much had changed.

'I've something to tell you,' she said as they sat near the fire outside under a star-filled sky. She heard her voice wobble and forgot the speech she'd planned. 'Freddie, I'm expecting a baby.'

He looked at her in horror. 'You can't be! Are you sure?'

'Of course I'm sure.' She reached out to grasp his hand, but he shook her off and stood up, staring down into the fire that was crackling cheerfully, a beacon in the darkness around their humpy.

'Aren't you glad about it?' she asked when he didn't speak. 'We'll be a real family now. And I'm sure things will go all right this time.'

He didn't turn round to face her. 'No, I'm not glad.

I wanted to wait, you know I did. How could it have happened? We were being so *careful*.'

'No way is foolproof except abstinence, the doctor said. And I'm glad. I want a child.'

'It'll be too much for you.'

'No, it won't.'

'What about the birth? We're so far from a doctor here.'

'Well, thanks to the Bush Nursing Association, there's been a nursing sister at the hospital in Northcliffe since March and she's a trained midwife.'

'Call that a hospital! It's a cottage, that's all.'

'Other babies have been born there and so will ours.'

'What if the nurse has been called out when your time comes? What will you do then?'

'The other women in our group will help me. I won't be on my own. Pam knows quite a bit about birthing. She was telling me the other day that she's helped other women.'

He didn't answer her, only kicked out at some pieces of burning wood that had fallen out of the fire.

She reached out to touch his arm. 'Oh, Freddie, think of having our own baby! You're not a real family till you have children.'

He shook her hand off and turned, and his face looked ugly in the flickering light, ugly and bitter. 'What do I care about babies? It's you I love. I can't bear it if I lose you.' He made a sweeping gesture with one hand to encompass the dark mass of bush that was waiting to be cleared from their block. 'If anything happens to you, this will all have been in vain.'

She was bitterly disappointed by his reaction to her news, as well as by his attitude to their new life. She loved it here. She wanted to shout at him, but she didn't. It'd do no good. The new Freddie just shouted back. 'This time it'll all go well, I'm sure. I'm feeling fine, better than I have for years. No morning sickness, even.'

'You've not lived through a winter here yet. It's winter that always makes you ill. We should find a way to get rid of the baby. It's still early days, easy enough to do.'

She stared at him in horror. 'Kill our own child? You can't mean that!'

'Oh, yes I do. They sell things to help women in your situation. You can't be far along, surely?'

'It doesn't matter how far along I am. I'd never do that, never!'

'It's going to be gruelling hard work when our cows arrive. You'll be in no fit state to milk morning and evening if you're expecting. We have to think of ourselves, our new life. Promise me you'll think about it. I'll find somewhere to buy whatever's necessary, even if I have to go up to Perth to get it, and—'

Her voice was thick with tears. 'Hard work doesn't kill you, but a mortal sin kills your soul. Never, ever ask me to do such a thing, Freddie, because I won't.'

He glared at her as if he hated her then got up and strode off into the darkness, tramping off along the track.

She sat on for a while in front of the dying fire, hugging her stomach, sending warm thoughts to the child growing there. If Freddie didn't love their child, she didn't know what she'd do. Children needed love to thrive and grow into decent, happy people.

How could he even think of killing their baby?

She was tired now, tired and feeling chill inside, so sick with disappointment that she thought she'd vomit. Freddie had let her down, turned into a stranger she didn't know. Was this why couples fell out of love? She'd seen it happen, however rapturous the start of a marriage. What if he continued to hate the thought of a baby? What would she do? How would she feel about him?

She didn't wait for Freddie to come back, but went inside the humpy and got into bed, huddling down on the floor, where they'd spread out their blankets on a piece of canvas, expecting to make love.

Tears rolled down her cheeks, but she didn't let herself sob, kept listening for him, trying to hang on to a belief that he'd return and say he'd been wrong, hadn't meant it.

Only he didn't and gradually her hope vanished and with it, some of her love for Freddie. She knew it, couldn't help it, wept over it.

She lay there for a long time and the fire outside died right down, leaving everything in darkness.

But he didn't come back.

Gil heard footsteps on the track and got up from his usual position by the fire. Surely they didn't have another thief? Well, he wasn't letting people wander round at night and rob others.

He went quietly towards the track and recognised

Freddie Dawson in the moonlight. 'Everything all right, lad?'

Freddie stopped, breathing deeply, looking so unhappy that Gil moved closer. 'Want to tell me about it? I may be able to help.'

The answer was a harsh laugh. 'No one can help. She's gone and got herself in the family way. We were taking precautions. It shouldn't have happened. And she won't do anything about it. This isn't the time to have a child.'

Gil listened in disgust. 'You should be rejoicing about that baby!' He couldn't help speaking sharply. 'I'd have given all I own to have a child.'

'Well, you can have this one if you like. *I* don't want it.'

'Come and sit by the fire. You need to calm down.'

But Freddie shook his arm off. 'The only way I'll do that is walk. And even then I have to go back and let her put a chain on me. We'll never be free to make a better life if we start having children. And that means we'll never get away from here.'

'You hate it, don't you?'

'Yes. But I was prepared to do it, to put up with it for a while, for *her*. I'd do anything to get her back to health. And she *is* better. Now she'll get ill again like she was last time she was expecting.'

'Having a child doesn't make you ill.'

'It did Irene. She nearly died last time. And the baby did die. Oh, what's the use of talking?'

Gil watched Freddie storm off along the dark track, still walking in the opposite direction to his home, walking quickly, shoulders hunched, his whole body radiating unhappiness.

Shaking his head, Gil went to make sure the fire was safe and then sought his bed.

Some people didn't understand how lucky they were.

When Freddie eventually returned, just before dawn, Irene had moved from feeling upset to feeling furiously angry with him. So she pretended she was asleep and was even more annoyed when he didn't try to wake her to say he was sorry.

Soon he was breathing so evenly and deeply beside her, she knew he was asleep. And perhaps that was for the best. She didn't want to quarrel with him, was afraid of what she might say. She'd never realised how protective you'd feel if your baby's life was openly threatened.

Surely by morning Freddie would have grown used to the idea and be starting to feel some pleasure at the thought of a son or daughter? He had to. She couldn't bear it if he didn't, because she couldn't imagine life without children of her own, wanted several. And she couldn't imagine life without Freddie, either. Not this new Freddie, but the loving man she'd defied her family and church to marry.

The following week, Gil received another shipment of timber and corrugated iron for building cowsheds, together with the news that the first batch of cows was on its way and the animals would be there 'in a day or two'.

'You'd think they could give us better notice than that,' he muttered, then set to work with the men to sort out the timber and plan how they could best use it.

During the next two days, he worked the men hard to build as many simple cowsheds with adjoining dairy area as they could, ignoring their grumbles about 'slave drivers' and insisting they work every hour of daylight.

He answered all grumbles about this hard work with, 'You can have a day off when the cows arrive. You'll need it to get used to them. In the meantime, it's getting cooler and wetter. We must have shelters ready for them. These are cows in milk not hardy young steers, you know.'

Even after the hard days' work, some of them went home to fashion bits of furniture for their own houses by the light of their oil lamps, or do other jobs needed to create a farm from nothing. He was beginning to spot the ones who had most chance of succeeding, and Andrew Boyd stood out like a bright star among these, while Norah and Pam were the most capable of the women.

The groupies made furniture from the crates that had carried their possessions out from England, and the wooden boxes in which tins of food arrived were much sought after too. Bits of tree trunks and pieces of wood from the block clearances were used ingeniously and anything straight enough was set aside, with pieces of log serving as stools and rough, home-sawn planks used for makeshift tables.

Those men who weren't as handy at woodwork, but eager to learn, went round to watch the men who were, or offered to help in return for being taught how to do it.

Freddie, however, kept to himself after the day's obligatory work was finished and though Gil kept an eye on him, he couldn't think what to do to help him settle down. It was Irene he felt sorry for, because she fitted in so well, and usually seemed cheerful enough as she went about her work.

But when she was with her husband, you could sense the strains between them, see the shadows in her eyes as she looked at him, the resentment in his and increasingly, the resentment in hers.

Gil was very frustrated with the Board's ineptitudes. He always seemed to be trying to make up for their poor planning. The timing of this delivery was ridiculous. The other groups were ahead of them in building and settling in, so maybe they'd be all right, but Special Group 1 had not had time to finish clearing the twenty-five acres set as a preliminary goal for each block.

Worst of all, there was no sign of the teams who came to build the wooden farmhouses. Not a single one had been built for this group. With winter coming on fast, that worried Gil greatly.

The wet season would be a testing time for them all.

Maybe he should suggest people order wood-burning stoves to put in their humpies for the time being. But not all would be able to afford that.

It was a fine, sunny day, if a bit brisk, and Irene got the washing done early. She left it drying on the makeshift line and walked across to see Norah, because she desperately needed to talk to another woman.

Norah was still working on her much larger pile of washing, using a tin tub standing on a small bench and water boiled on the small cooking fire in the lean-to kitchen. She was humming to herself, looking sweaty and ready for a rest, but not unhappy.

Irene called out from across the block and Norah turned, smiling when she saw who it was and waving a hand holding a scrubbing brush covered in suds by way of a greeting.

Janie was peeling potatoes at a rough outdoor table and looked sulky. She didn't bother to look up until her mother said sharply, 'Say hello to Mrs Dawson.'

The words came out tonelessly. 'Hello, Mrs Dawson.'

'Hello, Janie. I see you're helping your mother.'

'I don't like peeling potatoes.'

Irene looked at Norah, who gave a slight shake of her head and frowned at her daughter.

'If you'd put the kettle over the fire, Irene love, we could have a nice cup of tea,' Norah said. 'I'm nearly ready for one. There's some clean water from the well in that bucket and there's a fire in my kitchen.' She smiled as she said this.

'It's a good kitchen, the best of any I've seen,' Irene said enviously as she went into the lean-to. 'You've got it all set up so well.' Freddie had made her a lean-to of sorts, but hadn't really finished it off and one side was still open to the weather. She tipped water from the bucket carefully into the kettle. 'Shall I get some more water from the well?'

'If you don't mind.'

'I'm happy to help. And when you're finished, maybe we could have a talk?' She looked meaningfully at Janie.

Norah nodded.

After the washing had been mangled and hung out, Norah suggested Irene help her in the vegetable garden and the two women left Janie to finish peeling the potatoes and carrots.

'It's hard to keep on top of the weeding. That winter grass grows so quickly at this time of year. I want to put some more seeds in as soon as Andrew's fenced in some more land.'

'You've got green fingers.'

Norah laughed and looked down at her hands. 'Red today from the washing. But I'm enjoying gardening. I've not done it before, but it's so wonderful to eat something you've grown yourself. Just wait till you see what I grow next year. More than this! But you didn't come here to talk of gardening, did you?'

'No. I need your advice.' As the two women worked, Irene told her friend how much Freddie had changed since coming here and described his reaction to the news of the coming baby. She was sobbing by the time she finished her tale, felt Norah put her arms round her and leaned against the other woman, taking comfort from her strength.

After a moment or two, however, she straightened up. 'I shouldn't burden you with my problems.'

'What else are friends for?' Norah gave her another quick hug.

'It's just . . . I don't know what to do about Freddie and the baby.'

'There's not much you can do. He'll grow used to the idea. Didn't he want children in England?'

Irene frowned. 'We never talked about it then. It was just us he cared about, I think. When I lost the baby and was so ill, he was so wonderful. He came out here to Australia to make me better. Only . . . he hates it here, absolutely hates it.'

'Oh dear. I was right then. I said to Andrew that's why Freddie is unhappy.'

There was silence, then Janie screamed and yelled, 'There a spider. Mummy, a big black spider.'

'That child is driving me mad,' Norah muttered. 'She won't give me a minute to myself. But I'll have to go and see what this one is. I'm still trying to work out which spiders are poisonous and which aren't.'

When they got back to the humpy, they found Janie standing away from the outdoors table where she'd been sitting peeling potatoes, with a stick in her hand, weeping.

'It's there! It's there!'

There was indeed a furry black spider as big as the palm of the hand on the edge of the table, but even as they watched, it began climbing down and went placidly about its business, walking away in the other direction. It wasn't trying to attack the child.

'It's a huntsman spider,' Irene said. 'We had one at our place yesterday. Gil said to leave it alone and it'll leave you alone. If you get one indoors you can kill it or put it outside.' She looked at the child. 'I quite like spiders. They catch mosquitoes for us.'

'I don't like them!' Janie began weeping again. 'I don't like it here.' She was hysterical and wouldn't listen to her mother, so Norah gave her a shake, then said in a calm voice, 'You're being silly. Now calm down this minute.'

So Janie wept more quietly.

'I don't know what to do about that child,' Norah said as the two women went back to work on the garden. 'She's naughty nearly all the time and miserable the rest. She tries to come between me and Andrew, and she won't have anything to do with the boys – or they with her, now.'

'I suppose it'll take time for her to get used to you remarrying.'

'She had the whole of the voyage out here to get used to Andrew and the boys.'

'But you were still sleeping with her then, so not much had changed.'

Norah sighed. 'Well, I can't sleep with her now. I've a husband and I want to be with him.'

Irene saw the glow in her friend's eyes as Norah spoke about her husband and drew her own conclusions. About time too, was her main thought.

She walked slowly back to her block to start cooking Freddie's tea, wondering what sort of mood he'd be in tonight. Not a good one, that was sure, but some evenings were worse than others.

14

During the next two weeks, the groupies worked hard, bringing order to their own homes as much as they could, getting ready to receive the cows and continuing to clear land so that each family could start with the same amount of usable land. Gil told Andrew privately that since he got so few directives from the Board, he was just doing what seemed fair and practical.

It was cooler now and rained more often, sometimes a downpour so heavy the air they pulled into their lungs seemed almost liquid. The rain also turned the rough tracks to mud, which made it miserable working out of doors or walking into town. Once they stopped working, the men were chilled to the marrow, in spite of the sacks they wore round their shoulders to keep the worst of the rain off. But Gil had to keep them working. Besides, he knew they couldn't afford to slack off, whatever the weather. Fortunately the rainy spells were only intermittent.

The 'day or two' for delivery of the cows stretched into several days and at least they got the cowsheds finished.

Grass was springing up everywhere, 'winter grass'.

In the early spring they'd seed more pastures on the land they'd cleared and he assured them that the grass would grow really quickly once the weather warmed up.

He worked all day with the men and slept at night in his humpy now because a tent was uncomfortable in the rain. Unlike the others, he hadn't had time to build on a lean-to kitchen, so he paid Pam to cook for him. When he went back from her place, he realised how little he'd done to make his own into a home. He'd do something about that, but later. There was far too much to do for the group at the moment.

But he smiled sometimes because he'd definitely done the right thing coming here, and he knew Mabel would be proud of him. He'd thought of burning her letters and letting her rest in peace, but it seemed wrong to do that. She wrote so well. Maybe some-time in the future people would want to read them to see what life had been like in Australia during the war.

He wasn't sure he'd ever read them again, didn't need to now.

As well as fencing Norah's garden, Andrew built a fowl pen and like most of their group, they sent off for some laying pullets. Everyone bought at least one, while the settlers with more money to spare or large families bought several. If they could produce eggs cheaply, they could feed their families better.

When the Boyds' four pullets arrived, Janie showed some signs of interest for the first time, making a pet of one which had a twisted foot and couldn't walk as fast as the others. She made sure that the other chooks, as people called chickens here, didn't push it out of the way when they were fed and it would follow her around with its slow, lopsided gait.

Andrew watched this without comment. One day he saved that pullet from the others, which had started pecking it and beckoned Janie across. 'I'll make you a separate corner for your little friend near the house, but only if you agree to look after her all on your own. Your mother has enough to do. The twisted foot won't affect the eggs she lays, and as long as she's producing, we'll keep her.' He thrust the wriggling hen into her hands.

When he took time the very next day to make a special enclosure for 'Fluffy', Janie's hostility towards him lessened just a little.

The pullets' eggs were a godsend, adding variety to the monotonous diet, making cakes and scones a more regular feature, not a rare treat possible only when someone was able to buy a tray of eggs at the store.

What with the chickens and the extra milk from looking after the cow, things weren't going badly, Norah felt. She didn't mind the cold or even the wet days, because it wasn't like snow or ice. Besides, every night, whether they made love or not, she and Andrew would snuggle up together in bed and chat about their day's doings. She loved that.

Even Janie's sulks didn't seem to upset her as much these days. She felt in glowing health and was busy from dawn till dusk.

*　　*　　*

Andrew was working on a cowshed two farms beyond the central camp ground when two trucks carrying cows drove slowly past, bumping in and out of the ruts, sometimes seeming to pause and decide whether to get out of a particularly deep rut or settle into it, but always just managing to escape and continue.

The men delivering the cows looked tired.

Gil put down his axe and yelled, 'Stop work!' Then he strode across the uneven ground towards the trucks, which had pulled up a bit further on. One of the men greeted him by name.

'Thought you'd vanished from the face of the earth, you old devil!' the truck driver said affectionately. 'You look a lot better than last time I saw you.'

Gil nodded. He felt a lot better, too. He exchanged news quickly, congratulated his old friend on the birth of a fourth child and studied the animals.

'Two for each family we brought this time. It'll give the groupies time to get used to them before they get their full quota of six.' He lowered his voice. 'How's it going? Lost any of your group yet?'

'One death, one thief, one runaway wife.'

'Not bad going. You'll lose more of them by the end of the winter. Some of the poor sods seem to think it's going to be sunny all the time here. It might not snow, but I can't stand mud. I'd rather be working up north where it stays warm all year round, but my wife has family in Bunbury so we've settled there.' He looked back down the track in disgust. 'Worst road in the area you've got.'

'Yeah. Going to have to corduroy some of the worst

patches.' He'd been keeping some tree trunks to do this with. The men had been amazed to think of laying trunks across the track to form a road surface. But then the poor sods had been amazed at a few things since they got here. You used what you had, and they had felled trees here, not tarmac.

His companion swiped at the water running into his eyes and cursed it cheerfully.

'Tell me which are the best animals, mate. You must have some idea by now.'

His friend looked sideways at him. 'Choosing your own?'

'Nope. Can't manage any of my own at the moment. I'll get mine later. It's just that some of these fellows are less likely to make a go of it, so why waste good beasts on them? Give us a ride, eh?' He clambered on the outside of the open truck, holding on to the rails and yelled at the men who'd been working with him, 'Meet you back at the camp ground. We'll assign the cows then and you can take them home with you.'

When he arrived there, he picked up the metal bar hanging beside the store hut and clanged the iron triangle they used to summon people to meetings or in case of emergencies. He rang it good and loud, knowing that those on the nearer blocks would send children running to warn those on the outer blocks, as agreed. Their version of the 'bush telegraph'.

While he waited for the groupies to gather, he supervised the brewing of a huge supply of tea in a former kerosene can. You couldn't beat a hot drink for putting heart into you on a day like this.

He'd have to remind the women to let him know if they had any trouble using the cream separators and other dairy equipment. He'd already demonstrated their use with the milk from the cow Norah was tending.

So many things to do.

He smiled again. Such a nice busy life.

Andrew, who had been working with Gil, stood looking down at the square tin of black tea simmering at the edge of the fire, tendrils of steam curling lazily up from it. He remembered suddenly how people in Pemberton had greeted their train with a similar brew when they first arrived. What a long time ago that seemed now! They'd thought it primitive to brew tea that way, but it tasted just as good as any that'd been brewed in the finest china teapot to a tired, thirsty man.

He shook the rain from the brim of his hat, an Australian style hat which he'd purchased to keep the sun off and now found equally useful for keeping the rain out of his eyes. After taking another gulp of the hot liquid and sighing with pleasure as the warmth slid down him, he went over to study the cows.

Gil came to stand beside him. 'You get two each from this lot.'

'We've got one cow already.'

'You can keep that.' He winked.

'Are you sure?'

'Yes.'

'I can't believe the dairy only wants the cream. There'll be a lot of milk going to waste once we get the rest of our cows.'

'Piglets fatten up well on it.'

'Where would I get some of those?'

Gil tapped the side of his nose. 'I know a man who has a litter for sale.'

Andrew grinned. How Gil knew so many people in the area constantly amazed him. They'd fallen lucky with their foreman. Without him, they'd have struggled even harder to make sense of the mess into which they'd been dumped. Special group, indeed! Sudden afterthought, more like.

Two hours later he and Norah started driving their new cows home, cows which Gil had helped him choose without letting the others see that he was doing it.

The three children walked with them, Jack whistling cheerfully as usual, Ned lost in his own thoughts and Janie grumbling about the rain.

'Right,' Andrew said when they got back. 'We all need to be able to milk these cows. What if I was ill, or your mother was? How would you manage then? Anyway, it's a job which children can do, milking is.'

Janie looked at him in horror. 'I don't like cows. I'm not doing it.'

'You'll do it,' he promised grimly. 'We all will.'

She looked pleadingly at her mother.

Norah shook her head. 'We can't have one person being lazy. We all have to help.'

Janie began to cry and when the two boys laughed at her, cried even harder.

Andrew's voice cracked out like a whip. 'Stop that, young lady!'

She stared at him in shock, then edged away from

him and nearer to her mother. But Norah merely said, 'Do as your father tells you.'

They took the cows out to the proper cowshed Andrew and the other groupies had built, and the presence of Blossom seemed to soothe the newcomers, because they were soon standing in a little group, tails swishing, jaws moving as they ate some of the hay he offered them.

'I'll get the water hot and scour out the buckets,' Norah said. 'Gil said the Dairy Company will be coming to collect the cream every morning from tomorrow onwards. Andrew, we'll need somewhere to stand the cream can near the gate, somewhere off the ground.'

He smiled. 'I know. I've got the rest of the day off, so I'll cobble something together. The boys can help me.'

'And Janie can help me separate the cream.'

When she'd got everything clean, Andrew settled down beside her and they started milking. Jack was soon wanting to have a try and proved to have a fair touch, almost as good as his father's. Ned tried next and wasn't nearly as good, but remained his usual cheerful self and kept trying.

Andrew ruffled his son's hair. 'You'll soon learn. Your turn now, Janie.'

She moved forward a little, then shook her head.

'No work, no tea,' he said.

She moved closer to the cow, but it swished its tail at her and with a shriek, she fled across to the house and disappeared.

When the cream was separated, Norah set the can carefully on the shelf Andrew had built her in the dairy, eyeing it with satisfaction.

At teatime, she set four places only.

When she called everyone to table, she pulled Janie aside. 'Your dad said no work, no tea. You can sit at the end of the table but you get no food.' It upset her to see her daughter go without, but a stand had to be made.

Mute and hunched, Janie watched them all eat. With all the milk to spare, Norah gave the boys as much to drink as they wanted, already planning to buy some rice and make puddings with it regularly.

In the morning, she got her daughter up early, gave her a glass of milk and took her along to the cowshed. 'We'll do the milking together and you'll see that there's nothing to be afraid of.'

Janie was stiff at first, wincing each time the cow moved, but like the boys she was big for her age, taking after her mother, and old enough to help.

When Andrew and the boys joined them, no one commented on the fact that Janie was milking, so they had another lesson and between them, got the three cows finished quickly. After that Andrew carried the lidded cream cans to the entrance to their block and set them on the rough bench he'd made.

Within half an hour the dairy truck had collected the cream and the boys were fetching the empty cans back, claiming further glasses of the morning's skim milk and chatting about what they and their father would be doing during the day.

Soon they fell into a routine, and by the end of the week, even Janie had lost her nervousness with the cows and was milking them when asked. She never managed to work as quickly as the two boys, but she did what she had to, and made considerably less mess when she helped clear up and wash out the pails and separator and cream cans.

But underneath, the child was unhappy. It showed in the droop of her mouth and the listless way she moved around. She was so unlike her old self it worried Norah a lot. Nothing they said or did seemed to make a difference to her.

They could only hope that time would work a gradual cure.

Gil watched his group carefully, noticing more than most people realised. The one he worried about most at the moment was Freddie Dawson. What was wrong with the man? He'd chosen to come here, it was rebuilding his wife's health, why was he so surly? He was a misery to work with these days.

Something about Irene still drew Gil's eyes to her whenever they were together. But she had eyes only for Freddie, didn't notice the foreman's interest in her.

Well, why should she? Gil thought. She wasn't a loose woman like that Susan Grenville had been. No doubt the Dawsons would sort themselves out one way or the other, people usually did. And if he could help them, he would.

He bought the piglets and left word here and there that he was looking for more, before delivering the little creatures. Andrew had converted his original cow shelter into a pen for the two piglets. Freddie was working with a gang of men today, but had assured the foreman that he too had an enclosure ready for the piglets. But it was such a sorry excuse for an enclosure, one which even small piglets would soon escape from, that Gil nearly took the lively little creatures away again.

Then he looked at Irene and her unhappy expression stopped him speaking his mind.

'It's not good enough, is it?' she said.

'No. The piglets will get stronger and they'll soon be able to push their way out of that.'

Tears filled her eyes and she bit her lip.

He couldn't bear to see her upset. 'I'll help you sort it out, shall I?'

'Why? You've got enough work of your own to keep you busy from dawn till dusk.'

'I don't mind. The cows look good. Milk coming nicely?'

'Oh yes. We've plenty to spare for the pigs.' Her smile was genuine this time. 'I like milking the cows. They're such gentle creatures.'

He'd chosen their two with care, for that very reason. 'Good. And as for your pig pen, I can always spare a few minutes to help a neighbour.'

'Thank you. I'll do what I can to help you—'

'In your condition, you need to be careful.'

'Oh. You know, then? I wasn't going to tell anyone yet.'

He smiled. 'We all live so close together that if someone sneezes the rest hear it. Congratulations.'

But more tears welled up in her eyes and escaped, and she pressed one hand against her lips as if to hold them back. He couldn't bear it and before he knew it, had his arms round her and she was sobbing against his chest.

'Tell me,' he said when she stopped weeping.

'Freddie doesn't want the baby.'

Gil knew that, thought less of the man for it, and didn't know how to comfort her. 'He'll come round.'

'He's showing no signs of it.' She fumbled in her apron pocket and found a handkerchief, blowing her nose and scrubbing at her eyes, then straightening her shoulders. 'I'm sorry. I shouldn't be burdening you with my troubles.'

'A foreman's here to help and you'd be surprised what people tell me.'

'No.' Her voice was soft and there was even a faint smile on her face. 'I'd not be surprised. You're equal to anything.' She moved away from him.

His arms felt empty without her. He was annoyed at himself for feeling like that but he couldn't help it. She was such an attractive woman, the prettiest in the group, but what attracted him more than that was the sort of woman she was, gentle but hard-working, ready to try anything, pleasant to others. He could see no fault in her.

Taking a deep breath, he said as cheerfully as he could manage, 'Let's see to this pig enclosure then, shall we? And don't forget the manure will be really useful. You'll need to shovel it out and make yourself a muck heap.'

Talking to fill in the silence that seemed fraught with her pain and emotion still, he set to work, remaking the fences and putting on timber cross pieces to stabilise the pig shelter. This was a simple structure, made mainly of corrugated iron that formed a wall and bent over in a quarter circle to form a roof high enough for pigs but not high enough for a man to stand under. It was built to shelter the animals against the prevailing winds, and at least Freddie had got that right. Well, more or less right.

By the time Gil had finished, the shelter was built to last a good few years and he and Irene were in a fair way to becoming friends, chatting comfortably as she passed him things.

Which was better than nothing, surely?

A couple of weeks later, on May 7th, there was an official proclamation and naming of the townsite.

'It was already called Northcliffe,' Gil said, shaking his head in amusement. 'Trust government officials to be behind the times.'

But the group used this occasion as an excuse to have a Saturday gathering and as the weather co-operated, a good time was had by all.

Some of the men joined the new Returned Soldiers' League, which had formed a chapter in Northcliffe, but not all of them bothered. They were too busy, working on their new farms.

Or in the case of Freddie, too disenchanted with everything to bother.

15

The huge tree on Pam and Ted's block was in exactly the wrong place, right in the middle of the approach to the house if they were to have pastures of decent size on either side. Ted wanted the tree felled as soon as possible and when the rainy weather eased, Gil agreed to bring a team to have a go at it.

'You'll need to take care,' he warned the men. 'Trees like these are known as "widowmakers". They can drop branches without much warning. So if I yell "Run!" then you move away from it as fast as you can. Right?'

Things started well and the men worked up a sweat, using their axes to chop out the base of the massive trunk. They were all learning to fell trees, a necessary skill here.

Gil mostly left them to it, because they had to learn to do this sort of thing without him. He kept a careful eye on their progress, however. He didn't trust the bigger trees.

They were nearly there, ready for the tree to fall in the direction they'd planned when suddenly there was a loud crack and one of the big lower branches shuddered. As everyone knew, branches like this could weigh a ton, especially after a rainy period, so Gil yelled, 'Run!' at the top of his voice.

The men scattered, but as Andrew, who was directly underneath it, swung round, his foot turned over on a small stone and he fell headlong. There was another cracking noise right above his head and he tried to roll to one side to avoid the branch, but didn't manage to do so completely. The earth shuddered as the heavy branch thumped down on to the ground and the fallen man vanished from sight beneath the thrashing foliage of its side branches.

'Andrew! Are you all right?' Gil shouted.

There was no answer.

'Stay back!' he ordered the others. 'The rest of the tree's going.' He could have wept for his own help-lessness, couldn't see whether his friend was all right, but didn't dare move forward.

The huge tree creaked and groaned, falling slowly down amid the noise of branches breaking as they hit the ground. They sounded like gunshots and for a moment Gil was reminded of the war.

The tree had fallen slightly to the side of where they'd planned, coming down very close to where Andrew must be lying.

Gil prayed as he'd never prayed before that his friend would be still alive, but not till the last sounds had died away did he move. Even then he kept looking anxiously at the other branches jutting upwards from the fallen forest giant. 'Keep back. Let me check that it's safe first.'

As he approached the foliage and branches under

which his friend lay, he was able to see that Andrew had been protected from the rest of the tree by the huge branch. Taking great care of where he set his feet, Gil crept closer.

'Is he all right?' someone called.

'Can't see his face yet, but he's not moving.'

Step by step Gil threaded his way through the mess of branches, some broken off, some still attached to the fallen tree. And at last he was able to push the final piece of foliage aside. Andrew's chest was moving slightly. He closed his eyes for a second, groaning in sheer relief. *His friend was alive!*

Praying that the other wasn't too badly injured, Gil looked round at the bigger branches nearby, which were jutting up at all different angles. None of them seemed poised to fall in this direction, so he pushed through to kneel beside the still figure. Andrew was still unconscious. There was a bad bruise and grazing on his forehead and his left arm was trapped beneath a side branch, but fortunately not beneath the main piece that had fallen. The side branch was big enough to do serious damage to a man's soft body, though.

He turned to call back. 'He's unconscious but trapped. Two of you come and help me get him out. The rest stay back.'

Two others pushed their way through to join him.

'We need to get the branch off him first,' one said.

Gil stuck his arm out to stop them rushing in. 'Don't try to lift it yet. It's heavy and if you let it drop, you could do more damage to him. Get something to wedge underneath it then it can't fall back on him.'

He waited, alternately giving directions and keeping an eye on the injured man.

When the others brought some sawn-off pieces of a smaller tree, he helped wedge these under the heavy branch. Two stood ready to slip other pieces of trunk underneath as they eased away the branch that had done all the damage. Even to move it slightly was an effort.

Pam had come running from the house and was standing just beyond the fallen tree, watching, her tightly clasped hands up near her mouth. Gil was relieved that she had enough sense not to try to help.

The way Andrew's arm had been trapped suggested to Gil that it might be broken, but to his relief it was only the forearm that was trapped, not the shoulder. *Only!* He cursed under his breath. Of all the rotten luck. A man engaged in physical work needed both arms. If it was broken, Andrew would be out of operation for weeks. He tested the safety of the propped-up branch. 'Right. Let's pull him away.'

Even when they moved Andrew, he didn't stir or groan, which worried Gil far more than the prospect of a broken arm.

Once they were away from the tree, he stopped them. 'Lay him down carefully and let me look at his arm. It has to be broken, or at least fractured after being walloped by that branch.'

'Shouldn't we wait for the doctor?' Pam worried.

'What doctor? The one from Pemberton?'

'Well, the nurse at the hospital, then.'

'Do you want Andrew to be jolted into town in my

cart? That'd make the injury worse, I'm sure. Look, I've dealt with broken legs on animals, and done quite a bit of first aid during the war. Sometimes, if it's a clean break, you can jiggle it back in place. I can't do much if it's shattered, though. He might even lose his arm if that's the case. If I'm in any doubt, I'll do nothing and we'll send for the nurse or doctor.'

He began to get Andrew's shirt off. 'It hurts like hell to touch a broken limb, so I want to check it before he regains consciousness. Ah. The skin isn't broken. That's good. If he's lucky, it's just a fracture.'

Surrounded by a totally silent group of people, he felt his way carefully along the forearm, then felt it again and sat back on his heels with a sigh of relief. 'It's not shattered, but I can feel a bump where the bones are bent. I'm going to straighten it if I can and bind it to a splint while he's unconscious.'

He stood up and looked round. 'Someone get me one of those pieces of scantling off the cart – they're the thinnest planks we have. Saw it to the right length for fingertips to elbow. Pam, have you got something we can bind the arm in place with?'

'Yes. I've an old sheet I use for cleaning rags. I can tear that up. And shall I send my Joe to tell Norah?'

Her son was standing by her side, watching wide-eyed. He was ten and a sensible lad, so Gil turned to him. 'Just tell Mrs Boyd that her husband's hurt but alive. He has a broken arm and we're bringing him home. Tell her to stay there and get ready for him.' He made the boy repeat the message and then saw him run off along the track in the direction of the Boyds' house.

There was a sound of sawing and as Gil stood waiting for the splint, he kept an eye on his friend. It was still worrying him that Andrew hadn't regained consciousness, hadn't even groaned when they moved him and set the arm. That always hurt like hell. He'd seen a lot of injuries during the war and done a fair amount of first aid. Give him a screaming patient over a totally unconscious one any day, if you wanted the man to recover.

What the hell was Norah going to do if Andrew died? No, don't think of that. His friend wasn't going to die.

They brought Gil the materials for the splint and stood round as he felt the arm again, then took a firm grasp and pulled carefully until the bone was as straight as human touch could make it. If Andrew had been conscious, he'd have been screaming in agony and they'd have had to hold him down. Gil had seen that happen more than once.

But Andrew didn't even react.

When there was nothing more he could do, Gil bound the arm carefully to the narrow piece of wood and let out a sigh to release the tension. 'Now, let's get him on the cart. And make sure that arm doesn't get jolted in any way.'

'Do we need to take him to the hospital?' someone asked.

'I don't think so.'

'I still think we should take him to the doctor in Pemberton,' Ted said.

'That'd be dangerous. Head injuries are unpredictable.

I think we should get him on the cart and take him home, then someone should fetch the nurse to look at him. And if she thinks we should get the doctor, we will. But I'm not jolting him around, not while he's unconscious.'

'I'll get some blankets for him to lie on,' Pam said. 'And a pillow for his arm.'

When the cart was ready, they lifted the unconscious man gently. Even when one of the bearers stumbled as they carried him to the cart, Andrew still didn't react.

Bad, Gil thought. *That's bad.*

He drove along the track slowly and carefully, with Ted sitting in the back making sure the injured man didn't bounce around more than was unavoidable.

Norah was waiting in the doorway, looking pale but in command of herself. She ran to the cart as it drew to a halt. 'How is he?'

'Broken arm and knocked unconscious,' Gil said briefly. 'I've set the arm. One of the lads is going for the nurse.'

As Norah looked at her husband, anxiety sat like lead weights in her stomach. He was pale, his hair wet and dirty. She reached out to take a dead leaf out of his hair, upset by the livid bruise on his face, with the dried blood where the skin had been torn open by something sharp.

She'd never seen him so still and it seemed wrong. Every minute he was awake, he was doing something. He was the most active, energetic man she'd ever met.

Gil touched her arm gently. 'Let's get him inside

and warm him up, Norah. Have you got any hot-water bottles?'

'One.' It was a modern rubber one, too, not an old-fashioned earthenware one. Andrew had shoved it in as an afterthought to protect something else. They'd not expected to need hot-water bottles in a warm country. No one had told them how cold the nights were in winter.

'Show us which bed, then heat some water and fill the bottle. We'll ask round and see if anyone else can lend you another bottle or two. We have to keep him warm, especially during the coming night. I don't need a doctor to tell me that.'

'Janie, go and get the kitchen fire burning up.' She tried to speak calmly, but heard the wobble in her voice. 'And if there's not enough water, fetch some more from the well.'

For once, her daughter did as she was told without arguing.

Norah helped them settle Andrew, then went into the lean-to kitchen. It seemed to take a long time for the kettle to boil and she kept wanting to go back inside, to be with him.

Janie hovered beside her. 'Is he going to die?'

'*No!*'

Norah carried the filled hot-water bottle into the humpy, wishing there were some way of heating the place up. They'd talked of ordering a stove, but had decided to see how they went on without. The warmth from the fire in the lean-to did come through the metal wall that backed on to it.

'Ted's gone off to get you some more hot-water bottles,' Gil said.

'What else can I do?' Norah asked. There must be something. She'd go mad if she had to just sit there and watch him.

Gil spread his arms wide in a helpless gesture. 'You can pray he regains consciousness. The head wound's more worry than the arm. Just – keep him warm.'

The words seemed to echo inside her head. She'd had no experience whatsoever with serious head wounds. They were something feared by everyone because they could knock the senses out of a person and leave them a drooling idiot.

Gil patted her shoulder. 'If necessary, I'll go into Pemberton and fetch the doctor to him. We'll make sure someone stays with you.'

The men left her with Andrew and a short time later, there was the sound of pounding footsteps and the boys, who'd been working elsewhere, burst through the door.

Norah held up one hand. '*Quiet!* Your father's broken his arm and he's unconscious.'

'He's not going to die, like Mr Roberts did, is he?' Jack asked, his voice shriller than usual.

'No, he's not.' She spoke more confidently than she felt, but it reassured her as well as the boys to say it aloud.

Janie looked from one person to the other, then back at the bed, but held her tongue, thank goodness.

'What can we do?' Jack asked.

'Nothing. Just wait and pray. I'll need your help tonight milking the cows, though.'

Jack nodded. 'We can do them for you, so that you can look after Dad. We'll be very careful and keep everything clean, I promise.'

'Thanks. You're a good lad.'

He put his arm round his brother and stayed there, watching, his face white and anxious.

Irene turned up, stayed for a while, then, when it was clear there was nothing anyone could do and Norah wasn't going to fail under the strain, she suggested taking Janie back with her for a while.

Norah found it a relief not to have to keep an eye on her daughter.

Pam arrived soon afterwards and offered to have the boys.

'I'm not leaving him,' Jack said at once. 'Mum needs us for the milking.'

Norah looked at her friend, hoping Pam would guess that she wanted the children out of the way.

Pam nodded as if she understood. 'The boys could come across to us after milking and have tea with my lot, then spend the night, if that's any help.'

'Thanks. I appreciate that.'

'I'm *not* leaving him,' Jack said again.

'It'd help me not to have to feed you or worry about you.'

He studied her face, then thrust his hands in his pockets and kicked at the edge of a blanket that was hanging on the floor. 'I want to help.'

'As soon as your dad comes to his senses, you can

help a lot. And you can come back early in the morning to milk the cows. Till then, we need peace and quiet here. And I need you to keep an eye on your brother.'

Ned hadn't said anything, was still staring at his father, looking close to tears. She went to give him a quick hug, but it was all the energy she could spare and she soon went back to her husband. Bringing in one of the rough stools Andrew had made, she set it beside his bed. She felt shaky and close to tears, but refused to let them fall. Her thoughts were bleak, though. To lose her man so soon after she'd found him was more than she could bear to think of, so she tried to set that dreadful thought aside.

Only it kept coming back to worry her.

Time passed and as Gil had promised, there was always someone with her. The groupies had set up a roster, it seemed. It comforted her a little to know people would rally round like that, as neighbours would have done in the streets back in Lancashire.

The two boys crept in and out of the humpy very quietly to look at their father and there was always another adult nearby. After a while, she asked the boys to make sure all the animals had enough water, then check the chickens and collect any eggs. Anything to keep them busy.

She tried to talk sense when anyone spoke to her. Some told her of people they knew who'd been knocked unconscious and recovered just fine. She wished they wouldn't, wished it was Gil sitting with her. He was a restful person and she didn't want to talk, just watch over her husband.

But the nurse had been unavailable, due to a difficult birth, and on her advice, Gil had gone off to Pemberton to fetch the doctor. Head wounds worried everyone, it seemed.

The hours dragged past so slowly Norah thought the clock must have stopped. Andrew lay as still as a corpse, his chest rising and falling slightly, his breaths warm if you held your hand near his face. She did that from time to time, for the sheer comfort of it.

And she waited.

In the early evening, Pete turned up to help with the milking.

'Let the boys do it,' she whispered. 'If they manage all right, they can take over. It'll give them something to do.'

He nodded and shepherded the lads out, then came back to assure her that they were good milkers, though Ned was a bit slower than an adult would be. 'You can leave it to them.'

'Did Janie come to help?'

'No.'

Just wait till she saw her daughter! She'd give her a good telling-off.

When they'd finished cleaning up after the milking, the boys came to stand white-faced and anxious beside the bed. There was no one else with them because Pete had stayed outside.

'I heard someone say he's going to die.' Jack's voice broke on the words.

She cursed whoever had been so careless as to say

that in the boys' hearing. 'I told you before: he'll not die if I can help it!' She went across to put her arms round them and they both clung to her, trying not to cry. It was the first time they'd come to her for comfort in this way, and she drew comfort in turn from the feel of their bodies against hers, drew strength from their need for her – and from Andrew's even greater need.

When Jack stepped back, he dashed away tears with one hand. 'Boys shouldn't cry,' he said gruffly.

'There's no one to see you but me,' she said gently. 'And it's natural to be upset when your father's injured like this.'

He looked at her as if unsure, his eyes bright with more tears.

'I've cried too. I love your father very much.' She moved back to Andrew's side. 'I'll be with him every minute, I promise. And Pete's come to stay with me overnight. Best thing you can do is get a good night's sleep and be fresh to take over the milking in the morning. Jack, you're in charge of that from now on.'

He nodded and drew himself taller. He was a reliable lad, older than his years in some ways, perhaps because of his mother's death, and very protective of his younger brother.

She wished they got on better with their stepsister.

Janie hadn't even come back to see how Andrew was and Norah felt angry about that.

One of the women from the second group of arrivals, a family they'd not had much to do with, came across after milking with a bowl of stew for her and Pete.

'Is there anything I can do to help?' she asked.

'No. But this is very welcome. It's kind of you to think of us.'

'Well, if you need me or my husband, remember we're happy to help. I'll cook some tea for you tomorrow as well, if you like.'

'Thank you. You could take the rest of the tin of meat that I've got open. It needs using up. And there are some potatoes.' She knew the family hadn't much money. The encounter warmed her as she continued her vigil. She forced some stew down to keep up her strength, but let Pete eat most of it.

The hours ticked slowly past. Pete wasn't a talker and went to bed early. She refilled the hot-water bottles round Andrew when they grew cool and tried not to despair as the hours crawled past and her husband didn't move. It was cold and she sat with a blanket round her, but she couldn't lie down, had to keep watch, had to.

Surely Andrew would wake soon? She'd never heard of someone being unconscious for such a long time, wished desperately that they weren't so far from a proper hospital here. She and Janie were so healthy, she'd not really thought about that aspect of coming here, and even if she had, she'd not realised how far the distances were between towns in Australia – if you could call such small places towns!

What was keeping Gil? Norah kept listening for the sound of his cart, but heard only frogs and a boobook owl calling somewhere. She was glad to have Pete staying with her, just in case, though there was not

much he could do. He offered to spell her on watching
Andrew so that she could get some sleep, only she
didn't want to sleep.

Maybe she'd be able to sleep tomorrow night if –
no, *when* Andrew was awake.

She picked up his hand and raised it to her lips.
The flesh was warm still, breath was coming and going
from his nostrils – she kept checking that. It was proof
that he was still with her.

Please, she prayed over and over, *let him stay alive.
I've only just started to love him.*

When he left Norah, Gil drove the cart into Northcliffe,
spoke to the nurse, who had a very sick child under
her care, then got a lift to Pemberton. He knew the
doctor had a motor car and would bring him back,
otherwise he'd find someone else who could help him.
People always rallied round in emergencies.

But when he got to the town, he found that the
doctor was out at a farm dealing with a difficult birth
and wouldn't be back until the early hours, or even
later.

In fact, it was six o'clock in the morning before the
doctor returned. Gil, who'd been sleeping on his
veranda, stood up to greet him and explain why he
was there.

The doctor sighed wearily. 'You were right not to
move him. Give me time to get a quick wash and something to eat, then I'll drive back with you.'

'I could do the driving, if you like, and you could
get a bit of rest.'

'Good idea.'

It was nine o'clock before they got to the Boyds' farm. Gil was praying that Andrew would have woken, but when Pete came to the door and shook his head slightly, he realised his friend was still unconscious, even before they went inside the humpy.

The doctor checked Andrew carefully, approved what Gil had done to the arm, then moved away from the bed and gestured to them to follow him. He went outside and hesitated, looking at Norah.

'Is he dying?' she asked, unable to wait a second longer to find out.

'I hope not. But I try not to discuss such things in front of unconscious patients, ever since one who recovered told me he'd heard every word that was said within his hearing while he was unconscious, and proved it too.'

'Oh.'

'I won't conceal from you that we're fairly helpless with this sort of injury. And the longer Mr Boyd remains unconscious, the less chance he has of recovering fully.'

She wasn't aware that she was wringing her hands till he reached out to still them.

'On the other hand, your husband is clearly a strong, healthy man in his prime, and this is an accident, not an illness, so it's far too soon to give up hope.'

'What must I do?'

'What you're doing already. Keep him clean and warm – and pray. I'll come back in two days' time. I'm sorry I can't come sooner, but I have other patients. I don't even have another nurse I can send to help you.'

'I can do what's necessary for him.'

'Don't forget to get some sleep yourself. You'll need all your strength once he recovers.'

'What about his arm?'

'Mr Matthews has done what's necessary. He's a sound fellow, your foreman. Keep the arm splinted for a week or two. Nature does a wonderful job of healing broken bones as long as they're put back into the right position. Just leave her to get on with it. It's the head injury that's more serious.'

When his car had driven away she went back to Andrew's side, to find that Gil had taken Pete's place.

'You need to sleep,' he said abruptly.

She nodded, feeling the stress of the long, anxious night catching up with her.

'I gather the children are being cared for?'

'Yes.'

'I'll keep an eye on the cows and chooks, see that the children are managing. And Norah?'

She turned.

'Don't give up hope.'

She dredged up a ghost of a smile because he was being kind. But no kindness could take away the sick worry about Andrew that went with her to bed and kept her awake for a while, tired as she was.

When Norah woke in the early afternoon, she found that Irene was sitting with Andrew and Janie was by her side.

'There's no change, I'm afraid,' her friend said.

With a quick smile at Janie, Norah went to check on Andrew herself.

'Gil's gone to organise the men's work for the next day or two,' Irene said. 'Then he's coming back to help you.'

Janie came to stand closer to her mother and Norah hugged her absent-mindedly but her attention was mainly on that still figure and she put her daughter gently aside. 'Not now, love.'

When she went outside to relieve herself, Janie followed. She hadn't asked about her stepfather, or expressed any anxiety, just hovered.

Before Norah went back inside, she told Janie to go and check on her pet chook, then went to take Irene's place by the bed. 'Thanks for looking after Janie. Did she behave herself?'

'Yes. She was no trouble at all.'

'She isn't when she's away from her stepbrothers. I don't know how to make that girl see that we're one family now and she has to be part of it.'

'I know. But she has been worried about him, Norah.'

'Has she? Or was she worried about what would happen to us without him?'

'From what you've told me, she's had a lot of losses for a child that age,' Irene said gently. 'I think she's frightened of having to face another set of changes.'

Norah wasn't sure about that. She didn't feel sure about anything at the moment.

At her friend's urging she had something to eat and drink, bread and jam which seemed utterly tasteless, and a cup of tea which grew cold because she forgot to drink it. In the end, because she was vaguely thirsty, she gulped down the cold liquid.

Then she sent a protesting Janie back with Irene and continued sitting beside Andrew. She talked to him, explaining what was happening, assuring him she'd be there when he woke up. His arm was only a simple fracture, the doctor said, and would be all right in a few weeks.

Gil came in while she was doing this and nodded approvingly.

He didn't bother her, but sat quietly to one side. Strange, she thought, how Gil seemed almost one of the family now.

The second night passed even more slowly than the first. She kept watch for part of it, slept for the rest, trusting Gil more than she trusted anyone else.

16

Irene served the evening meal and looked at Janie, who was picking at her food. 'Eat up, dear. It'll do your father no good if you starve yourself.'

'He's not my father.'

It was a statement she often made, but Irene thought Janie sounded far less certain this time.

Freddie looked at the girl in disgust. 'Of all the ungrateful brats! Of course he's your father now that he's married your mother.'

Irene tried to shush him, because this was no time to be scolding the girl, but he ignored her.

'Who do you think is paying for the bread you put into your mouth every day?' he went on. 'Andrew is.'

Janie continued to stare at him mutely, her eyes wide and frightened.

'Who's providing the roof over your head?' Freddie went on. 'Well, answer me? Who?' When he got no answer, he thrust his face closer and said even more loudly, 'Your *father*, that's who.'

Irene tugged at his sleeve for the second time. 'Leave her alone. She's upset.'

He shook his wife's hand off. 'Upset about his accident or about being away from her mummy? I'm fed up with people making excuses for her. She's an ungrateful brat, that's what she is, and she'd feel the back of my hand if she were mine.'

Janie burst into tears and ran out of the humpy into the darkness.

'You're a brute!' Irene threw at her husband and hurried after the child. She didn't see Janie at first and stopped to stare anxiously around as her eyes grew accustomed to the darkness. Then she heard a muffled sob and moved round the side of the house to find the girl leaning against the wall, sobbing in a despairing way.

'Come here. No, don't pull away. You're upset. Let me hold you.'

Gradually Janie relaxed against her and the tears slowed down. 'I want to go home. I don't like Australia.'

'You will like it once you get used to it. And if you were nicer to them, people would like you, of course they would.' Irene prayed Freddie wouldn't come and interrupt them. She'd thought for a while that what Janie really needed was friends her own age, or someone outside the family to talk to. There were no other little girls of Janie's age in the group, and at that age, a year or two made a big difference.

'What don't you like about it?' she asked when the silence continued.

Words poured out of the child like a dam bursting its walls, and it was what Irene had expected: no aunts or grandma here, no friends, two stepbrothers who banded together against her, a man she didn't know taking her place with her mother.

And most of all, it seemed to the listener, the child didn't know how to stop being unhappy and start accepting the new life.

A bit like Freddie.

Irene made soothing noises and let Janie get it off her chest. 'It's very different here,' she said at last when Janie fell silent, 'so it may take some time for you to get used to it. But if it's any help, I've left my nieces and nephews back in England and I miss them. I liked being an auntie. Maybe I could be your auntie now and you could be my niece? Would you like that?'

Janie was quiet for so long, Irene began to wonder if she'd said the right thing. Then the child said in a tight little voice, 'You won't want to. Everyone hates me here.'

'Nonsense. Your mother loves you and Andrew wants to love you too, but you won't let him.'

'He doesn't.'

'You're wrong. He's a kind man. Haven't you noticed how he helps people? Don't you think he wants to help you too?'

'He can't now. He's going to die and then we won't have a home any more. We didn't have a home after Granddad died. That's why Mum married *him* and came here.' She shivered, and not from the cold.

'Your stepfather's not going to die. Your mother won't let him. She loves him too much.'

'She doesn't love me any more, she only loves him.'

'Of course she loves you. You can love lots of people at the same time.'

Janie digested this for a few minutes, then said uncertainly, 'Can you?'

'Of course you can. I come from a big family and Mam loves every single one of us, all her grandchildren too.'

Irene stayed outside talking until they were both shivering in the cold, damp night air, because she didn't trust Freddie not to interfere if she tried to have this important conversation in his presence. But in the end, she guided the little girl inside, persuading Janie to lie down on the makeshift bed.

Freddie scowled at Irene. 'You'll catch your death of cold standing outside in weather like this. In my opinion that child needs a good smacking, not somebody being soft with her.'

She rounded on him then. 'If that's the sort of father you're going to be, one who smacks unhappy children, I dread to think what our family life is going to be like.'

'So do I. You must be as fertile as your damned mother to have got yourself pregnant after all the care I've taken.'

Irene glared at him. 'It takes two people to make a baby!'

'Yes, but which two? I've been as careful as a man can be. Maybe you've been meeting someone else. You're always off talking to other people instead of staying home waiting for me.'

Irene was so taken aback by this accusation, she could hardly breathe for a minute or two. She gaped at him, seeing a bitter twist to his mouth and no signs of the love that usually warmed his gaze. She might be able to help this unhappy child, but nothing she said or did seemed to help Freddie.

'Well?' he shouted when she didn't speak. 'I haven't heard you deny it.'

'Shh now!' she said with a glance at the child.

'To hell with her. Answer my question. Have you been with someone else?'

'You *know* I've never been unfaithful, Freddie, and if you don't, then our whole marriage is a mockery.' With that she got ready for bed, ignoring him but waiting for him to say he was sorry, hadn't meant it. He had a hot temper, but he was always sorry when he said hurtful things.

But this time he didn't apologise, didn't say a single word to her.

Janie wasn't the only one to weep into her pillow that night.

In the middle of the third night, Norah was drowsing on her bed, which she'd pulled alongside Andrew's. She was holding his hand, had been for a while, though his was limp and unresponsive.

When she felt his fingers twitch in hers, she came fully awake with a start. Had she imagined that or had he really moved?

She waited a long time and had given up hope, thinking she must have imagined it, when his hand moved again. It definitely did. And this time he gave a low groan as well, the first sound he'd made since the accident.

She was out of bed in an instant, turning up the lamp that had been left burning low on a shelf between two uprights. As she came back to him, she saw his head move slowly from side to side. He winced, groaning again as the bruised part of his forehead touched the pillow.

She took hold of his hand. 'Andrew, love. Can you hear me?'

His eyes opened and he stared at her, looking totally puzzled as if rousing from a very deep sleep. Then he closed them again.

When she bent to kiss his cheek, he looked at her again, his eyes crinkling at the corners as if he was trying to smile.

'You've been hurt in an accident, but you're going to be all right.'

He stared at her for so long she began to wonder if he'd understood what she said, then he opened his mouth and croaked, 'Thirsty.'

'I'll get you a drink. Don't try to move.'

When she brought a cup of water back to him, his eyes were closed again. She hesitated, but she wanted to get some liquid into him. 'Are you still awake?'

'Mmm.' He looked at her and tried to reach out for the cup, but must have jarred his arm, because breath whistled into his mouth as if it hurt.

'You've broken your arm. Don't try to sit up yourself. I'll hold you up and help you drink.'

He took about half the water in the cup then pulled back from it, so she let him lie down again and put the cup on the ground beside the bed.

'I'll just wash your face and hands. You'll feel better then. After that you need to sleep, love, so that you can get well again.'

She had a damp washcloth ready, had tried to think what might be needed when he awoke. The cloth was cold, so she warmed it against her own cheek for a few moments then gently cleaned his face and hands, knowing how that freshened you up.

He closed his eyes as she did this, murmuring, 'Mmm.'

When she'd put down the washcloth, she turned to find him asleep again, breathing as softly and evenly as a child. Was it her imagination or did he have a bit more colour? She didn't try to wake him, but watched for a few moments, then turned down the lamp. When she got back into her own bed, she reached out for his hand again.

He'd seemed to understand what was going on and he'd had a drink of water. Surely they were signs that he would get better again, properly better, not like a lad down their street back home, who'd had a bang on the head and lost half his wits as a result.

No, she mustn't think of that, must concentrate on Andrew's recovery, on finding ways to help him. She'd have to deal with the cows and everything else on her own until his arm healed, but she could manage. The children would help more and . . .

She fell asleep, still holding his hand.

Janie woke with a start when Mr Dawson shook her.

'Time for you to go and help look after the animals at your place, young lady.'

She pulled away from him, looking round for Irene.

'She'll be back in a minute. Your family will need your help today, so I decided to wake you up.'

'I don't like cows.'

He laughed harshly. 'Neither do I. But we both have to deal with them. I'm going outside now. When I get back, I expect to see you up and dressed, ready to start work. If you're not, I'll pull you out of bed myself.'

To her relief it was Mrs Dawson – Auntie Irene – who came back first.

'Oh, you're awake, Janie. That's good.'

'Mr Dawson woke me. He said I have to go and help milk our cows. I don't, do I?'

'You ought to see if you can help, dear. Your mother's going to need you. Do you want a drink of yesterday's milk before you go or shall you wait for the fresh milk?'

'I don't want anything, thank you.' Feeling that nobody understood her, Janie went towards the door, turning to look pleadingly at the woman smiling at her.

'We all have to do our share of the chores, dear, even the ones we don't like.'

So Janie went outside. Last night it had seemed that Mrs Dawson understood. She'd even said to call her auntie. But this morning everything was bad again. No one cared how she felt. No one.

With dragging feet, Janie walked across to the next block and peeped in at her mother, who was making a pot of tea in the lean-to.

'Your father woke during the night. He's going to be all right,' she said with a smile. 'Isn't that wonderful?'

'Yes.'

'Have you come to help with the animals? The boys have just started on the cows, but you can see to the chooks.'

Her mother went back into the humpy, so Janie followed.

When she looked across at the bed she saw *him* staring at her. She was glad he wasn't going to die. She didn't like it when people died. But that didn't change the fact that she hated it here, or that her mother now loved him more than she did Janie.

As she walked past the cowshed, Jack said, 'You're late. The hens need feeding and the eggs collecting. And you didn't help at all yesterday.'

'She's here now,' Ned said in his softer voice. 'Did you see Dad, Janie? He's woken up. Isn't that marvellous?'

'Yes.'

'You don't sound glad.' Jack scowled at her.

'Well, I am.'

A few tears went into the bucket of water she got from the well and carried across to the chooks, but though Jack turned his head to watch her go past, he didn't notice. He didn't care whether she was unhappy or not. They weren't really her brothers, whatever anyone said.

As the boys finished milking, Gil came in to join them.

'We're just finishing, Mr Matthews,' Ned said. 'We made sure everything was clean.'

'That's a good lad. Now, let's get that cream separated and down to the gate ready for the truck.' As a few people had found to their cost, if the cream wasn't ready, the truck just drove straight past. It had a tight schedule and didn't wait for anyone.

No one seemed to notice or need her, so Janie wandered back to the house, where her mother told her to stir the porridge and make sure it didn't burn. They'd had milky porridge every day since the cows arrived and she was sick of it. She thought of letting it burn, but didn't, because she'd still have to eat it and then scour the pan out.

It was horrible here. No one loved her any more.

When Gil went into the house and saw that Andrew was awake, he closed his eyes and said a thank you to fate, or God, or whatever was out there watching over the Boyds. Then he helped Norah tend to Andrew's needs, calling out to Janie to stay outside until they'd finished.

Andrew ate a small helping of porridge, with his friend's help then looked down at his arm. 'I shan't be able to work till this is better, so I shan't be earning any money.'

'No. Sorry.' There was silence, then he made the offer he knew his friend would refuse. 'Um – have you enough to tide you over? It'll be over a month before you can use that arm again, the doctor said, and even then you won't be able to do the heavy work.'

There was no answer. 'Look, we're friends, aren't we? And friends help one another, so if you haven't enough, I can lend you some.'

'We can manage.' But Andrew's expression was

grim. Gil could understand that. No one liked to use up their savings, especially in circumstances like these, so far away from family and friends. What if something else bad happened and the Boyds had nothing to fall back on?

He realised with surprise that he'd turn to them without hesitation if he was in trouble. It was the first time he'd made real friends since Mabel's death. Dear Mabel! The memories no longer brought that overwhelming rush of anguish, but he still missed her – and missed being married, sharing his life with someone.

Was it too much to hope that one day he'd find someone to love again?

Someone who wasn't already married.

The children milked the cows again in the evening, and did a good job, too. The boys were annoyed at having to sleep away at Pam's again, because they wanted to help look after their father, but everyone thought it better to let Andrew and his wife have another night where it didn't matter if they were up and down.

Janie shrugged when told to sleep at Irene's again.

Norah was relieved to be having a quiet night, felt very tired now that the crisis was over.

'Thank you,' Andrew said abruptly as they settled down for the night.

'What for?'

'Looking after me so well.'

'That's what a wife's for.'

'I'm sorry the burden of caring for the animals will

fall on you from now on, but I'm sure I'll be able to do some of the jobs around the place as soon as this dizziness goes.'

He'd nearly fallen when he tried to stand up and if she hadn't been there, might have hurt himself again. 'The boys have taken care of the cows and milking. They're both good lads and Jack is very capable. We'll manage just fine. You concentrate on getting better and don't try to do too much. The doctor will be coming again tomorrow and he'll tell you what to do – and what not to do. And I'd be grateful if you'd pay attention to his advice.'

He chuckled and held out his hand to her. 'You sounded quite fierce then.'

She lay there, her hands enlaced in his, enjoying being alone with him for once. 'I can be very fierce, if necessary. If you try to do too much too soon, I'll stop you.' She hesitated before adding, 'I'll be really careful with the money, too, make it spin out. I'm a good manager.'

'I know you are. I'm not happy to have to use our savings, but that's what the money's for, a rainy day.' Silence then, 'Do you think my arm will heal properly?'

'The doctor said Gil had done a good job of setting it.'

'I hope you paid the doctor for his services.'

'Not yet. It'll be quite expensive, I should think. He'd had to come a long way.'

'We'll pay him tomorrow then. I've always paid my way. Always.'

She saw him move his head and grimace. 'Is your head still aching?'

'A little.'

'Shall I turn the lamp off?'

'Leave it burning low. I'd like to see your face if I wake in the night.'

In the morning, it was all bustle. Gil turned up to help Andrew again, and the children did the milking, with Gil checking that everything was done properly and then putting an expression of pride on Jack's face by praising him for a job well done.

Even Janie looked after the chooks without being told, washing the eggs and carrying them carefully to the kitchen.

When Norah praised her for that she looked pleased.

The doctor arrived in the early afternoon, and was delighted to see that his patient had recovered consciousness and was in full possession of his senses. He left some powders for the headaches, which should go away in a few days, and checked the arm, nodding approval.

'I shan't come again unless you send for me, because you seem to be making a good recovery, Mr Boyd. Just remember, don't try to use that arm too much until it's healed properly, or you could weaken it.'

'I'll be careful. Now, how much do we owe you?'

The doctor hesitated, then glanced round and asked bluntly, 'Can you afford to pay me?'

Andrew's expression was grim. 'Yes.'

When the doctor had gone, he said to Norah, 'I don't want people thinking we need their charity.'

'I know. Gil's going to show Jack how to trap possums for meat, and we have the eggs now, plus plenty of milk, so we shall do all right for food.'

His fierce expression softened. 'You're wonderful.'

Those words gave her a warm glow that lasted for a long time.

All seemed set fair for the Boyds, then later the next day, more cows were delivered to everyone in the group without any warning. There was no hiding the two new animals from Andrew, who had made them turn his bed round so that he could see out of the door and was talking about getting up and seeing which jobs he could do one-handed.

When their new cows were brought up to join the others, he insisted on being helped to the door, where he sat on the rocking chair, looking pale but determined.

'They're not a bad pair,' the man said, slapping one on the rump. 'Gil chose yours for you. He knows his cows, that chap does. Had an accident, have you?'

'Yes. And it couldn't have happened at a worse time.'

'There's never a good time for an accident, is there? Just be glad you've not lost an arm or a leg.'

He drove the final few cows away up the track to the next farm, whistling cheerfully, and Norah set the children to work, refilling the cows' water trough. The three of them were sleeping at home again now, and they'd be needed, with the new cows to settle in and the chooks to look after, not to mention the cooking and other household chores still to be done.

The boys worked hard and Jack in particular was a great help, bringing wood for the cooking fire and trying to chop up more with an axe that was too big for him, until Norah stopped that.

'It's dangerous you using that big axe, Jack. We don't want any more accidents.'

When they eventually sat down to a simple tea of corned beef and boiled potatoes, Nora let Andrew explain to the children that they'd have to be very careful with money until he was earning again.

He smiled at Jack. 'And if you can catch the occasional possum, we can make stews and not have to open tins of meat. Gil says parrots aren't bad eating, either. The less we have to buy at the store, the better.'

Janie pulled a face at the mention of possums. Norah knew she didn't like the meat – well, it wasn't nearly as good as beef or lamb – but this was no time to be fussy.

At least Janie was tending the chooks conscientiously, though not with the cheerful willingness of the boys.

That was a good sign – wasn't it?

17

In the month that followed, Norah worked harder than she ever had in her life before. She was up at dawn and out to supervise the milking, whatever the weather, trying to fit in her household duties around the things they had to do on the farm. She used old flour and sugar sacks to keep the worst of the wet off herself, and kept a fire burning in the lean-to kitchen all the time.

Even with the warmth from that coming through the corrugated iron wall next to it, it was miserably cold inside the house because there was no way of heating it. It was a good thing they'd not bought the wood-burning stove, though, because they needed the money while Andrew was incapacitated. Though he didn't complain, he spent a lot of time huddled under the blankets, grateful when she could refill his hot-water bottles.

Several times he grasped her hand and said, 'You're a grand lass,' or simply, 'Thank you.'

It was enough to make her feel happy, in spite of all their worries.

During the first week he suffered a lot from headaches, but then, to her relief, he improved suddenly and began to get his old energy back. From then on, he insisted on getting out and about and worked alongside Norah, using his sound arm when he could to steady things for her or pick smaller things up. It was good to have his company and his advice was always sound, but she worried that he was pushing himself too hard.

Their whole lives now revolved around getting the cream out to the entrance to the block in time to be picked up, so that they'd earn a few shillings a week at least to be credited against their purchases at the store.

By the end of the second week, Andrew had decided that he and the boys could do some further clearing of the smaller bushes and trees for an hour or two in the middle of the day.

'Are you sure you should be doing this?' Norah asked.

'I'll not be doing much except supervising the lads. Janie could help us clear the undergrowth, too. It's light work but it'll help once I get fit again and can work on the bigger timber.' He scowled at his arm, still in its sling. 'I'm glad we've not got any monster trees like that devil which hit me. Make sure you never stand under Karri trees, Norah.'

'I won't. And Gil's being a big help. That kangaroo meat he gave us was nicer than the possum, don't you think?'

'Yes. He's a good friend.'

The boys didn't complain about the strange assortment of food. They were always hungry. Janie pulled a face sometimes, but Norah ignored that. And Andrew's appetite was coming back, thank goodness, though he'd lost some weight since the accident.

But all in all, things could have been worse.

Freddie and Irene quarrelled more during the first two weeks after the accident than they had in the whole five years of their marriage before, usually about the baby. After that he grew morose, refusing to discuss his feelings with her.

When she was sick in the mornings, he didn't offer any help or comfort, just watched her with a disgusted expression.

She didn't know what to do about the situation, tried several times to talk to him, and got nowhere.

One evening Gil called in on his way to see the Boyds. 'I just wanted to let you know that Freddie will be late back.'

'Oh? Is he finishing a job?'

Gil hesitated.

'Or is he drinking again?'

Gil picked up the heavy bucket of water she was fetching from the stream and carried it to the house for her, a job Freddie had done before but hardly ever bothered to help with now.

'You shouldn't be carrying heavy buckets like that. At least don't fill them to the brim.'

The sympathy made her want to cry. Well, she cried easily these days. She blinked hard, but the tears wouldn't be held back and next thing she knew he'd put the bucket down and was letting her weep against him, patting her shoulders. That made her weep all the harder.

After a while, the storm of emotion subsided and she was just going to pull away, when a voice roared, 'Get your hands off my wife, damn you!'

They jerked apart as Freddie strode up to them.

'So it's him!' he yelled at Irene.

'He was just comforting me.'

'Is that what you call it?' He turned to Gil, fists bunched.

She pushed between them, terrified that Freddie was going to start a fight. 'He carried the bucket of water back for me, then saw I was upset. *That's all!*'

Gil set her gently aside. 'I don't need to shelter behind you, Irene.' His expression was scornful as he faced the angry man. 'There's nothing between us, except me feeling sorry for her, because of the way you're treating her lately. You don't deserve to be a father.'

Freddie swung a wild punch at Gil, which the older man countered easily.

'Stop it!' The foreman's voice rang with authority and made Freddie hesitate. 'I'll swear on the Bible that I've never touched your wife in that way, if it helps.'

For a moment, all hung in the balance, then Freddie muttered something and strode into the humpy.

'Will you be all right?' Gil whispered.

Irene nodded. 'He'd never lay a finger on me.'

'If he does . . .'

'He won't.'

But she wasn't nearly as sure of that as she sounded

and waited till Gil had gone on towards the Boyds' block before following her husband into the humpy.

He thrust the Bible her mother had given her into her hands before she'd done more than cross the threshold. 'Swear on that!'

She looked at it in puzzlement. 'Swear what?'

'That the child is mine.'

She was so outraged at this she nearly refused, but was worried if she didn't swear, he'd go after Gil again. So she took the Bible from him, the book her mother had bought them when they were married to record the births and deaths of their new family in. The thought of Mam brought tears to her eyes and she hugged it close. She'd have given anything to be near her family again.

Then she saw the way Freddie was looking at her and straightened up, staring him in the eyes as she said loudly and clearly, 'This is the only time I'm going to say it, so listen carefully and remember it if you ever get such stupid ideas again. I swear by this holy book,' she raised it to her lips and kissed it, 'that the child I'm carrying is yours and that I've never, ever been with another man, not before we married and not since.'

Then she shoved the book at him so hard he took an involuntary step backwards and nearly dropped it. She went out into the lean-to kitchen to prepare their food because she didn't even want to look at him.

Tears splashed into the frying pan, making the fat sizzle, but by breathing slowly and deeply, she gradually stopped them flowing. She wasn't going to spend her life weeping or putting up with such treatment.

He'd disgusted her tonight and destroyed the trust that she'd fondly imagined lay between them. It had been weakening since their arrival, she'd sensed that, but been powerless to stop it. She'd racked her brains but couldn't think of anything that would mend matters. And anyway, it took two people to make a happy marriage. Freddie had always been volatile, radiating happiness one day, down in the dumps the next. But lately he'd been unremittingly miserable.

More tears threatened but this time they didn't fall. Something had died in her tonight, something that had been ailing for a long time. She had done her best for Freddie. Now it was up to him to draw closer again – or not. But she wouldn't let him hurt her baby. She felt fiercely protective of this innocent life. She wanted it so very much. What was a family without children?

What was a marriage without love and trust?

Freddie and Irene had another quarrel just before they left for the sing-song on the Saturday evening. He'd been in a foul mood all day, though he was usually a bit more cheerful on fine days. But he was coming down with a cold and wasn't feeling well.

She tried to be understanding, but honestly, it was only a cold! Everyone got them from time to time. The world didn't stop turning because you had the sneezes and sniffles for a few days. It wasn't as if he had a weak chest as she did.

She got their meal ready early and set it down in front of him.

'Not stew again!'

'It's a bit hard to cook anything else but stew or a fry-up when you don't have a cooker or an oven,' she snapped. 'But if *you* can do any better, you're welcome to take over the cooking.'

'I'd be happy to laze around at home all day like you women do. You want to try working on the roads. It's no wonder I've caught a cold, getting soaked through day in, day out. They treat us like navvies. And what a primitive way to make roads. I can't believe they haven't provided proper ones for the new settlements, or cleared the blocks properly for us.'

She didn't rise to the bait. This was a much-repeated complaint of his.

Everyone had been surprised when Gil started the work teams laying halved tree trunks down to form the surface of the road, starting with the muddiest patches. Corduroying, people here called it. It worked quite well, too, and though it made for a bumpy ride, that was better than getting bogged down in mud and having to unload everything to get out of it, then reload before driving off. Corduroying made sense because there was certainly no shortage of timber.

Irene preferred to walk along such roads to trying to avoid the hidden muddy hollows. She hated it when mud squished into her shoes. But Freddie always wanted jobs to be done the English way, 'the proper way' he called it. That was yet another cause for his grumbling and resentment.

'Given how close a friendship you have with our dear foreman,' he said suddenly, 'how about using your influence to get me assigned to other work? He favours

Andrew Boyd all the time. *He* gets put in charge of things. Given the way Gil looks at you, whether he's touched you or not, I'm sure he'd do anything you asked him.'

That took her breath away for a minute or two. She didn't intend to keep denying that she had any sort of *close friendship* with Gil, so continued to eat her meal, then, when she couldn't force another spoonful of stew down, she cleared her plate away, and started getting ready to go out.

But the words lingered. Did Gil really look at her that way? He'd never said or done anything to make her think he fancied her, had always treated her with respect.

Freddie lingered at the table, blowing his nose from time to time and frowning into space. When she looked at the little clock her sisters had given her for a wedding present and saw how late it was, she couldn't help saying, 'It's time to get ready.'

'I don't think I'll go tonight.'

'But I've been looking forward to the sing-song all day long.'

'Go on your own, then. You're good at doing things on your own, you are.'

She hesitated, then thought, *why not?* 'I will, then.'

She got ready, picked up the biscuit tin full of drop scones that she'd made earlier as her contribution to the supper, and went to the track to wait for the Boyds. She didn't have to wait long.

'Do you mind if I come with you tonight? Freddie isn't feeling well. He's got a bit of a cold.'

She saw by Norah's searching glance that her friend had immediately guessed something was wrong.

Andrew smiled. 'We're always happy to have your company, Irene.'

So she walked along with them, though it felt strange not to be holding her husband's arm.

Freddie caught up with them halfway to the camp ground.

'How's the cold?' Andrew asked.

He shrugged. 'I'll live.' He made no attempt to walk beside his wife.

'Trouble?' Norah whispered.

You couldn't pretend in such a small community. Irene glanced sideways to make sure Freddie wasn't within hearing. 'Yes. I'll tell you about it tomorrow.'

Norah squeezed her hand and began to talk about something else.

When they got to the camp ground, Freddie walked off without a word of farewell to join Len Binton, with whom he'd been spending quite a lot of his spare time lately.

Irene's heart sank. He'd been coming home smelling of booze and complaining about how expensive it was for a man to get hold of a drink or two when there weren't any pubs. Was he going to do that tonight as well? He'd frightened her a little last time he got drunk.

Gil washed and dressed in clean dry clothes, ready for the evening out. He felt relaxed and happy. They'd nearly finished corduroying the worst bits of road and could go back to clearing the blocks again, so that everyone had the same amount of land cleared for them before they were left to clear further land on their own, which the Board would pay them to do.

Maybe then he could do something to his own block soon. He'd hardly touched it, though of course he'd have his allotted acres cleared by the working teams along with the others. It didn't really matter, though he would like to make himself a bit more comfortable. He hadn't even had time to build a lean-to kitchen.

Well, he'd have years to sort his own place out. He wasn't short of a quid or two and at the moment it gave him more satisfaction to help the groupies, who were a hard-working lot, on the whole. Nearly all of them had buckled down and learned the new skills they needed here, putting up with hardship – mostly cheerfully – and making the best of it in spite of the incompetence of the Board. A grand bunch of folk, they were.

Two or three times now, on fine Saturdays, they'd arranged sing-song suppers, each family contributing a plate of food and gathering at the camp ground to sing and gossip and exchange ideas by lamplight. They built big fires to counteract the cold and dressed warmly.

He noticed that Freddie and a couple of other men had somehow got access to some booze, but as long as they didn't go wild with it, he'd turn a blind eye. It was Irene he felt sorry for, especially tonight with Freddie ignoring her. Didn't the man realise what a treasure she was, so pretty and gentle-natured, yet hard-working?

He'd noticed Norah keeping an eye on Irene and inviting her to sit with them. Janie too seemed to enjoy Irene's company and once he'd heard the child address her as 'Auntie Irene', which was a good sign. It wasn't good that the two boys still avoided their stepsister, that she deliberately turned her back on them, and stayed as far away from Andrew as she could.

On this particular evening, Andrew had dispensed with his sling and looked happier than he had for a while. He and Norah must have been practising their singing, because they did a couple of new duets, which everyone enjoyed. After that, it was the old favourites, with everyone joining in.

But where was Freddie Dawson?

Gil wandered round the outside of the group, staying back from the others so that he didn't get trapped into conversations. He went right round the people sitting round the camp fire. No sign of Freddie and Len Binton was missing, too. What were they up to?

As the evening drew to a close, Gil waited for them to reappear. Len eventually strolled back along the track from the direction of his humpy and rejoined his wife and children. His gait wasn't quite steady, but he wasn't rolling drunk, at least.

It'd be as well to find out where they were getting their booze from, Gil decided. He waited, expecting Freddie to join the group again, but he didn't.

When it was time to return home, Irene looked round for her husband, but there was no sign of him, hadn't been for most of the evening. Anger had been simmering in her and now it welled up, giving her the courage to pin a smile to her face and act as if it was normal for a woman to be left to walk home on her own.

Andrew insisted on lighting her to her front door while Norah took the other lantern and saw the children home. 'Will you be all right?' he asked when they got there.

'Of course I will. Just let me get a lamp lit and then you can go home to Norah and the children.'

As he stood in the doorway, she fumbled with the matches. She was so upset she was all fingers and thumbs and dropped the box, scattering the matches over the floor. 'Oh, no!'

He set down his lantern and came to help her pick them up.

'If it's not one man, it's another!' a voice roared.

They both jerked to their feet to see Freddie standing there, swaying and clearly the worse for wear.

'What the hell do you mean by that?' Andrew asked.

'First it's Gil, now it's you. She's a whore, that one is – an' if you'll stand still for a minute, I'll thump you and teach you to stay away from my wife.' He squinted then launched a blow at Andrew, missing him completely and staggering into the doorpost as the force of it swung him round. 'Fight fair, damn you.' He steadied himself against the door frame.

'Better come home with us for tonight,' Andrew said to Irene, keeping an eye on the drunken man.

'Thank you, but no. You get off and leave him to me.'

'I can't do that, the condition he's in.'

'He'll be worse while you're here.'

'Come here, you!' Freddie lurched towards her but she only had to sidestep for him to miss her completely and fall on the floor, where he lay muttering to himself.

'He'll not harm me,' she insisted as Andrew still didn't move. 'Even at his worst, he's never laid a finger on me.'

'Does he get drunk often?'

'Only recently.' She shook her head, beyond tears. 'He hates it here.'

'He makes that plain enough.' He waited, but Freddie showed no signs of getting up. 'If you're sure . . . ?'

'I am, yes.'

She waited till Andrew had gone then turned to find Freddie had somehow got to his feet again. Before she could move away, he slapped her face hard. Although this shocked her rigid, she didn't wait for another blow, but darted out into the lean-to where she picked up her frying pan.

When she went back into the humpy, Freddie was waiting for her, still swaying on his feet.

'I'll teach you t'behave yourself,' he announced, slurring the words.

'It's you who needs to learn a few manners,' she countered.

When he raised his fist, she clanged him on the arm with the frying pan and he yelled in shock, then rubbed the place she'd thumped.

'That hurt, you bitch!'

'You hit me first. And get it through your stupid

skull that if you hit me, I'll always hit you back, always! Even if I have to wait till you're asleep to do it.'

For a minute they stood there glaring at one another. His breaths rasped in his throat and he sneezed suddenly.

She could hardly breathe at all, shock and fear of what he'd do next holding her motionless.

'Y're not worth the trouble.' With some difficulty, he got into bed, not bothering to get undressed. He dragged the blankets over him and closed his eyes. He sneezed a couple of times more, blew his nose loudly on a corner of the sheet, then murmured something and grew quiet. A short time later he began snoring loudly.

Only then did she lower the frying pan.

She was beyond tears, couldn't understand how they'd got to this stage. But she wasn't putting up with him thumping her. She'd never tolerate that sort of treatment, would leave him first.

She lay awake for most of the night, staring into the darkness. She heard the frogs calling for a while, then they fell silent. She watched the setting moon send a spear of light into the humpy through the open gable, and saw it gradually move across the few pieces of furniture, then vanish as the moon moved down the sky.

In the morning she was up before he was awake. He was breathing stertorously, the cold in the head obviously gaining ground. Serve him right. She only relented enough to find him a couple of handkerchiefs, laying them on a stool.

She dressed quickly and went to light the fire and get the kettle boiling, then got everything ready for the milking.

He didn't come to help her and it took a long time to do the work on her own, but she got the cream to the entrance in time for the truck. But only just.

When she went back into the hut, he was gone. She told herself she didn't care, but she did.

And what was he doing on a Sunday? Where could he have gone? There was no group work today.

Andrew was working on a cupboard he was making from the wooden box that tins of kerosene came in. His arm was a lot better, but he wasn't stupid enough to do any heavy work with it yet. Thank goodness it was his left arm he'd broken.

The wood was cheap, splintery stuff, soft enough to saw easily. He'd not have bought wood like that, but when it came free, it was good enough to make shelves that could hold clothes. The square kerosene tins were also useful and once empty, could be made into all sorts of things after they were washed out thoroughly and clear of the smell.

He heard someone walking towards the rough shelter he used to store things, and where he did woodwork and other household jobs on rainy days. It had been fine for a few days, but looked as if it'd rain later on. He saw it was Gil, so moved into the open to greet him. 'You look worried.'

'I am. About Freddie next door.'

'Don't talk to me about that one! You'll never believe

what he accused me of last night.' He described what
had happened.

'He accused me of the same thing a few days ago.'

'Has the man run crazy?'

'He's certainly not thinking straight. I'm worried for
Irene. He's not even carrying the water for her – and
her in the family way, too.' He kicked a small stone to
one side. 'I saw him walking down the track towards
Northcliffe today, so I came up to ask if Norah would
go over and see how Irene is.'

'Good idea. She can take Janie with her. You'll stay
till she gets back? I'm sure Norah can find you something to eat.'

Gil grinned and pulled a small tin of corned beef
out of his pocket. 'I was hoping you'd invite me. This
should pay my way.'

Andrew stiffened. 'We can still afford to feed a
friend!'

'I'd rather contribute my share.'

'You've done a lot for us since the accident. That's
enough.'

Gil shrugged and put the tin away. 'It's what friends
are for.'

The two men looked at one another and each gave
a small nod, then they changed the subject and began
to talk about less personal matters.

Norah came back an hour later, having left Janie to
keep Irene company.

Gil put his tools down the minute he saw her. 'Well?'

'She doesn't know where he's gone.' She looked

round to check that the boys weren't within hearing, and added, 'She's got a bruise on her cheek. I sent Janie outside and asked if he'd hit her and she said yes.' She saw Gil's fists clench and added quickly, 'But she hit him back with the frying pan and threatened to hit him while he was sleeping if he touched her again.'

Gil's worried expression relaxed a little. 'Good on her.'

'I can't abide chaps who beat women,' Andrew said. 'I didn't think he was that sort. He was quite cheerful on the ship, but he's changed since we got here.'

'Well, we all know he doesn't like milking cows or doing heavy physical work, though what else he thought he'd be doing on a farm beats me.' Gil looked at Norah. 'You'll keep an eye on her? It'd make things worse if I went near her, but I can't help worrying about her.'

'Yes, of course.'

Norah didn't say anything to Andrew, but it had become increasingly clear to her that Gil was deeply smitten with Irene. She hoped he'd have the good sense not to do anything about his feelings because that could lead only into great unhappiness for both of them. She wasn't sure whether Irene knew how he felt.

Poor Gil. He looked so lonely sometimes.

18

Freddie hardly noticed his surroundings as he walked along the track towards Northcliffe. His head was full of the cold and he felt rotten, but he was sweating and it wasn't raining, so hadn't bothered with his overcoat. His anger carried him along at a brisk pace. He knew a fellow in one of the other groups was selling sly grog, as they called it here. Freddie intended to arrange a supply of this illicit, home-made booze for himself, because he was sure it'd be cheaper than buying it through Len. Sometimes you needed a nip of something to cheer yourself up, especially when you had a cold, as he had now.

He got to the next group of farms, which had more land cleared than his group and proper wooden houses instead of pigsties like the one he was living in, and asked for the man who sold booze by name.

The fellow he spoke to winked and told him where to go.

When he got there, Freddie bought two bottles of clear spirit, which had no taste, but had a fiery kick. He paid his money – less than he'd paid Len, so it was worth the trip – then set off back home. But he was shivery now and he'd developed a cough, which seemed to be getting worse by the minute.

He decided to sample the brew. Everyone knew a drink was good for coughs. The warmth of the raw spirit felt good as it trickled down his sore throat. Noticing a clearing to one side with a fallen log in it, he stopped for a rest. He sat down, waited till another bout of coughing had passed and raised one of the bottles in a mock toast. 'Down with Australia!' He took another good swig. 'Ah, that's better.'

A few swigs later he was feeling warmer and had stopped coughing. It seemed stupid to go the long way home by the track when he could cut through the forest, so that's what he did.

He felt nicely relaxed now. Birds were calling everywhere, little creatures scuttled away as he passed and in the distance he saw a group of kangaroos, with two joeys hopping around them like bouncing bundles of sticks. At the sight of him, the little ones dived head-first into their mothers' pouches and the whole group took off, bounding away through the trees.

He grew tired and was feeling a bit light-headed, so stopped for another rest, sitting on the ground with his back against a tree, closing his eyes for a minute or two.

When he woke it was dusk and he was shivering. He cursed himself for taking the shortcut. You could follow a track after dark but it was much harder to find your way through the forest.

It began to rain and he hunched up his collar, not feeling hungry only thirsty. He took a nip of booze every now and then to help him on his way, had to because his chest was feeling really rough now, and he kept coughing up phlegm. He'd never felt this rotten with a cold before. Everything was worse in Australia. No wonder they had to bribe people to come and settle here by giving them land.

Tears came into his eyes as he thought of England. He should never have left, hadn't realised how home-sick he'd feel.

His limbs felt heavy and he had to force himself to move forward. When he stopped for another rest, he admitted to himself that he was lost. Maybe he should stay here till dawn? Yes, that would be the thing to do. He might be going in the wrong direction. Once the sun rose, he'd know which way to go.

He was chilled through, but there was nothing he could do to keep warm, so he huddled in a hollow at the foot of a large tree, which kept most of the rain off, at least. He took another nip or two, his head spinning.

He'd done it all for Irene, come here to save her life, and was she grateful? No, she wasn't.

He slid slowly sideways, curling up into a ball, shiv-ering again. He'd get up in a minute or two and move about to keep himself warm. He just needed a bit of a rest first.

When Freddie didn't come home by dusk, Irene was really worried. Where could he be? He hadn't made any close friends here, was rather scornful about most of the other groupies, and there simply wasn't anywhere to go. Besides it had rained several times today and Freddie didn't like getting wet.

She pulled the stew off the heat and left it to one side of the fire to keep warm. She wasn't hungry, so paced to and fro, looking at the clock from time to time, always surprised at how few minutes had passed since she last looked.

But eventually, the slow hands crawled round to nine o'clock and she couldn't bear it any longer. She lit the lantern, put on her warm coat and tied a shawl round her head as well, treading carefully through the darkness, trying to avoid the puddles and mud, stopping every few minutes to listen and call his name.

When she got to the next house and banged on the door, she heard Andrew exclaim in surprise and the door opened.

'Irene! Is something wrong?'

'Yes. It's Freddie. He's been out all day and hasn't come home. I can't think where he can be.'

He drew her inside and Norah insisted she sit down and wrap a blanket round herself. 'I'd better go and tell Gil. We might have to get a search party together. If you stray off the track, it's easy to get lost after dark.'

'I'll come with you,' she said at once.

'I'll go faster on my own and anyway, you don't want to risk falling, not in your condition.'

So she stayed with Norah. From the other side of the humpy, the children called out, asking what was wrong and were told to get back to sleep.

It was over an hour before Irene heard voices. Norah

had dozed off but woke up when the door opened and Andrew came in, accompanied by Gil and Pete.

'No sign of him?' Irene asked.

Andrew shook his head. 'None, I'm afraid.'

'I saw him earlier today walking towards Northcliffe,' Gil said.

Irene frowned. 'I don't know why he'd go there.'

Pete cleared his throat. 'He – er, might have been going to buy some grog.'

She saw Gil look at him sharply, but Pete was avoiding the foreman's eyes.

'Where would he get booze from?' Gil asked.

'There's a fellow with a still just outside town. Makes a brew every now and then. Good stuff it is, too.'

'You should have told me about it.'

Pete shuffled his feet. 'Aw, it's only a drink or two. The bloke can't make more than a dozen bottles at a time.'

Rain suddenly began to patter on the metal roof of the humpy. Gil sighed. 'We called out all the way here and there was no answer. We can't do anything till morning. Perhaps they've had a booze-up somewhere and are sleeping it off.'

'Freddie wouldn't have joined in that sort of thing,' Irene said. 'He mostly drinks on his own. In England he didn't drink in the pub but bought jugs of beer and brought them home.' She looked at Gil. 'Can't you search for him tonight?' Even as she spoke, thunder rumbled in the distance and the rain began pounding down so hard on the metal roof they had to raise their voices to be heard.

'We'd get nowhere in weather like this,' he said gently. 'We'll go at first light, I promise you. Can we stay here, Norah?'

'Yes, of course. We'll make up a bed on the floor for you men. Irene can have Andrew's bed.'

As the sky began to turn from black to grey, Gil woke abruptly. It was still raining outside, but at least they'd be able to see where they were going. Norah got up and he heard her in the lean-to, getting the fire burning, coaxing it into a blaze.

Irene jumped suddenly out of bed and ran to the door. He heard her being sick outside, poor thing, and remembered that Mabel had been sick in the mornings, too. Afterwards Irene went into the lean-to and he heard the women's voices, low and companionable.

As he got up and roused the others, the women came into the humpy with some bread and jam, and a pot of tea. The men ate quickly, drank the warm liquid down to the last dregs, then set off with sacks round their shoulders to protect them from the rain.

When they were out of Irene's hearing, Andrew said abruptly, 'I hope he found shelter somewhere. He had a really bad cold on Saturday.'

'There's a providence that usually looks after drunken fools.'

There was no sign of him on the way to the camp ground, so Gil harnessed his horse and set off in the cart with Andrew, leaving Pete to direct the teams about where to work today.

They had no difficulty finding the man who brewed

the booze. At first he tried to pretend they were mistaken, but Gil cut him short. 'We know you're selling booze, and we aren't looking to interfere in that, but we've a man missing, so tell us what you know.' He described Freddie.

'I sold two bottles to him yesterday morning. He didn't say much, just paid and walked off with one in each pocket. He kept coughing and sneezing, but he hadn't even got an overcoat on, the fool. He looked feverish and was very hoarse.'

With a sigh, Gil drove slowly back, stopping to check anything resembling a track. But they found no signs of Freddie and of course the rain had washed out any footprints.

When he got back to the camp ground, he clanged the metal triangle as loudly as he could. He'd arranged with Pete to do this if they needed to make a full search.

The other men came tramping in and listened as he explained about Freddie. Dividing them into pairs, he arranged a careful search of the sides of the track from Northcliffe to their own group's blocks.

It was a long day, with no signs of Freddie. But just as it was getting dark, Ted stopped. 'Shh! I think I heard something.'

He and his partner listened intently.

'Sounds like a wounded animal to me,' the other man said.

'Let's go and find out.'

They found Freddie delirious, calling out then shaking so hard his voice fractured and was lost. They couldn't rouse him, so carried him back to the track and cooeed to let the others know he was found.

As they stood there, wiping the rain from their faces, they heard the call passed on from one group of searchers to the next. When Gil arrived with the cart, they lifted him on to it, but someone had to sit with him because he kept thrashing around. The other men were cold, but Freddie's skin was burning with fever.

Irene turned white at the sight of her husband and pressed both hands to her cheeks with a little moan. She had reason to be upset, Gil thought. Freddie was in a bad way. Congestion of the lungs, if he'd ever heard it, the phlegm rattling in the sick man's chest as he alternately shivered and gasped for breath.

She pulled herself together. 'Bring him inside.' She turned back the bedding and they laid him down. He was still thrashing round.

'I'll go and fetch the nurse,' Gil offered.

She looked down at Freddie then at Gil. 'It won't do any good. I've seen people in this state, been like it myself, too. He's beyond human help now, isn't he? Only God will decide if he lives or dies.'

He didn't try to fool her, admired her courage. 'Yes. But I'll still fetch the nurse. We have to try everything.' So once again he set off into the darkness, encouraging his horse and letting it pick its own way.

Freddie gradually quietened. He opened his eyes and stared round, seemed aware that he was in his own bed and gave a long groaning sigh.

'Would you like a hot drink?' Irene asked.

He didn't seem to understand but she went and

brought a cup of tea. With Andrew's help, they got a few mouthfuls down him. His breath was rattling in his lungs and it seemed painful for him to breathe, so they propped him up. He lay with eyes shut for a while, then looked at her again, really looked at her.

'Stupid,' he said quite clearly. 'Should have stuck to the track.'

'Well, you're home again now.'

He fumbled for her hand. 'Safe with you.'

'Yes.'

Norah arrived. 'I'll stay with you as long as necessary.'

Irene clasped her hand for a minute. 'Thank you.'

'Is he making sense or is he delirious?'

'I think he was making sense a few minutes ago, but now he's delirious again. He keeps throwing off the covers.'

For a few minutes they fought to keep Freddie covered, but he was too strong for them, so they had to let him kick off the blankets and lie there with the sweat congealing on his skin. Then he started shivering and when they pulled up the covers again he let them.

'Stupid bitch,' he said clearly at one stage. 'Don't want a child.'

Irene bent her head for a minute or two, fighting against tears. They'd both made the child, not just her.

Time seemed to stand still as the two women tried to care for the sick man. At one stage they had to call Andrew in to hold Freddie down on the narrow stretcher bed. Then a few minutes later he seemed to be sleeping. But not for long.

It was three hours and nearly dawn before Gil

returned with the doctor, who'd been attending someone in Northcliffe's tiny hospital. Andrew was standing outside, drinking a cup of tea and staring out at the block. When they got out of the doctor's car, he said simply, 'He's bad.'

The doctor went inside.

'I'll get you a cup of tea,' Andrew said.

'Thanks.' Gil waited, because that was all he could do for her. 'I had to wait for the doctor to see to a bad injury, couldn't get him here any quicker. We were lucky I didn't have to go into Pemberton.' He took a few gulps, sighing with pleasure. 'Your wife's a wonderful woman, very capable.'

Andrew smiled. 'Yes. So I've found out. I'm a lucky man.'

The doctor came out with Irene beside him, giving bad news out of hearing of the patient again, Gil guessed.

'There's nothing I can do for him, I'm afraid, Mrs Dawson. If you can get liquids into him, that'll help. But it's in God's hands. Pneumonia is – unpredictable.'

She nodded and went inside again.

The doctor looked at Gil. 'Do you need a ride anywhere?'

'No. I'll stay and look after their cows.'

When the doctor's little car had chugged away he turned to Andrew, 'You go back and do your milking. I'll see to things here. They can call out if they need my help with Freddie.'

'He's been a lot quieter for the past hour or two.'

As the day passed, Gil did what was necessary for

the animals, kept the kitchen fire stoked up, chopped up some firewood for Irene. When darkness fell again, he went inside and insisted the women take turns to eat something.

'I'm not hungry,' Irene said, 'though I'd love a cup of tea.'

'Pam's brought some soup across,' he said.

'Good.' Norah looked at her friend. 'You'll have a bowl of that, Irene, and no arguing. You have to eat. Stay with her, Gil, and I'll get some for all of us.'

He nodded and took her place by the bed, watching Irene as often as the sick man. From time to time she looked across at him and gave a faint smile, but for the most part, her attention was on her husband.

The hours passed slowly and it seemed to him that Freddie grew weaker.

Another night fell, a fine one this time, with stars twinkling in the sky. They'd taken it in turns to sleep for an hour or two, but now they were all gathered in the humpy, trying to ease the coughing fits, to persuade him to drink, to keep him covered.

But for all their efforts he was growing weaker.

As dawn was breaking, the sick man opened his eyes, looked at his wife and rasped, 'You'll be – better off – without me.'

'Don't say that! Try to get better.'

He looked beyond her to where grey light was showing through the gable. 'Don't – want to. Had enough.'

Within minutes his breaths stopped.

Gil had just come back in. He hesitated in the

doorway, then turned and went to set some water on to boil. The man had just given up. He'd not have done that if he had a wife like Irene, not to mention a child on the way.

Irene was holding Freddie's hand and had closed her eyes for a few seconds, because they were burning with tiredness and lack of sleep. She didn't realise he'd stopped breathing till Norah reached out to touch her.

'He's gone, love.'

Even before she opened her eyes, she realised how quiet it was without the tortured sound of his breathing. She looked down at her husband's still face on the pillow and reached out to close his eyes gently. In death he looked like the old Freddie again. No scowl or sulky look, just a peacefully sleeping face. She was glad about that. It was how she wanted to remember him.

'He was young and healthy.' She reached out to stroke his cheek. 'How could he have died so quickly?'

'They do sometimes with pneumonia, and the strongest seem as vulnerable as the weakest. I've seen it before. Shall I lay him out for you, Irene?'

'We'll do it together.'

Later that day Gil and Andrew brought round a coffin they'd pieced together hastily from green wood, sawn into rough planks by the men in their group.

Gil watched Irene, but to his relief she was holding up well. Too well? Would she collapse afterwards? Bereaved people sometimes did once they'd buried their dead.

He couldn't help wondering what she was going to do now. Would she leave Australia and go back to England? How would he bear that?

They took the dead man to Pemberton, because there was still no cemetery in Northcliffe. There they obtained the death certificate, a mere formality given that the doctor had seen Freddie before he died, and made the necessary arrangements.

The following morning, the poor young man was buried, prayed over by a cleric who'd never met him and attended only by his wife, Norah and Gil.

Inevitably it brought back memories of Mabel and comrades who'd been killed during the war. Well, at least Freddie had left the baby as a lasting legacy. Poor Mabel hadn't even managed that.

When it was over, they waited for Irene to lead the way back to the truck. She stood looking down at the coffin, but neither of them hurried her.

It was a dry-eyed woman who eventually turned to them and said in a calm, cool voice, 'Can we go home now, please?'

'Of course.'

Norah went to link arms with her and the two women walked slowly back to the truck, with Gil trailing behind them. Irene turned just once to look back at the man who was already filling in the hole.

It wasn't till they got back to the block that she began to weep, not loudly but in a soft, despairing way.

'Do I have to leave the block straight away?' she asked Gil as he supported her into the house. 'I don't have anywhere to go yet, can't seem to think what to do.'

'No, of course you don't have to leave.' But he knew the Board had rules about this sort of thing and would expect to have the block back quite quickly, not to mention stopping payment of Freddie's wages.

Well, to hell with them. It was Irene who mattered most. He'd delay writing to inform them for a few days, that's what he'd do.

The two women went inside and Gil turned to Andrew, who'd walked across the cleared land to join them. 'I'd better get back to work again, I suppose. I'll see to her stock.'

It was all he could do for her. And at least it would mean he'd see her every day, be able to watch over her.

19

It was two days before Irene managed to pull herself together. Gil didn't intrude on her grief. He went to milk the cows for her every morning and evening, lit the fire for her every morning in the sorry excuse for a kitchen lean-to that Freddie had cobbled together, and made sure her water buckets were full.

On the second day he talked to Andrew, putting his thoughts about Irene into words for the first time very hesitantly, afraid of a rebuff.

Andrew didn't reply at once, but sat gazing into the fire they'd lit outside the humpy, since it was a clear night. 'I'll ask Norah. Women understand these things so much better than men do.'

Gil nodded his thanks. Somehow he hadn't been able to speak to Norah himself.

Soon afterwards he took his leave, walking slowly and thoughtfully home to a nearly bare humpy and a cooking fire that hadn't been lit for several days. It seemed even lonelier tonight.

Andrew found his wife in bed. 'I need to talk to you, without the children overhearing. Do you think you could put on a coat and come outside? I can soon get the fire we sit round blazing up.'

'Yes, of course. Is it something Gil said?'

'Yes. It's – rather delicate.'

She threw back the blanket and got out of bed again. 'I can guess.'

'You can?'

'Haven't you noticed the way he looks at her? If ever I saw a man in love, he's one.'

When they were out by the blazing fire, they sat on the rough bench he'd made and he put his arm round her. After telling her what Gil had suggested, he waited patiently for her response.

'It's too soon, really, but I'll talk to Irene tomorrow,' she said at last. 'I'm glad she let Janie sleep there tonight. I didn't want her to be on her own. And I've told Janie not to wake her in the morning, but to let her sleep on.'

'Janie's seemed a bit more settled lately,' he ventured.

There was another long silence then Norah sighed. 'She's quieter, but she's so different from what she was like in England that I'm still worried about her.'

His breath caught in his throat. 'Does that make you sorry you accepted my offer?'

She raised the hand she was holding to her lips and kissed it. 'No, love, never that. But I'm at my wits' end as to what to do next to help her.'

'She'll settle down, given time.'

'Yes, I suppose so.'

But it was Irene who most needed their help at the moment. Janie's problems would keep.

*   *   *

The following morning Norah went across to Irene's once the milking was over, meeting Gil on his way back from dealing with her friend's cows.

'Is she up?'

He nodded. 'Only just, though. Your little lass is fussing over her.'

'It's a bit early to speak to her about your suggestion, really.'

'I know. But the Board won't let her stay here for more than a week or so. They see the land as belonging to the man, not the woman. I should have notified them of Freddie's death immediately, can't delay it much longer.'

'I suppose not.' She walked on to the humpy.

Janie and Irene were having breakfast at the rough table outside, just bowls of porridge and when Norah got close, she had to hide a smile as she saw how lumpy it was. Her daughter never managed to make good porridge, because her heart wasn't in it.

She made small talk with Irene, waiting till Janie had finished eating and her friend had pushed a half-empty bowl to one side. 'Get off home now, Janie love, and peel me some potatoes. Do more than usual, fill the big pan right up, and don't forget to make sure they're covered in water or they'll go black. I'm going to make some potato cakes with the leftovers.'

Janie scowled. 'I was going to stay and help Auntie Irene today.'

'You can come back later. I need to talk to your auntie privately about something.'

'It's not fair. You're always having secrets from me.'

Norah stiffened. 'Secrets from you, indeed! Grown-ups have things to discuss that don't concern children. I won't put up with cheekiness.'

Janie bit her lip, then swung round and stamped off towards their own block. There was quite a path marked between the two farms now.

'She's been a big comfort to me,' Irene said.

'Good.' Norah hesitated, unsure how to approach this. 'Look, Gil's asked me to speak to you. He has to notify the Board about Freddie and you won't be able to stay here much longer than a week. Have you – um, thought about your future?'

Tears welled in Irene's eyes. 'I lay awake half the night worrying about what I'm going to do and I couldn't think of anything. I suppose I'll have to go and live in Perth, but the baby's going to make it difficult to support myself later on, even if I get a job now.' One of her hands went instinctively to settle on her stomach, where the baby was starting to show. She was sure she hadn't been this big at this stage last time.

'I'm glad I'm having it, though.' She heaved a big sigh. 'I suppose I should go home, only I haven't got enough money.'

'Do you want to go back to England? If you do, we'll find the money for you, somehow, take up a collection. People are usually generous.'

Irene bowed her head, pleating the material of her skirt.

Norah didn't say anything, giving her friend time to think out her answer. This was so important.

When Irene raised her head, she said simply, 'No. I

don't really want to go back to England. I was ill every single winter with a bad chest, and the doctor told me to get away to a sunnier place, if I could. Since I've come here, I've felt well all the time, no wheezing, no gasping for breath, even in the cold weather. I've not felt this good since I was a child.'

'So if you had a choice, you'd stay?'

Irene nodded.

'Then you might like to consider Gil's suggestion.'

'Oh? What is it?'

'He knows it's early days, but he'd be happy to marry you and provide for the child. He's always longed for children, only his first wife couldn't give him any.' She stopped, because Irene's expression was so shocked.

'*Get married again!* With Freddie only just buried? How could Gil *ever* think I'd do that?'

'He knows it's too early, but he has to speak to you now, because otherwise you'll be leaving. He loves you, Irene. The way he looks at you – well, haven't you noticed?'

'I've noticed how kind he was, but I didn't think about him in that way.'

'He says he'd not touch you till you felt ready, if that's what's upsetting you.'

There was another silence, then Irene shook her head. 'No. The whole idea of getting married so soon is wrong. What would people say?'

'They'd say you were being sensible.'

'Well, sensible or not, I can't do it. Tell him thank you, but no. I'll just – move up to Perth and find a job, manage somehow.'

To give Gil a bit more time, Norah risked saying, 'I'm not telling him anything for you. You must give him your own answer.'

Irene looked at her in shock.

'But I will tell you one thing. I married Andrew for convenience. When my father died, I lost my home and had to go into lodgings. And the thought of living in one room, answering to a landlady, seeing Janie go without – well, it upset me. So when the curate's wife suggested I marry Andrew and come here, I had a good think and agreed to meet him.' She could feel herself flushing as she added, 'And I liked him, so I agreed to marry him and now – now we've grown to love one another. So it can work.'

'That's different.'

'How?'

Irene looked down, biting her lip. 'Your husband had been dead for a few years.'

'I know, but women do what they must to provide for their children.' Norah stood up. 'I'll tell Gil to come and see you. When would be convenient?'

'Can't you give him my answer? *Please*.'

'No. He's done you the honour of offering for your hand in marriage. The least you can do in return is think about it carefully and then speak to him yourself.' She walked away before she interfered more than this and told Irene she'd be stupid to refuse such an offer.

You couldn't make other people's decisions for them, though sometimes you itched to do it.

★　★　★

Irene sat on at the table, letting the winter sunshine warm her face. Her thoughts were in a turmoil. This was the last thing she'd expected, the very last.

As if you could bury one husband, then marry another within the week! It was a shocking idea. The other groupies would be horrified.

She was horrified.

And yet . . . she was touched by his kindness.

Somewhere a kookaburra let out a trail of crazy laughter and she smiled in sympathy. They didn't have a pretty call, but she loved to hear it. She loved the frogs that called at dusk, too, droning on and filling the early night with their harsh undertone of sound. Something moved and she turned slightly to look towards the uncleared bush. Kangaroos. One had a baby sticking out of its pouch.

Irene's hand went to her own baby, which had been a source of great comfort to her over the past few days. It'd helped her stay strong because she was all the baby had now.

It could have more, though, it could have a father.

She clapped one hand to her mouth, though she'd not spoken the words aloud. She was shocked that she could even think like this, so went to start clearing out the humpy. But when she tried to go through Freddie's clothes and possessions, she began weeping and couldn't stop.

In the end, she lay down on his bed, pulled the blanket up over herself – the blanket which still smelled of him – and drifted into sleep.

She didn't want to face any questions or make any

decisions today. Couldn't. Tomorrow would be time enough.

Gil worked himself hard, trying to keep his thoughts and hopes at bay. In vain. He kept seeing Irene's wan face at the funeral. He shouldn't have spoken so soon, he definitely shouldn't.

When he went in the evening to milk her cows, there was no sound from the humpy. He hesitated, then peeped through the half-open door and saw her lying on the bed, fast asleep. There were dark circles under her eyes and he ached to cherish her, hadn't the right.

Would she even consider his offer?

Why should she? He was older than she was, never had been particularly good-looking, with his gingerish hair. The other young men he'd grown up with had always attracted women far more easily than he had.

Then had come the miracle of Mabel, who had loved him as much as he loved her.

He'd consider it a second miracle if Irene agreed to marry him.

After finishing the milking he trudged back to his own home. Home! It was a mess, a camp, a temporary resting place. How could he think of offering to bring her here?

Needing to keep busy, he lit a good fire, then mixed up a batch of damper and set it to cook in the embers. He opened a tin of corned beef and forked out chunks, not tasting it, just knowing his body needed feeding.

Then he lit a couple of lanterns because it was growing dark and he wanted to study the humpy inside and out. It wouldn't take much to build on a kitchen. He'd collected a pile of poles from the small trees they'd felled, because poles came in useful for all sorts of things. He could make a start on a lean-to tonight. Why not?

When he heard someone approaching he swung round. Andrew. He didn't say anything, just waited.

'Norah says Irene needs time to think about it. She says not to bring it up until she does.'

Gil nodded.

'Smells good.' Andrew indicated the camp oven with one toe.

'Damper. I'd offer you a piece, but it won't be ready for a while yet.'

'What are you doing, working so late?'

'Making a start on a lean-to kitchen. Should have done it before. Been too busy helping you lot.'

'Then it's about time someone helped you.' Andrew rolled up his sleeves.

They didn't talk much, but they got a lot done.

When his friend had gone home, Gil cut himself a big chunk of damper and slathered it with jam. He ate it slowly and with relish, watching his billy boil and the tea in it brew till it was dark and strong. A full pint, that old billy made, perfect for a thirsty man. Good tea, too, especially if you put a couple of gum leaves in to give it additional flavour. He'd missed that sort of tea while he was overseas.

He set to and did another hour's work, so tired by the time he went to bed that he slept soundly.

But when his alarm clock rang the following

morning, he was up in seconds. If all he could do for her was milk the cows, then that's what he'd do.

He hoped she wouldn't take too long to give him her answer, though. It was agony waiting.

Irene woke feeling disoriented. She realised she was in Freddie's bed and her heart stabbed with unhappiness when she remembered why.

She suddenly remembered Gil's offer, and the way Norah had refused to give him her answer. *No.* That's what the answer would be. She couldn't possibly marry him or anyone while she was carrying Freddie's child, grieving for her husband.

She got up and found that the cows had been milked and a bucket of clean water set ready in the lean-to. That made her sigh. What a kind man Gil was! She didn't want to hurt him, must tell him very gently.

She made some porridge, smiling at the memory of Janie's lumpy offering. Everyone was being so kind to her, so very kind.

After breakfast she felt like lying down again, but didn't let herself. Instead she decided to sort out the money and count it carefully. She opened the leather pouch which contained their savings and looked at it aghast. There was hardly anything left. Where had all their money gone?

The answer was obvious, but she didn't let it come to the forefront of her mind for a few minutes, just shut the leather pouch, stroking the gold initials on it, then opening it again. Freddie must have spent the money on drink. That was the only way twenty pounds could have gone down to a meagre three pounds seven shillings and twopence. How could he have done that?

She didn't weep because she was too upset for that. Instead she searched through every item they possessed. Her mother had given her two pounds, 'just for a rainy day'. She'd kept it in a little pouch embroidered for her by one of her sisters. That money was gone, too. She had the remains of her housekeeping money, five shillings and threepence ha'penny. In all, that made three pounds twelve shillings and fivepence ha'penny. She'd not last long on that. And she had no family to turn to for help here. Cold fear shivered through her and settled in her belly.

Unless she married Gil.

No. Fear wasn't a reason to marry someone, no one should do that to a decent man. She didn't love Gil, hardly knew him. She had loved Freddie, faults and all.

Hadn't she?

But it seemed she hadn't known him as she thought she had and as if her love had faded.

She made piles of the coins, arranging and rearranging them, doing the same to her thoughts. But it always led her to the same conclusion.

She couldn't do it, just – couldn't marry anyone. Not even Gil.

Later that day, Norah went across to see her friend, making Janie unhappy by refusing to let her go too. The boys had gone off with their father today. She worried that they weren't getting any schooling, but they loved helping the men and Andrew said a few months without lessons wouldn't hurt them.

She was a bit worried about leaving her daughter alone in the humpy. But she was only a short walk away and would be back within the hour. Before she left, she gave Janie some chores to do, hardening her heart to the hurt look on her daughter's face at being left behind.

It looked like rain again, so Norah took her umbrella, hurrying along the faint path that made a shortcut between the two properties.

She found Irene standing by one of the beds looking down at a pile of Freddie's clothing.

'Do you think people would buy these from me?' she asked.

'Some might take a piece or two. But people haven't got a lot of money to spare for clothes at the moment, you know.'

'Perhaps I could sell them in Perth, then. I shall have to look for a job there, because there's nothing here.' Irene brushed away a tear impatiently, then told her friend about the missing money.

Norah hugged her. 'I don't know what to say. I think we could lend you a pound, but that's all. We had to use some of our savings while Andrew was unable to work, and we have to think of the children.'

'Thank you, but I'd not take it. I shall manage somehow. I think my baby will have more chance of making a good life for itself here in Australia, don't you? Isn't that why you and Andrew brought your children here?'

'Yes. But who can ever be sure? I love the outdoor life we lead here. I even like milking the cows.'

Irene nodded slowly. 'I do too. I'll miss them.'

'You're going to tell Gil no, aren't you?'

Silence.

'Irene?'

She shrugged then nodded.

'Only you can decide that. But I like him and so does Andrew. He's a good man, would stand by you through thick and thin.' She looked out as the rain grew heavier. 'It seems to be setting in. Gil says it'll soon be spring and then the rain will mostly stop until next winter. Remember the lovely warm weather when we first arrived?'

'Yes. I really enjoyed it.'

Irene sat on after her friend had left, lost in thought. She too loved the warmth. You never got days and days of sun in Lancashire. The air was never sparkling clear there, either. Maybe that was why she'd had a bad chest, the dirty air. She remembered struggling for breath, thinking she wasn't going to live.

She couldn't go back!

That was one decision made, at least. Two, if you counted Gil. She straightened her shoulders and began packing. She had to be strong now, for the baby's sake.

20

Janie watched her mother go striding across to Auntie Irene's house and kicked the leg of the table as she stared at the pile of potatoes. It was all she ever seemed to do, peel potatoes, fetch water, make porridge.

She went to feed the hens first. Her lame little hen came over to peck some grains from her hand. She picked Fluffy up and stroked her. The hen made a soft noise and nestled against her, seeming more interested in cuddling Janie than in eating. Well, the mash they boiled up every couple of days from potato peelings and other scraps smelled horrid, but the hens seemed to love it.

When she set Fluffy down, the hen stayed near her feet so instead of putting her pet back into the chook pen, she left her outside, scooping up some of the mash and putting it back into the bucket to save for Fluffy. This creature loved her and showed it. No one else did.

She went back to the house, with Fluffy trailing behind her and set down the bucket of mash next to the outside table. They did their chores here when it was fine. By the time Janie had finished peeling the potatoes her hands were stiff with cold and she had run out of clean water. They never left her enough water. It wasn't fair!

Picking up the bucket, she took it across to the well, hanging it on the big hook and letting it down into the water at the bottom. When she wound it up, it was too full for her to carry, so she leaned over the top of the well to tip some out. Of course it splashed down her front and that made her even colder.

As she walked slowly back to the humpy, a gust of cold wind blew raindrops in her face. She glanced up at the sky, where the clouds were so low they seemed almost to touch the treetops. More rain coming.

Setting the bucket of clean water on the low shelf in the lean-to, she looked round for Fluffy. There was no sign of the little hen, so she went outside again, making the soft clucking noises that usually brought her pet to her side. Only this time they didn't.

Janie looked further away but could see no sign of the hen, so walked all round the humpy searching. From the rear she saw a movement in the distance. Even as she watched, Fluffy disappeared into the bush, no mistaking that it was her, because she walked so lopsidedly.

'Come back!' she called, but the hen didn't reappear. She ran towards the place she'd seen Fluffy vanish, forgetting to look where she was going. Suddenly her feet slid from under her and she went flat on her backside in a patch of mud.

She began to cry but got up and ran on. Her mum would be furious at her if she lost one of the hens.

When she got among the trees, Janie saw her pet walking away from her, so ran on, calling out.

But Fluffy ran here and there, refusing to come to her, and could duck under bushes, while Janie sometimes had to go the long way round.

Suddenly she couldn't find Fluffy at all. She stopped, looking carefully round, but there was no sign of her. Shivering now, she turned to go back.

It wasn't long before she realised she was lost and stopped in bewilderment. How was that possible? She hadn't come very far into the woods. But though she went this way and that, she couldn't find her way out. Everything looked alike.

It was raining hard now and her hair was plastered to her head, her clothing heavy with water and her feet squelching in her boots. She huddled against a big tree, sheltered a little from the rain, unable to think what to do.

She was going to die here, catch her death of cold like Mr Dawson had and die.

When Norah got back she found a pan of peeled potatoes standing out in the rain, but no sign of her daughter. She went to check the latrine, which now had a proper wooden seat and pan, with a little corrugated shelter over it, thanks to Andrew's hard work. But no one was there.

She cupped her hands round her mouth and called out as loudly as she could, 'Janie! Where are you?' After waiting a minute, she shouted again, 'Janie, come back here this minute!'

But there was still no answer.

What could have happened to the child? Could she have run away? No, of course not. Janie didn't like the bush and always stayed close to the house and her mother. And anyway, her coat was hanging on its usual hook, so she couldn't have gone far.

Norah did another quick tour of all the outhouses and as she was walking back, she saw Fluffy coming towards her from the bush behind the house, clucking softly. 'How did you get out?' She scooped up the little hen and put her back into the pen, shutting the gate firmly.

Could Janie have gone across to see Irene by another route? She must have. It was the only explanation. Sighing, Norah picked up Janie's coat and the umbrella, then walked as quickly as she could to her friend's house.

'Is Janie here?'

'No. I've not seen her today.'

'She's not at home and I can't think where she can be because her coat is still on the hook. I thought – hoped she'd be here.'

Irene reached for her own coat. 'I'll come and help you look.'

The two women walked back to the Boyds' block just as the boys came into sight.

'Dad sent us home early,' Ned called out. 'Can I have a cup of tea. I'm frozen cold and—'

'Have you seen Janie?' Norah interrupted.

'Course not. She stayed at home with you. None of the girls work with us men.'

'She's missing.'

Jack shushed his brother. 'How long has she been gone, Mum?'

'I was only away for an hour, and I've been searching for her for about an hour since I got back. I can't think where she can be. She didn't even take her coat.'

Jack, who'd been listening to Pete's tracking tales, walked all round the humpy studying the ground.

When he called out, Norah thought he'd found Janie and went running, disappointment flooding through her as she found him standing beside a muddy puddle. He pointed to the ground and there, half obliterated by the rain, were a child's footprints, one very distinct handprint and some slide marks.

'I think she fell over here,' he said. 'And if so, she was going in that direction.'

They all stared down at the marks and his ideas did make sense.

Norah went towards the bush, which wasn't far away at this side of the block.

Jack came to pull her back. 'Don't go in there, Mum. We don't want you getting lost as well.'

'But why would she have gone away from the house?' She suddenly remembered Fluffy. 'Oh, no! She can't have been so stupid.' She explained about the hen wandering around loose.

Jack looked longingly into the bush, but he'd heard too many tales of people getting lost. 'I'll go and fetch Dad and Pete. We'd better not go after her.'

'We could cooee,' Ned suggested.

'You and Mum do that. I'm going for Dad. Better

go back indoors, Mum. You and Mrs Dawson are soaking wet.'

Norah was impressed by the sheer sense of what Jack was saying. Her older stepson was very like his father, practical and dependable. She watched him run off towards the track then she and Ned started to cooee. But there was no answer.

Remembering Irene's condition, she shepherded the others inside, going into the lean-to to get the fire burning up and set the kettle on to boil. A hot drink never went amiss.

Then she found a towel and they all rubbed their hair a bit to stop it dripping down their necks.

'It's no use changing our clothes,' Ned said with relish. 'We'll have to go out again with the search party to find her.'

'You're going nowhere, my lad.' In spite of his protests, she took him into the children's half of the humpy and got him out of his soggy garments and into dry clothes. By that time Irene had got them all cups of hot cocoa, which shut him up for a while longer.

'Perhaps she'll come walking in of her own accord before they get back,' Irene said. But her voice was uncertain.

Norah shook her head. 'If she was close by, she'd have come inside already on such a cold, rainy day. I'm worried sick to think of her out there without a coat.'

After that, they didn't say much, just sipped their tea and waited for the men to come.

* * *

Jack was so out of breath when he found his father that it took him a minute to explain what had happened.

Andrew immediately called Gil over. 'Janie's missing.'

'Pete's the best tracker. You get back to Norah. I'll find him and we'll follow you as quickly as we can. We need to start our search before it gets dark.' He put two fingers in his mouth and let out a shrill whistle, then gesticulated vigorously to a group of figures a few hundred yards away.

He looked up at the leaden sky, shaking his head in dismay. No let-up in the rain.

Pete came hurrying across the rough land, the other men from his work team following him. 'What's wrong?'

'Janie's missing. We need to start searching for her before it gets dark.'

Pete nodded and the men turned to make their way towards the Boyds' farm. It was at times like this they all wished they had better forms of transport than Shanks's pony. It took so long to get anywhere on foot.

There was no sign of Andrew on the track. He must have moved quickly to get so far ahead of them.

When her husband burst into the humpy, Norah walked straight into his arms. 'Oh, Andrew, love, she's still missing. I'm that worried!'

'We'll find her, I promise. The others are following but I ran on ahead. Have you any idea where she went?'

'Yes. Come and see.' Explaining as they walked she took him to the puddle. Already the signs of Janie's fall had almost been wiped out by the heavy rain.

'Thank goodness Jack saw her footprints here before it was too late.'

'I'll get my axe. We need to mark the way as we go. No use all of us getting lost.'

'I'm coming with you.'

'You should stay here.'

'I'll go mad if I have to sit waiting. Irene will stay with the boys and be here if anyone – *when* someone finds her.'

By the time the other men arrived, Andrew and Norah were ready to leave. Gil sent them off with Pete, while he went in a slightly different direction with Ted.

The men pushed through the forest, stopping every few minutes to cooee and listen carefully. But there was no sound of the child's voice, only the monotonous dripping of the rain from the trees and the crackling and rustling of twigs underfoot as they tramped along.

Norah kept up with the two men, and managed the loudest cooee of all, her voice rising at the end more shrilly than theirs. Apart from that, she said nothing, holding her fears tightly inside herself. Whenever they stopped she listened as hard as she could, but heard nothing except the calls of the other group.

She looked up at the sky and then at Andrew. 'It's getting dark.'

'We'll get lanterns, keep on searching.'

'It'll be too dangerous. You won't be able to see your own marks on the trees.'

*   *   *

Back at the house, Irene and the two boys were sitting wrapped in blankets. Jack, who'd been thinking hard, said suddenly, 'What if she's gone round in circles? People do in the bush, Pete says.'

'They'll still find her eventually.'

'They don't always find people who're lost.'

He sat frowning and a few minutes later said, 'I think we should go outside and cooee again in case she's closer to us than to them.'

'Your father said to stay in the house.'

'It's worth a try, don't you think? I'll only be a few steps away. There's no danger in that.' He looked at her pleadingly. 'I can't just sit here. She's smaller than Ned, even if she is a year older than him, and she doesn't know the bush at all because she always stays near the house. *Please.* Just let me go outside and try.'

'You won't go out of sight of the house?'

'No. I promise.'

He went outside and sent shrill calls echoing through the nearby bush, then stood listening. But there was no answer.

Glancing guiltily back at the house door, he walked towards the edge of the bush, taking care not to make any noise that might bring Irene out. The wind was blowing strongly, sending rain slicing into his face. Janie wouldn't walk into that wind, he decided, but away from it. He walked away from the wind and when he was further along the edge of the uncleared land, he sent another call through the forest, then another three for good luck.

Standing motionless, he strained to hear the slightest sound, giving her plenty of time to reply.

Was that something? He listened again, but wasn't sure.

Casting a quick guilty glance over his shoulder, he moved in the direction of the sound, breaking off branches as he went so that he'd be able to find his way back. When he'd gone fifty paces into the bush he stopped and called again.

This time he was quite sure he'd heard something. He looked up at the sky. It was getting dark fast. No long twilights here in Australia, as there had been in England. Did he have time to find her? He hoped so. He couldn't, just couldn't go back and leave a little girl alone in the forest. She must be terrified, poor thing.

Taking care to continue breaking off branches, leaving them hanging by shreds of bark as signposts to the men who would surely follow him, he walked on, stopping to call every twenty paces and hearing a reply every time, definitely a reply and getting louder.

Who else could it be but Janie?

Irene went to build up the fire in the lean-to, filled the kettle and put it on to boil. 'I'd better go and get another bucket of water,' she told Ned. 'Don't go away.'

When she went outside, she looked round for Jack, and realised suddenly that she hadn't heard him cooeeing for a while. She couldn't see any sign of him, either. Surely he hadn't broken his promise?

She set the bucket down and walked all round the humpy, but there was no sign of him. From the forest, however, came a distant call. He *had* broken his promise and gone searching for his sister! She was more afraid than angry, terrified that he'd get lost as well.

Ned peered round the corner of the humpy. 'Where's our Jack?'

'Gone into the bush.' She grabbed the boy. 'You're not going after him. There are two children lost in the bush and you're not making it three.'

'Jack won't be lost. We play trackers sometimes and he can always find his way back.'

'I pray that's so. Whatever happens, your father's going to be very angry with him when he finds out what he's done.'

'Oh, Jack'll be all right.' Ned looked up at the sky. 'It's getting dark, so it'd be no use going after him. He'll be lost all night. What an adventure!'

That idea seemed to fill him with such relish she kept a firm hold of his jacket as they went back into the humpy to wait.

The minutes seemed to tick past very slowly. She felt she had failed Norah and Andrew.

What if they got so cold they came down with pneumonia? She shivered at the thought.

After a while, Janie decided it was stupid to sit doing nothing, getting colder and colder. She stood up and began jumping up and down to keep warm. Then she realised she'd not been making any noises for some time. If there was one thing that had been dinned into all the children, it was that if you were lost, you had to shout every few minutes.

She cupped her hands round her mouth and tried to do that. But her voice broke down into sobs. With great difficulty she made herself stop crying and call again. This time she managed to make a noise.

But it still wasn't loud enough. She could do far better than that. She took deep breaths and cooeed several times, then waited and listened. She knew you didn't keep on making noises, so decided to do three calls then count to a hundred, then do three more.

She didn't try to walk on through the forest, though, because she didn't know which way to walk.

The next time she called, she looked up at the sky and saw in dismay that it was getting much darker. That wasn't the grey of rain clouds, it was darkness coming on fast. What if she was lost here all night? What would she do then? It was so cold.

She almost missed the distant call, and had started counting again when it suddenly dawned on her that she'd heard a faint answering sound. Surely she had? She listened again.

Nothing.

She must have been mistaken.

Tears filled her eyes and she sagged back against the tree trunk, jerking upright as another call rang out again. She hadn't been mistaken. Someone was looking for her.

Eagerly she called back, waiting . . . waiting . . . and yes, there it was again.

As the caller came gradually closer, tears of relief ran down her cheeks, mingling with the rain. Then she heard the noise of someone coming towards her and called out, 'I'm here. I'm here.'

When Jack walked into the clearing where she was standing, she looked behind him, expecting to see his father or the foreman. But there was only Jack.

She began to sob. She wanted a grown-up to pick her up and hold her tight. She wanted her mother.

Jack was so glad to see her safe and sound he stopped dead and let out a groan of relief. Then he moved towards her. She seemed very little with her clothes sticking to her body and her hair flattened by rain. She was crying so hard, he put his arms round her and gave her a hug.

'It's all right. Shh now, it's all right. I've found you and we'll be able to find our way back.'

She put her arms round him. 'Oh, Jack, I was so frightened! I didn't mean to get lost. I was chasing Fluffy. I'm ever so sorry.'

'Shh. It's all right. I'm here now.'

He couldn't get her to stop crying for some time.

When she did, she looked round anxiously, her face a white blur in the darkness. 'It's nearly night.'

'I know. We have to stay here. We can't find our way back in the dark because I won't be able to see where I've broken off branches. But I'll easily find my way in the morning, I promise you.'

She shivered and huddled against him.

'We shouldn't even try to move,' he decided after thinking it over.

'But it's getting colder and colder, and I don't have a coat. What shall we do?'

'We'll cuddle up to one another to keep warm and if you turn your back to me, I'll wrap my overcoat round you. It's a good thing my aunt bought this one too big for me.' He moved a strand of wet hair from her eyes and pulled her close again. 'I'll look after you. I'm your big brother. That's what big brothers do.'

'You didn't want a sister.'

'Well, you didn't want a brother. But we've got one another now, so we should make the best of it.'

Silence, then, 'All right.' A few seconds later she added in a rush, 'And thank you for coming after me. I'm not frightened now I've got you. Well, not very.'

He looked round and seeing a leafy bush in the last of the light, said, 'Let's see if we can make a little shelter.' He began to pull the branches off the bush and pile some on the ground. 'They'll be lumpy, but they'll be warmer to sit on than the wet soil and mud.'

She started to help him and got a bit warmer with the activity. After they'd made a pile to sit on, they stacked some branches round the front of the hollow in the tree trunk, which gave a little protection from the cold wind.

Soon it was dark. They sat down together, huddling close. A short time later he felt her head droop against his chest and heard a soft, steady sound of breathing. She was asleep.

He felt suddenly very protective, not because it was his duty but because she was his sister now, and she felt soft and helpless as she lay cuddled in his arms, like a kitten he'd once had.

As he shifted slightly to get more comfortable, he decided he'd better stay awake. His dad and the other men might come hunting for them with lanterns. If they did, he needed to be awake to call out if he saw any lights coming through the trees.

He hoped his dad would come and find them soon, because it was bitterly cold.

21

When the searchers returned to the Boyds' humpy, Irene burst into tears at the sight of them.

'I'm sorry. I told Jack to stay near the humpy. He *promised* me he would.'

It was a minute or two before they could calm her down and find out what was wrong.

Andrew looked at Pete. 'Would it be too risky to go looking for him?'

'Well . . . I've been talking to the kids about what to do if they get lost in the bush. Jack was the smartest of them all and I reckon he'll have done the right thing.' Pete looked across at Irene. 'Do you know at which spot he went into the bush?'

She took a minute to consider this. 'Not exactly, but it'd be behind the house not in front and towards the right as you look at the bush.'

'That's a start.' Gil picked up the lantern. 'Get that other lantern, Andrew. Pete, you'll come, won't you?'

'I will if he's left signs; if he hasn't, we'll have to wait till first light.'

Norah stood up. 'I want to come too.'

Gil shook his head. 'Not this time. Trousers are easier when going through the bush, won't slow us down as much.' He looked at her skirt, which had several new tears in it from their recent foray.

When they went round to the rear of the house, Pete held up one hand. 'Stay back.' He walked slowly along the rough ground and stopped to finger a low-hanging branch. 'Ha!'

'Have you found something?'

'Yes. Look.'

The others moved forward and saw a broken branch hanging from a strip of bark at just below a man's eye height.

'Told them to leave signs if they ever got lost,' Pete said in satisfaction. 'Clever lad, that one. Let me go first and you two stay behind till I tell you to move forward. We don't want to destroy the clues.' He moved on, casting around and eventually calling to his companions.

By the time they'd gone about a hundred yards into the bush, the lights of the house had disappeared, but the hurricane lanterns shed pools of brightness in the rustling darkness around the two men.

Pete stopped. 'Time to call out, I reckon. Hold my lantern. And keep quiet afterwards.'

As the sounds he made echoed through the forest, they waited. Nothing. He raised his hands to his mouth and sent the call ringing out again. Waited again. With a sigh of disappointment, he reached for the lantern and they moved on, still finding broken branches. 'We're definitely on the right track.'

After the next call, he stiffened. 'Did you hear that?'

Andrew shook his head. 'My hearing isn't as good as yours. Comes of toiling in a noisy workshop.'

'I heard something. Yes, there it goes again.' Pete answered it, then moved on again.

It took them about ten minutes to find the children. Jack didn't get up to greet them, because he was still sitting holding Janie, who was clinging to him, her white, frightened face turned towards their rescuers.

As the boy looked up, his father saw that his son was crying, but didn't comment. A lost lad was entitled to shed tears of relief at such a time. Hell, Andrew's own eyes were brimming over. 'I'll take her. You hold my lantern, son.'

Janie held up her arms and was lifted into Andrew's care, then Pete and Gil helped the boy up.

'We've found you, love,' Andrew told the weeping child gently. 'You're quite safe now, Janie.' Without thinking, he pressed a kiss on her forehead.

She looked up at him in bewilderment, then flung her arms round his neck and cuddled closer, not saying anything, but shivering with cold.

'Hold her a minute,' he said to Gil, and slipped off his coat, wrapping it round her and taking her back. 'There. Better get you back to your mother now. You need warming up.' He looked past her to his son, who'd now got Pete's coat round his shoulders and whose shivering was quite visible.

'I'm sorry I disobeyed Mrs Dawson, Dad, but I could hear Janie calling and didn't want to lose her again. She must have walked round in a circle. We didn't move once I'd found her, just as Pete said.'

'You did the right thing, son. I'm proud of you.'

'I broke off branches as I went.'

'That's what led us here,' Pete said. 'Couldn't have done it better myself.' He had to clear his throat and swallow hard, he was so relieved to have found them.

As they neared the humpy, Gil called out, 'We've got them!' and people spilled out.

Norah surprised herself by bursting into tears as she kissed first Janie, then Jack, who wriggled in embarrassment.

Then they all went inside. When the children were dry again, they sat wrapped in blankets, sipping cocoa and telling their stories. Everyone kept reassuring one another that they'd been sure the children would be found.

'I'll go and get a couple of hours' sleep now,' Pete said. 'Coming, Gil?'

'I'll walk Mrs Dawson home first. You get on your way, mate.'

When they'd left, Janie said in a sleepy voice, 'My brother found me and my new daddy carried me back.' She put her lips closer to her mother's ears. 'They don't hate me. I thought they did, but they don't.'

The words had been perfectly audible to the others, but Andrew only winked at his sons and when Ned would have made a comment, Jack shushed him up quickly.

'Better set that alarm clock of yours,' Andrew said to Norah. 'The milk truck waits for no one.'

Before they got into their narrow stretcher beds, she pulled him towards her and gave him a long embrace. 'I think it's going to be all right now. With Janie, I mean.'

'I think so too.'

Only when the humpy was silent and Andrew's breathing had slowed right down did she allow herself to weep out her relief.

The following morning Gil was awake well before dawn, because he'd not really settled, only dozed on and off. His thoughts kept going back to Irene, who had said very little as he took her home. He kept trying to remember whether she'd given any hints as to what her answer would be to his offer of marriage.

Ah, he was an old fool! Why would she want a fellow like him, twelve years older than she was?

But just in case, he put on a clean shirt and did his best with his hair, gazing in the small shaving mirror, fingering the greying hairs at each temple and frowning in concentration as he soaped his face and slid the safety razor across it. He should have bought some new razor blades. These were blunt. He didn't want to go to her with cuts on his face.

She didn't come out when he arrived to milk the cows but there was a curl of smoke rising from the lean-to.

He went across to it, had to see her, just to make sure she was all right.

She came to the door and gave him a very solemn look. 'I should have given you an answer before now, Gil. I'm sorry about that.'

'It's important, shouldn't be rushed.'

'Everything seems to be rushed at the moment. How long before I must move out?'

'A week or so.'

'And what about the cows and chooks? What do we do with them?'

'They go back to the bank, but in practical terms they'll be given to another family.'

'I see. Would you like a cup of tea?'

He just wanted to be put out of his misery but she obviously wanted to take things slowly. 'That'd be nice.' At least it gave him an excuse for spending time with her.

When they were sitting down, she took a few sips of her tea, then drew in a deep breath and turned to him. 'I'm grateful for your offer, Gil. It's very kind indeed of you. But I can't accept. It's too soon. I'm still trying to get used to the idea that Freddie's no longer here.'

'I know that. I'd not have said anything, only you'll be leaving soon.'

Briefly her hand rested on his. It might have been a burning brand from the fire, because it seemed to mark his flesh with warmth. 'What shall you do?'

'Sell everything I can and go to Perth – or Fremantle. Try to find a job until the baby arrives.'

'It'll be hard.'

She nodded. 'Yes. I'm terrified. But that's no reason to take advantage of you.'

'It's me who was trying to take advantage of you, lass. I'm a lot older. Why should you want a fellow like me?'

'Don't talk like that! You're a wonderful man, would make someone a fine husband.'

'But not you.'

'No. Not me. It's too soon.'

They both sipped again, then he had a sudden thought. 'I can give you an address to go to in Fremantle, if that's any help. Nelly's a cousin of mine. She'll put you up if I ask her.'

'You'd do that?'

'Of course I would. I'll write to her at once and find someone going to Pemberton to get it in the post tonight.'

'Oh, Gil, I feel even worse about turning you down.'

His voice came out harsher than he'd intended. 'Don't say that! I don't want you accepting out of gratitude. It's love I feel for you, not pity.' He stood up, not caring that he'd overturned the cup. 'I'll go and milk the cows.'

Her voice floated after him. 'Thank you.'

He strode across to the cow shed. At least Irene would be all right with Nelly, who had a big heart. She'd tried to help him, too, after the war. But she'd failed because he'd needed time and another purpose in life before he pulled out of his miseries. He looked round. He loved it here, would make it his home, even if he couldn't get his heart's desire.

By the time he'd finished milking the first cow, Irene was there to separate the cream, not saying a word, just getting on with it.

He was glad she didn't try to force a conversation. What was there to say now that wouldn't rub salt into the wound?

★　★　★

When Irene left Northcliffe, Gil arranged for her to have a lift to Pemberton on the milk truck. He set the men off on their day's work and went off to his own block to finish the lean-to. He didn't feel like company today.

But he didn't make much progress. He kept wondering where she was now, if she'd got on the train yet.

Strange, though. This time, sad as he was, he didn't feel the urge to get drunk. That urge seemed to have left him totally now and he didn't care whether he ever had another drink or not.

Instead he wandered round his farm, then couldn't resist going over to hers. He had to do something about it, what with the cows and everything, so no one would be surprised to see him there. But it was her he thought of, not the cows.

It was while he was walking round that the idea came to him. Why shouldn't Andrew and his family move across to this farm? The soil was much better, there were fewer large trees and a permanent stream ran across one corner of it. It was worth a lot, a stream that ran all through the long dry summer. Many of them didn't. He'd seen it running when they arrived here. You could make a dam with a stream like that and have water through the worst of the droughts. And there were always drought years here.

And he knew exactly how to word his letter to the Board about this so that they'd accept his recommendation. Quite a few people had walked off the land already and he'd been instructed to do all he could to retain the best settlers. So he'd tell them he was obeying their instructions, and he'd bet none of them would question that.

He walked into Irene's humpy and saw a neat pile of bedding on the stretcher beds, which he'd promised to dispose of. Fool that he was, he should have brought his cart. Well, the stuff wouldn't run away, would it? They had no more thieves in their group, just ordinary folk, some of whom worked harder than others, all of whom had their dreams. The things would still be here tomorrow and he'd take them over to his own house for the time being.

He waited for Andrew to pass by on his way home after a day's timber clearing on a farm at the other end of the group's land. 'Got a minute?'

His friend nodded and changed direction.

Gil led the way and they walked in silence up the slope to the unoccupied farm. He stopped by the buildings and spread out his arms. 'It's about this place.'

Andrew looked at him in puzzlement.

'It's much better land than yours. I think you should transfer to this one.'

'Is that allowed?'

'Yes. If you're agreeable, I'll write to the Board and fix it up.'

'You're sure it'd be better.' Andrew smiled wryly. 'I've not got enough experience to tell if it'll be worth all the trouble. I've made things more comfortable at our place than they are here, built sheds and things.'

'I'm very sure. And I'll help you move them. They're easy to pull down, tin sheds are.'

'I'd have to talk to Norah. She's made a garden, loves working on it.'

'You can make another garden and move some of the plants. She's not done the main spring planting yet.'

'Can you give me a day to think about it?'

'Yes. One day. But that's all. I have to let the Board know quickly, before they send someone else.'

When Andrew got home, he could smell the food from a distance and it made his mouth water. A man got ravenous doing so much physical work. Norah did wonders with the few ingredients they could rely on and usually managed to produce something tasty for them.

Since it was fine, they sat at the outside table, well wrapped against the cold, because that was pleasanter than squashing inside the congested living area. He looked round and smiled at the three rosy-faced children. Today Janie smiled back at him. She was sitting between her two stepbrothers, not next to her mother and looked happier than he'd seen her for a long time.

Thank heaven she and Jack had recovered so easily from their chilly adventure!

Once the meal was over he said, 'You kids can clear up today. Your mother and I have something to discuss. Jack, you're in charge of the lanterns. Put them somewhere safe before you start the washing up.'

The boys pulled a face at this, because neither of them considered washing up men's work, but Andrew had decided early on that since the chores were done under such difficult conditions, they'd all share them.

Everyone was looking at him anxiously, so he added, 'There's nothing wrong and no one's in trouble, it's just something Mr Matthews suggested. We'll tell you about it later.'

There was enough moonlight for him and Norah to see their way so he offered her his arm and they strolled round their small domain.

'What is it?' she asked. 'What has Gil suggested?'

'He thinks now that Irene's left, we should move to her block.' He explained the advantages.

She was silent for so long he stopped walking. 'Don't you want to go?'

'Not really. We've done so much here, it's beginning to feel like home.'

'We can move nearly everything to the other block.'

'We can't move my garden.' She shrugged. 'But Gil knows more about farming than we do, so I think we should take his advice.'

'It's not easy, though, is it?'

'No.'

'You are happy here, aren't you?'

Her smiled was glorious. 'Oh, yes. Never doubt that, love.'

So he had to kiss her, a rare treat with the kids always nearby. He took his time over it, leaving her gasping and clinging to him, something which pleased him greatly. 'I do love you, Norah.'

'And I you.'

When he told the children, they were much less

worried about the move, though Janie needed re-assuring that he'd build another chook pen for Fluffy because Mr Dawson's pen was crooked and the chooks kept getting out of it.

Irene didn't reach Pemberton in time for that day's train, so she had to use up some of her precious money on lodgings. She hated to spend even a penny she didn't need to and resolved to manage without food on the journey, though she'd take a filled water bottle.

But without being asked, her landlady made her some sandwiches and when she tried to pay, refused to accept the money. She was warmed by this gesture from a complete stranger. Maybe there would be other kind strangers to help her along the way.

She arrived in Fremantle two days after leaving the farm, weary now and feeling dishevelled. She found a lad with a handcart who knew where Gil's cousin lived and walked with him through the streets, tired as she was, because it was cheaper than taking a taxi.

A plump woman of about Gil's age opened the door and smiled. 'You must be Mrs Dawson. My cousin wrote to me about you. Come in, come in! We've only got a sleepout, but you're welcome to stay there.'

'Can I ask how much it is? I'm – a bit short of money.'

'I wouldn't charge a friend of Gil's, but I'd appreciate a hand round the house till you find a job. There's always too much to do.' She laughed comfortably, then looked at her guest in concern. 'Are you all right, dear?'

Irene couldn't hold back the tears. 'You're so kind. Everyone's been kind to me.'

'Gil looked after me when I was a lass, so if he says you need help, I'm happy to oblige. What sort of world would it be if we thought only of making money?'

There it was again, Irene thought, someone praising Gil. What a lovely man he was! Her thoughts hovered like butterflies for a moment as she realised that she hated the thought of not seeing him again, but she couldn't dwell on that, had too much to do.

With Nelly's help, she found a job within two days, working as a general help in one of the bigger houses. She could walk there from her lodgings and they treated her kindly enough. The lady of the house even gave her some clothes that would fit round her stomach, which was expanding more rapidly than she'd expected.

After some argument, Nelly agreed to accept a couple of shillings a week for the room and further money towards food.

Irene tried to make the best of her new life, but the evenings were lonely, sitting in her little room, staring out at the garden. Nelly invited her to join them, but she didn't do that every evening. They had a right to their family life.

To her surprise, she missed the farm more than she had expected, missed the other groupies . . . missed Gil most of all. He had been there, solid as a rock, a true friend, and now she was on her own.

Oh, she was wanting the moon. You couldn't have everything, could you? She'd turned down his offer and still felt it had been the right thing to do. There were no jobs in Northcliffe and here she'd found one easily. What if she did have to look out on to the next house's side wall from her little bedroom instead of at trees and slopes? What if she didn't hear birdsong when she woke, or smell the tang of eucalyptus leaves crushed underfoot as she walked through the edges of the bush?

There was one thing that still worried her. How was she to care for the baby after it was born and earn a living for them both? There'd be no Gil to help her solve those problems.

No use meeting trouble before it met you. There were several months to go. She'd just count her blessings and save her pennies. She was grateful she'd managed so well. Very grateful.

Thanks to Gil.

'If you move on Sunday,' Gil told Andrew, 'I'll bring my cart and help you.'

'Thank you. I was going to ask if we could borrow it.'

'You can borrow me, too.'

On the Sunday morning, Gil turned up early and with everyone pitching in, they made short work of clearing out the humpy. Well, they'd not had a chance to accumulate many possessions, just the bits of furniture Andrew had made from the crates food and kerosene arrived in.

At noon, Norah provided a quick meal, then they set to work again. The men were dismantling the cowshed and dairy, then the other rough shelters for the pigs and hens. She went across to her new home to start unpacking, but found the lean-to and humpy very lacking in shelves and other small conveniences a man's clever fingers could provide, so she set up the stretcher beds and made them up ready for tonight. Andrew would sort out the other problems over the next few days.

At the old farm, the children were in charge of catching the hens, and did this with much laughter. Then the three of them walked across to the new farm, each carrying a hen, with Janie crooning to Fluffy and the little hen nestling against her.

They set the chooks down in their new homes and checked to make sure they couldn't escape, then watched them exploring, pecking everything in sight.

'Dad's buildings and fences were much better than these!' Jack said scornfully. He picked up a stone and hammered one of the fence poles into the ground more securely.

All the animals seemed mildly indignant at the changes to their lives, even the cows swishing their tails more than usual. They stopped so many times that it took ages to get them into their new enclosure, where they lowed dolefully as if hard done to.

'He didn't make much cop of this place, did he?' Gil said to Andrew, looking at the wobbly fences and trying not to think of Irene.

'No. He'd never have made a farmer, poor fellow. He was a townie to the core.'

Gil insisted on working right through until dark, but refused to join them for the evening meal.

'This place reminds him too much of Irene,' Norah

said to Andrew as they settled down to sleep. 'He's missing her.'

'I'd miss you if you went away.' He reached out and fumbled for her hand, holding it.

She smiled in the darkness, then her mind turned back to their next tasks.

'Tomorrow Janie and I will move as many of the plants as we dare.'

'Move them all. They might survive. What have we to lose?'

'I'd rather leave them for the next people than destroy them. Some are far too big to move.' She sighed happily. 'We've been so lucky, haven't we?'

But his hand had gone slack in hers and his breathing had deepened. Her bed was close enough for her to tuck his hand under his covers, then she snuggled down. She was longing to share a double bed with him properly, and for them all to have a more normal home life.

Well, it would come. They were over the worst now, surely?

22

The rest of the winter seemed to pass very quickly to the hard-working groupies. Men worked all day for the Board, then all evening for themselves, making furniture from anything to hand ready for the coming move into proper four-roomed houses – even though they'd not yet been given a date for these to be built.

Women worked at anything needed, whether it was men's work or not, and in the evenings they sewed or taught their children. Some were determined not to let their education lapse, others weren't worried about schooling, thinking more of the contribution the children's work could make to establishing the farm. All the youngsters did their share, willingly or not, working far harder than most of them had ever done in their lives before.

Each family now had six cows and the Boyds seven, because somehow Gil had managed not to account for the first cow sent to the group. Life centred on getting the cows milked and the cream to the gates for the pickup truck. The few shillings a week the cream brought were very important to everyone.

Another family walked off their block in August,

which made everyone feel let down. Why hadn't they asked for help? Everyone knew they weren't happy. They simply didn't have the right touch with animals or a feeling for the land, and the misery on their faces showed they knew it. But you couldn't force your help or advice on people, now could you?

The family didn't tell anyone what they were planning. One morning before it was light they trekked into Northcliffe and begged a lift into Pemberton, abandoning their furniture – a pitiful collection of oddments – and taking only their clothes and blankets.

They left debts behind, but they didn't leave a word of explanation or thanks for the help that had been freely offered to them.

Gil took charge of those possessions worth salvaging and suggested he sell what they could and put the money towards something the whole group could use. He knew he should have reported these items to the Board and given the meagre proceeds to the bank which was funding the groupies. But he felt the bank had enough money and his groupies were working so hard they deserved what little extra he could squeeze out for them.

It'd been like that in the Army. You learned what you could and couldn't do to bend the rules and regulations. He hadn't done that to be greedy nor had he taken things for his own profit, but to make himself and the lads – all of whom might die the next hour, the next day – happier or more comfortable.

When he reported the family's disappearance, the Board sent another family to take the place of those who'd left, just as they had with the Dawsons. The newcomers were a capable couple in their early thirties, with a daughter of Janie's age and two sons of five and three, hard-working folk, who fitted in straight away. Everyone was pleased to see the two little girls at once become friends because though Janie now got on better with her stepfamily, she was the sort who couldn't manage without a friend or two.

Gil complained to the Board on a monthly basis that they'd not yet built proper four-roomed houses for SG1, as they had for other groups. The reply, if officialdom bothered to send one, was always that the matter was 'in progress' and that each group must wait its turn.

There was much grumbling when they heard that a school was being set up for some of the other Northcliffe groups and that a woman had been appointed as teacher.

But most of all, life for the settlers was work, family, comradeship, followed by more hard work. And when that work was on land that they would one day own, they didn't grumble. There was such a freedom to this life, a chance to be your own master.

As August moved into September, spring brightened the floor of the forest with dozens of different wild flowers, orchids so tiny you had to bend close to see how beautiful they were, so many of these flowers, unknown to the English settlers. Pete taught the groupies their names: donkey orchids, spider orchids. There was one even he didn't know, pink and smelling like chocolate. Wild flowers of all colours sprang up like delicate frills along the edges of the tracks, and peeped shyly out from under bushes. Then there were kangaroo paws, with leaves like tall grass and long stalks with furry looking green and red flowers on the end that did look a bit like an animal's paws.

Northcliffe was expanding rapidly, with more buildings going up, but the town site was a cause for much complaint by everyone. In the wet weather, it was covered in puddles and the stretches of slippery mud were a trap for the unwary that caused quite a few falls. The drains dug to keep the area from flooding were almost as much of a hazard. Even in the hot weather the ground there never completely dried out. You didn't have to go down far to find dampness.

Whoever had chosen that site for the town wanted his head examining, in Gil's opinion.

There were occasional bouts of upset stomachs in the group, and one of the smaller, weaker children died, after which Gil was even more watchful that everyone set up their lavatories properly. There was a regulation sanitary pan, with lid and ring, sold at the store, but some families tried to economise by using kerosene tins instead. Whatever receptacle they used had to be emptied regularly or he let forth his sergeant's roar and tore a strip off them, then stood over them till they did the noisome deed.

He was always busy – but never too busy to think about Irene and wonder how she was. One day, after much thought, he risked writing to her, just a friendly letter asking how she was.

The following week he received a reply. There was nothing romantic about it, but she said how lovely it was to hear from him and asked after the Boyds and others. That meant he had an excuse for replying and best of all, it gave him a flicker of hope. He reread her letter every night as he sat by his lonely fire, even though he knew it by heart, tracing the lines of her signature with his forefinger.

It was agony to wait a further week to write again, but he did, composing the letter in his mind, going over it again and again, till he knew by heart what he wanted to say and felt fairly certain it wouldn't upset her. He wrote it without a single change or hesitation on the day he'd settled on in his mind as 'right' and sent it to the post in Pemberton the next day.

They needed a post office in Northcliffe, needed a lot of things.

But they were managing, making progress, making farms together.

As September turned into October and edged towards November, the weather grew much warmer again, though the nights could still be chilly.

Norah's new garden was full of plants, which she watched over carefully for fear of wild animals intruding: peas, beans, marrow, cauliflower, lettuce, cabbage and tomatoes which didn't need greenhouses to grow here. After rabbits got in and ate some of the young plants, Andrew fenced it off with wire netting, digging the netting in at the bottom and putting rocks along it, so that no wild creatures could spoil the harvest.

They all welcomed the fresh greens, seemed to crave green food, somehow. Norah had ensured they had dried peas all through the winter, cooking them the Lancashire way till they were mushy and serving them sometimes in a cup with vinegar, a treat the children loved.

After perusing the catalogues she'd sent away for more seeds and cuttings of fruit bushes, asking advice on how to grow them from Gil, who laughed and confessed he'd never been a gardener. So the groupies all pooled their knowledge of the old world, asked other groups and learned together what would grow here in the new world and how best to encourage it.

On Norah's birthday Andrew bought her a grape vine, which he had sent for from a catalogue. The sight of it reduced her to tears.

'It'll take years to fruit,' he said apologetically. 'If you don't like it, I can—'

'I do. I love it. I want apple trees too, once the house is built and we know where we stand.'

The vine was a source of great interest in the area, and when Gil said you could take cuttings from the wood which would have to be ruthlessly pruned at the beginning of the following winter, she rashly promised cuttings to all her neighbours.

Much of their shopping was done by catalogue, with the staple groceries bought in the Northcliffe store, huge bags of flour and sugar, tins of jam and corned beef. Sacks of apples in season. And sometimes farmers or smallholders came in from Manjimup or Pemberton selling their produce, heavy sacks of potatoes and onions, cabbages and cauliflowers.

'It's such a good life here,' Norah said to a friend on one of their sing-song evenings. 'I don't think I've ever been as happy.'

'Hard work, though,' Pam said ruefully. 'I nearly didn't come tonight, I was exhausted. You never seem to flag.'

'I do get a bit tired at times, but only when I've worked harder than usual, like on washdays. Normally I'm all right the next day.'

'Lucky you.' But Pam didn't say that with any malice.

Most of the women were good friends now, Norah thought contentedly. And even Janie was happy with her little friend. She was so glad they'd come here, happiest of all that she'd married Andrew.

By December the weather was hot and there'd been no rain for weeks. Grass that wasn't near a water source had turned a beige colour, looking like straw. Andrew was glad to have the creek bringing a stripe of green across his block and blessed Gil for suggesting they move here. He watched the level of the water anxiously, but it kept flowing, albeit at a reduced rate.

As the dry weather continued, he dug out a deeper pool, where water would collect to be scooped up for their garden. It was hard work and the hole had to be lined with stones, but quite pleasant to stand bare-legged in the water in such hot weather.

The children paddled whenever they were allowed, but downstream and he didn't let them stir up too much mud, insisting they walk about gently. Plodging, his grandma had called it when he was a lad.

Norah began making preparations for Christmas, but it didn't feel right, somehow, to celebrate in such warm weather.

'We'll kill one of the chooks,' she said rashly one day. 'We can buy another couple of pullets.'

Janie's eyes filled with tears. 'I won't let you touch Fluffy. And I won't eat any of them.'

Both parents tried to make her understand. 'This is a farm, love. Animals are for food, whether they lay eggs or provide us with meat.'

But the child remained so distressed they decided to order a joint of pork from the butcher instead.

'Silly baby!' Jack said, but he said it fondly these days. 'I'd eat the chooks any time.'

Janie stuck her tongue out at him.

A few minutes later their heads were together over a book which Norah had brought with her. Jack was helping Janie with the long words. All their books had been read and reread.

'Living here seems too good to be true,' she said to Andrew one night. 'And they say we'll be getting our houses soon.'

He looked at her in surprise. 'Where did you hear that?'

'At the store.'

'Gil hasn't said anything. It can't be true, surely?'

'Well, I heard it from a woman in another group who's already got her house. She says it's lovely to have four rooms again. And the men building it told her they would be starting on Special Group One soon. Why would they say that if it wasn't true?'

A few days later Gil confirmed that their houses would indeed be started within a couple of weeks and everyone went round smiling at the thought of having a proper home at last.

Gil had a private word with Andrew that same night. 'I, um, I'm going up to Fremantle to visit my cousin. I've got someone to keep an eye on my place and milk my cows. It's just for a few days, before they start building the new houses. I haven't had a break since I got here, and I've still got some things stored in my cousin's shed. I'll probably bring them back with me, or sell them up there.'

'Hope you have a good time.'

'Mmm. We'll do a bit of back burning near your farm after I return,' Gil added, looking round with a frown. 'I don't like to see so much dry grass and leaf litter. But don't start that without me there. You have to be very careful not to let the fire get away from you.'

When Andrew later told Norah about Gil, she beamed at him.

'It's Irene he's going to see, really.'

He looked at her in puzzlement.

'Don't you men ever tell one another personal things? He's been writing to Irene regularly and she to him. She told me about it ages ago in one of her letters. And she was due to have the baby last week. I've been waiting to hear how that went, she said she'd drop me a line. But there hasn't been any word. Perhaps the baby's late. That'll be why he's going up to see her, to find out if she's all right.'

'But she turned him down and he hasn't said a word about it and . . .' A smile slowly creased Andrew's face. 'The sly devil. He's been courting her.'

'Don't say anything. If she turns him down again, he'll not want people knowing. But I hope she won't. It's clear from her letters that she's not happy living in a town. I miss her. She was a good friend.'

Norah fanned her face with a bit of newspaper folded like a fan. 'It's been so hot today. I can't believe I was ever cold. Remember the mud and rain in winter?'

'Only too clearly. But it's hard working in the heat, too. Gil insists we all drink a lot of water. As if we need telling! I sweat so much, I'm always thirsty and even lukewarm water from my bottle tastes good.'

She went to bed and her last thought was a hope that Irene and Gil would get together. She liked them both so much.

The day Gil left for Perth was a scorcher, hotter than anything they'd had before. He warned them all to be particularly careful with fires, not to let sparks fly, if they could help it, and to be sure to wear their hats to keep the sun off.

Then, feeling he'd done his duty, he got on the train, heaved a sigh of relief and felt himself start to relax. He didn't know if he was doing the right thing, but he had a feeling it was time to go and see Irene. He'd got to know her better through her weekly letters, and that had only made him love her more. She was always cheerful, never said a word against anyone.

He hoped she was feeling more positive towards him, because he didn't know what he'd do if she turned him down again. But surely she'd not have continued writing if there wasn't hope?

Fremantle seemed full of people and noise. He'd grown used to quietness, rustling trees and space, felt uncomfortable here. He walked slowly through the streets, with his old kitbag slung over his shoulder.

Whether things went well with Irene or not, he intended to make a proper home for himself in Northcliffe. His humpy was as well fitted up as it could be now, because he'd been able to work on his own farm as the groupies grew more independent. It was fit for a wife.

When he got to the end of his cousin's street, he stopped and drew a deep breath, then squared his shoulders and strode towards his fate.

Three days after Gil left, Andrew got up early because he smelled smoke. You couldn't be too careful with the woods dry as tinder and another 'century' expected, a day over a hundred degrees Fahrenheit. He stood outside, sniffing, but the smoke was only faint and he could see no sign that it was nearby, so he got on with his morning chores, joined by Norah and Jack as they milked the seven cows.

You couldn't make a living from so few cows and he intended to get more, but not till after his family had a proper home again and after the rest of the lower part of the block was cleared.

After a hasty breakfast he set off for the place he'd be working today, leaving the children at home, because he didn't like having youngsters around when they were felling the bigger trees. He'd never forgotten the branch which had knocked him senseless and wasn't risking his lads or little Janie.

Norah had planned a washday and got the children to help her fetch water from the well Andrew had dug near the site they'd chosen for the proper house they'd have one day. She stopped to gaze round in pleasure. They'd chosen the site with care and she loved the view down the slope towards the road, not to mention the nearness to the stream which would make it easy to water the garden.

As she worked the smell of smoke grew stronger and in the end she decided to go and check where it was coming from. From time to time, small bush fires were ignited in the forest, by lightning or who knew what chance. Usually they burned out quite quickly, but it never hurt to keep watch.

The sky seemed overcast, which surprised her. When she looked up, there were no clouds to be seen but the blue seemed darker somehow. As she went round to the other side of the humpy, she saw smoke billowing up into the sky. That was causing the dull light. A trickle of unease ran down her spine, because the wind was blowing in their direction. But the smoke was still a long way from their block and other bush fires had burned themselves out.

She went back to her washing.

A short time later Jack came up to her. 'Mum, I think that bush fire's coming this way. Shall I go and have a look?'

She dried her hands on her pinafore. 'I'll come with you to check it again. The day seems to have got darker.'

When they walked round to the other side of the humpy, they saw a pall of dark smoke hovering above the forest, much closer than before. The wind was rising and even as they watched, the smoke billowed up in great black clouds.

Her heart began to beat more rapidly. She should have kept checking, but she hadn't realised it was possible for a big fire to spread so quickly.

'Shall I fetch Dad?'

'No. I don't want you getting trapped in the open. We've been warned about that. But just in case the fire carries on this way, we'll bring the animals closer to the house.' She ran back round to the front of the humpy. 'Janie! Ned! Help your brother bring the animals into our garden. We don't want them frightened by the fire.'

She blessed Andrew's care in fencing off their own garden from the stock. Now, his sturdy fence would be used for the opposite purpose, to keep the animals safe.

The cows milled about, seeming upset equally by the smoke and by the presence of the other creatures. One of the pigs ran into the house and Ned rushed to chase it out. The chooks fluttered here and there, finally settling on one of the rough benches near the house.

'Shut the house door!' she called. 'Then start drawing water. We'll fill everything we can to dampen down the ground round the house.' She was very worried now, but tried not to let it show.

The children seemed to understand the seriousness of the situation without being told. They worked hard, Jack drawing water from the well in the big bucket, Ned and Janie going further afield and bringing water up from the stream in smaller buckets, tipping them into her washtubs and empty kerosene cans, even into her mixing bowl.

It grew darker and darker and the smoke made it difficult to breathe. She found four tea towels, soaked them in water and instructed the children to tie them over their mouths and noses.

'I still think we should run away down the road,' Ned said, stopping to look at the fire.

Jack gave him a shove. 'Don't be stupid! Remember what Gil and Pete told us. Fire can move faster than people, so you stay where you are and try to make yourself safe.'

'Don't quarrel, boys.' Norah spoke as calmly as she could. 'And listen. If the fire sweeps over the house, we'll have to leave the animals and go down to the stream. Thank heaven Andrew dug out a pool. We could go and lie in that. Now, keep on bringing me water. I'm going to soak everything I can, even the ground.'

The four of them toiled hard, dampening down the

area closest to the house. The outbuildings would have to take their chances, Norah decided.

The cows were moving to and fro, eyes rolling in fear. One suddenly ran towards the fence, mooing loudly. Jack rushed to head her off before she could trample her way through it. From then on, they had to keep an eye on the animals as well as continue fetching water.

It was getting harder and harder to breathe and the noise of the fire was so loud they had to shout to make themselves understood.

'It's getting close to the fodder store,' Jack said. 'Oh, no! Look.'

The shed erupted into flame.

Nora stopped briefly, saddened to see flames destroy Andrew's hard work, then filled her bucket again. 'It's the house that matters. We have to save the house if we possibly can.'

Every time she looked the fire was closer, but slowed down in its approach to the house by the cleared land. Trees seemed to catch fire spontaneously with a great whooshing roar, even before the fire reached them. Burning twigs and leaves whirled in the air, landing ahead of the main fire, setting smaller fires here and there.

One burning brand landed on the cow shed and even as she watched, it too burst into flame.

'It's the other side of the house as well now!' Jack yelled.

She swung round to see a long finger of fire burning across the ground at the far side of the house. 'Dampen everything that side again,' she yelled, and set off running, trying not to slop too much of the water on her skirt.

The four of them continued to toil. Norah poured water over them all, sick with worry for the three children's safety. She counted them under her breath every time she turned back from a new task, one, two, three.

By now all their faces were black with smoke, the whites of their eyes seeming unnaturally bright against the dirty skin. The heat seemed to beat around them. 'Wet yourselves again,' she called hoarsely because their clothing was drying quickly in the heat. She watched as they poured buckets of water over one another, Jack supervising the others. Then he came and poured one over her, something she'd forgotten to do.

She paused as she rewet the material covering her mouth and nose to consider their position.

Should they run down to the stream and lie in the water, or should they stay and fight on to preserve the house? How did you know when to give up?

All she could think of was getting more water, keeping things damp if possible, keeping themselves and the stock wet, surviving any way they could. She'd try to save their possessions, but it was their lives that really mattered.

And still the fire grew higher around the little house, roaring like an evil monster, while an unnatural darkness covered the land, the black smoke shot through with vivid flashes of flame as leaves filled with eucalyptus oil flared up.

★   ★   ★

As they worked, Andrew and the others kept smelling smoke, seeing a distant plume of it. But the bush fire seemed a long way away and they'd seen other bush fires come and go.

But this one didn't go. Indeed, as the wind rose, it grew bigger so suddenly, it took them all by surprise when they realised how quickly it had moved in their direction.

Pete came over to them. 'I think we'd best get off home and check that everyone's all right. If the fire keeps going in that direction it'll probably bypass us, but you can never be sure with bush fires. They can swing round and they move as fast as a train.'

The men all gathered their tools and set off for the camp ground. But the fire seemed to be outpacing them.

'It's turned a bit, even in this short time. It's going to hit the furthest farms,' Pete said. 'Those with families there give the others your tools and get off home.'

They did that, running along the track. But the monstrous cloud of black smoke with the line of living flames at its base, reared up in front of them, seeming terrifyingly close beyond the camp ground.

They found their way barred suddenly by a wing of fire that had outflanked the rest and was roaring along the side of the track. It was clear that Andrew's farm was now encircled.

One of the men grabbed his arm and pulled him to a halt. 'You can't run into that. You'd be dead before you'd gone a hundred yards. We'd better move back. It's going sideways at the moment, but you never know when the wind will change direction.'

'I can't leave Norah and the children on their own.'

'You've no choice, mate. You can't get to them,' another man said. 'By heck, I never thought a fire could move so quickly. Did you ever see anything like it?'

But they had to grab Andrew and drag him back before it would sink in that he couldn't get through to his family.

23

In Fremantle Gil knocked on his cousin Nelly's door, relieved when it was she who opened it, not Irene. 'I had to come up to Freo to get the rest of my things—' he began, but was cut off short as she hugged him, laughing and crying at the same time.

'I'm so glad to see you, you've no idea. Come in, come in!' She tried to tug him inside, but he held back.

'How's Irene? Will she – want to see me?'

She stared at him, then smiled and nodded as if he'd confirmed something. 'Aaah. I guessed how things stood when I saw your letters. Regular as clockwork you wrote. Not like my cousin Gil, that, I thought.'

'Shh.' He looked anxiously over her shoulder, not wanting Irene to be embarrassed by this teasing.

'It's all right. She's feeding one of the babies.'

'Babies?'

'Yes. She had twins. Little girls. The prettiest things and healthy too, the nurse says, even if they are a bit small.'

'Twins.' He couldn't move for a moment or two out of shock, then smiled. 'That's a turn-up for the books, isn't it?'

Nelly nodded, her face more serious now. 'Though

how Irene's going to manage with two of them to care for, I don't know. I don't mind her not paying me any rent, but I can't afford to feed them and I haven't the time to watch them for her.'

He lowered his voice. 'I asked her to marry me before, but it was too soon after her loss. Do you think I should ask her again?'

Nelly pursed her lips. 'Let's see how she greets you first. That'll tell me a lot.'

'I thought she'd have written to tell me her news.'

'She's been too busy to write and anyway, one man's twins is a lot to saddle another man with, don't you think?'

His throat felt thick with emotion. 'If they're hers, I'd welcome them any time.'

Nelly gave him an extra hug for that, then led him inside, calling out, 'Look who's come to see us!'

Irene was sitting in a chair, holding a sleeping infant who, to judge by the dribble of white at the corner of its mouth, had just finished feeding. When she saw who the visitor was, her face lit up. 'Gil!'

Just to hear his name spoken by her in such a warm, welcoming tone gave him hope. 'I had to come to Freo to get the rest of my things—' he began, then stopped and said, 'No, I didn't. I'll not lie to you, now or ever. I came to see you, to make sure you were all right.'

Nelly looked from one to the other, then winked conspiratorially at her cousin and nodded encouragement. 'I'll go and get you a cup of tea, Gil, then make up a bed for you in our Jimmy's room. You are staying for a day or two, aren't you?'

He nodded, but his attention was on Irene. He walked across the room and knelt beside her, reaching out to touch the soft skin of the infant's cheek. 'She's beautiful. What have you called her?'

'This one is Jenny and the other's Mary.'

'Lovely names. Is the other as pretty as this one?'

'I think so.'

He looked at her across the top of the baby's head. 'Most important to me is: are you all right? Really all right?'

'Oh, yes. I'm recovering quickly, they tell me.' She smiled again. 'Australia seems to agree with me.'

'Did you know it was twins?'

'Towards the end, the midwife said it might be. Told me to eat for three.'

'Why didn't you tell me?'

She hesitated, her eyes searching his face as if she was unsure of herself.

'What is it, Irene? You know you can tell me anything. My feelings haven't changed.'

She nodded then her eyes went from one infant to the other. 'I realise that, but I didn't know if it was *fair*. To you, I mean. Two babies. It's a lot to ask a man to take on.'

'If you knew how I'd longed for children, you'd not say that. Oh, Irene, I was going to tread so carefully, wait to be sure of your feelings, but I can't. I want to marry you, and the sooner the better. Am I asking too much?'

Her smile was tender and luminous. 'No, Gil. I'm the one who's doing that. But if you're sure . . .'

'You'll marry me?'

She nodded.

He let out a yell of triumph and pulled her into a hug, baby and all, then plonked a kiss on the baby's head.

The noise brought Nelly running into the room. 'What's the matter?'

He stood up and waltzed his cousin round the room, then into the hallway and back. 'She's going to marry me!'

Both women were laughing and crying at the same time, but soon stopped when the baby on Irene's lap, disturbed by the noise, started to cry gustily, setting her twin off crying too.

'They always do that,' Irene said. 'If one cries, so does the other.' She looked at Gil. 'You're sure?'

'It's my heart's desire.' He didn't ask if she loved him, didn't dare. It was enough that she wanted to marry him, needed him, would be bringing him the family he'd ached for. 'Let's get married quickly then you can come back to Northcliffe with me. I'll get a special licence or whatever you have to do.'

She looked surprised, then nodded. 'I'd like that. I've imposed on Nelly for long enough.' She turned to the other woman. 'I can never thank you enough for all you've done.'

'I was glad to help you. Especially now it turns out we're going to be cousins.'

Gil wept briefly when he went out to the lavatory, understanding absolutely at that moment why women wept when they were happy.

★   ★   ★

Andrew went through all the agonies of hell in the hours he had to wait to see whether his family was safe. The wind turned again, not much but enough to drive the bush fire away from the rest of the farms.

He helped light small fires that would run towards the main one and leave a strip of burned-out vegetation to prevent the fire if the wind changed direction yet again. But every minute or two he would gaze in the direction of the main fire, hear its roar as it moved along, see its hungry red mouth swallowing everything in its path.

As soon as he could, he moved forward, but there were still things burning between him and his family, charred trees could drop limbs, logs flare into life again and hot embers on the ground burn through a man's shoes.

People stopped to lay one hand on his shoulder as they passed, not saying anything – what was there to say till they knew? But it showed they cared and that warmed his heart.

He was aware of an acrid taste in his mouth, men coughing from the smoke, small jobs to be done. But his main attention was on the fire. It had passed. It was dying down. How soon could he cross that piece of ground?

One of the women insisted he have something to eat. He wasn't hungry but it was easier to do as she asked and swallow what she thrust into his hand. And anyway, he didn't know what he'd be facing, had better keep up his strength.

Later, he had no idea how much time later, Pete

came to stand beside him. 'I reckon another hour and we can go through. But you're to stay behind me, Andrew, no going ahead on your own. And we'll follow the track, even if it's longer, because it'll have less burning stuff on it.'

He nodded. 'An hour.'

It was the longest hour of his life. For most of it he paced to and fro, leaving the work to the other men now, unable to do anything but watch and wait.

'We'll give it a try now.'

Andrew stared at Pete, unable to take in the sense of the words for a minute or two, then realised it was time to find out if Norah and the children were still alive. He couldn't hold back a deep sobbing breath as he followed Pete and didn't care who heard him.

It was hot still. Smoke curled up from the remains of trees, silver ashes floated through the air together with blackened specks of soot, while charcoaled wood crunched underfoot. Trousers that were dirty already took on a coat of black dust.

Let them be alive, Andrew prayed over and over as he walked slowly forward behind Pete. *Please, God, let them be alive.*

'I think it's passed, Mum.' Jack took hold of her arm to stop her going to fetch yet another bucket of water.

Norah stared at him, feeling stupid with stress and fatigue, then his words sank in and she looked round.

Yes, the main fire had passed, but with it had gone months of Andrew's work. The humpy was still standing, but no other building on the farm had escaped the blaze. Black, twisted skeletons of the various sheds and the larger cowshed and dairy, sagged in mute testimony to the power of the fire.

She turned slowly round, looking at one after another. Destroyed. Several months' hard work destroyed in just an hour or two.

When Norah stopped turning, Janie came to press against her on one side, Ned on the other and Jack stood beside Janie, his arm round his little sister's shoulders. No one said anything for a while, then Norah spoke. 'We're alive. Whatever else we've lost, we're all safe. Your father must be worried sick, though.' It took her a minute to recognise her own voice, so croaky was it.

She hugged them one by one. 'You did well, worked so hard. I'm proud of you.'

'I thought we'd have to go and lie in the stream,' Jack said.

She looked down at herself and at them, blackened faces, mouths shockingly pink against the dirty skin of cheeks and chin, ashes and cinder ash smeared across their faces and clothes. 'Eh, we look a right old mess, don't we?'

That drew a smile from them.

No use changing their clothes, she thought. They'd only get dirty again. 'We'd better fetch the animals some water before we do anything else. Their throats must be sore from the smoke.'

So they busied themselves tending the stock, moving lethargically to and from the well now that the worst was past. She shooed the pigs out of her garden, where they'd been feasting happily on her young plants, but did it gently, not really angry at them.

The animals didn't go far away from the circle of unburnt earth round the house, though, and she didn't even think of trying to lead the children away from the farm.

Let Andrew come to them.

And let him come soon.

She felt shaky now that the danger had passed. She'd worked like a fiend to cast water over everything in sight, taking turns with Jack to haul it up from the well. Now, her arms were aching and weak and just for a minute she needed to lean on her husband.

How long before he could get through to them?

Only then did she realise he might have been hurt by the fire and her breath caught in her throat at the utter horror of that idea.

She didn't think she could bear it if she lost him now.

Andrew walked along the track, choosing his footing carefully, but not really taking in the destruction to each side of him. He would willingly lose everything he possessed in the world as long as he could keep his family safe.

When they got near the entrance to his property, he moved to the front of the group, leading the way on to his land. His house came into view at the top of the slope. It was a poor thing, but it had stood against the fire storm and surely that was – yes, it was a group of people.

He began to run forward, heedless of where he put his feet and only when Pete yanked him to the left did he realise he'd nearly fallen headlong over a log that was still burning.

Muttering thanks, he went on more sensibly, but his eyes were raking the figures, counting and recounting them. Four. One woman and three children. Four. All of them safe.

Thank you, God!

Breaking into a run up the last part of the slope he ran towards them, trying to gather them all into his arms at once, sobbing unashamedly. 'I thought I'd lost you. I thought I'd lost you.' He kissed them one after the other, then kissed them again for good measure.

It was several minutes before they could stop weeping for joy and speak sensibly.

The other men stood a little way off, exchanging smiles, studying the desolation that had been a farm, and waiting.

As she found her voice again, Norah explained how they'd managed, giving praise to the children.

He told her of his agonising wait to get through to her.

The other men came nearer.

'Can you manage tonight?' one of them asked. 'If not, the wife says you're welcome to come to our place.'

'I've not even looked inside the humpy,' Norah said, her voice still shaking, her arm still linked very tightly in her husband's.

'Let's do it now,' he said.

So the five of them walked inside, nodding as they saw that things were untouched. Everything was covered in soot and ash, the whole place reeked of burning, but that could be dealt with.

'Do you want to stay here tonight or go to a neighbour's?' he asked.

'Stay here,' she and Jack said at the same time, then smiled at one another.

'Be it ever so humble . . .' Andrew murmured. 'That's how I feel too. I want to stay here.'

He went back to the door to look at his burned outbuildings. 'So it's all to do again. Will this land never let us settle in peace?'

'We can do it,' Norah said from beside him. 'We'll all help you.'

'We weren't insured against fire. I don't think anyone is here.'

'But we have a home and our land. All the animals are safe. We can do it.'

He nodded, but there was a bitter twist to his mouth. He'd worked so hard.

Gil and Irene arrived in Pemberton too late in the day to travel on to Northcliffe, especially with two tiny babies to care for. He found lodgings and arranged transport for themselves and a pile of trunks and boxes the following morning, then sat down to watch his new wife feed their daughters.

When it came to supplementing their mother's milk with a bottle of baby milk, he took one of the twins, taking care not to hurt Jenny's soft skin with his rough fingers, but rejoicing in the sight of her sucking vigorously on the rubber teat.

'There aren't many men who'd do that,' Irene said as she performed the same service for Mary.

'There aren't many men who've longed for children as I have. And anyway, twins are different.' He smiled at her. 'I hope you're not regretting what we did yesterday, Mrs Matthews.'

'Never. But I had to wait, to grieve for poor Freddie, to be certain I cared for you enough. You do understand, don't you?'

He nodded. She'd said this a few times. 'Of course I understand. Stop worrying.'

'Worriting, we say in Lancashire.'

'Whatever you call it, you're not to do it.'

The driver of the truck Gil had hired turned up at six o'clock in the morning. He took his hat off as he came into the kitchen, where they were feeding the babies.

'Do you still want to go?'

Gil looked at him in surprise. 'What do you mean? Why shouldn't we want to go there?'

'I heard last night that they'd had a bush fire through that group yesterday. Bad one. It destroyed some of the buildings and if the wind hadn't turned it, everything would've gone up in smoke.'

Gil stiffened. 'Was anyone hurt?'

'No. Miracle, that. One family was trapped on the farm and folk were anxious about them for a while, but they did the sensible thing and stayed put near their well, the fellow told me.'

Gil looked at Irene. 'If there's been a fire through the group, it'll be no place for you and the babies.' He saw her open her mouth to protest and repeated firmly, 'They haven't got good lungs like we have, too young yet and it'll reek of smoke. It's not safe for them, Irene.'

Their landlady, who'd been listening and exclaiming, said at once, 'You can stay on here, Mrs Matthews. Your husband's right. You have to be careful with babies that young.'

Gil could see how disappointed Irene was, but she looked down at Mary, covered by a shawl as she fed from the breast, and nodded slowly.

'I'll take most of our things and come back for you as soon as it's safe.'

The landlady took over the second baby and the bottle. 'I'll look after them, don't you worry, Mr Matthews.'

As he got ready, he prayed it wouldn't be too bad. Buildings had been lost, his companion had said. Which buildings. Not his friend Andrew's, surely?

And . . . not his own. Please, not his home, just when he'd got it halfway decent and was bringing his new family to live there!

24

In the morning, Norah woke to find Andrew already up. Flinging on her clothes, she went out to look for him, pausing in the doorway, not wanting to rush too hastily into a private moment. She knew how upset he was by their losses, how hard he was trying to put a brave face on it.

She was upset too, but so relieved that no one had been hurt, that the pain about the waste of all their months of hard work didn't yet seem quite real.

The animals had stayed near the house during the night. Now, the cows and pigs were drinking from her wash tubs, which Andrew must have filled with water because their wooden drinking troughs had been destroyed with everything else. The poor creatures' hides were dirty with ashes and soot, and she could see a few burns from flying debris. Otherwise, they too had survived.

So not everything was lost.

Andrew was standing fifty paces away with his back to her, next to what had been the dairy. His hands were clenched into fists and he was motionless, staring at the twisted, charred frame which had been a sturdy wooden shed yesterday, built by his own hands.

She remembered him calling her to come and see it when he'd finished, the pride in his voice, the sparkle in his eyes.

She began to walk towards him, but he didn't turn, though he must have heard her coming because her feet made crunching noises on half-burned twigs.

A quick glance showed her he had tears in his eyes and she looked quickly away from his face. She couldn't think what to do but hug him, so she did, not a woman's hug for her lover, more a mother's hug for her hurt child. He didn't put his arms round her immediately then, with an inarticulate noise, he gathered her to him and buried his face in her hair.

'We're all alive,' she said quietly. 'Keep fast hold of that thought, my love.'

She could feel him nod but he didn't say anything, just continued to hold her close.

After a while, she decided to give him something to do to take his mind off things. 'We'd better make arrangements for milking the cows and separating the cream. Can't leave the poor things with full udders, can we?'

'How do we separate the cream? Everything was burned.'

'We'll borrow Gil's cart and go into Northcliffe and replace what we can. I still have my savings. We're not penniless.'

His voice was harsh, with an edge to it. 'Money won't buy buildings, won't take us back to where we were.'

'No, we'll take ourselves back, step by step.'

'And what if there's another bush fire? And another. What if we lose everything again? We've not been lucky here. First we drew the worst block of land, now this!'

She'd never seen him so discouraged. 'We'll just – do what we have to,' was all she could manage.

He gave her another quick hug then pushed her to arm's length, looked at her and smiled. Just a slight lifting of the lips, but it lifted her heart with it.

'I was lucky in one thing, at least, the most important thing of all.'

She was a little puzzled. 'What do you mean?'

'Lucky to find you, to marry a strong woman who'll work by my side, who'll brighten my darker moments and gild my happy ones.'

A tide of warmth ran through her and the words echoed in her mind. She would never forget this wonderful compliment, never. 'As you do for me.'

He kissed her, and she kissed him back sweetly and gently.

She tried to pull away and he wouldn't let her, so she laid her cheek against his and tried to lighten the tension. 'I really like this sort of work, you know, being outdoors and working with animals.' To her relief, his smile still lingered and the bitterness had gone from his face.

'I like it too. So . . . we'll start again. Together.'

His next kiss wasn't gentle, it was full of passion and need. It lasted a long time, making her head spin with pleasure and the wonderful knowledge of how much she was loved.

Then she heard giggles and he must have too,

because he stiffened and moved his lips from hers. Together they looked back at the house to see the three children grinning at them from the doorway.

'Look at them,' she said. 'What grand children they are.' She let go of him and held out her arms.

Janie immediately set off running towards her. A few seconds later Ned followed, then Jack, and they were all hugging and kissing one another, a rare demonstration of their love, but something to hold on to in the hard times to come.

'I'm hungry,' Ned said, when the moment had passed.

'You're always hungry. All right, I'll come and get you some food. Andrew love, if I send Ned out with one of my mixing bowls, can you wash Blossom's udder and get some milk from her for breakfast?

And so the work began.

But the fire had done one good thing, Norah thought later. It had bound them tightly together as a family, and for that she was deeply thankful. So far away from home, they had only one another so needed strong love to support them all.

Gil sat beside the driver as the truck jolted along the road to Northcliffe. He didn't really want to make conversation, but forced himself to pay enough attention not to upset his garrulous companion. Billy obviously loved talking.

When they got into Northcliffe, they saw no one in the town centre.

'Don't stop,' he told Billy. 'I want to see if I've still got a house left.'

There weren't any signs of men working this side of the camp ground and he wondered where they were. But the first few farms were untouched, thank goodness, and cream cans were standing by their entrances as usual.

The camp ground was empty too. Gil's anxiety rose as the truck slowed down to enter a burnt landscape. Where was everyone? Had someone been killed?

'Damned bush fires!' the other muttered as they drove into the part where the fire had struck, a desolate landscape, all black tree trunks and scorched earth.

There was no edge of pain to his companion's voice, Gil thought, no real understanding of what it meant to stand helpless as fire raced through a piece of bush, destroying what you'd created with your own hands. Billy was just echoing what unaffected people always said.

But Gil had seen the effects of bush fires before, had helped a friend who'd had one go through his place, and seen how devastated both land and man were afterwards. Besides, this was his group, his *friends* who'd suffered.

Above all, he prayed no lives had been lost. Land endured and plants regenerated, buildings could be replaced but people couldn't.

They were driving even more slowly now. On both sides of the track stood blackened trees, some with shreds of curling leaves clustered here and there, most bare. Some had tumbled over, others pointed what remained of the charred trunk upwards in a final jagged salute to the fire.

Some of the larger fallen trees were still smouldering, giving off little wisps of smoke and he made a mental note to send men to shovel earth over them to make sure they didn't erupt into another fire.

Every now and then a group of trees near the track was only half burned, the lower leaves scorched and curled, but some of the upper branches still showing clumps of green. Bush fires were like that, moving on sudden whims, sparing some, totally destroying others.

The air smelled strongly of smoke, so acrid his breath caught in his throat as he drew it in.

Where was everyone? Had the fire damage been worse than he'd heard?

Was his own home still safe?

Damnation! He should have stopped in Northcliffe for the latest news, not rushed blindly on.

Before Andrew could set off to borrow the cart, which was in Pete's keeping while Gil was away, Norah insisted on everyone eating a proper breakfast. Then together they wrote out a list of basic necessities and she handed over her savings to pay for them, knowing he didn't have enough of his own money left.

'I hate taking it from you,' he said.

'It's not mine or yours, it's *ours* now.' She went to the door with him and looked across the burnt land. The paddocks might not have any grass left on them at the moment, but that would grow again. They'd need the fences mending, though, to keep the animals from straying. Some of them looked intact, but were badly burnt. Even as she watched, one of the pigs pushed down a section of blackened fence, raising a cloud of sooty ash. Then it set off for a stroll.

Andrew cursed it under his breath.

Norah realised he could do more here than she could. 'Why don't I go into town to get these things?'

He hesitated. 'Don't you have things to do here?'

'I think it's more important that you fence in the animals than I clean the house, don't you? And I'll buy a loaf from the baker's. We'll make do with sandwiches and porridge for the moment.'

'You're right. I can do more here.'

'I'm sure Pete will drive me back afterwards with the things I buy.' There would be too much to carry, that was sure.

'He has his own work to do. I don't like to bother him.'

'Well, I can ask, can't I? We really need some help, love.'

'If he's too busy, bring what you can and I'll go back for the rest later. We'll manage somehow.'

Andrew hated asking for help. She'd noticed it before, this stubbornly independent streak in her husband, so she didn't comment or argue. But if Pete didn't help her to bring everything back, she'd be surprised and disappointed. It was such a pity Gil was away, because he'd have been here first thing this morning, helping out. And Andrew would have accepted his friend's help more easily, wouldn't have had a choice about it if she knew Gil.

She set off to walk into town, taking Janie with her to help carry things and leaving the boys to help their father mend the fences. All three were dressed in yesterday's filthy, torn clothes.

It was going to be hard going setting things to rights, rebuilding what they'd lost.

'The turn to my place is just round the bend, to the right,' Gil said. He hadn't let the driver turn into the camp ground, because his anxiety to see his home was all he could focus on.

The truck edged forward slowly, weaving in and out of tumbled branches and trunks. Twice they'd had to stop to move a fallen, half-burned tree trunk, using the jack as a lever. He could have got off and walked as fast as this, but the truck was loaded with his and Irene's things.

As they left the main track and bumped up the hill to his place, he saw that his house was still standing. The fire had gone through further down the slope, but where he lived was green still. 'Oh, thank goodness!' he exclaimed in a voice choked with relief. 'Thank bloody goodness!'

Billy looked at him. 'Your place looks all right, mate. You're lucky.'

'Yes.' As he glanced back along the main track, he noticed two figures approaching from the burned part. 'Stop!' He was off the truck and running towards her before the driver finished braking. 'Norah! How have you and Andrew fared?'

'Oh, Gil, I'm so glad you're back.'

She clutched his hands so tightly, he was terrified for a moment or two. 'No one's hurt?'

'No. The house is all right, but we've lost all our outbuildings, every single one. I was caught at the farm and Andrew had to wait out the fire at the camp ground. The children and I just kept wetting everything down.'

He could guess how hard that had been. 'What about your stock?'

'We drove them into the garden. They're alive but hungry. Andrew's rebuilding the fences now, fetching poles from the unburned bush along the track. Only a few hundred yards and the fire would have missed us. It was only a spur fire, not the main one. No one else got hit so badly.' She snapped her mouth shut, a bleak look on her face.

He bit back a curse at the unkindness of fate. 'Where are you going now?'

'To the store. We need stock feed and other things. I was hoping Pete would give me a lift back with them on your cart. We'll have to milk in the open till he can build us another cowshed. Good thing the weather is warmer.'

'We'll go up to my house and I'll lend you a few things to start you off.' He shoved her and Janie into the cab of the truck, and clung to the back as it jolted up the slope.

At his house, he checked that everything was all right, which it was apart from the smell of smoke and drifts of ash here and there. With the driver's help, he lugged all his things inside, then turned back to Norah. 'What do you need most?'

'I've got a list.'

'Good. Give it me and I'll get them for you, then I'll bring them out to you myself.'

He turned to the other man. 'Will you take her home with these things then come back for me and take me into town to buy what they need, Billy?'

'We can't ask you to do all that,' she said quickly, conscious of Andrew's pride.

Gil grinned at her. 'Try stopping me.'

The driver grinned at her too. 'Same goes for me, missus. I'm my own boss and if a man can't help someone after a bush fire, he's as worthless as teats on a bull!'

When the truck chugged up to the house, Andrew came running out.

'Norah! Is something wrong?'

Janie slid out of the cab and she followed. 'No. Quite the opposite. I met Gil on the way into town and he lent me some things. He said he'd go into town and buy the rest for us.'

Andrew's expression brightened and he helped them unload.

Only when the driver had left did he think to ask, 'How did Gil get on in Freo?'

'I forgot to ask him. It can't be good news or he'd have told me, surely?'

'We'd better not say anything about Irene, unless he does.' He looked down at the pile of clean buckets and bowls. 'Well, let's get those poor beasts milked. At least we can do that properly now.'

He was, she could see, still grim-faced and trying to hide it. Sighing for his pain, she went into the house to start shaking the ash out of things and tidying up the children's room. She was glad they still had their possessions. They'd lost a lot, but not everything.

If only Andrew didn't lose the will to start again. She couldn't imagine living anywhere else now.

Armed with Norah's shopping list, Gil went back into town, where he found his horse and cart behind the store and Pete inside buying hardware.

'Where is everyone?'

'Those who can be spared are cutting trees and making slabs. A couple of men are down at the timber mill getting what they can.'

'For what?'

Pete looked at him as if he'd lost his wits. 'To help the Boyds, of course. They were worst hit by the fire, so we'll work on their place first, build them a few sheds. The others only lost a few bits of fence.'

Gil felt a tide of warmth run through him. This was what it'd been like when he was growing up, neighbour helping neighbour through the bad times. He hadn't expected the group to reach this stage so quickly, but the news only made him more certain he wanted to put down roots in this community.

'Let's go through the details,' he said brusquely to cover his feelings. 'Oh, and this is Billy. He's volunteered to help us take the stuff out to the Boyds' farm.'

Pete immediately shook Billy's hand and slapped him on the back. 'Good man, good man! I was going to have to make several journeys.'

'I'll go and ask that builder fellow if he can spare some dressed wood in a good cause,' Gil said. He turned to the storekeeper. 'I hope you'll give us a good price on the stuff we're buying. This is no time to be thinking of profit when a family's lost so much.'

The man pursed his lips, then nodded. 'Cost price.'

'Thanks.' Filled with determination, Gil went off to see what else he could scrounge for his friend.

Ned was the first to hear the truck coming back and went to fetch his father, who was felling some more small trees further down the track to use as fencing poles.

By the time they got back to the farm, not only was the truck parked outside the house, but the cart was just drawing to a halt and men were gathered round both vehicles. Other men could be seen in the distance, walking along the track towards his farm. Women too.

Janie came flying across to him. 'Daddy, everyone's coming to help us,' she shouted. 'All our friends.'

Norah had been talking to the driver, but turned to beam at her husband. 'Isn't it marvellous?'

'Come and help us unload,' Gil yelled from the rear of the truck. 'There's another load of timber to come out yet.'

Andrew couldn't move. He'd never have asked, never. But he hadn't needed to. Half their neighbours were there. Even as he looked there was a squeaking sound and Ted came up from the track pushing a handcart he'd built himself. It had been the cause of much teasing, with its solid wooden wheels made from a tree trunk and the squeak that no amount of oiling would stop.

Now, the cart was full of tools and small pieces of wood, the sort you needed for crosspieces or slats.

'Thought you might like some help with the rebuilding,' Ted said cheerfully. 'We all had a few bits and pieces to spare.'

'Good man!' Gil said as Andrew seemed lost for words. 'We'll need to clear up the mess before we can make a start. Do you want the sheds in the same places?'

Andrew's gulp was quite audible and Norah could see that he was fighting against tears, blinking furiously.

'We're so grateful for your help,' she told Ted, to give her husband time to pull himself together.

'We've money to pay for the timber.' Andrew gestured to the pile that had been unloaded. His voice was rough, sounding almost ungracious.

'They've given you the first load free,' Gil said. 'And the hardware at cost price. A couple of men are down the track, felling trees and splitting them into slabs for your shed walls. Your animals won't complain about how green the wood is. Now, where do we build?'

'In the same place,' Andrew managed. 'Thanks. I can't—' He broke off again.

One man nudged another and jerked his head. They walked over to the ruined cowshed and began knocking the remains of it down, heedless of the black dirt that flew everywhere.

Andrew pressed one hand against his mouth for a moment then took a deep breath. 'I don't know how to thank you enough.'

'Argh, you'd do the same for us,' someone said.

The men were fidgeting, seemed at a loss for what

to say, embarrassed by the emotion, so Norah intervened again. 'I'll brew us all a big pot of tea. It's thirsty
work clearing up a mess like this.' She had a former
kerosene can that Andrew had converted into a square
bucket. That'd do.

'You're right there, missus,' someone called. 'Make
mine sweet and strong.'

'My Pam's coming over later to help you, soon as
she's finished at our place,' Ted told her. 'We're all
here for the rest of the day, so she's bringing some
food. She's been cooking since dawn. Some of the
other women will be along later, and they'll be bringing
food, too.'

The men exchanged jokes and mocking insults as
they split up into pairs and found small trees for poles
or felled bigger ones to make slabs. The milled timber
soon started going up to frame the buildings again,
and the second load the truck brought out from town
contained some battered sheets of corrugated iron for
roofing, pieces they'd been given for nothing.

The women helped Norah clear out the house and
hang up the bedding and clothes that reeked of smoke.
Some prepared food for the whole group of workers,
others began to repair the damage to the garden, one
took a gaggle of children to find wood for the fire in
the unburnt bush, using the squeaking handcart to
bring it back, again amid much laughter. And for once,
no one scolded the children for dirtying their clothes.

Everyone worked as long as they could that day,
some staying until it was too dark to place a nail
correctly. They snatched something to eat now and

then, not caring what it was, and they drank gallons of tea.

When they'd gone, there was only Gil left and a stew simmering on an open fire.

'You'll eat with us?' Norah asked.

'If you've enough.'

'We've always enough for our friends.'

As she served the meal, she was unable to stop smiling. In this morning's bleak mood, she hadn't expected to feel so happy by evening. And Andrew was the same, she could see.

'They're good folk, our group,' Gil said quietly as he and Andrew waited for Norah to sit at the table with them.

'The best,' Andrew said and blew his nose loudly.

When they'd finished eating, Gil stared down at his plate. 'I've some news of my own to tell you.'

Norah exchanged worried glances with her husband. 'You don't have to say anything if you don't want to. You don't owe us any explanations.'

Gil leaned back in the chair they'd brought from England, the one Andrew usually sat in, smiling round at them all. 'It's good news. Don't you want to hear it?'

'Good news?' Norah leaned forward eagerly.

'Irene and I were married in Freo a couple of days ago.'

'Married! You're married! Oh, Gil.' Norah got up and plonked a kiss on his cheek.

'You married Auntie Irene?' Janie asked. 'Is she coming back here to live?'

'She is indeed. She'll be living with me and working with me on my farm.'

Janie clapped her hands together and cheered loudly. The boys nodded approval in a less demonstrative way.

'So will the twins,' Gil said when the noise had died down.

'*Twins?*' Everyone gaped at him.

He nodded. 'Would you believe it, she's had twins. Two little girls, called Jenny and Mary.'

'That's wonderful.' It was Norah's turn to mop her eyes.

When the meal was over, Andrew walked down to the main track to see his friend on his way. Pete had taken the horse and cart earlier because he would be fetching another load of newly felled timber the next day. Gil would send a message to Irene in Pemberton and arranged with the truck driver to fetch his wife and children home a day or two later.

The two men stopped at the entrance to the Boyds' farm. Gil clapped Andrew on the back and they stared at one another for a minute, then nodded and went on their way. Good friends didn't always need words.

25

Gil brought Irene home from Pemberton three days later. His friend Andrew was well on the way to being set up again on his farm. Now it was time for Gil to start his new life.

Irene was waiting for him, bright-eyed, so pretty his breath caught in his throat. He kissed her tenderly, then turned to cuddle the babies. 'They've grown, even in a few days!'

'Do you think so?'

'I'm sure of it. They're a pretty pair. I can see we'll have all the lads round courting when they grow up.'

She laughed. 'We've a little time before that happens. I've just fed them, so let's get everything in the truck. With a bit of luck, we can get home before they need feeding again. And I've bought plenty of tins of baby milk powder.'

The sun was shining brightly, and his nostrils were filled not with the stink of charred wood, but with the fresh smell of her skin and hair. She said she didn't use perfume, but she always smelled sweet to him. He'd buy her some perfume next Christmas, though. Lily of the valley, perhaps. No, that had been Mabel's favourite. He'd ask Norah what else was nice.

As they jogged along, he thought about Mabel, fondly now, without the old desolation. She'd approve of his new family, he was sure. He looked at the woman in the front of the truck, sitting beside the driver, the babies crammed in at her feet in little nests of blanket and his heart skipped in his chest with joy.

An uneven patch of road had him clinging on in the back and laughing.

When they got to the shack, he and Irene each carried a baby into their new home. He stopped dead in surprise. The new table he'd built was covered with baked goods: a cake, freshly baked damper, a plate pie. There was a pan and when he peeped into it, he saw some stew.

'Who are these from?' Irene asked.

'The other groupies, I suppose. The food wasn't here when I left for Pemberton.'

'How kind of them!' She looked round and beamed at him. 'You built them a cradle.'

He'd been busy helping Andrew, so it'd cost him some precious hours of sleep, but it was worth it. 'Can't have my daughters sleeping on the floor, can I? You said they always like to sleep together, so I built it wider.'

'They do.'

Jenny stirred in her mother's arms, her rosebud mouth opening and shutting as she searched for food.

'Let's put them down for a minute or two and get our things in, then when Billy's gone I'll deal with these two.' She looked round. 'You've done a lot of work on this place.'

'I want you to be comfortable. Though it looks like we'll be getting a proper house in the next few weeks. Andrew and Norah have got theirs going up this very week.' He pulled the rocking chair forward. 'Sit down and I'll pass you whichever baby you're feeding first.'

'Jenny. She's always more hungry than Mary.'

That night they slept chastely side by side on two stretcher beds because Irene's body hadn't recovered from the birth yet, so consummating their marriage would have to wait.

'I'm so glad to be back,' she said sleepily.

'Not half as glad as I am to have you here.'

'Mmm.'

He lay listening to her soft, even breaths. He hadn't expected to be as happy as this ever again.

A few days later, men turned up with a load of timber to build the first of the farmhouses.

'It's scheduled for Lot Seven,' one of them said, pulling a crumpled piece of paper out of his pocket.

'That's changed,' Gil told him. 'Lot Twelve is the one to start on.'

They looked at him suspiciously. 'It says Lot Seven.'

The man held out the paper for him to see, but he pushed it aside. 'Look, there's been a bush fire through, and Lot Twelve was badly hit, lost all their outbuildings. Let's give their spirits a boost, eh? Let's build them the first proper house in this group.'

The men looked at one another and shrugged. 'No one up in Perth is going to know where we build it, are they?' one said.

The other smiled. 'By the time they send an inspector out to check on it, it'll be up and they're not going to pull it down again, are they?'

'If anyone asks, I'll tell them I misheard the lot number you told me,' Gil offered.

'You're on, mate.'

Andrew saw the truck pull off the track at his farm and put down his hammer. There wasn't any more timber due. He had his farm buildings up now. 'Can I help you?'

'We've come to build your house. Yours is the first to go up.'

'House?' It took a few seconds for him to realise what they meant. 'The farmhouse, you mean?'

'Yeah. We'll drop this stuff off today and be back with some more tomorrow. Better work out where you want it.'

Norah came out to join them and Andrew picked her up and swung her round. 'It's our house! They're building our house first.'

After the men had left, they walked together to the spot they'd chosen, the children tagging along behind them.

'This is still the best place to put it.' She looked down the slope towards the entrance to their farm.

'Shall we have a celebration when it's finished?'

The children crowed with delight.

'Oh, yes. We'll invite all our friends, have a sing-song and then . . .'

'Then what?'

'Then we'll settle down to work and make this the best farm in Northcliffe.'

When the house was finished, Andrew picked Norah up and carried her over the threshold.

She clung to him, laughing, looking up at his dear face with its strong features. 'Happy again?'

'Yes. But though this place sets the seal on it, what makes me happiest of all is you, my family and the best neighbours on earth.' He looked round. 'It's not exactly free land, is it, as we thought when we read that brochure?'

'No. We buy it with our sweat and toil.'

'But we have the freedom to do that here, which we'd never have had in England. Still glad you came?'

'More than ever.' She hesitated, then added shyly. 'Talking of family, we're going to have another member in a few months.'

'I wondered.'

'Yes, I thought you'd guessed.'

'It'd be hard to miss it, living as closely together as we do. Are you glad?'

She laid her head on his shoulder. 'Very glad. I don't know what the children will say, though.'

'The boys will love their baby brother and spoil him to death. Or baby sister. And having seen the way Janie cares for that lame chook of hers, I think you'll have trouble keeping her away from the baby.'

They stood on the front veranda, watching the children carry the first of their possessions across from the humpy. Sunlight slanted through the trees, whose leaves were already starting to grow again. One of the cows mooed, and not to be outdone a pig squealed a reply.

Then the children arrived and all was bustle and noise – just the way Norah liked it to be.

ABOUT THE AUTHOR

Anna Jacobs grew up in Lancashire and emigrated to Australia, but she returns each year to the UK to see her family and do research, something she loves. She is addicted to writing and she figures she'll have to live to be 120 at least to tell all the stories that keep popping up in her imagination and nagging her to write them down. She's also addicted to her own hero, to whom she's been happily married for many years.

CONTACT ANNA

Anna Jacobs in always delighted to hear from readers and can be contacted:

BY MAIL

PO Box 628
Mandurah
Western Australia 6210

If you'd like a reply, please enclose a self-addressed, business size envelope, stamped (from inside Australia) or an international reply coupon (from outside Australia).

VIA THE INTERNET

Anna has her own web domain, with details of her books, latest news and excerpts to read. Come and visit her site at
http://www.annajacobs.com

Anna can be contacted by email at
anna@annajacobs.com

If you'd like to receive an email newsletter about Anna and her books every month or two, you are cordially invited to join her announcements list. Just email her and ask to be added to the list, or follow the link from her web page.

READERS' DISCUSSION LIST

A reader has created a web site where readers can meet and discuss Anna's novels. Anna is not involved in the discussions at all, nor is she a member of that list – she's too busy writing new stories. If you're interested in joining, it's at *http://groups.msn.com/AnnaJacobsFanClub*